Praise for

"Wonderful . . . [Kelton] deftly uses characters from past entries while constantly folding in new personalities. This is arguably the best ongoing Western series in the genre today. It shouldn't be missed."

—*Booklist* (starred review)

"As always, Kelton's history is accurate and his characters clearly drawn and believable."

—*The Dallas Morning News*

"Once again, Kelton offers an exciting tale in which the bad guys are really bad and some of the good guys are, too. His characters are sharply defined, the historical background is vivid, and the gunplay can't be beat."

—*Publishers Weekly*

Praise for *Hard Trail to Follow*

"An engrossing, entertaining chase played out through two intriguing main characters. Mr. Kelton's attention to detail and his well-crafted minor characters bring additional richness to the book's sense of place and reality. This novel will likely further enhance Elmer Kelton's hard-earned reputation as one of America's premier Western writers."

—*The Dallas Morning News*

"An exciting and satisfying Western tale."

—*Publishers Weekly*

Forge Books by Elmer Kelton

JERICHO'S ROAD

—— AND ——

HARD TRAIL TO FOLLOW

Elmer Kelton

A TOM DOHERTY ASSOCIATES BOOK | NEW YORK

This is a work of fiction. All of the characters, organizations, and events portrayed in these novels are either products of the author's imagination or are used fictitiously.

JERICHO'S ROAD AND HARD TRAIL TO FOLLOW

Jericho's Road copyright © 2004 by the Estate of Elmer Kelton

Hard Trail to Follow copyright © 2007 by the Estate of Elmer Kelton

All rights reserved.

A Forge Book
Published by Tom Doherty Associates
175 Fifth Avenue
New York, NY 10010

www.tor-forge.com

Forge® is a registered trademark of Macmillan Publishing Group, LLC.

ISBN 978-0-7653-9352-4

Our books may be purchased in bulk for promotional, educational, or business use. Please contact your local bookseller or the Macmillan Corporate and Premium Sales Department at 1-800-221-7945, extension 5442, or by e-mail at MacmillanSpecialMarkets@macmillan.com.

First Edition: January 2018

Printed in the United States of America

0 9 8 7 6 5 4 3 2 1

CONTENTS

JERICHO'S
ROAD

For Jerry Hunt,
Art and Margie Hendrix,
avid collectors

1

After several years as a Texas Ranger, Andy Pickard concluded that the average criminal he dealt with was about as intelligent as a jackrabbit. That said, even a dullard could pull a trigger and hurt somebody. A case in point was the reluctant prisoner trudging along ten paces ahead of Andy, dragging his feet and wailing about the insensitivity of law enforcement.

"It ain't fair," the handcuffed man whined. "You're a young man, barely growed, but you're ridin' my horse and makin' me walk."

Andy said, "You shot mine."

"I didn't mean to."

"I know. You were shootin' at *me*."

The prisoner stumbled over his own feet and almost fell. "How much further we got to go?"

"A ways yet. It'll give you time to consider changin' your occupation."

Deuce Scoggins had earned a reputation as a second-rate horse thief who could not tell a mare from a gelding and knew no better than to peddle them in the first town he came to after he stole them. His trail had led Andy across several counties along the Colorado River, but a string of angry victims had made the path easy to follow. Confronted, Deuce had fired one shot in panic, killing

Andy's horse, then had thrown up his hands and begged for mercy. Andy had made him strip the saddle, bridle, and blanket from the dead animal and transfer them to his own.

"Where'd you get this horse?" Andy asked him.

"Won him in a poker game."

Andy doubted that. Deuce was not smart enough to win a poker game. He had stolen this horse like he had stolen just about everything else he had. Deuce's sweat-streaked shirt was much too large, loosely draped over thin shoulders, the grime-edged cuffs almost covering his dirty hands. He had probably lifted it from somebody's clothesline.

Andy asked, "Did you ever think about gettin' a job and makin' an honest livin'?"

"Work? I tried once. Ain't much I can do good enough that anybody'll pay me for it."

"You're not very good at this, either."

Andy wondered if he was being fair, comparing Deuce's intelligence with that of a jackrabbit. He might not be giving the rabbit enough credit.

Deuce grumbled, "Even an Indian would treat a man better than this."

"You don't know Indians." Andy did. Through several of his boyhood years he had lived among the Comanches. "Be glad you *don't* know them. They'd make it a mighty short acquaintance."

The afternoon was almost done when they rounded a bend in the wagon road and saw the crossroads town ahead. Its largest buildings were a courthouse, a new jail, and a church.

Deuce brightened, seeing that his long walk was almost over. He said, "I heard their old jailhouse got burned down. It wasn't no nice place. I was in it once."

"Too bad you didn't go in the church instead."

"Can't you take these handcuffs off before we hit town? It's embarrassin' to let people see me this way."

"A little embarrassment might be good for you. There was a time when they would've necked you to a tree limb. As it is, they'll likely just send you to the penitentiary."

"I already been there. It ought to be against the law to put a man in a hellhole like that."

Sheriff Tom Blessing stood in the doorway of the red-brick jail. Recognizing Andy, he grinned broadly and raised his big right hand in greeting. He looked more like a farmer than a lawman, for indeed he was a farmer first. Despite his years he still had the muscled body of a blacksmith. "Bringin' me a guest, Andy?"

Andy grinned back at him. "I hated for your new jailhouse to stand empty. The taxpayers have put a big investment in it."

Andy dreaded the handshake because Tom could bend a horseshoe double, and he could break the bones in a man's hand. He had been sheriff here so long that many people in town could not remember anyone else serving in that office. He showed no sign that he was ready to yield any ground to his age. He said, "Come on in here, Deuce. I've got a nice cell with your name on it, all swept out and waitin' for you."

Deuce sounded like a lost soul crying in the wilderness. "I'm hungry and I'm thirsty, and this Ranger has wore my feet down plumb to the bone."

Tom offered no comfort. "Write a letter to the governor." He led Deuce past barred iron doors and pointed him to a cell. When Deuce was inside, Tom slammed the door hard. That reverberating impact always reminded Andy of a gallows trapdoor dropping. There was something coldly final about it.

Tom told Deuce, "I'll bring you a bucket of water directly. There's a slop jar under the cot. Make yourself at home." He winked at Andy.

Deuce was wanted in several counties, but Andy had brought him here because this was the nearest jail, and the sun was almost down. He did not care to risk camping with the prisoner on the trail. Here he could get a good night's sleep without worrying that Deuce might try to escape. Tom would keep the horse thief in custody until the several counties that wanted him sorted out their priorities.

Tom asked, "Did he give you any trouble?"

"Not after he shot my horse. He went to blubberin'. Thought I was fixin' to kill him. I let him keep on thinkin' so till I got the cuffs on him."

"Some Rangers *would've* shot him for killin' their horse. Whose is that you're ridin'?"

"No tellin'. Somebody's probably lookin' for him."

"I'll check my notices." Tom fingered through a stack of papers on his desk. "I got a message for you somewhere. Yeah, here it is." He handed a paper to Andy. "Your captain sent a wire to all the sheriffs around here, not knowin' just where you'd turn up. Wants you to report in to him."

Andy felt uneasy, wondering what the captain might want. Maybe the state's finances had turned tight again and the Ranger force was being trimmed. It had happened often before. His several years of service were no guarantee that he would escape the next cut.

He asked, "Reckon the telegraph office is still open?"

"I expect so. The operator's not anxious to go home of an evenin'. His wife's been burnin' the beans lately on account of him bein' a sorry poker player."

Andy mentally composed a brief message on his way

down the street. In the telegraph office he wrote it out on paper, reporting the capture of Scoggins. He read it over and penciled out every word it could spare. The state disliked paying for long messages, so Ranger reports tended to be spare on detail. He remembered one Farley Brackett had sent: *Five fugitives met, three arrested, two buried.*

He told the telegraph operator, "If I get a reply, I'll be stayin' the night at the jail."

"I'll fetch it over soon as it comes."

Andy stayed to watch him tap out the message. He still marveled at the progress he had seen in just the few years he had been a member of the Rangers. It seemed unreal that he could write a few lines here and know they would be received miles away in an instant. The telegraph had done much to tighten up law enforcement across Texas. Word of a fugitive could race past him and alert officers to intercept him down the road.

Andy could not imagine how it might ever get much better than that.

Back at the jail he found Tom standing in front of the woodstove. The sheriff said, "I'm heatin' some leftover beans and corn bread for the prisoner, but I expect you'll want somethin' better. I'll go with you down to the eatin' joint soon as I get Deuce taken care of."

Tom had a farm a few miles out of town, but he often spent the night in the jail rather than make the ride twice, once out and then back in the morning.

Andy said, "If it wasn't already so late I'd ride out and pay a visit to Rusty Shannon. Maybe I'll do it tomorrow."

Tom smiled at the mention of the red-haired former Ranger. "I used to worry a right smart about Rusty. He pined away for a long time after Josie Monahan died. He's fared some better since he made up his mind to marry her sister Alice. She's been like a tonic to him."

"He deserves a run of good luck for a change. He had enough bad to do for a lifetime." Rusty had been like a brother to the orphaned Andy, teaching, counseling, providing a benchmark when Andy seemed about to lose his way. "If it wasn't for Rusty I don't know where I'd be now. In jail, like as not. Or dead."

Tom had a benevolent smile his prisoners seldom saw. "You never were that bad of a kid. All you needed was guidance."

Andy had been taken by Comanche raiders when he was a small boy. They raised him until he fell back into Texan hands at about the time his voice started to change. His reintroduction to the white man's world had exposed him to many pitfalls. Even now, in his midtwenties, he sometimes found himself facing situations where the choice was difficult to make. He had always leaned heavily on Rusty's advice. When Rusty was not around, he tried to visualize what Rusty would do.

He said, "Too bad Deuce Scoggins didn't have somebody like Rusty to point the way for him when he was young."

Tom shrugged. "Might not've made any difference. There's some people that nobody can help. They've got no skill and no trade. They're too shiftless for honest work, and every time they come to a fork in the road they turn the wrong direction. I've seen a lot like Deuce, driftin' to God knows where. I've got to watch myself so I don't get to thinkin' the whole world is that way." Tom's eyes narrowed. "You've been a Ranger for a good while now. You ever find yourself gettin' cynical?"

Andy had to think a minute before he remembered what *cynical* meant. "I still find there's more good folks than bad ones. If I try, I can even feel a little sorry for Deuce."

"Don't tell him so. It might encourage him to get worse."

The telegraph operator found Andy sitting with Tom at a table in the restaurant, hungrily emptying a bowl of thick beef stew. He waved a sheet of paper. "Got a reply to your message. Thought you'd want to see it right away."

Andy read it slowly, his finger tracing the lines. Rusty had been more successful in teaching him about farming and being a Ranger than about reading and writing.

"Any answer?" the operator asked.

"Just say, 'Will comply.'"

That ought to be short enough to satisfy the money counters, he thought.

The operator picked up a biscuit from the table and took a big bite of it as he went out the door. Tom asked, "New orders?"

Andy nodded. "Captain says our company is bein' cut again. Says headquarters in Austin wants to reassign me to the Mexican border."

Tom frowned. "If you've ever thought about resignin', this might be the time. A man can get killed down there."

"A man can get killed anywhere. Deuce might've shot me if he hadn't hit my horse instead."

"But it's like a holy war along the Rio Grande. Been that way since the battle of the Alamo and doesn't show any sign it's fixin' to change. You're automatically somebody's enemy on sight. It just depends on how light or dark your face is."

"Sounds like the Indian wars."

"The Indian wars are over with. This one's not. Do you speak any Mexican?"

Andy swallowed a mouthful of stew. "Just a few cusswords I've picked up."

"You'll have every chance to use them, and probably pick up a bunch more."

The captain had not given Andy a deadline for showing up in Austin. Because the horse he had taken from Deuce was undoubtedly stolen, he left it in Tom's custody and bought one at the livery barn. Rangers were obliged to furnish their own horses, but the state was supposed to pay for one killed in the line of duty. Andy trusted that he would be reimbursed. If not, he would still eat, though it might be a while before he could afford a new hat or a pair of boots.

Tom approved of the black horse. He rubbed his big hand down the back and the shoulder and finally patted the animal's neck. "Got long, strong legs. He'll serve you well in a chase."

"I hope I'm the one that does the chasin'."

"If not, you'll sure be glad for those good legs."

WHEN ANDY PREPARED to leave town the next morning, Tom said, "Sorry I couldn't provide you a featherbed."

The jail cot had been hard as a cement floor.

Andy smiled. "At least the price was right."

Tom said, "I'll ride with you as far as Shanty's farm. Then I'll be cuttin' off and goin' home."

"I'm glad for the company."

"If they send you by San Antonio, be sure to go and visit the Alamo. It'll help you understand the trouble you'll run into when you get to the Rio Grande."

Riding down the street, Andy saw two women pull a buggy up near a general store.

Tom said, "That's Bethel Brackett and her mother."

"I know." Andy hesitated, wondering if he should ride

over and greet them. He realized they had seen him, so he had no choice. "Give me a minute, Tom."

Tom smiled. "Take all the time you want. If it was me and I was thirty years younger, I'd take the whole mornin'."

Dismounting, Andy extended his hands to help the older woman down. She said, "We had no idea you were in town, Andy."

"Passin' through on duty. You're lookin' fine, Mrs. Brackett."

He turned toward the younger woman, who had been driving the horses. Bethel seemed reluctant at first to accept his help. "Andy Pickard, I ought not to speak to you."

"What did I do?"

"It's what you don't do. You don't ever come to see a girl. You could be dead and I wouldn't know about it for six months."

He thought her pretty, even if at this moment she was being petulant. He said, "If I ever die, I'll write you a letter and let you know."

"You could've let me know you were here."

"Didn't get in till late yesterday. Can't stay. I've got orders to report to Austin."

She frowned. "Even my brother Farley breaks down and sends us a few lines every six months or so. I'd write to *you* if I knew where you'd be."

"Half the time I don't know that myself." Andy could not tell whether she was angry or just a bit hurt.

She turned at the door. "If you run into my brother somewhere, tell him Mother and I are all right." She went inside, leaving him embarrassed and not knowing what to do about it.

Tom had watched quietly. He drew in beside Andy and said, "That little girl thinks a lot of you."

"Hard to tell it, the way she acts."

"A woman likes to have some attention paid to her, and you ain't done it. She'd follow you in a minute if you was to just ask her."

"Follow me to what? A tent camp in the brush with a Ranger company? She was raised better than that."

"You won't be a Ranger forever. Sooner or later you'll get a bellyful of cold camps and short rations. You'll start lookin' for a place to light."

"I don't know as I could ever be a farmer like Rusty. Followin' a mule down a corn row is too slow a life for me."

"Lots of Rangers go in for sheriffin' when they get tired of the service. They can uphold the law and still sleep in a decent bed most nights. If you was to decide to give it a try I'd hire you as a deputy."

"Much obliged, Tom, but so far I'm satisfied with what I'm doin'."

A FORMER SLAVE, Shanty York had inherited a small farm when his owner died. At first he had trouble keeping it because some neighbors objected to a black man's being a landowner. Several of them burned his cabin one night. Rusty and Tom and other friends rebuilt it and none too gently elevated Shanty's antagonists to a higher level of tolerance.

The old man looked frail. Nevertheless, he was working in his garden when Andy and Tom rode up. He seemed always to be busy so long as there was daylight to work by. Shanty took off an unraveling old straw hat and wiped a tattered sleeve across a black face shining with sweat.

His broad smile displayed a solid row of white teeth. So far as Andy knew, he still had all the ones God had given him. "Mr. Tom! Andy! You-all git down and grab ahold of this hoe awhile."

He reached out his hand, and each man took it. For most people Shanty would precede their names with *Mr.*, as he did with Tom. But he had known Andy since the day Rusty had brought him home, a hurt and frightened boy who spoke only Comanche. Shanty had helped care for Andy's broken leg and patiently coached him word by word into remembering his forgotten English.

Tom exchanged a few pleasantries, then rode on toward his own farm. Shanty said, "You'll stay and eat with me, won't you, Andy?"

Andy said, "I wish I could, but I've got orders. Just want to drop by and see Rusty before I go."

Shanty kept smiling. "You don't need to worry none about Mr. Rusty. He's doin' fine, him and Miz Alice. I don't know as they've told anybody yet, but she's in a family way."

Andy chuckled. "The old rusty-haired son of a gun. I didn't know he still had it in him."

"It's in Miz Alice now. She glows like the sunrise."

It was useless to ask Shanty how *he* was doing. If he were on his deathbed he would declare that he was fine. His face gave little clue to his real age, but his short gray hair and the droop of his shoulders showed that he was getting old. Andy asked, "Anything I can send you from Mexico?"

"Any necessaries, I can get right here to home. Can't think of nothin' I'd want from way off yonder."

"The Rio Grande is pretty far, all right."

"Too far for these weary old bones. You be careful you

don't come back speakin' Mexican. Took us long enough to get you over speakin' Comanche."

Andy reached into his saddlebag and lifted out a small sack. "Brought you some rock candy to sweeten your disposition." He knew the old man loved candy, but Shanty rarely splurged on such luxuries.

Shanty's eyes teared a little as he struggled for words. "I thank you mighty kindly."

Andy stalled, not wanting to leave. Every time he rode away he wondered if this might be the last time he saw the old man. He asked, "Would you like me to milk your cow for you before I go?"

"She's dried up for a little while. She's in a family way too." Shanty stared at him, his eyes serious. "You be careful, boy. They tell me there's lots of wicked goin's-on down along that river."

"There's wicked goin's-on everywhere." Andy reconsidered what he had said and wondered if his experience with lawbreakers *was* making him a little cynical. Tom Blessing had warned him about that.

He turned once in the saddle to wave at Shanty, then reined the black horse in the direction of Rusty Shannon's farm. The familiar terrain brought back memories, most of them pleasant, a few he did not want to dwell upon. Not far from here he had been part of an unlucky Comanche raiding party, come down from the high plains to steal horses. In a skirmish with Rangers and settlers his horse had fallen on him. Rusty had recognized that he was white and took him to his farm to heal. At first Andy had given him reason to regret his generosity, trying to escape back to his Comanche friends. He had eventually realized that the Indians had reached the end of their time as free-roaming horsemen of the plains. He had gradually accepted his place in the white world, though sometimes he still found himself thinking like a Comanche, feeling like a Comanche. He leaned heavily upon instincts that were sometimes so strong they puzzled him.

Like now, for instance. He sensed a horseman's approach before he saw him. As he crossed over a rise in the wagon road he saw a man on horseback, moving diagonally toward him. He recognized one of Tom Blessing's brothers. They stopped and visited a few minutes, but Andy did not mention what his instinct had told him. Most people did not know how to accept it.

Riding by Rusty's field, he saw that the corn was tall and green, promising a good yield. He remembered a time he had found the crops beaten into the ground by a hail so devastating that Rusty had reenlisted in the Rangers awhile to make up for the financial loss.

Alice stood in the cabin's open dog run, slicing a ham suspended from a rafter. She did not see him right away. She was a slender woman with light brown hair almost to her waist. He had always considered her handsome, though her sister Josie might have been prettier. Josie's death had dealt Rusty a blow that for a time threatened to break his spirit. Eventually he had worked his way up from the darkness and had come to accept Alice.

Andy had been pleased, though he had one reservation: he feared Rusty might regard her as second best, a substitute; that Josie still held first place in his heart. Alice deserved better than that.

She gave Andy a sisterly hug, then pushed him off at arm's length to look him over. "Don't the Rangers ever feed you? You look like you haven't eaten in a month."

He grinned. "I eat Indian style. When I can get it, I eat all I can hold. When I can't get it, I live off of what I ate before."

"I'll slice some more ham and see how much you can eat for supper. I've managed to put some weight on Rusty. If you'll stay around a week or so I'll fatten you up too."

"Can't. I've been ordered to Austin."

She appeared disappointed. "A few days of company would be good for Rusty. He hasn't been away from the farm much since plantin' time."

"I guess he figures he did enough travelin' when he was a Ranger. A man can get awfully tired of it."

"Don't you get tired of it, Andy?"

"Now and then. But soon as I rest up a little I'm ready to go again."

"There'll come a day when you'll decide it's been enough, like Rusty did. You'll want to settle down." Her eyebrows lifted. "Are you goin' to see Bethel Brackett before you leave?"

Andy looked down. "Already saw her, in town." He abruptly changed the subject. "Where's Rusty at?"

Her eyes told him she still wanted to talk about Bethel, but she said, "He went lookin' for a heifer. He thinks she's had her calf, and she's hidin' it out."

"Summer calves can be hard to raise."

"A farmer is ready to take a rain or a calf any time."

She went into the kitchen side of the cabin. "I'll start supper when I see Rusty come to the barn. How about some coffee while you wait?"

"I can get it myself."

Rusty had done his bachelor cooking at the fireplace, but Andy noted that a new iron stove had been installed. A shop-made table and sturdy wooden chairs replaced the crude homemade kitchen furniture that he remembered.

Coming up in the world, he thought.

He watched Alice, trying to discern sign of her pregnancy. All he saw was a brightness he had not found in her eyes before. He said, "Shanty tells me there'll be three of you by-and-by."

She looked startled. "How could he know? We haven't told anybody."

"Guess he saw it for himself. He said you glow like the sunrise." He studied her face. "I believe he was right."

"I have reason enough. I'm happy here. I couldn't ask for things to be any better."

Andy looked at the mantel. Always before, he had seen a picture of Josie there. It was gone now.

Alice turned to see where his gaze was directed. She said, "Lookin' for Josie's picture? Rusty took it down. He said he didn't need a picture to remember, or to keep pushin' the past into his face. Said yesterday's gone. Today is all we've got."

"You think he really sees it that way?"

He saw a flicker of doubt in her eyes. "Sometimes when he holds me I can't help feelin' that he's thinkin' of Josie." She blinked and turned away. "I've tried real hard to be a good wife to him. Lord knows he deserves it. I wouldn't ask him to forget Josie, ever. But maybe with time I can be as much a part of him as she ever was. Even more."

"Maybe you already are."

"No, not yet, but I will be. I'm a Monahan, and you've never seen a Monahan give up."

Andy heard a milk cow bawling. He walked to the door and saw that Rusty had ridden up to the log barn. He said, "I'll see if he needs any help."

"Tell him supper will be ready by the time he gets through with the milkin'."

Rusty pumped Andy's hand as if they had not seen each other in years. It had been only a few months since

Andy had ridden by here on his way to an assignment. They exchanged small talk about crops and rain and local politics. Andy squinted. "I see a little more gray in your hair."

"You've got the sun in your eyes."

"Alice looks fine."

"She does, doesn't she?"

Andy pointed toward the milk cow. "You'll be needin' all the milk Old Boss can give. I understand you-all are expectin'."

Rusty was surprised. "Alice told you?"

"Shanty did. That old man sees things nobody else can."

"He ought to. He's been around since the Colorado River was just a creek. What brings you over this way?"

Andy told him he was due for reassignment to a company on the Rio Grande. That brought concern to Rusty's eyes. He repeated what Tom Blessing had said: "A man can get himself killed down there."

"A little risk never stopped *you*."

"It would now." Rusty glanced toward his cabin. "I've got responsibilities."

"I don't."

"You've got a responsibility to yourself. If you stay too long you're liable to get all shot up and have to quit anyway. Then you may be too crippled to do much of anything else."

"I'm doin' a job that needs to be done. When I stop feelin' that way I'll turn it back to them like you did."

2

As cities went, Andy always found Austin agreeable provided he did not stay long. His first visit here had been with Rusty and Tom Blessing. He had spent his early years in Indian villages and later in the sparse farming community where Rusty lived. The size of this city had amazed him. It was the state capital, Texas's seat of power. That fact had been driven home to him by a tempest that boiled up in 1873 upon the transfer of the governorship from the state's reconstruction administration back to the Texans who had supported the Confederacy. Many former Rangers, cast adrift after the war, had participated in the forcible removal of a reluctant Unionist governor.

The place looked peaceable now after several years of stable and generally benevolent government. Andy rode up Congress Avenue toward the capitol building. The street was wide enough that several spans of mules or oxen could turn a wagon around without crunching its wheels against the wooden sidewalks. After seeing the town several times, Andy was still in awe of the wagon and carriage and horseback traffic and the busy-looking pedestrians along the street. It took a lot of people to govern the state, he thought. Or perhaps, as Tom had once suggested, it took one to do the work and two to watch him.

He paused in apprehension at the door of the Rangers' state office, wondering what was in store for him. He straightened his back and stepped inside, trying to look confident. A clerk sitting at a rolltop desk turned and viewed him over the rims of reading glasses set low on his nose. His annoyance over the interruption was but thinly veiled. "Yes?"

"I'm Private Andy Pickard. I was ordered to report here for reassignment."

The clerk did not recognize the name. His face was pale, the mark of a man who spent his days in an office rather than out in the field. Andy wondered if he knew which end of a gun the bullet came out of. After riffling through some papers he withdrew one and studied it. "Oh yes, Pickard. Do you know Major Jones?"

"Met him. He's visited camps where I've been." Major John Jones was well-known for spending a minimum of time in the office. He was usually on the trail in his buggy, inspecting the far-flung Ranger outposts that were his responsibility.

The clerk said, "Luckily you have chosen a day when the major is in. Unfortunately at this moment he has company. You may sit if you choose to wait."

Andy seated himself in an uncomfortable straight-backed wooden chair that he supposed was meant to discourage long visits. He became aware of loud and angry voices beyond the door of the major's office. He glanced at the clerk, asking a silent question. The clerk rolled his eyes. "The major is having a discussion with a representative of the treasurer's office. The gentleman is explaining why the Rangers must do more but do it with less money and fewer men."

Andy could not follow all that was being said, but he

caught words like *stingy* and *waste* and *efficiency*. The latter seemed to receive special emphasis.

The door swung open. A man as pale-faced as the clerk strode out but turned to fling final words back at the major. "If it were up to me we would disband the Rangers. That would stop this needless drain on the state's resources."

Major Jones followed him, shaking his finger. "And I hope the next person to face a holdup man is yourself. I'd like to see how long it would take you to call for the Rangers."

A gust of hot wind seemed to follow the treasury representative's retreat.

Major Jones's fists were clenched. He said, "There goes a man who can make me forget the biblical injunctions against profanity."

As his anger subsided he became aware of Andy standing at attention. He said, "I remember your face, but your name is a puzzle to me."

"Private Andy Pickard, sir. I was ordered to report to you for reassignment."

"Oh yes." The clerk handed Jones a couple of sheets of paper. Jones glanced at them, then beckoned Andy into his office. He was known for quick perception and attention to detail. He could drop in on a camp unannounced and in a few minutes have a firm grasp on the situation there. If he found shortcomings he saw to it that they were being corrected before he left for the next place to be inspected. He believed in Ranger regulations, but his own conduct was based on higher rules. If he visited a camp on a Sunday, he personally conducted religious services.

The major was a small man, but he had a firm handshake and a strong, steady gaze that seemed to see into the hidden part of a man's mind. "Have a seat, Pick-ard."

Some officers might offer a man a drink at this point, but not Major Jones. He said, "As you may know, the legislature has seen fit to cut our budget again. Some from the settled parts of the state say we don't need Rangers now that the army has the Comanches and other hostiles safely tucked away on their reservations. I have argued to little avail that outlaws present as much of a challenge now as the Indians ever did. Would you not agree?"

Andy was inclined to defend the Indians, but he knew that was not what the major wanted to hear. "Yes, sir."

"I am keeping as many Rangers as I can, given the funds the state has allotted to me. Your record tells me you are one whose services I should retain. I am transferring you to a region that needs all the law enforcement it can get. Are you familiar with the Nueces Strip?"

"I've heard of it. Never been there."

The major turned to a map of Texas on the wall behind his desk and put his finger on the lower part. "It is that region between the Nueces River and the Rio Grande. Mexico still claims it in spite of the treaty Sam Houston won from Santa Anna. The scarcity of law has made it a gathering ground for robbers and cutthroats from both countries."

"I heard Captain McNelly whipped them a few years ago."

"Leander McNelly and his men put down much of the worst trouble, but fighting still goes on. Mostly it's between the races—white against Mexican, Mexican against white." He lowered his chin and stared hard at Andy. "How do you get along with Mexicans?"

Andy shrugged. "All right, I guess. Never knew very many. They haven't settled much where I come from." He had known a few Mexican boys among the Comanches. Like himself, they had been captured on raids and gradually assimilated into the tribe as potential hunters and warriors.

Jones said, "Mexicans dominate the Nueces Strip, at least in numbers. Some still consider themselves to be living in Mexico and not subject to American law. At the same time many Americans in that section do not recognize that Mexicans have legitimate rights, especially ownership of property. They drive them from their lands, or try to. They would like to see every Mexican banished to Mexico, or killed. It is not for us to choose sides. It is our responsibility to put down violence from whatever quarter it may arise."

"Sounds like that would take a lot of Rangers."

"Far more than we have, which sometimes drives us to actions we would not normally consider. Captain McNelly used extreme measures, but the situation called for them. He was up against desperate men."

"What do you mean, extreme measures?"

"At the worst, summary executions. We would prefer to observe all the niceties of the law, but outlaws respect only force. McNelly knew how to get their attention. He stacked the bodies of a dozen dead bandits in the town square in Brownsville. Afterward he conducted a raid across the river into Mexico and shot every suspect he came across. No doubt he killed some who did not deserve it. They were simply in the wrong place at the wrong time. This caused us no end of diplomatic trouble. It is easy to criticize him now from the comfort of an Austin office, but you have to give him credit. He put a damper on border jumping for a while."

Andy was troubled by the thought of shooting suspects.

"It's been preached to me over and over that everybody has a right to be tried by a jury."

"No bandit summons a jury before he shoots someone. Mind you, I do not advocate summary justice. However, under extreme circumstances we may have little choice. Now, after what I have told you, do you think you can handle this assignment?"

Andy nodded. "I'll do my duty as I see it, sir."

"Your commanding officer may sometimes see it differently than you do. If so, will you obey him?"

"If I can't, I'll give him my resignation."

Jones mulled that over. "Well enough, but surely you would not desert him in a crisis."

"I won't quit in a fight, but I might resign afterward."

Jones dipped a pen in an inkwell and began to write an order. "How soon can you start?"

"Right now. I'm travelin' light."

"It is a long way to ride alone. I have assigned another Ranger of your acquaintance to the same place. Find him and you can travel together."

Andy thought of several he hoped it might be—Len Tanner or either of the Morris brothers.

Jones said, "His name is Farley Brackett."

Hearing that name was like biting into a sour apple. Andy and Farley had ridden together on several missions, but their relationship had always been prickly.

Jones said, "From all I know of him, Brackett is a good man to have at your side in a fight."

Andy knew that to be true but was tempted to tell Jones that Farley started some of those fights himself. The war had left a visible scar on his face and invisible scars on his soul. In the first years after the Confederate defeat he had been an unreconstructed rebel, a constant thorn in the side of Union authorities. He had brought trouble to Rusty Shannon's door and therefore to Andy as well.

The major handed Andy the order he had been writing. "Stop at Ranger headquarters in San Antonio as you pass through. They can tell you exactly how to find your camp on the Rio Grande. It is moved from time to time."

"Yes, sir." Andy sensed that the major was finished with him. He thought he should salute or something, but he simply backed to the door.

The clerk was waiting for him. He said, "I hope you've got a little money."

"A little. Not much."

"It'll have to stretch. We have no traveling money to give you."

"I don't eat much."

"That's good. You may have to live off of the land."

That was neither new nor news to Andy. "Any idea where I'll find Farley Brackett?"

"He put his horse in a stable down the street. Beyond that, I suggest you investigate all the dramshops."

Brackett did not have a reputation as a drinking man, but perhaps that was because he seldom had the opportunity, Andy thought. Whiling away the hours in Austin might tempt him to make up for time lost in dry and spartan Ranger camps.

Andy went to a livery barn where he and Rusty and Tom Blessing had stabled their horses on a visit several years ago. He recognized the proprietor as the same dried-up little man who had been there before, charging a shameless price for oats, hay, and corral space. Andy said, "I'm lookin' for a Ranger named Farley Brackett."

The hostler pointed to a stall. "His horse is here. I doubt Brackett has gone far afoot. Most of the Rangers I know had rather be whipped with a wet rope than to walk a hundred yards."

"If he comes in, tell him Andy Pickard is lookin' for him."

The hostler eyed him with curiosity. "You've got some older, but I believe I remember you. Ain't you the one that spiked them Union soldier boys' cannon so they couldn't use it to keep that Yankeefied governor in office?"

Andy suspected a lot of people in Austin remembered that incident. It had been a wonder someone was not killed. "I didn't spike the cannon, but I was with the ones that did."

"It was a hell of a show for a little while. Too bad it fizzled out before anybody got a chance to kill one of them damn Yankees."

Like many Texans, the hostler was still engaged in the war between the states, at least with words. Living among the Comanches at the time, Andy had been only dimly aware of the war. He knew a lot about its aftermath, however. To some degree it was still going on, just as the war between Texas and Mexico continued along the border years after it had been relegated to the past elsewhere.

He walked back over to Congress Avenue and entered the first bar he came to. It was moderately busy. He noted that most of the patrons wore suits. Men who wore suits in Austin were usually either lawyers or state employees. No wonder people complained about the waste of their tax money, he thought. This was a weekday. These men were supposed to be working.

Farley was not there. Andy waved off a bartender's question and returned to the street. A second barroom gave him no better result.

As he approached the third he heard a familiar voice

raised in challenge: "I don't give a damn whether you like Rangers or not."

The reply came in an equally angry voice, though the words were muffled. Andy heard boots striking hard upon a wooden floor. A man hurtled out through the open door, speeded along by strong hands that gripped his collar and the seat of his britches. He sprawled on his stomach in the street. Farley Brackett stood in the doorway, making a show of dusting his hands. He said, "Come back in and I'll finish windin' your clock for you."

The man sat up but for the moment looked too confused to continue the contest.

Farley's eyes reflected surprise as he recognized Andy. "Badger Boy! What the hell you doin' here?" He did not appear pleased.

Badger Boy was an English version of the name by which Andy had been known among the Comanches. No one used it anymore except Farley, and he usually said it in a mocking way.

"Lookin' for you. I ought to've known to wait and listen for a fight."

"Wasn't no fight to it. I was just standin' there havin' me a peaceful drink when that gink asked me if I wasn't a Ranger. Don't know how he figured out I was. They never have got around to givin' us any badges."

"Some people claim they can tell a Ranger on sight, just by the way he walks and talks."

"I wasn't talkin' at all till that bird started to hooraw me. He said he never seen a Ranger that didn't smell like a skunk."

"If you try to whip everybody that doesn't like us, you'll be too busy to do anything else."

Farley transferred his irritation from the stranger to

Andy. "You're a little young to be preachin' gospel to me, Badger Boy. I've been shot and shot at more times than you've had birthdays."

"A little preachin' might do you good, but I know you wouldn't listen to it."

"That, I wouldn't," Farley said, and went back into the bar. Andy remained on the sidewalk, debating with himself about following. He considered riding on alone and letting Farley follow in his own good time or not at all. He knew from past experience that Farley could be poor company, chronically dissatisfied and critical. But the major might not be pleased. He liked his Rangers to work together as a team, not pull against one another like stubborn mules.

He walked into the room and found Farley leaning against the bar, a drink in his hand. The war scar on the side of his face accentuated his frown. "You still here? I figured you left."

"The major says we're supposed to head south and report for duty on the border."

"I don't remember him sayin' I had to ride with *you*. Every time we work together somethin' bad happens to me. You're a damned jinx."

"I'm not crazy about the notion either, but if you don't like it you can resign."

"That'd make you happy, wouldn't it? Well, I'm not quittin'. Go find you a girl or somethin' and leave me in peace for what's left of the day. We can start the trip fresh in the mornin'."

Andy doubted how fresh Farley would be if he spent the evening in this bar or some other, but that was Farley's problem. "I've got my horse in the same stable as yours. I figure to leave soon after daylight."

Walking outside, he met the stranger Farley had

thrown out. The man seemed to have gathered his wits, and his expression indicated that he did not consider the argument settled. Andy pointed his thumb at the door. "He's still in there," he said. He stood around a few minutes, listening to the sounds of a vigorous scuffle and the cheers of bystanders from inside.

Farley tumbled out the door and fell on his back on the sidewalk. Andy looked down at him and tried not to grin. "Enjoy yourself."

Farley rolled over and pushed to his feet, muttering under his breath. Face crimson and fists clenched, he stalked back into the barroom.

Andy's growling stomach reminded him that he had not eaten anything since breakfast. He had noticed a restaurant as he walked down the street. He met a policeman hurrying along the wooden sidewalk. The officer said, "Somebody told me there's a fight down thisaway."

Andy pointed. "You might look in that bar yonder. There's a right smart of noise comin' out of it."

By the time Farley got himself untangled from this mess he might be ready to travel, Andy thought.

AWAKE AT DAYLIGHT, Andy sat on the edge of the wagon-yard cot and looked at Farley, still sleeping, his blankets spread on a pile of hay. "Time to get movin'."

Farley did not respond. Andy had heard him come in during the night but had no idea what time it was. Farley had been talking to himself.

Andy said, "I'm fixin' to go get some breakfast. Then I'm hittin' the trail with or without you."

Farley still did not respond. Andy could see his chest rise and fall with his breathing, so he knew at least that Farley was not dead.

The hostler had a fire going in a small iron stove in the front office, a steaming pot on its top. He told Andy, "Got coffee here."

"Thanks, but I'm goin' for breakfast."

"You might want to take some coffee to your partner. By the looks of him as he staggered by here in the wee hours, he's liable to need it."

"His legs ain't broke. Let him come and get his own coffee."

The hostler seemed startled at Andy's lack of concern for Farley. "I thought you was Rangers together."

"Rangers, but not together any more than we have to be."

After breakfast Andy brushed the black horse, then saddled him. Farley was sitting up but still on his blankets. He appeared to have trouble focusing on Andy. "Where you goin' so early?"

"South, like we were ordered. You can catch up to me or not, that's up to you."

Farley rubbed a hand over his bruised and swollen face. His knuckles were red, the skin broken. "I must've had fun last night. I just can't remember much about it."

"Last time I saw you it looked like you were comin' out second best against a man who didn't like Rangers."

"It taken me a while, but I finally convinced him. It's what happened afterwards that I can't remember much about. The last I knew, him and me had a couple of drinks together, us and some policeman."

"A couple?"

"Maybe three. I never let myself get drunk."

Andy tied his blankets behind the saddle and started to lead the horse outside. Farley called, "Ain't you goin' to wait for me?"

"No." Andy mounted in the street and turned south to

intersect the San Antonio road. He crossed the Colorado River on a wooden bridge and turned to look back northward toward the capitol building. Though he liked Austin, he never felt at ease in large cities. This one was home to maybe five or six thousand people.

He was a couple of hours down the trail when he heard a horse coming up behind him. "Badger Boy! Wait up."

Farley pulled in beside him. "Damn it, you'd make a man kill his horse tryin' to catch up with you."

"Told you I was leavin' soon after daylight."

"You could've waited. I was sick this mornin'."

"You look like a herd of cattle ran over you. For all I care you could've stayed in Austin."

"I was just havin' a little fun. Looks to me like I've earned it. Don't get much chance when we're out in the field."

"It's a good thing the major didn't see you."

"He knows that a man has to let off some steam now and again. Else he'll blow up like a boiler with the valve stuck."

Andy remembered how Farley had let off steam in the early years after the war, provoking the carpetbag state police into one fight after another. He had been like a wolf luring dogs into chasing him, then turning on them in a fury of slashing teeth. They had learned to pursue him only at a safe distance. Now he directed his belligerence at lawbreakers for the most part. That made him useful to the Rangers, though he tended to act first and plan later.

After a long, smoldering silence Farley remarked, "That's a good-lookin' black horse. Where did you steal him at?"

Farley had never gotten past a bone of contention involving a sorrel horse his father had given to Rusty

Shannon and that Rusty had passed on to Andy. Farley always contended that the horse was his own and that his father had no right to give him away.

Andy said, "I always figured if you're goin' to steal a horse, you'd just as well steal a good one."

THE WAGON ROAD south from Austin skirted the eastern edge of rough limestone hills where the Edwards escarpment rose out of the western portion of the coastal plain. To the east lay farming settlements along the Colorado and Brazos rivers. To the west, stock farmers and ranchers were freely expanding their operations now that they no longer slept with their guns, worrying about Indian raids. German enclaves such as Friedrichsburg and Neu Braunfels had sunk deep roots. The hill country had appealed to Andy from the first time he saw its long green valleys, its bubbling springs, its clear-running creeks and rivers. Someday, if he ever left the Rangers, he thought he could make a life for himself there.

Traveling at a pace that would not be hard on the horses, Andy and Farley took two days traveling from Austin to San Antonio. Farley said, "Last chance for a little relaxation. Ain't goin' to be much fun from here south."

"If you'd had much more fun in Austin you'd still be there."

"It'll be all business when we get to the border. Go on ahead if you want to, but whatever trouble they got down there can wait another night or two."

Andy did not feel like arguing. "We can tell them we needed to rest the horses." He would welcome the chance to look around the historic city. "We'll need to find Ranger headquarters."

"Tomorrow is soon enough. If they know we're here they'll want us to start south right away whether our horses are tired or not."

Andy had never been to San Antonio, though he had heard many stories about its turbulent past. The town had been a crossroads of early Texas history. Several pitched battles had been fought there, first for Mexico's freedom from Spain and later for Texas's freedom from Mexico. Though other cities in the state were rapidly gaining in importance, San Antonio remained the jewel in its crown—if a sprawl of picket *jacales* and single-story buildings of stone and adobe could be considered a jewel.

As soon as they found a convenient wagon yard and put their horses away, Farley disappeared. He had been to San Antonio in his hell-raising days after the war and knew where he wanted to go. Andy asked the stable's manager how to find the Ranger headquarters, then walked about, familiarizing himself with the center of town. Street traffic was heavy. A man had to look both ways before crossing over lest he be stepped on or rolled over by horses, wagons, and ox-drawn carts with high, solid wooden wheels that groaned and squealed on dry hubs.

He had known the population would be heavily Mexican, but seeing it for himself made him feel like an outsider. As a boy with the Comanches he had listened to Kiowas talking. He had felt helpless because he could not understand a word. He found himself just as lost trying to decipher some meaning from the Spanish he heard spoken all about him.

He had learned Comanche and relearned English. With time he should be able to pick up at least enough Spanish to get him by, he thought.

A strong German element was also evident, spilled

over from early immigrant settlements founded in the 1840s. He despaired of ever learning to speak German. Spanish would be challenge enough.

He came unexpectedly upon what he recognized as the Alamo, at least the battle-scarred remains of the church that had been the center of the original mission complex. Much of the rest was gone, lost to new construction and bustling commercial uses. He was disappointed to find that even the old sanctuary had been turned into a warehouse. He thought it an undignified fate for a building where brave men had fought, bled, and died for Texas. Perhaps it would someday be turned into a shrine befitting the blood sacrifice that patriots of both Texas and Mexico had made there.

In the Ranger office Andy looked at a map that appeared to be the same as the one on Major Jones's Austin wall except that more trails had been added, some ranches and small towns penciled in. A lieutenant traced one of the trails with his finger. "With some exceptions, you'll find most white ranchers friendly to the Rangers. With some exceptions, you'll find most Mexicans distrustful and unfriendly. Both sides have cause." He turned back to face Andy. "Have you got anything against Mexicans?"

"Major Jones asked me the same question. No, I don't."

"Many people do, Rangers included. It's not one-sided, though. Many Mexicans have a hard grudge against whites too. Especially Rangers. They say we use our authority and our guns to help the gringo ranchers run them out of the country."

Andy reflected a minute. "Do we?"

"We're not supposed to, but some take it to be their duty. Old wars don't die easy. They linger on like an incurable disease."

"I try to treat everybody just alike."

"That's a fine ideal. I hope you can live up to it when you've been on the river awhile. A man can lose his religion there if he doesn't get killed first."

Andy was not sure just what his religion was. Old Preacher Webb and others had counseled him about Christianity, but remnants of Comanche beliefs lingered as well. Sometimes the two seemed much the same. Other times they conflicted.

Andy asked, "When I get down there, what'll my duties be?"

"They'll be whatever Lieutenant Buckalew tells you to do. If he says ride, you'll ride. If he says shoot, you'll shoot. Don't waste his time or yours askin' questions."

"Yes, sir."

"When the lieutenant isn't around, you'll take orders from Sergeant Donahue. You may find that the lieutenant and the sergeant don't always see eye to eye."

"In that case, which one do I listen to?"

"The one who's there at the time." The officer turned toward a small safe. "How long since you've been paid?"

"I was out on assignment the last payday. And I had to buy a horse. About all I've got in my pocket is a whittlin' knife."

"I'll advance you a little travelin' money against your wages. We can't have a Ranger beggin' his way down the road. Keep account of your expenses. Maybe the state'll see fit to reimburse you. Or maybe not."

Andy normally wasted little time worrying about money, but once in a while the need could not be ignored. He had feared he would have to accept a wound to his pride by asking Farley to lend him a few dollars. But Farley might have no money left either after a couple of days

and nights in San Antonio. It would give Andy deep satisfaction if Farley had to touch *him* for a loan.

His stomach rumbled loudly enough that he was sure
the officer must have heard. He asked, "Where can I get
a decent meal cheap?"

The lieutenant seemed to approve of the word *cheap.*
"There's a fair-to-middlin' chili joint down the street
a couple of blocks and around the corner. It's not the
Menger Hotel, but it's fillin'. And the cook washes his
hands once a day whether they need it or not."

"Sounds like the place for me."

He started to leave, but the officer snapped his fingers
and said, "Almost forgot. There's another Ranger who'll
be headed the same way as you and Brackett. He came
up to deliver a prisoner. Maybe you know him. Name's
Len Tanner."

Andy grinned. "I've known him since I was this high."
He held his hand flat at chest level. "I lost track after he
got transferred away from my camp. Where do you reckon
I'll find him?"

"Go where you hear the loudest talkin'."

Len had a reputation for a loose jaw. He could talk the
bark off a live-oak tree. Andy had first gotten to know
him when an accidental horse fall and broken leg took
him out of Comanche hands and thrust him back into the
life of a white boy. A jovial spirit who came and went as
the mood struck him, Len had spun enticing tales of high
adventure and eventually had talked Andy into joining
the Rangers.

The café's proprietor had laughing eyes that offset the
fierceness of his black beard. His body was shaped like
a pickle barrel. He asked, "Cowboy?"

"Nope," Andy said. "Ranger."

"Ain't nothin' too good for a Ranger. I'll give you a choice: beefsteak or chili. Same price."

"That bein' the case, I'll take the beefsteak."

The man laughed. "Some of the biggest ranchers in South Texas come in here to eat. It's the only time a lot of them ever eat any of their own beef."

Andy took that to imply that most preferred to eat their neighbors' cattle. It also implied that the operator of the chili joint was not choosy about the source of his meat supply.

Andy said, "It doesn't sound like rightful ownership means much around here."

"Not unless a man is ready and willin' to fight for what belongs to him. There's people here who can steal your socks without takin' your boots off."

The cook poured a cup of coffee for Andy without being asked. A cast-iron skillet clanged as he placed it atop the stove. He plopped a huge spoonful of hog lard in it to heat and melt. He said, "The secret to a good steak is to fry it deep in plenty of hot grease."

Enough of it, Andy thought, and he could develop a belly like the cook's.

The cook said, "I ain't seen you before. Where are you stationed?"

Andy told him he was being reassigned to the border. The man's face went serious. "The trail down to the Rio Grande can be risky, especially the lower part. The more Rangers the better. You never know who's liable to pop out of the brush lookin' for somebody to shoot."

"I'll have another Ranger with me. Maybe two if I can find Len Tanner."

The name brought a flicker of recognition from the

cook. "I believe that old boy was in here yesterday. He talked till my ears hurt."

"That's him."

The cook turned Andy's steak over in the skillet. "If I was you I wouldn't noise it around too much about bein' a Ranger. I rode awhile with McNelly's outfit. Down in that border country the Mexicans called us *rinches,* and they didn't say it sweet. I decided to move up here for my health."

Mention of Captain McNelly stirred Andy's curiosity. "What kind of a man was he?"

"As good a feller as I ever knew. He had a hard job to do, and he done it despite bein' sick most of the time. Some days he was almost too weak to stay in the saddle, but he wouldn't let go. He meant to clean up the border if he had to kill half the population. He *did* kill a lot of them. Some claim he went too far." The cook shrugged. "All I can say is that bandit raids tapered off right smartly by the time he got through."

Andy said, "From what I hear, they're back. Maybe not as strong as before McNelly, but bad enough."

The cook lifted the steak on a fork and dropped it onto a platter. "Want a little advice? No extra charge."

"Sure."

"Don't trust every smilin' face you see. You never know for sure who's your friend and who wants to see you dead. When in doubt, shoot first."

Andy asked, "What if I kill somebody innocent?"

"There's damned few innocent people down there. They might start that way, but they get over it."

Andy's back was to the door, but he sensed that someone had entered the room behind him. The voice was Farley's, and he sounded agitated. "Eat quick and let's get movin'."

"I thought you had some celebratin' to do."

"Done done it. I'm ready to go."

"What's the big hurry? It's already late in the day. We can't get far before dark."

"We can get far enough. I'll go fetch our horses while you finish your supper."

Farley left in a trot. The cook said, "Don't eat too fast. Ain't good for the digestion."

"I just hope he didn't kill somebody."

Before Andy had finished eating his steak and red beans, Farley was back and leading Andy's black horse. He shouted from outside, "Come on. Let's move."

Andy kept his seat until he had emptied the platter and finished his coffee. He paid the proprietor out of the money the lieutenant had advanced. The cook said, "Mind what I told you. They'll smile when you're lookin' and stab you when you turn your back."

Farley was fidgeting as if he had ants in his underwear. "You damned sure took your time."

"I don't see why we have to rush away from here like a couple of thieves."

Farley did not answer. He set his horse into a long trot. He did not bother to look back and see if Andy was following.

Andy caught up to him as they passed through the southern outskirts of town. "Who did you shoot?"

The question surprised Farley. "I never shot nobody."

"The way you left, I thought maybe you did."

Farley looked back. "It wasn't nothin' like that. I ran into an old friend of yours, and I was afraid he'd want to ride with us. I can't listen to Len Tanner all the way to the border. I might shoot him to shut him up."

Annoyed, Andy said, "All this rush was to get away from Len? Where did you find him?"

"I was visitin' a couple of ladies I know. He was there doin' the same thing. You're too young to understand."

"I'm old enough. Seems to me like you ought to find yourself a good woman and leave those other *ladies* alone."

"What woman would look twice at this scarred face unless she was paid to do it?"

"There's bound to be some. You've been searchin' in the wrong places."

"And you're stickin' your nose in where you've got no business."

Andy choked down his irritation. Though Len's chatter could be a trial, he would prefer it to riding with a morose Farley Brackett. "I've got half a mind to go back and find him."

"If you do, you'll go by yourself."

"That might be an improvement."

Farley grumped, "You're damned hard to get along with. Must be you ain't got all the Indian out of you."

3

Andy looked back a couple of times as they put the historic old town behind them. He hoped he might see Len catching up. He said, "Len's a good Ranger, you can't take that away from him."

Farley said, "That don't mean I've got to appreciate his company. A man can put up with just so much jaw."

Andy knew of no one who disliked Len except some of the criminals he had sent away to board with the state. Farley was a good Ranger too, but Andy knew many people who did not care for much of his company, himself included.

He asked, "When are we goin' to stop and camp?" He hoped Len would catch up.

Farley said curtly, "You already had your supper, and I brought mine with me." He held up a pint bottle.

Andy had rarely seen him drunk, for Farley could hold a prodigious amount of whiskey without showing its effects. He had a stern will that did not permit interference with whatever he set his mind to do. Len, on the other hand, did not drink on duty or when he thought he might be called to duty. Even a modest amount of whiskey could start him to singing in a voice loud but seriously off-key.

At dusk Farley said, "We better call it a day. We been pushin' the horses pretty hard."

Farley had been pushing. Andy had just been trying to keep up.

Farley added, "We don't need no fire. It's warm enough, and we ain't cookin'. A fire just draws visitors."

Andy knew Farley was concerned about just one visitor, Len. They pulled off the trail a little way, unsaddled and hobbled their horses. Dragging one foot, Farley smoothed the rocks from a small patch of ground and spread his blankets. He hoisted the bottle without offering to share it. Andy would have refused it anyway. He had not developed a liking for whiskey and could not understand why others so readily did. It always burned his throat on the way down and kindled a fire in his stomach when it got there.

Farley said, "I don't suppose you seen my mother and sister before you left?"

"I did."

"How were they?"

"Fine. They're the *likeable* members of the Brackett family."

Farley accepted the implication without visible reaction. "You serious about Bethel?"

"I might be if I wasn't a Ranger."

"That's easy fixed. You could quit."

"If you don't like me ridin' with you as a Ranger, you sure wouldn't like havin' me for a brother-in-law."

"I'd seldom ever see you."

Andy said, "I guess that's right. You hardly ever visit your womenfolks."

"It's better that way. All I ever brought them was trouble."

Andy kindled a small fire. Farley demanded, "What's that for?"

"I want to boil a little coffee after that ride."

"Never could see why some people got to have coffee all the time. It's too much trouble. With whiskey, all you have to do is pull the cork."

Andy heard the strike of a horse's hooves and saw a lanky rider approaching in the dusk. A familiar voice shouted, "Hello, the camp. You there, Andy?"

Farley groaned. "Oh hell."

Andy stood up and waved his arm. "Come on in, Len."

Len Tanner swung a spindly leg over his horse's rump and stepped to the ground. "I'd about give up on catchin' you fellers. I thought you'd wait for me in town."

Andy saw no need to explain and hurt Len's feelings. "Farley was in a hurry to leave. It's a right long trip to the river."

"I know. I had to deliver a prisoner all the way up to San Antonio. He was wanted for usin' his knife a little too free. That's a common failin' in this part of the country. Got some of that coffee left? I ain't had no supper."

Farley muttered, "I suppose after a few days in town you was too broke to feed yourself."

Andy figured Farley might be right about that. Wages slipped through Len's fingers like sand. He always said he could travel lighter without the weight of silver in his pockets. He was too skinny to carry much extra weight anyhow.

Len said, "I'll ride with you fellers if you'll have me. It always shortens the miles when I've got somebody to talk to."

Farley grunted and moved to where he had spread his

blankets. "I'm hittin' the soogans. If you find me gone in the mornin' it'll be because I made an early start."

Len said, "Eager, ain't he? He wouldn't rush if he knew the border. It was easier fightin' Indians. At least when you saw one you knew he was your enemy. Down yonder you're never sure."

Andy asked, "How come you to transfer from the San Saba? That was a nice place to be stationed."

"The captain volunteered me. I guess they needed a man with experience."

More than likely the captain had heard Len's stories one time too many, Andy thought.

They set out the next morning soon after daybreak. Len began to tell about his experiences since he had been sent down to the border. Andy listened eagerly, but Farley quickly lost patience. He stopped and dismounted, lifting his mount's left forefoot and examining the shoe.

"I think there's a stone lodged in here," he said. "You-all go on. I'll catch up to you by-and-by."

Andy suspected Farley was trying to get out of earshot. He would probably drag along behind. Andy had rather listen to Len's stories than to Farley's grumbling anyway.

He had noticed a bright, shiny star on Len's shirt. Sometimes Rangers made their own badges. "Where did you get that?"

"A Mexican cut it for me out of a silver peso. Looks pretty good, don't it?"

"Looks like a target."

"Ain't nobody hit it yet. Been a couple tried."

"White or Mexican?"

"One of each. Most Mexicans don't like Rangers, and a lot of whites don't like Rangers gettin' in their way when they're tryin' to take what belongs to the Mexicans. We get shot at from both sides."

By noon Farley had not caught up. Andy could see him poking along a couple of hundred yards behind. Len asked, "Reckon we ought to stop and wait for him?"

"He likes his own company. Let him make the most of it."

"I figure he must've been born in the dark. Me, I was born in the daylight."

Andy enjoyed studying the changing landscape. It was gently rolling, mostly open except for watercourses lined with trees and many varieties of brush. Wide areas were flat enough for farming, though little had as yet been broken by the plow. Cattle of many hues grazed the tall, summer-curing grass. Some hoisted their tails and ran for the thickets. Others watched placidly as the riders passed, for this was a much-used public roadway. They were accustomed to wagon, cart, and horseback traffic.

He said, "Sure looks peaceful."

Len shook his head. "Wait till we get down into the brush country. Plant, animal, or human, everything there is lookin' for a chance to draw blood. They've all got stickers, horns, knives, or shootin' irons."

Farley grudgingly rejoined them as they stopped at an abandoned adobe hut from which windowsills and the roof had been removed. The mud walls were gradually disintegrating, most of their plaster covering gone.

Len said, "Sure feels good to sleep indoors now and again."

Farley spread his blankets outside, by himself.

As the next day waned toward dusk they began looking for a place to stop. They came upon a little creek that appeared to be a favored camping site. A half dozen Mexican ox carts were there. A couple of dark-skinned men walked out to meet the riders. They spoke in Spanish. Andy could not understand a word.

Len said, "I've picked up a little Mexican lingo. They're invitin' us to share the camp with them."

Andy asked, "They can see your badge. I thought all Mexicans hated Rangers."

"Just the same, they'd feel safer camped with us. There's gringos around who would be glad to do them harm."

Farley said, "They might wait till we're asleep, then carve their initials on our gizzards."

Len argued, "They're just freighters, haulin' goods from the Gulf of Mexico to San Antonio. They know if they hurt anybody they couldn't get away. An ox team travels awful slow."

"I don't trust anybody I can't understand. We need to find a place where we're by ourselves, or at least with people who talk our language."

Andy said, "The worst people I ever knew spoke our language real plain. They just didn't think the same way we do."

Farley snorted. "Stay here for all I care. I'm goin' on."

Andy glanced at Len and shrugged. They traveled a while longer. Farley turned from the road and followed a cow trail about a quarter mile. "Them people might come huntin' for us after dark. They'll play hell findin' us out here."

Andy was not keen on making a dry camp. He asked, "What have we got that they'd want?"

"Our horses. Our guns. We're gringos, and we're Rangers. That by itself might be enough."

Len said, "Can't fault anybody for bein' what they was born. The big dealer dealt us each a hand the day of our birth. It's up to us to play it out the best we can."

Farley said, "I was born cautious."

Not all that cautious. Andy remembered when Farley's

reckless disregard for reconstruction law had made him a target of the carpetbag state police and brought bad trouble down upon his family. But Farley was selective in what he chose to be cautious about.

Len said, "If you-all are nervous about my badge, I'll take it off." He stuck it in his pocket. "If anybody jumps us now, it won't be because we're Rangers."

Toward noon the next day Andy began seeing dust rising in the south. It troubled him for a time because it was too localized to be a dust storm.

Len said, "It'll be a trail herd on its way north. Lots of them swing by San Antonio to supply their wagons."

The point man, riding at the front of the strung-out herd, was white. He gave the three Rangers a silent and distrustful study, then moved on past them. Len observed, "It's a steer herd bound for the Kansas railroad, I'd guess. Cow herds are generally headed farther north, like to Wyomin' and Montana."

Wyoming and Montana were exotic-sounding names to Andy. He said, "I wonder how it'd be to go up there ourselves."

Len shook his head. "The sight of a snowflake makes me shiver. Feller told me one time he was up in Wyomin' and seen a hat movin' along on top of the snow. When he went to look, he found a cowboy under the hat, and the cowboy was on horseback."

Andy grinned. Len declared, "It's the gospel truth. At least that's what the feller told me."

Farley's face was without expression. Andy could count on one hand the number of times he had ever seen Farley smile at a joke, or anything else. Farley nodded toward the cattle. "Notice how many different brands they've got on them?"

Len said, "A lot of those are Mexican brands." He

pointed out that they were larger and more intricate than most of Texas origin.

Andy asked, "You think they're stolen?"

"Let's say they was got awful cheap. They swum the Rio Grande in the dark of the moon. Come daylight, they was citizens of Texas."

Andy said, "Maybe we ought to arrest this whole outfit."

Farley said, "Didn't the Comanches ever teach you how to count, Badger Boy? There's a dozen or fifteen of them and just three of us. I doubt you'd find a church-goin' man amongst them."

Len said, "There's a chance these people bought the cattle in good faith from somebody else who brought them across the river. Anyway, the Mexicans they belonged to may have made up the loss already, swimmin' Texas cattle back in the other direction."

Farley said, "Sounds like everybody breaks even."

"Not everybody. There's losers, and they're generally the little fellers. Besides, it's bigger than just cattle. People get killed."

A swing rider approached. He had a sober bearing that indicated he might be the boss. He said, "I hope you-all ain't Rangers."

Andy said, "Why? What difference would it make?"

The drover spat. "The Rangers gave me trouble over the Mexicos in this herd. I had to pull strings in high places."

Farley said, "We're Rangers, but we ain't been given any orders yet. It's no hide off of our butt if you take these cattle to Timbuktu."

The trail man said, "Kansas is far enough. Time we get there they'll all be talkin' American."

The Rangers pulled away from the herd to get out

of the dust. It struck Andy as curious that more than half the horsemen appeared to be Mexican. He said, "If these cattle were stolen from south of the river, the Mexicans with this outfit are robbin' their own countrymen."

Len said, "Some don't feel like they owe Mexico nothin', or Texas either. Santy Anna stabbed them in the back. After preachin' that his soldiers ought to be proud to die for Mexico, he gave away Texas to save his own hide. They don't see that anything is wrong if they can get away with it. That includes shootin' a Texas Ranger or a Mexican *rurale*. It's open season on anybody who gets in their way."

"Some of these drovers are gringos."

"Thieves don't pay much attention to each other's color as long as they're all fillin' their pockets. Afterwards they may try to cut each other's throats. Why, just last spring . . ." He started retelling a story he had already told twice on this trip.

Farley dropped back a hundred yards.

LEN DISMOUNTED IN front of an abandoned adobe house. He rubbed his mount's right foreleg. "Feels to me like my horse is comin' up lame."

Andy looked to the west, where the sun cast a rosy glow through low-hanging clouds. "He may just be gettin' tired. It's time we stopped for the day and gave the horses a rest."

Farley argued, "We've got an hour of daylight left."

Andy said, "You want Len to have to walk and lead his horse?"

"It wouldn't hurt him none. Might make him tired enough to quit talkin'."

Len said, "You go right on ahead if you want to. I ain't goin' to ruin a good horse."

Andy said, "I'm stayin' with Len."

Farley seemed about to argue the point but gave in. "You two need lookin' after. Anyway, they ain't goin' to pay us extra for reportin' in early."

Andy saw a well beside the house and led his black horse over to examine it. Looking down into the water, he saw no sign that it harbored any drowned rats or other small animals. Though the house appeared not to have been occupied in a long time, the windlass had a reasonably new rope. It was probably a gift from someone who passed this way often. Andy turned the handle and brought up a bucket of water. He poured it into a small wooden trough and brought up a second bucket so there would be enough for his horse. He cupped his hands and tentatively tasted the water to be sure it was good before he drank his fill.

Len started to walk through the door but stopped abruptly and stepped back. Andy heard a buzzing sound that he recognized instantly as a rattlesnake's warning. Len said, "I believe I'll sleep outdoors tonight." He handed his reins to Andy. "But I'll make sure this gentleman doesn't come out huntin' for me." As soon as Andy had led his and Len's horses away, Len shot the snake.

Holstering the pistol, he said, "Welcome to South Texas, where everything scratches, stings, or bites."

They searched around for sign of more snakes, then hobbled the horses. Andy built a small fire in a rock-lined hole that travelers had used before him. He let the fire burn down to red coals, then set a coffeepot on top of them.

He said, "Indians would make supper out of that snake. It tastes a little like chicken."

Len grimaced. "Help yourself. I've been hungry lots of times. I've eaten mesquite beans and jackrabbit. I've eaten horse and mule meat, but I ain't never been hungry enough to eat a rattler." He went on to describe at length a couple of times when he was desperate enough that he almost ate the tops from his boots.

Muttering to himself about liars and those who listened to them, Farley went out to gather some dry wood. He came back and dropped several dead mesquite limbs near the fire. "Riders comin'," he said. He went to his saddle lying on the ground and pulled his rifle from its scabbard.

Andy followed his lead by drawing his pistol. He counted seven horsemen, one a smooth-faced boy of fourteen or fifteen. The others were older and had not felt a razor in at least a couple of weeks, nor water either except to drink.

Farley said with some relief, "At least they're Americans."

Len's right hand rested on the butt of his pistol. "That don't guarantee nothin'. They may not like the law, so we better not tell them we're Rangers. They've got us outnumbered."

The riders stopped a respectful distance from the Rangers' camp. One rode forward with his right hand raised in a sign of peace. He slouched in the saddle. "Howdy. Looks like you-all have made yourselves to home."

Farley did not offer a welcome. "You got any quarrel with that?"

The rider shook his head. His whiskers were coal black, a sharp contrast to the washed-out gray of his eyes. "None at'all. We're just travelers like yourselves, lookin' to water our horses before we ride on a ways more."

Farley said, "The water's free for everybody."

The man said, "We come upon a bunch of Meskins back yonder. They eyed us like coyotes that found a mess of quail. I've got a hunch they been trailin', waitin' to hit us in the night when we're asleep. It'd ease our minds if we could camp with you-all."

Andy saw doubt in Len's and Farley's eyes.

The visitor said, "The more there is of us, the safer we'll all be."

Farley was slow to lower his rifle. "Maybe. What say you-all camp over on the other side of the house?"

The man waved his arm, and the other six rode in closer. He said, "My name is Burt Hatton. Me and the boys here, we just delivered a herd to San Antonio. There's people that'd gladly shoot us for the money them cattle brought. Failin' that, they'd at least try to take our horses."

Andy did not like the looks of the men. They reminded him of a wolf pack circling a small buffalo herd and looking to bring down a calf.

Len was uncharacteristically silent. As the men moved away, he said, "Andy, you look like you smelled a skunk."

"It's just a feelin' I've got."

"Me too. Seems to me like I've seen that hombre before. With all the whiskers it's hard to be sure."

The drovers made camp on the opposite side of the adobe ruin. Once their horses were unsaddled and hobbled, Hatton walked back over to the Rangers' campfire. He asked, "You-all headed for the border?"

Len was usually the first to speak, but he kept his silence. His badge remained in his pocket.

Farley said, "We thought we'd go down there and take a look around."

"I hope you've been told what kind of country you're gettin' into."

"We've got a pretty fair notion."

"You'll find more Meskins than white people. Damned shame, seein' as this country is supposed to be American. We've chased a lot of them across the river, but they keep birthin' more and more of them here. Seems like they're bound and determined to outbreed us. A white man has got to keep his guns strapped on all the time."

Andy was a little disturbed by Hatton's tone. "If a man owns his land, how can you run him off of it?"

"They'll sell out when you put the proposition to them right. A Meskin gets real agreeable if you stick a pistol up against his ear and cock the hammer back. Especially if you can bribe a couple of Rangers to stand behind you."

Andy saw anger rising in Len's eyes. He had seldom seen Len yield to ill humor. Len turned away from the campfire. "I'm goin' to see about the horses."

Andy followed him. He kept his voice low. "A Ranger wouldn't ever do that. Would he?"

Len frowned. "There's some that might. They think the border country would be a lot better off if all the Mexicans was moved to the other side."

"That's what they did to the Indians. They pushed them all north of the Red River." Resentment stirred when he thought about his Comanche friends forced into exile on a cramped reservation away from their former range. Yet he realized it had been the only way to curtail their raiding.

Len said, "The law says you can't put people off of their property, but some gringos ignore the law. They tell the Mexicans they can either leave or die. More often than not they sell out for whatever they can get. It usually ain't much."

"I wouldn't be a party to such as that."

"Me and you, we're just privates. We've got no say. If

a sergeant says 'Fire,' all we can do is ask what at." Len looked worriedly back toward camp. "I'd swear that Hatton looks familiar."

"Maybe he's in your fugitive book."

Rangers carried a book with handwritten descriptions of fugitives. They consulted it often and kept it as up to date as possible. They took special pleasure in marking off a fugitive as captured or killed.

Len said, "Might be. I'll read it after a while when that bunch can't see me."

Andy returned to the campfire. He heard Hatton talking to Farley about border outlaws. "There's one in particular you better be on the *cuidado* for. Guadalupe Chavez has got a big ranch over yonder, stocked with good Texas cattle his bunch has stole. Used to have considerable land on this side of the river too, but Jericho Jackson ran him off of it."

Andy asked, "Who's Jericho Jackson?"

Hatton seemed surprised that Andy did not know. "Just about the biggest man on the Texas side of the border these days. Took over a large part of what Chavez claimed north of the river. He ain't a man to be crossed, not even by the likes of Guadalupe Chavez. They're blood enemies."

Andy said, "This Chavez, what kind of man is he?"

"A real bad hombre. His pistoleros come across the river lookin' for somethin' to steal and gringos to kill. He tells his people that someday he'll fly the Mexican flag again over everything from the Rio Grande to San Antonio."

Len said, "I hear that Jericho Jackson ain't no angel either. It's like he built a wall around his ranch and don't let anybody in that ain't an outlaw like he is."

Andy said, "I remember Preacher Webb talkin' about a place called Jericho. It had walls, but they fell down."

Len nodded. "That was on account of a soldier called Joshua, but I ain't met anybody around here by that name."

Hatton's eyes flashed in irritation. "I wouldn't go talkin' against Jericho. It can get a man hurt." He pushed to his feet. "Maybe the boys have got supper fixed." He stalked away.

Farley turned on Len. "What did you provoke him for? He was tellin' us things we need to know."

"I remember where I've seen him before. He was with a bunch we caught drivin' stolen horses. We got most of the horses back, but the ones they rode was faster than ours. We suspected they was workin' for Jericho Jackson, but it's hard to get anything on him. People like Hatton do his dirty work for him."

Farley chewed on what Len said. "You reckon there's paper out on Hatton?"

Len grunted. "There ought to be. I'd wager that the cattle they delivered to San Antonio still had Rio Grande mud on them. We better stand guard duty tonight, or we're liable to find ourselves dead in the mornin'. Or at least afoot. Notice the way he kept lookin' at our horses?"

Farley said, "I figured since the men was all white that we had no need to worry."

"White, Mexican, down in this country there's meanness enough to go around."

Andy asked, "So what do we do?"

Len made a wry smile. "What would your Comanche brothers do if they smelled Apaches?"

"They'd sleep with their eyes open and a war club in their hands."

Len said, "We'll do better than that. After good dark we'll move our horses, then we'll keep watch."

Andy half expected Farley to put up an argument because the idea was Len's, but he didn't. They made a show of stringing a rope between two trees and tying their horses and the pack mule to it. Before moonrise they quietly led the animals farther out into the brush and retied the picket line. They returned to camp but remained in the shadows beyond the campfire's dying light.

After a time Andy felt himself dozing off. Farley punched him with his elbow. He whispered, "Rub a little tobacco in your eyes. That'll keep you awake."

And maybe blind me, Andy thought. He declined the offer of Farley's tobacco.

He felt himself nodding again just before Len gently shook him. "They're comin'."

The fire had burned down to flickering coals that yielded little light. Andy could make out shadowy figures moving stealthily into the Rangers' camp.

He recognized Hatton's voice, raised in disappointment. "They're gone."

Someone else said, "They can't be gone far. Their camp stuff is here."

Farley raised up. "Yes, we're still here, and you sons of bitches ain't gettin' our horses."

Pistols blazed on both sides, and then a rifle. Men shouted and cursed. A youthful voice cried out in mortal pain. Hatton's men backed away, quickly lost in the darkness. Andy heard Hatton shout, "Pick him up and let's get out of here."

The smell of gun smoke was pungent. Andy heard horses moving away from the Hatton camp. His heart pumping with excitement, he said, "We must've hit somebody."

Farley said, "I thought they would just come after our horses. But they was after us too."

Andy said, "No witnesses, no charges."

Len said, "No use tryin' to follow them in the dark. I can't see that they done us any harm."

He was mistaken. At the picket line they found Farley's horse down. Andy knelt to examine it and found it was dead. "Stray bullet must've got him."

His first reaction was relief that his black horse had not been hit. But he realized that this would complicate the completion of their trip.

Farley declared, "Damned if I intend to walk all the way to the river."

Len said, "We can borrow a horse at the McCawley ranch, a little ways south. Till then we'll take turns walkin'."

Farley asked, "Who's McCawley?"

"Big Jim McCawley. He married into the Chavez family."

The name got Andy's attention. "Chavez?"

"He married Guadalupe Chavez's sister, but don't hold that against him. There was a time when even Lupe Chavez was considered good folks. That was before Jericho and others tried to take everything away from him and his family."

Farley said, "I don't know as this is a good idea, havin' truck with Chavez's kinfolks."

Len shrugged off Farley's objection. "Big Jim's always been friendly to the Rangers. We've brought back stock of his that was run off by thieves."

"I'd be friendly too if they recovered my property."

"You'll be surprised how many *ain't* friendly." A smile spread across Len's face. "Once you see Big Jim's daughter Teresa, you'll be glad we went there."

Andy said, "You sayin' she's pretty?"

"Wait till you see her eyes. Dark as coffee beans. They melt me plumb down into my boots."

Farley said, "But she's Mexican, ain't she?"

"One look at her and you won't even think about that."

"Mexican is Mexican."

4

Hatton and his men had galloped more than a mile when Burt Hatton shouted for a stop and reined his horse around. "Let's see about that damned kid."

Jesse Wilkes held the wounded boy to prevent his falling from the saddle. "I'm afraid he ain't goin' to make it."

Hatton listened for sound of pursuit but heard none. He dismounted and raised his arms. "Lift him down to me." He lowered the groaning youngster to the ground. "I wish to hell you'd stayed home like you was told. Let's have a look at you."

He felt the warm stickiness of blood on his hands. He fished a match from his pocket and struck it for light. In the few seconds that it burned, he saw what he had feared. He heard a faint bubbling sound. "Of all the bad luck, they got him in the chest."

Wilkes said, "I'm afraid he's goin' to die."

Hatton made no comment.

The boy whimpered, "Where's Aunt Thelma? Take me to Aunt Thelma."

"You'll be all right," Hatton said, knowing he lied. "We'll carry you to a doctor."

"It hurts. Oh God, it hurts."

Wilkes was always finding fault. He said, "It was a mistake to let the boy come along. Jericho told us not to."

Hatton retorted, "We didn't let him come. He done that on his own."

The boy was a nephew of Jericho's wife. Given the responsibility of raising him, she had spoiled him so that he took advice from nobody except her. He had begged to help Hatton and his crew drive the cattle to San Antonio. It should not have been a dangerous trip. It became so only when Hatton took a notion to bushwhack three strangers for their horses and gear. It had looked easy.

Whose damn-fool idea was it in the first place? Hatton asked himself, though he knew it had been his own. He had not intended for Jericho to know about it. Hatton and the others would not have had to split their booty with him.

The boy cried, complaining about the pain until his voice began to fade.

Fearfully Wilkes said, "He's dyin', Burt. Do somethin'."

"Damn it, shut up."

In a few minutes the kid shuddered and was gone. Hatton shuddered too, and cursed under his breath. "Just my luck."

Wilkes said, "Better it had been one of us. It'll be hell to face Jericho. He's been known to kill a man for bringin' him bad news." He looked at Hatton, making it plain he expected Hatton to be the one to carry the message. "You know how he dotes on that woman of his, and she dotes on this boy."

Hatton frowned, considering his options. An idea took a little edge from his dark mood. "He don't have to know how the shootin' came about. We can tell him we got ambushed, and it wasn't our fault."

"Jericho'll see right through you. His eyes cut like a knife. Why would anybody pull an ambush on us?"

Hatton's spirits lifted a bit more. "Jericho hates Lupe Chavez like he was strychnine. He'll believe it if we tell him we ran into some Chavez bandits. We'll tell him they didn't give us a chance."

"*You* tell him. I wouldn't lie to him for a hundred dollars. What about the kid? We goin' to take him all the way home?"

"It's too far, and the weather is too warm. Come daylight we'll find a place to bury him. Jericho is goin' to ask a lot of questions. Everybody remember: Chavez's outfit ambushed us."

Wilkes grumbled, "I still say he won't believe it."

Hatton's voice was deep and dangerous. "You tell him different and I'll kill you."

BIG JIM MCCAWLEY's place was not fancy, but it was large. A long Mexican-style rock house dominated a gentle knoll. It was surrounded by smaller, flat-topped buildings, mostly adobe, some of pickets, scattered haphazardly down the slope. Off to one side lay corrals with fences of stacked stones or upright tree branches bound tightly together with rawhide thongs dried to the hardness of steel. Everything appeared to have been built from raw materials close at hand.

Andy and Len walked their horses so Farley could keep pace afoot. He chose to lag behind a little so he did not have to listen to Len's long-running commentary on everything from the weather to the crowned heads of Europe, and now and then a detailed description of Teresa McCawley. Andy carried Farley's saddle and roll. Len carried his bridle and blanket.

Len said, "He ought to be gettin' in a little better humor now that he can see the ranch."

Though Farley had ridden for long stretches while Andy and Len took turns walking, Farley had been grouchy as an old badger awakened from sleep. He seemed somehow to blame Andy and Len for the loss of his horse, though Andy knew that was illogical.

Once while Len was taking his turn at walking they came upon a long-horned cow with her calf. Not accustomed to seeing a man afoot, she took Len for a threat to her offspring, lowered her head, and charged. Len's long legs carried her in a wide circle until she gave up and trotted away with her calf, wringing her tail in agitation.

Farley almost smiled.

Andy asked Len, "You sure McCawley will lend Farley a horse?"

"Better than that, I'll bet he'll give him one. He'd take the shirt off of his back for somebody in need. He was a Ranger himself once, long before the war."

Andy saw dust rising from behind a corral fence. As the breeze swung around from that direction he could hear men yelling encouragement. He saw a figure bobbing up and down, riding a pitching horse. He said, "Maybe Farley can have that one."

Len said, "It'd give him somethin' to cuss at besides us." His grin showed that the thought pleased him. He pointed his thumb toward a corner of the corral. "I see Big Jim over yonder."

A large man stood outside, watching the show from between the upright tree branches that constituted the fence. In size and stature he reminded Andy of Sheriff Tom Blessing. The rancher turned his head as the two riders approached. His big hand dropped quickly to a pistol on his hip, then eased away as he decided the visitors presented no threat.

Len raised his hand. "You know me, Mr. McCawley. Name's Len Tanner. I'm a Ranger."

McCawley's eyes lighted up. A pleasant grin spread across a face ruddy and deeply lined, seasoned by many years of sunshine and hard weather. Gray hair in need of a trimming curled over his ears. "Sure, I remember you." He shook Len's hand, then shifted his attention to Andy.

Len said, "This is Andy Pickard. The tired-lookin' bird draggin' his feet back yonder, that's Farley Brackett. Him and Andy are Rangers too."

McCawley looked at Farley's saddle, which Andy held in front of him. "A saddle by itself ain't worth much. How come your man ain't got a horse to go with it?"

Andy was content to let Len do the talking. Len explained that they had been set upon by outlaws. "There was one that called hisself Hatton. I'm pretty sure he was with a bunch of horse thieves that our scoutin' party jumped a while back on the river."

McCawley's eyes went grim. "Hatton. Yes, I know him. He runs with Jericho Jackson's coyote pack. I had him in my sights once, but my horse scotched and I missed."

"I heard somebody holler like he was hit, but I don't know if it was Hatton."

Andy rode up to the fence and looked over. The bronc had stopped pitching. It was circling the in-side of the corral in a lope, its bay hide shining with sweat. A grinning Mexican cowboy held a hackamore rein high and tight. Three other cowboys stood in-side the fence, watching, hollering for him to spur the bronc in the flanks. One was Mexican, two were white. Having heard so much about racial strife in the borderland, Andy was a little surprised at the camaraderie.

McCawley said, "That's Pedro Esquivel in the saddle. He's *puro jiñete,* a natural bronc rider." He turned and saw Farley at last approaching the corral. "I suppose your man is hopin' for a horse?"

Andy said, "Yes, sir, but not that one."

McCawley smiled. "I've got several he can pick from. Nothin's too good for a Ranger."

Len said, "We'll see that Farley either pays you or brings your horse back."

"No need. It's a small thing against the debt I owe the Rangers. If the horse stayed here some thief would probably take it anyhow. We get hit by all kinds, Mexican and white."

Andy knew instinctively that he was going to like this man. The more he looked at him, the more he was reminded of Tom Blessing, solid as an oak, comfortable as a well-worn pair of handmade boots.

Farley trudged up to the corral, shoulders drooped in weariness. Sweat rolled down his face. Len introduced him to the rancher and said, "Mr. McCawley's goin' to fix it so you don't leave here afoot."

Farley always seemed to have trouble expressing gratitude. "I'll pay you when I can."

"I already told your friends that it's a gift."

Farley shook his head. "I'll pay you. I don't like leavin' debts behind me."

McCawley shrugged. "Whatever suits you." He looked at the western sky. "It'll be sundown directly. How about you-all comin' up to the big house with me? We'll have supper pretty soon."

What he called the big house was modest in size and far from new. The stones that constituted its walls were of varied sizes and hues. The building had been con-

structed for utility rather than for beauty. It reminded
Andy of houses he had seen in San Antonio.

McCawley said, "I've promised my wife, Juana, a new
house for years, but we're land-rich and cash-poor. If we
could stop the raidin' and thievin', maybe I could lay
aside enough money to build what she deserves."

The place might be old, but evidently McCawley's wife
was making the best of it. A well-tended flower bed
reached across the entire front, broken only by the doorway. It held roses, brilliant crepe myrtles, and several
other colorful and eye-pleasing plants Andy could not
identify.

The three Rangers removed their hats as they stepped
over the threshold, past a heavy wooden door carved with
cattle brands and horse figures. A heavyset, middle-aged
Mexican woman spoke to them in Spanish, took their
hats and placed them on a rack in the nearest corner.
Andy assumed at first that she was McCawley's wife,
then realized she was a servant.

McCawley said, "Juana's in the kitchen. You-all come
on back." He led them into a room dominated by a large
fireplace where the cooking was done. Andy remembered
that Rusty Shannon had bought an iron stove for Alice.
Maybe McCawley was waiting for that new house before
he installed so modern a convenience. Through a window he saw an outdoor Mexican-style baking oven in an
open patio.

The room smelled of fresh bread, reminding Andy that
he had eaten nothing since breakfast but a strip of jerky.

A slender, black-haired woman was bent over a table,
slicing strips from a hindquarter of beef. McCawley said,
"Juana, we have company."

She turned. Andy saw that she was no longer young,

but she still had smooth olive skin and large, expressive brown eyes so dark that they looked black. She smelled faintly of lilac perfume. Or maybe it was the flowers in pots scattered not only in the parlor but in the kitchen.

"My wife," McCawley said.

Andy felt awkward, not sure he should speak English to her. But he knew no Spanish. He bowed from the waist. "How do, ma'am? I'm pleased to make your acquaintance."

Len said, "Howdy, Miz McCawley."

Farley grunted something unintelligible.

She said, "Welcome to our home, gentlemen. If you would like to wash up, you will find water and soap and fresh towels in the patio. Supper will be ready in a little while."

McCawley said, "These men are Rangers."

She smiled, skin crinkling at the corners of her eyes. "Then you are doubly welcome. Our house is your house."

The Spanish-style patio sat in the center of the house. Flowers of many hues had survived summer's heat beneath the edge of the overhanging roof.

Len commented in a loud whisper, "She talks English purt near as good as me and you, don't she? I'll bet she was somethin' to look at when she was twenty years younger."

Andy said, "She still is." For a moment a vague image came into his mind's eye, a faint recollection of his mother. She had been killed by Indians when he was a small boy. He had no clear memory of her face, but sometimes he imagined he could hear her voice. He thought he heard an echo of it in Mrs. McCawley's. "She seems like a real pleasant woman."

Farley said, "But she's a Mexican."

Andy hoped McCawley had not overheard, but he had.

The rancher said, "Yes, she's Mexican. There was a time when her family owned all this land." He made a sweeping motion with his hand. "Don Cipriano Chavez, her father, fought beside Sam Houston against Santa Anna. But that didn't help him when Americans decided they wanted his land. They killed him and Juana's first husband, and they tried to take away the property he had on this side of the river."

Len asked, "Then how come you to have this ranch?"

"After I married Juana, most of the land grabbers left this place alone. They knew I was a Texian, and I proved I would fight them. Some people called it a marriage of convenience, to save what her father left to her. But it was a lot more than that." McCawley looked back toward the door, his expression softening. "I was just a wanderer. I had no real aim in life except to survive. She gave me purpose. The land is in my name now, but it'll always be hers. And the children's."

Andy asked, "How many children?"

"I have a daughter and a stepson. Our daughter, Teresa, will be here in time for supper. She teaches the ranch children in a schoolhouse we built here."

"And the stepson?"

McCawley frowned. "Tony is away, with his uncle." His expression indicated that he did not want to dwell on this topic. Andy did not press him on it. He said, "You said bandits hit you pretty often."

"White renegades feel like this ranch is Mexican because of my wife. Mexican bandits feel like it's an American outfit because of me. We're fair game for all of them. Especially Jericho's bunch."

"Can't the Rangers stop him?"

Andy saw Len shake his head.

McCawley said, "Some of them don't want to. Jericho

never lets himself get caught at anything he could go to jail for. He's like a general who runs an army from the rear and never goes out on the battlefield. And because he concentrates most of his attention on ranches in Mexico, a lot of the Rangers look the other way. They've never forgotten the Alamo and Goliad."

Andy said, "I thought McNelly stopped most of the bandits, white *and* Mexican."

"For a while. But he's gone."

Mrs. McCawley stepped out into the patio. "Teresa's here, and supper is ready."

McCawley motioned toward the door. "After you-all."

Andy waited for Len but not for Farley. His attention went immediately to a pretty girl with long black hair. McCawley introduced her as his daughter, but Andy had realized that the moment he saw her. She had the same dark brown eyes as her mother. They looked at Len and Andy, then dwelled for a moment on Farley before shyly cutting away. She waited for the men to sit. Farley did, but Andy and Len stood until she decided to seat herself. Andy was surprised at Len's sudden good manners.

Mrs. McCawley was last to the table. Light from the window revealed strands of gray hair that Andy had not noticed at first. She bowed her head and recited a prayer in Spanish. She crossed herself at the end of it, as did her daughter.

McCawley said, "Eat hearty. One thing we've got plenty of is beef. There ain't enough bandits to take it all."

Conversation lagged at first. Andy was too hungry to talk until he had emptied his plate. He was slower eating the second helping. He noticed that Teresa kept taking quick glances at Farley. He supposed she might be fascinated by his scar. It made him look a bit dangerous. Andy had been told that many women were drawn to men who looked dangerous.

To McCawley he said, "You've mentioned havin' trouble with Jericho. What about Guadalupe Chavez?"

A look passed between McCawley and his wife, and McCawley considered before he answered. "Some of Lupe's countrymen run off stock from time to time, but he leaves us alone."

Andy noticed that McCawley used the familiar form of the name, Lupe instead of Guadalupe.

Mrs. McCawley said, "My father was Cipriano Chavez. Lupe Chavez is my brother."

Andy stared at the girl. Her gaze was studiously fixed on her plate, though she had stopped eating. He thought she looked too innocent to be kin to a bandit whose name was known up and down the border. He remembered something the hole-in-the-wall cook in San Antonio had said, that very few innocent people lived on either side along the Rio Grande.

He remembered something else. McCawley had said his stepson was with an uncle. That uncle must be Guadalupe Chavez, Andy thought.

He had a feeling that whether or not his service on the river was pleasant, it should at least be almighty interesting.

After supper McCawley led the Rangers out onto the broad front porch, where he lighted a pipe while Len and Farley smoked cigarettes. He said, "You-all heard enough in there to raise a lot of questions. I feel like I owe you some answers."

Andy said, "You don't owe us nothin'."

"I want you to understand how things are. I was poor

as a whip-poor-will when I first came to this part of the country. That was back in the fifties. Jobs were scarce. I served a little while with the Rangers, but half the time the state couldn't afford to pay me. Old Don Cipriano had land on both sides of the river, and he put me to work as a vaquero. By that time Americans were movin' into this part of the country in considerable numbers. They wanted land. They found that most of it was owned by Mexicans, so they started pushin' them out. The old man thought they'd leave him alone because he'd fought for Texas independence.

"Some of those Johnny-come-latelys hadn't fought for Texas, but they thought they had a right to whatever part of it they wanted. They took control of the courthouse and ruled that the old man's land grant wasn't legal anymore. When he fought back, they ambushed him and Juana's husband. Lupe hunted down the leaders and left them layin' dead as a skinned mule. Then he took a fast horse and went to Mexico."

Len said, "And after that you married Mrs. McCawley?"

"When a respectable time had passed. I was in love from the first time I saw her. Besides, I was grateful to the old man and wanted to save his land for her if I could. I had to face up to some hard men. I even had Jericho in my sights once. I ought to've killed him, but I let him go because there was a time when we used to be friends." McCawley looked regretful. "He's hated me ever since. I guess he figures he's beholden to me, and it grates on his soul to owe anybody."

Andy said, "At least you've given Lupe Chavez a reason to like you, marryin' his sister and savin' her land."

"No, Lupe doesn't like me. To him I'm just another gringo, and he hates them all. He'd be glad to come to my funeral if he didn't have to kill me himself. He leaves me alone on account of his sister."

Farley asked, "But you're American. Ain't it tough, standin' up against your own kind?"

"People like Jericho aren't my kind."

Andy thought he understood. "For a long time I thought of myself as Comanche. But there were some Comanches I had no use for." He explained to McCawley about the years he spent with the Indians.

McCawley said, "Then maybe you can understand the position I'm in. Sometimes I feel like I belong to both sides, and other times I don't belong to either one."

After dark the Rangers unrolled their blankets in the yard. Len lay on his back, looking up at the stars. He asked Andy, "What color would you say Teresa's eyes are?"

Andy said, "Brown. Dark brown."

"But they're not brown like anybody else's. They're different. They're . . ." He considered for a moment. "Damned if I can say just what color they are. But they're the prettiest eyes ever I seen."

Andy said, "Sounds to me like you're in love. But as I remember it, you've been in love lots of times before."

"Not like this."

Farley said, "She's Mexican."

Len's voice was defensive. "Half of her is white."

Farley gave the matter some thought. "I'll admit, I kind of liked lookin' at her."

After breakfast McCawley led them back out to the corrals. A dozen horses stirred in a single pen, warily watching the men who entered the gate. He said, "Take your pick, Farley."

Andy had always known that despite his faults Farley was a good judge of horses. He strode among them, making them walk, watching how they moved. He soon made his choice. "I like that stockin'-legged red." He had always shown a partiality to sorrels.

McCawley said, "You've got a good eye. He'll take you there and bring you back."

The Rangers saddled up. Andy shook McCawley's hand. "Please tell the womenfolks again how much we enjoyed their good cookin'."

"And you-all watch out that the next time you run into bandits, it's of your own choice and not theirs."

THE RANGER CAMP was similar to one Andy had known on the San Saba River. It was a row of pyramid-shaped canvas tents and a set of crude but effective corrals built of tree branches tied together with rawhide. The tents could be moved on short notice as the need arose and the corrals quickly put together at the new site with whatever materials happened to be at hand.

A broad-shouldered man emerged from a tent and stood with big hands placed solidly on his hips as he watched the three riders approach. He gave Andy and Farley a critical study, then shifted his attention to Len. He said, "Look what the north wind just blowed in. I figured you liked San Antonio so much that you wasn't comin' back."

Andy could not be sure whether the man was joking or not. He sounded serious, even disappointed that Len *had* come back.

Len took no offense. "I left as quick as I could, Sergeant. Brought you two men."

"Prisoners?"

"No, Rangers."

The sergeant squinted, one eye almost closed. "It's hard to tell. They got an outlaw look about them."

This time Andy was seventy-five percent certain that the sergeant was not joking.

Len said, "Sergeant Donahue, this is Farley Brackett and Andy Pickard. They been transferred here from out in West Texas."

Donahue studied Farley with suspicious eyes. "Brackett? Seems to me like I've heard that name."

Len said, "He's got a considerable reputation up yonder where he comes from."

"Good or bad?"

"Depends on who you ask."

Farley gave Len a cautioning look.

Donahue nodded. "Well and good, but we judge men by what they do here and not by their reputation somewheres else." He spoke to Andy. "You appear too young to have much of a reputation as yet. Are you here lookin' to get one?"

"I'm just here to do my job, whatever that is."

"Well, boy, you better watch these border Meskins. They'll grind you up and make tamales out of you. I just got one rule when it comes to them. If you're in doubt, shoot." He punctuated that statement by jerking his head. "Come on, you'd best report to Lieutenant Buckalew and get on the pay roster. That don't guarantee you'll get any pay, of course." He did not look back. He had the air of a man who has no doubt that his order will be obeyed. The three Rangers followed him, leading their horses.

Entering the headquarters tent, the sergeant introduced Andy, Len, and Farley to the lieutenant. Buckalew welcomed the newcomers with more enthusiasm than Donahue had shown. He said, "You men are a welcome

sight. As you will soon discover, this company is somewhat under strength. There's been a dearth of state ap-
propriations. I see you brought your blankets. I hope you
brought lanterns as well. You will have more use for them
than for a bed."

Len put in, "They're good men, Lieutenant. You tell
them what to do and they'll get it done or bust a gut."

The lieutenant smiled. "They don't have to go that far.
All I'll ask is that they work thirty hours a day and eight
days a week."

Len reported on their confrontation with Hatton and
his bunch. The lieutenant listened intently, glancing at
Andy and Farley from time to time for confirmation.

The sergeant demanded, "Are you sure they wasn't
Meskins?"

Len said, "They was blue-eyed gringos, every one."

Andy had not noticed the color of their eyes, but he
nodded agreement with Len. "They were white men."

The lieutenant said, "You think they were part of the
Jericho outfit?"

Len said, "I can't say for sure that they belonged to
Jericho, but I'm pretty certain they're part of a bunch we
swapped shells with some time back. You was there that
day, Lieutenant. Remember, they was tryin' to get away
with some of Big Jim McCawley's horses."

"I remember. Think you killed anybody?" He asked
the question hopefully.

"Somebody hollered like he was hurt."

"I wish we could shoot them all, Jericho's bunch and
the Chavez gang too."

Sergeant Donahue interjected, "Or euchre them into
shootin' one another without costin' us anything."

Once the formalities were taken care of, Len headed

for the mess tent. A dark-faced Mexican cook used a wicked-looking butcher knife to cut a quarter of beef hanging from a tree branch. He dropped the slices one by one into a tin pan. Finishing, he chased the flies away and wrapped a bloodstained tarp around what remained.

Len said, "Pablo, we're hungry."

Pablo had a long, drooping mustache and a pitted face that showed he had survived a long-ago bout with smallpox. He looked westward to gauge the position of the afternoon sun. "Always, Tanner, you are hungry. You will wait like everybody."

Keeping an eye on the butcher knife, Len lifted the lid from a cold Dutch oven and found leftover flat-baked bread. He tore off a chunk. "Try it, Andy. It ain't bad when you get used to it. Mexicans don't know about bakin' biscuits."

Andy gave Pablo a questioning glance before accepting. He knew that getting crossways with the cook was about the worst mistake a man could make in camp. He saw that Pablo was awaiting his verdict on the bread. He took a bite and nodded. "Tastes mighty fine to me."

Pablo grinned. "Any time you are hungry, you come see me. We find you somethin' to eat." He shook the knife at Len. "You got enough. You wait for supper."

Len broke off another piece of bread. He said, "Another good thing about camp cooks is they've always got a givin' disposition."

The sergeant came looking for him. "Tanner, the lieutenant says we need to get the new men off to a quick start. In the mornin' you'll take Brackett and Pickard and patrol up the river. They need to get acquainted with the lay of the land."

Len asked, "We got to take Farley?"

"He needs to learn the country." Donahue frowned. "What's the matter? Don't you and Brackett get along?"

"I get along with Farley just fine. As long as I don't pay any attention to him."

Donahue grunted. "Just be damned sure you pay attention to *me*."

5

Burt Hatton came to a fork in the road and glanced with foreboding at a sign which stood on the left. It said: THIS IS JERICHO'S ROAD. TAKE THE OTHER.

He wished he could take the other and keep going. Facing Jericho was always unpleasant when things did not go as Jericho wanted. Hatton turned in the saddle and looked at the men who followed. One led a riderless horse. He said, "Don't none of you forget what we've agreed to say. We got jumped by Lupe Chavez's bandits. The kid got shot before we could reach cover."

He hoped Jericho would be mollified at least somewhat by the fact that they did not lose the cattle money.

Jesse Wilkes always looked as if he had sucked on a sour persimmon, and he had more complaints than a dissatisfied mother-in-law. He argued, "I still say you can't lie to Jericho. He reads faces like me and you read a paper."

"Let me do the tellin'. You-all just nod. Maybe he won't ask many questions. He'll be busy figurin' out some way to get even with Chavez."

"Whatever he comes up with, it'll be us that get sent to do the job. He don't do anything the law can grab him for."

Hatton's voice sharpened. "You've got nothin' to belly-ache about. You get your share."

"Money's hard to spend in the graveyard."

"You can always leave if you're a mind to. Go back to East Texas. Maybe they've forgot about that murder charge they had out on you."

Wilkes seemed to shrivel. "They don't ever forget."

"And neither does Jericho, so keep your mouth shut and let me talk to him."

Wilkes went quiet, but his eyes still reflected his anxiety. Hatton had not chosen him as a member of the bunch; Jericho had done that. Hatton often found it hard to fathom Jericho's thinking. It was too bad Wilkes didn't catch that bullet instead of the kid. If it ever became necessary for Hatton to sacrifice somebody to save the rest, Wilkes would be his first pick.

Hatton's eyes kept searching the crooked wagon track ahead. Jericho kept a guard on this road in case some stranger came along who couldn't read the sign or chose not to heed it. The guard moved around often, so Hatton could never predict just where he would be. The regular guards knew Hatton and his riders, but sometimes Jericho put a new man on the job. Sooner or later he might assign somebody who was too slow on recognition and too fast on the trigger.

A horseman casually rode out from behind the leafy green cover of a mesquite tree and stopped in the center of the road, waiting. He had a rifle in a scabbard and a pistol on his hip but nothing in his hands except his bridle reins. A telescope hung from a leather string around his neck. He said, "Been watchin' you-all with the spyglass, so I knowed it was you. Been a long time on this trip, ain't you?"

Hatton wondered if the guard was being subtly critical. "It takes a while to drive a herd all the way up to San Antonio."

"Jericho's been gettin' a little nervous, wonderin' if maybe you-all decided to take the cattle money and look for greener slopes."

Curtly Hatton replied, "He knows me better than that." Should he ever succumb to that ambition he knew he had better travel a long way, for Jericho would send somebody to track him down. Jericho would not care how long it took. Forgiveness was alien to Jericho's nature. He never forgot, nor did he ever fully trust. Hatton harbored a suspicion that Jericho might have assigned one of the men riding with him to watch the rest. If there was such a spy in his midst—and Wilkes seemed the most likely candidate—Jericho would not be long in learning what really happened to his nephew.

Hatton tried to reason that he was wrong, that he was just being paranoid. A man was apt to get that way, working for Jericho.

The guard said, "I hope you'll tell him you saw me and that I was right on the job."

"Sure, I'll do that." But Hatton knew he would not. He had more important things on his mind than accommodating a lowly gun toter worried about staying on the payroll or hoping to be promoted to a more profitable position.

The nucleus of Jericho's headquarters had been built long ago in Spanish times when Indian raids were a periodic threat. The stone walls of the long main house were thick enough that no bullet would penetrate them. Narrow rifle ports allowed shooters inside to fire at an approaching enemy with minimum exposure. Beyond the outer walls that enclosed the major ranch buildings, the ground had been cleared of brush for two to three hundred yards to expose attackers as they came into good rifle range. The first brush removal had been done by the Spaniards. Jericho had maintained it for his own protection.

Most visitors were unwelcome, whether they were Mexican bandits or lawmen such as the Texas Rangers. He could stand them off if they ever came at him here in his stronghold. So far, none had tried. Even Guadalupe Chavez, who took pleasure in rustling the outfit's cattle, had never attempted to overrun the headquarters. Outlaws were welcome so long as they were white and were willing to operate under orders, though their stay was short unless they proved themselves.

Hatton hoped by riding directly to the barn that nobody would notice the riderless horse. That would give him time to present the money and put the boss in a good humor before delivering the bad news. But Jericho was at the barn, watching a hired hand shoe his favorite mount, a big gray capable of carrying a large rider. He watched the riders' approach, and his flinty gaze fastened hawklike on the lead horse.

Jericho stood more than six feet tall, broad-shouldered and muscular. Women were drawn to him and considered him handsome, but they didn't see him as Hatton saw him now, coiled tight and dangerous like the spring on a trigger. Hatton wondered if even Jericho's Missouri-raised wife had ever seen him that way.

Hatton tried to head off the question by dismounting and immediately unbuckling his saddlebags. "The cattle brought a little more than we expected, boss. Got the money right here. I think you'll be tickled."

The big man was not to be distracted. "Where's the boy?"

Hatton swallowed. "It's a long story."

"Give me the short of it. Where's he at?"

Hatton stammered. "It's like this . . . we run into some of them Chavez bandits . . ."

Jericho seemed to tower over Hatton, his eyes cutting like blades. "You tryin' to tell me you got him shot?"

"It was . . . there wasn't nothin' we could do. They was on us so fast . . . we tried to shield the boy . . . but he was hit before we could . . . honest to God."

"Damn you!" Jericho's hard fist struck so quickly that Hatton did not see it coming. He fell backward, dropping the saddlebags and startling his horse into breaking free. The animal ran off a little way and turned warily to watch. Hatton shook his head and raised one hand to his aching jaw. He felt as if a mule had kicked him.

Jericho stormed, "I told you I didn't want him goin'. I told you to leave him at home."

Hatton found it difficult to speak. He had bitten his tongue hard enough that he tasted blood. He wanted to explain that the boy had trailed after them and had not let himself be seen until the second day out on the trail. He had declared that he would continue to follow even if not given permission. A reluctant Hatton had told him, "All right, stay, but make a hand."

One of these days, he thought, his soft heart was going to get him killed.

Hatton had seen many times how mercurial Jericho's moods could be. He could laugh one moment and roar in anger the next. His initial rage slowly cooled, and he took on a look of genuine sorrow. "He was a good kid. Didn't listen to advice worth a damn, but he was my wife's only nephew. Like a son to her, he was."

"I'm sorry. I wish it had been me." That was an exaggeration. Hatton was glad it had not been him. He wished it might have been Wilkes. If not him, any of the others. He got up hesitantly, afraid he might get hit again.

Jericho said, "Why didn't you bring him home?"

"It was too far, and the weather was too warm. But we found a churchyard and buried him in hallowed ground. I just wisht we'd had a preacher to read over him."

"What kind of a church was it?"

"I don't know. Always thought one church was like another."

"They ain't. I'll bet you buried him in a Mexican graveyard."

Hatton could not look into Jericho's accusing eyes.

Jericho asked, "Can you find that church again? My wife'll want to go there and see where the boy is restin'. Maybe even bring him home. He don't belong amongst a bunch of Mexicans, especially seein' as it was Mexicans that killed him."

"Remember the village where that Ranger got killed a year or so back? He's buried in the same churchyard."

"Damned poor company for the boy. We'll move him."

Jericho looked toward the house, his visage grave. "I sure dread tellin' Thelma. This'll just about kill her."

His wife was the only person for whom Jericho showed any real affection. He catered to her as if he were deathly afraid she might leave him. Hatton could not understand how such a strong man could allow himself to be so much at the mercy of a woman, any woman. It was the only weakness he had ever seen Jericho display.

Hatton had seen very little of Thelma Jackson. Neither he nor any of the other hands were allowed in the big house except for Jericho's office, to which there was an outside door. To Hatton she was a shadowy figure, more mystery than reality. Jericho was strict about shielding her from the unpleasant aspects of his business and the men with whom he had to deal.

Jericho's grieving gave way to a dark and brooding anger that would simmer beneath the surface until some resolution was reached. "Chavez." He spoke the name as if it were a curse. "He'll pay if I have to follow him all the way into hell." His voice dropped so low that Hatton could barely hear it. "Has Chavez got any kids?"

Hatton felt a measure of relief. Maybe things were going to work out. "I never heard nobody say. I know he's got a woman or two. You know them Meskins . . . they shell out like rabbits. Stands to reason he's got kids."

"Even if he doesn't, that stepson of McCawley's is ridin' with him, ain't he?"

"So I hear."

"That boy is Lupe's nephew. You know what the Book says: an eye for an eye. A nephew for a nephew."

Hatton wondered where Jericho had learned about the Book. He had never seen him read from it.

ANDY'S HORSE LOWERED its head to drink from the Rio Grande. The other horses and the little pack mule followed suit. The river was less impressive than Andy had expected. It appeared no wider and certainly less deep than the Colorado or the Brazos. It had passed through a lot of desert country before it reached this point on its long journey to the Gulf.

Len said, "Depends on where you look at it from. Some places it gets wide and shallow. Mexicans can ride a burro across it. Other places it gets narrow and deep enough to drown an elephant. It's them wide, shallow places where we got to watch for signs of border jumpers.

It's hard to hide tracks where a bunch of cattle or horses have crossed."

Andy asked, "If we find such a place, what're we supposed to do?"

"If they're headed south into Mexico, ain't much we can do. It's too late to help the owners. Their stock is gone unless they want to cross the border and try to take them back. The law don't allow us to do it for them. If the tracks head north, we may follow. Lieutenant Buckalew does. When Sergeant Donahue is in charge he usually tells us to leave well enough alone. He says Mexicans deserve to get robbed because they're all thieves anyway."

"Do we ever catch anybody?"

"Awful seldom."

"What could three of us do against a big bunch of bandits anyway?"

"Surround them. Give them to understand that we don't take kindly to their thievin' ways."

Ever since Andy had known him, Len had welcomed a vigorous scrap. He always maintained that an occasional good waking-up was healthful for the constitution, that it stirred the blood and loosened the bowels. As for Farley, he had been looking for a fight the first time Andy ever saw him, and he had not changed.

It could get dangerous, riding with two reckless companions.

Andy studied the land on the other side of the river. It looked no different from the north bank, though it was another nation. Over there he would be an alien and an enemy to most people. The thought was disquieting.

He had enjoyed the limestone hills and the fertile valleys of the San Saba River country. He found this region flatter and more desertlike, without the evident amenities he had found to the north. As someone had warned, most of the plants here had thorns, the animals had horns or tusks, and the insects had stingers. He remembered the homesickness that had afflicted him when he first fell back into the white man's world after his years with the Indians. Some of that emotion came over him now.

He supposed he might get used to it when he had been here awhile, but he was not sure he wanted to stay that long.

He expressed his feelings. Len said, "I felt the same way when they first sent me here, but you can find somethin' to like just about anyplace if you look for it. Else why would the devil live in hell?"

"I've never had a chance to ask him."

"You may run into him down here one of these days. He's got family by the name of Jericho and Chavez."

Farley growled, "This looks like the kind of country the devil would pick for his home. Anything you touch or that touches you is apt to bring blood."

Len said, "But there's pretty places too. I've been plumb out to where the Rio Grande pours into the Gulf. They got palm trees out there, just like in the Bible. I kept thinkin' I ought to see a camel someplace, but I didn't."

They came upon a small field irrigated by a ditch extending from the river. Up the slope stood a small picket house. A few spotted goats nibbled at brush and watched the Rangers approach. When the horsemen came close they clattered away, then turned to look again.

Len said, "These folks keep chickens. Sometimes when I come by here I buy a few eggs. Sure makes fat bacon taste better. Even beef jerky."

Andy saw a family working in a garden. At the Rangers' approach the woman shouted at two girls. All three retreated into the house. Andy heard a wooden bar dropped into place to secure the door. Len said, "They've had experience with gringos before."

The man stood at the brush fence, waiting to meet the riders alone. He bowed slightly and said a few Spanish words that Andy took to be a greeting, though his dark eyes conveyed a different message. He could not hide his dislike and his dread.

Len said, "Most of these people can tell a Ranger as far as they can see him. They don't like us and they don't trust us, but they'll accept our money." He spoke to the man. *"Huevos."*

"Tiene dinero?"

Len said, "He wants to see the money first."

Andy dug into his pocket and came up with two bits. "Reckon that's enough?"

"Two bits'll buy you the hen."

The man went into the house, returning shortly with several eggs in a small, crude basket woven of green willow stems. Len asked him something Andy did not understand. The man shook his head and replied with a shrug of his shoulders.

Len thanked him. "Says he ain't seen anybody cross the river in either direction except people who live close by. No bandits."

Farley said, "He wouldn't tell us anyway."

"If it's gringo bandits they'll tell you. If it's Mexicans they won't. Ask most white people along the river and they'll do the same except the opposite."

Riding away, Andy looked back. He saw the woman hastily hanging clothing on a line.

Len observed, "Them clothes ain't wet. That's a signal that Rangers are about. Anybody waitin' on the other side knows he'd best keep his feet dry."

Farley said, "I'll go back and yank them clothes down."

"No, folks behave better when they know we're around. The lieutenant had rather keep them out of mischief in the first place than to chase them afterwards."

At sunset they stopped to make camp. Andy removed the pack from the mule while Len scooped out a shallow hole in the dirt and filled it with dry leaves and small sticks. He lighted it with a match, blowing into the first weak, flickering flames to make them lick into the dry wood. He said, "We'll fix our supper, then we'll build this fire up to where they can see it. There won't be no cattle run across here tonight."

Andy pondered. "What's to stop them from goin' up the river to the next shallow place?"

"Us. This fire'll be here, but we'll be there. With another fire."

Farley argued, "Three of us can't be everywhere up and down the whole Rio Grande."

"No, but we can keep them wonderin' where we'll turn up next. It'll be as aggravatin' as a tick in the ear."

Farley dragged up more dry brush to keep the fire going. "I'd rather aggravate them with a bullet in the gut."

The fire went out during the night. Next morning after their meager breakfast Andy heard cattle bawling and determined that the sound came from the other side. Farley said, "Looks like somebody is fixin' to cross over."

Len agreed. "Let's ride to the bank of the river and show ourselves. It'll give them somethin' to fret about."

Len took a position at the edge of the water. Andy and Farley followed his lead. Andy asked, "How'll they know we're Rangers?"

"They won't know for sure, but they'll have to think hard about takin' the chance."

"Looks like they've got us considerable outnumbered."

"But they know they'd be easy targets in the water.

Most of them would never make it all the way across if we set our minds to stoppin' them."

Andy could see the men milling about, several gathering as if in conference.

After a while he heard distant shots.

Len grinned. "Looks like they've got theirselves in a fix. Somebody's caught up with them."

The gunfire increased. Andy watched several riders plunge into the shallow water, making for the north bank. "They're leavin' the cattle behind."

"Wouldn't you?" Len slapped his leg and laughed. "Look at them run. If they could fly, they'd do it."

Andy saw a man fall from the saddle just as his horse entered the river. Another made it partway across before he slid into the water and began floundering. A companion grabbed him and pulled him against his horse's shoulder.

Farley drew his pistol. "They'll blame us for this."

Len drew his rifle from its scabbard and laid it across his lap. "Ain't it a shame." He appeared to welcome the prospect of a confrontation.

Andy cautioned, "Have you forgotten how to count?"

"They'll be stringin' out of the river one and two at a time. They're tired and pretty well boogered. Us three can take them all on."

Andy had his doubts but decided to put his faith in Len's prior experience and Farley's fighting nature. The Rangers met the riders as they straggled onto the bank, their horses dripping. Len pointed his rifle in their direction and ordered each in turn to shuck his weapons. Two seemed prepared to argue, but Farley cut them short: "Don't make us finish what them Mexicans started."

Andy had thought some of these might be men who had attacked him and Len and Farley several nights ago, but he recognized none of them.

Len said, "Well, looks like you boys bit off a bigger chunk than you could chew."

One growled, "All we done was buy a herd of cattle across the river. Bunch of Mexican bandits jumped us and took them over. You seen it yourselves, didn't you?"

Farley was openly skeptical. "How about showin' us a bill of sale?"

"Mexicans don't put much store in such as that. Most of them can't read or write."

"I'll bet they can read brands."

The raider complained, "We lost a man over on the other side, and we've got another with a slug in him."

Andy turned his attention southward. "Looks like those Mexicans are comin' across to finish the job."

The man's eyes widened as he saw riders moving into the river. "Let us have our guns back."

Len shook his head. "No, the best thing you-all can do is see if them horses of yours are faster than what the Mexicans are ridin'." He waved the muzzle of the rifle, pointing it northward.

The man protested, "Them guns cost us good money."

"If you don't hightail it you ain't goin' to have no use for money. And tell Jericho the Rangers said howdy."

The raiders' reluctance to leave without weapons was quickly surpassed by their fear of the angry-looking Mexicans coming across the river. Andy watched the men move away in a lope. He said, "We ought to've arrested them and taken them back to camp."

Len said, "We'd've lost half of them between here and there. Anyway, whatever they done on the other side, that's Mexico's business. They didn't break no Texas law. Wasn't nothin' we could charge them for."

Andy asked, "How do you know they're Jericho's men?"

"I'm just guessin'. Jericho runs most of the contraband business along this stretch of the river, just like Lupe Chavez runs it on the other side." Len dismounted and began picking up the weapons. "Let's wrap these in a blanket and tie them on the pack mule. Them Mexicans have got guns enough already."

Andy unrolled his blanket on the ground. "Do you think you can bluff them like you bluffed the others?"

"What makes you think I was bluffin'?"

Andy counted ten horsemen coming across the river. Several more had remained with the cattle. Len squinted, studying them. "I don't see Lupe Chavez, but you can lay odds that these are some of his men." He remounted and again brandished his rifle. Andy and Farley followed his example. As the riders came up to face them Len said, "You boys are on the wrong side of the river."

A lean young man pushed forward, a challenge in his dark eyes and the set of his shoulders. "There was a time when the river didn't mean nothin'. South side, north side, it was all part of Mexico." He was dressed like a Mexican vaquero, but he spoke with little or no Mexican accent that Andy could discern.

Len said, "There's been two wars fought over that. If you ain't careful you'll start another." He softened. "I'm bettin' you'd be Big Jim McCawley's boy Tony. I heard you was ridin' with Lupe Chavez. Where's he at?"

The young man ignored the question. "I'm Antonio Villarreal. I'm Lupe Chavez's nephew, but I'm not McCawley's boy. Who are you to be blockin' the way?"

"We're Rangers." Len pointed to the handmade badge on his shirt.

The young man's face twisted. "Damned *rinches*."

Andy had learned that *rinches* was a term the Mexicans applied to the Rangers, and not in a complimentary manner.

Villarreal said, "If you'll give us the road we'll take care of your job for you. We'll fix them so they'll never come again."

"Like you said, that's *our* job. You did yours when you saved your cattle."

"I know you Rangers won't do anything about those thieves. If *we* don't, they'll be back."

"Catch them on your side of the river and you can feel free to shoot them all."

The young man's voice bespoke contempt. "Maybe someday we'll catch you *rinches* on the other side."

Andy studied the face. He thought he saw some resemblance to Tony's mother and half sister. He said, "We met your folks."

That seemed to pique Tony's interest in a negative way. "I guess they told you all about me?"

"They said mighty little, just enough to give us a notion you jumped the traces."

"My stepfather is a gringo."

"Everybody says he is a good man."

"He is still a gringo. When I was a boy I had to accept him as a father. Now I am a man, and he is not my father anymore."

Andy did not know whether to feel sorry for the young rebel or to be angry at him. He said, "I'd give anything I own to have a father."

"You can have mine. And next time you side with

Jericho's thieves we'll run over you like a freight train."

Farley spoke up. "You'll find the Rangers harder to bring down than that man you killed over there."

"He was a bandit. Anyway, he was just wounded. He's not dead yet."

Andy heard two shots echo from across the river. He winced. "I guess he is now."

Tony said coldly, "One less gringo bandit. The world is better off." He jerked his head as a signal and rode back into the river. The other men followed him.

Andy said, "He doesn't know how lucky he is. At least he's *got* a father. Stepfather, anyway."

Len said, "Too bad, but that's how it is down here. Most people choose sides accordin' to whether they're light-skinned or dark. That boy has set his eggs down on the Mexican side."

Andy pointed northward. The raiders had faded into the distance, swallowed up by the mesquite and other brush. "We could follow them and find out where they came from."

Len said, "They came from Jericho's little kingdom. Ain't much doubt about that."

Andy was intrigued. "Kingdom?"

"He runs it like he was a king. Nothin' happens in there without his say-so. Nobody pokes his nose onto Jericho's ranch unless he says it's all right."

"Not even the Rangers?"

"We go now and again, but he sees to it that we don't find anything or anybody we're lookin' for. If an outlaw needs a hidin' place, Jericho gives him one. They go out and do their devilment, then come back and give him a cut. He's built him a bank with stolen money, but he's managed to keep his hands clean. Even if the law was to bring him to trial, you couldn't gather up twelve men with guts enough to convict him."

Andy declared, "I'd like to see what he looks like. Have you ever met him?"

"Yep. And I'd pay money to buy back my introduction."

"What about that man they killed? Are we just goin' to go off and leave him over there?"

Farley said, "His friends did," and started north, following the raiders.

6

Following the trail was easy. The raiders made no effort to hide it. Though crossing with Mexican cattle was illegal unless properly cleared through customs, they had returned without contraband. They had little reason to fear the law once they were north of the Rio Grande. Andy carried the blanket into which the men's weapons had been piled. He had to tie the ends together and lash the bundle onto the mule. It was an unwieldy load.

He said, "These guns may not ride this way very long."

Farley grabbed a handful of the blanket and tugged to get a sense of the weight. "I don't see where we owe it to them renegades to deliver their weaponry back to them. We ought to've thrown it all in the river."

Len said, "Jericho's got lawyers up in San Antonio that raise hell every time we even wink in his direction. There's a little store at the crossroads. We'll leave the guns there."

Andy asked, "You think they'll come back and get them?"

"I would if the guns was mine. A man appreciates things when he has to pay out his own good money for them."

They came to a plain-looking building, a nondescript mix of stone and picket construction. Len said, "That's the store. The owner sells stuff to Jericho's men and buys their stolen goods. He'll treat us friendly enough, but don't believe his smile. It's all show."

Farley said, "If he deals with Jericho's thieves, why don't we arrest him?"

"A jury that won't convict Jericho won't convict his friends either. I'd about as soon stand in front of a Mexican firin' squad as face Jericho's lawyers."

Andy grinned at a sudden thought. "If we can't put those border jumpers in jail, we can at least aggravate them a little."

Len brightened with curiosity. "How?"

"Let's stop in the shade of that tree yonder." Andy dismounted and lifted the heavy bundle from the mule. He laid it in the shade and untied the corners that held it together. The rifles and pistols slipped and slid, clattering against one another. "Let's take these guns apart. Puttin' them back together will give those boys somethin' to do besides play cards and drink whiskey."

Len was always enthusiastic over a chance for harmless mischief. "I'd love to stay and listen to them cuss a blue streak."

Farley was not smiling. "I still wish we'd dumped the whole shebang in the river and let them swim for it."

They removed barrels and cylinders from the pistols and field-stripped the rifles. It took a while, but Len never stopped talking, laughing as he pictured their reaction. When they were done Andy mixed the pieces as if he were shuffling dominoes.

Len said, "I'd give a pretty penny to watch them sort out all this mess. By the time they put everything back together, they'll be wantin' to use them on us."

Farley said, "Let them come."

Andy retied the bundle and attached it to his saddle

horn. It still weighed the same but seemed less of a burden now. A middle-aged man came to the door, a smudged apron tied around his dough belly. He recognized Len. "Howdy, Ranger. Somethin' you-all need?"

"A little smokin' tobacco for me and Farley. Maybe a little *pan dulce* for the young'un here if you got any."

"Tobacco I got. He'll have to find the sweetenin' someplace else. I don't cater to the Mexican trade. Let them people in here and they'll be pilferin' stuff when I ain't watchin'."

Andy said, "Speakin' of pilferin', did you see a bunch of riders pass by a little while ago?"

The tracks indicated that the men had stopped here, but the storekeeper claimed no knowledge of them. "Ain't seen hardly anybody all day."

"They were tryin' to get away with some cattle on the other side of the river, but the owners caught up with them. They came back to this side in a considerable hurry."

"You don't say!"

Len said, "Anyhow, we've got some stuff that belongs to them. Reckon you can keep it till they come back?"

"Sure enough."

Andy brought the blanket inside and spilled its contents on the floor. A couple of cylinders rolled across the room. One disappeared behind some heavy-looking boxes. The storekeeper started to object but choked it off.

Andy said, "I hope you've got an empty box to put all this stuff in. I'll be needin' my blanket." He folded it and laid it across his arm.

The storekeeper grunted. "You won't want to be here when they see you've took their guns apart."

Cheerfully Len said, "They're welcome to come callin' at their convenience."

Farley said, "Tell them my name's Farley Brackett, and they can come see me if they ain't satisfied. I ain't had a decent fight since I left Austin."

The storekeeper gave Farley a quizzical look. "Brackett? Seems to me like I've heard that name."

"Lots of people have. Be sure you give it to them."

The three rode on. After a time Andy inquired, "Where does Jericho's land start?"

Len said, "We're already on it. He's got a six-shooter claim, at least. He says he bought out a bunch of Mexican owners. Ran them off is more like it, or he got a court to throw out the old grants like he tried to do with the Chavez family. Then he bought the land dirt cheap off of the county tax office."

The tracks led them eventually to a point where the trail forked. Andy saw a sign: THIS IS JERICHO'S ROAD. TAKE THE OTHER. "You ever been up this road?"

Len nodded. "Me and some other Rangers was trailin' stock headin' north. Jericho came out to meet us. Claimed the cattle belonged to him, and his men had just got them back from Lupe Chavez's ranch across the river. Even showed us some cattle with his brand on them. They wasn't the same ones we'd been followin', but we couldn't prove he'd pulled a switch on us. Sergeant Donahue wasn't anxious about it anyway. He said the more cattle that get stole out of Mexico, the better."

"In other words, just knowin' ain't enough. The only thing that counts is what you can prove."

Farley grumbled, "You get a little smarter every day, Badger Boy. But you still got a long ways to go."

Andy saw a dozen or so cattle grazing nearby. He rode over to look at them, moving slowly so they would not spook and run. "I see at least three different brands."

Len watched the cattle drift away. "And all Mexican.

Most of Jericho's cattle are natural swimmers. Show them a river and they'll jump right in."

The horse tracks split at the fork. Some riders had gone on northward. Others had swung to the west, following the trail marked as Jericho's.

Len said, "I've already seen Jericho's headquarters. The outside of it, anyway. If we stay with the other bunch we might find a new hangout. Someday that could be a handy thing to know."

Farley said, "I'll follow that bunch west. I'd like to know what Jericho's place looks like."

Len cautioned, "You're liable to learn more than you intended to. But I don't reckon it's my place to try and tell you what to do."

"Wouldn't matter none if you did." Farley rode off.

Len hollered after him, "Chances are we won't find one another again. We'll meet back at the camp." In a quieter voice he said, "And that'll be plenty soon enough."

If Farley attempted an answer, Andy did not hear it.

Andy and Len followed the northbound tracks until eventually the trail split again. Len said, "Ain't but one thing to do. You take the right hand and I'll take the left. When we've seen whatever there is to see, we'll back-track and meet right here."

Andy felt concern. "If you bump into somebody, you won't try to tackle them by yourself, will you?"

Len shook his head. "You know me. I ain't one to go lookin' for a fight."

"I don't remember you ever duckin' out on one."

"I'm just goin' to see what I can learn. I ain't got my fightin' britches on."

Andy knew Len's propensity for getting himself into trouble. He had that much in common with Farley. How-

ever, Farley met his challenges with a growl and Len met
them with a laugh. Andy conceded that Len had a point.
Sooner or later Jericho was likely to make a mistake, and
it behooved the Rangers to know as much as possible
about his ranch and what went on there.

He told Len, "You take the pack mule." The mule had
more or less attached itself to Len's horse. It would not
so readily follow Andy's.

Len said, "You won't have anything to eat."

"We'll be back together before time for that."

The sun bore heavily on Andy's shoulders. The back
of his shirt and the underarms were soaked in sweat.
Ahead he saw a windmill tower. That meant water. He
was pleased that the tracks he followed veered in that
direction.

Windmills were relatively new on Texas ranges. Railroads were first to try the idea, then farmers and ranchers had quickly adopted them to allow use of neglected
lands that lacked living water in the form of springs,
creeks, and rivers. Andy had seen a few windmills, but
they remained strange and exotic to him. He was fascinated by the notion of a mechanical device that could
harness the wind to pump water from unseen storage
deep in the ground. He wondered how much longer people
could keep coming up with such ingenious inventions.
Surely they must be nearing their limit.

This mill had a tower built of lumber that still looked
new except that it was already darkly stained by lubri-
cating oil spilled from its gears. The cypress fan looked
to be twelve or fourteen feet across. The sucker rod
clanked as it rode up and down, striking the walls of the
steel tube that enveloped it.

Water poured into a surface tank hollowed out of the

level ground. A few cattle turned and warily trotted away as Andy approached. He imagined the pleasant taste of cool water gushing from the end of the outlet pipe.

He failed for a moment to recognize an angry buzzing sound. By the time he realized he had disturbed a nest of wasps, they were attacking him and the horse. He tried swatting them away but seemed to make them angrier. The black horse squealed and kicked, then broke into pitching. Already off balance from fighting the wasps, Andy lasted only two jumps before he was jolted out of the saddle. Instinctively he tried to break the fall by extending his arm. He hit the ground hard. The arm twisted beneath him.

His left boot was caught in the stirrup. He felt himself jerked violently, then dragged as the horse pitched, squealed, and broke wind. He bounced on the rough ground. He tried to shield his face, but one arm felt numb and useless. His foot pulled free of the boot. The dragging stopped. The horse continued to run and pitch without him. A few more wasps stung Andy before they began returning to the nest. They swarmed around it noisily as if awaiting another target.

Finding himself lying awkwardly on the arm that had taken the first impact, he rolled onto his back. The arm began to ache as feeling returned. He examined it gingerly, fearing it might be broken. He satisfied himself that it was not, though it was badly scratched and bruised. The sleeve hung in strips, as did the rest of his shirt.

His face and hands burned in more than a dozen places where the wasps had stung. He felt his cheeks beginning to puff. His eyes pinched. He tried to push to his feet, but his whole body hurt. He managed to sit up and take stock of his situation as the swelling almost closed his eyes.

It had not occurred to him that the windmill and open tank provided a hospitable breeding ground for wasps in a region where water was scarce.

He began feeling nauseated as the venom took hold. Vision blurring, he was unable to see his horse. He did not know how far the animal might have run. He crawled on hands and knees to where his boot had fallen from the stirrup. Painfully he pulled it on. Thirst began to plague him, but he did not want to try for the windmill again. He could still hear the angry wasps.

He wished he and Len had not split up. He had no idea how far Len might go in following those other tracks. When he returned to the rendezvous point Len was likely to wait awhile before deciding to follow Andy and see what had delayed him. By then it would probably be dark, and he would be unable to see tracks until daylight.

No telling how long I'll be here by myself, he thought.

His canteen was empty, and Len had the pack mule with all their provisions. At the moment Andy was too ill to eat, but sooner or later he would be hungry as well as thirsty.

Damn wasps, he thought. They say the Lord had a purpose for everything He made, but I don't see any reason for wasps.

He crawled into the thin shade of a mesquite tree and wished it were as solid as an oak.

Dusk came. He knew he would be by himself at least until morning. His blanket had been tied to his saddle, and the saddle was still on the horse. He resigned himself to sleeping on the bare ground, hungry and thirsty.

As darkness closed in, he heard something moving about. He paid little attention at first, for cattle had been coming up for water. Most seemed not to notice him.

Those that saw or smelled him kept an uneasy distance. His blurry eyes made out the shape of a horse, his horse. It looked strange until he realized that the saddle had turned under its belly. He pushed himself to his feet, his legs aching. He spoke in a soft voice as he moved slowly and painfully toward the horse.

"Whoa, son. Gentle now. Whoa."

Grasping for the reins, he found one had broken off just below the bits. Holding the other, he patted the horse on the neck and rubbed his hand down its shoulder, then felt for the girth's buckle. The horse almost jerked away from him as the saddle dropped between its feet.

"Easy, boy. Ain't nothin' goin' to hurt you now."

Andy figured the wasps had become inactive for the night. Deciding to take a chance, he led the horse to the farthest end of the surface tank. There he let it drink. Hearing no buzzing, he took an even larger chance and walked to the end of the outlet pipe. Cupping his hand beneath the flow, he drank until his stomach ached.

He disliked tying the horse up short, but his rope had been lost. He had nothing to lengthen the one remaining rein. He tied it to a mesquite limb. He was disappointed to find that his blanket was gone. It had probably snagged on a bush and pulled loose.

He had already made up his mind he would be sleeping on the bare ground, so he was no worse off than before.

ANDY SPENT A long and fitful night trying in vain to find a comfortable position. The itching was so intense that he could not help scratching the bites. That made them burn worse than before. He knew there were ointments that might help, but they had just as well be on the far side of the moon. He tried to remember if the Comanches had any remedy. Nothing came to mind.

Thirst told him he was running a slight fever. He drank his fill before dawn set the wasps to stirring again. He could see better than the evening before, but he still felt as if he were peering through a slit in a wall.

"Damn you, Len, hurry up."

Andy figured it must be around noon when Len finally appeared, following tracks from the south. He reined up and stared at Andy as if he were an apparition. He declared, "You look like wild horses have stomped on you."

Andy warned, "Don't get too close to that windmill. There's a jillion wasps in there, and every one of them is mad."

"You let a few little old wasps do all that to you?"

"When they hit you, you'll think they're the size of a cow." He told how his horse had thrown him and run away, losing his blanket and rope.

Len said, "I'll see if I can find them."

He came back in a while, carrying both items. The blanket was dirty and torn. He said, "Bet you ain't had nothin' to eat. I'll fix you some dinner."

Andy had begun to feel strong hunger pangs, a sign of improvement. Len roasted bacon on a stick. Andy eagerly bit in without waiting for it to cool.

Len said, "I'm fixin' to do somethin' about that wasps' nest." He pulled several handfuls of dry grass and wrapped them around the end of a thin dead branch from a mesquite. He dipped the grass into the fire, then carried the blazing stick to the windmill tower. He shoved it under the nest. A few wasps came buzzing out, but most were consumed by the fire.

Andy heard Len exclaim, "Uh-oh!" The flames licked

upward along the tower's wooden leg, burning the oil spilled from the top. Len stepped back, swatting at a couple of wasps that had focused upon him as a target. "Looks like I've just played hell."

Andy said, "Throw some water on it."

"Too late for that, even if I had a bucket."

The flames intensified. Len backed away from the heat. "I think me and you had better mosey along. Jericho is apt to be a little put out about his windmill."

He saddled Andy's horse and shook out the dusty blanket, folded it, and tied it behind the cantle. Andy felt stiff. Swinging up onto the horse reawakened all of yesterday's soreness. The two horses and the mule danced uneasily, fearing the fire.

Len kicked sand over the small blaze on which he had fixed Andy's meager breakfast. "If they saw this," he said, "they'd know somebody camped here and set fire to the windmill."

"How else would it have burned?"

"Lightnin'."

Squinty-eyed, Andy looked up but saw no clouds. "Yeah, they'll sure be fooled, all right."

Riding south, Andy asked, "Did you find anything?"

"A few miles from where I left you, the bunch I followed stopped at an old Mexican ranch house. Jericho probably uses it as a line camp. Remind me to put it on the map when we get back to the company. What did you find?"

"A jillion wasps." Andy looked back. The fire had climbed up to the tower's platform. Once it burned all the wooden support and the cypress, the metal parts would crash to the ground. He said, "I'll bet that mill cost a hundred dollars."

"Jericho can afford it. His crew'll steal more than that between dinner and supper."

They had traveled a couple of miles when Len said, "Four riders comin' our way." Andy's vision had not improved enough for him to see them. Len said, "It's too late to hide. Let's just play innocent."

Len always had an innocent look about him, even when he was guiltiest.

As the horsemen came near enough for Andy to see them, he noted that a large man rode half a length ahead of the others. He said, "I'll bet that's Jericho."

"Yep, you're about to meet the big stud his own self. Don't act like you give a damn. He's built himself a little empire by makin' people afraid of him."

"From what I've heard, they've got a right to be afraid."

"Me and you can't afford to be. Show him the feather and he'll ride plumb over you."

Jericho Jackson looked to be more than six feet tall and stocky enough to weigh considerably over two hundred pounds. He was not fat, simply large. He rode a gray horse bigger than those of the three cowboys beside him. He had a reddish complexion and hair and beard of a strong rust color, not unlike Rusty Shannon's. His dark brown eyes fastened first on Andy, then on Len with a startling intensity. He recognized Len, though he probably could not have called him by name.

"Ranger, ain't you strayed a long ways from where you belong?"

"Rangers go anywhere they want to."

"Anyplace but my ranch. You lookin' for somebody?"

"Maybe. Who you got?" Len's voice had an insolent tone, one Andy was sure he had to work at. It was not his normal style. It would have been Farley's.

Andy recognized two of the riders. They had been with the men the Mexicans had chased back across the river. One leaned to Jericho and said something Andy could not hear.

Jericho said, "Seems like you've already made the acquaintance of my boys. They say you took somethin' that belongs to them."

Len said, "The guns? If they'll stop at that little gyp joint of a store they can get their property back."

Jericho switched his attention again to Andy. "You look like you been run through a coffee grinder, boy. You a Ranger too?"

"Private Andy Pickard. My horse drug me a ways."

"Probably because you took him where you and him wasn't supposed to be." Jericho leaned forward, his manner challenging. "You Rangers are always pokin' into my business, comin' on my land without so much as a by-your-leave. But when you're needed you ain't nowhere around."

Len said, "When did you ever need us?"

"Mexican outlaws murdered my wife's nephew. Never gave him a chance. It was one time we could've used your help, and you wasn't there."

Len and Andy looked at each other. Andy said, "That's the first we've heard about it."

"It won't be the last. I'm sendin' a protest to Austin."

Len said sarcastically, "They'll be tickled to hear from you."

"He was an orphan boy. My poor wife set a lot of store by him. I'll see that Lupe Chavez pays for what they done. When I do, you Rangers had better stay out of my way."

Andy said, "We can't, not if you break the law."

"It's a damned poor law that says you can't kill a Mexican when he needs it. As far as I'm concerned it's open season the year around on every saddle-colored son of a bitch this side of the river."

Jericho's red mustache seemed to bristle. Studying him, Andy was reminded of a book he had read about pirates. He seemed to remember that the character's name was Red Beard, or something like that. The longer Andy looked at Jericho, the larger he seemed to get. He doubted that he and Len could handle him in a fistfight even if the three cowboys stayed out of it.

Jericho's voice deepened. "You men are trespassin'. By rights I could shoot both of you."

Andy said, "Those who try to keep the Rangers away have usually got somethin' they don't want us to see."

Jericho glowered. "You-all are startin' to aggravate me. People with any sense are careful not to get my blood stirred up. Next time, stay off of Jericho's road." He looked past the two Rangers. "We been watchin' some smoke yonder. Know anything about it?"

Len turned to see. "We noticed it too. Grass fire, more than likely. You ought to caution your boys not to be careless with their smokin'. They could burn up the whole country."

Rusty had once said Len could talk the devil into joining the church.

Jericho pointed eastward. His manner was stern. "That's the shortest way off of my land."

Len pointed south. His manner was stubborn. "We're headed back to the river." He started, and Andy followed.

Jericho shouted after them, but Len did not acknowledge him. Softly he told Andy, "Act like you don't even hear him. He's a land grabber and a thief, but he's too much of a man to shoot us in the back."

They rode about a mile. Len abruptly turned to the east. Andy said, "Thought we were goin' to the river."

"That was just to show Jericho we wasn't afraid of him. It's a long way back to Ranger camp. You've got some bad cuts, and them wasp bites need attention. I'm takin' you over to the McCawleys'. Like Jericho said, you look like you been run through a coffee grinder."

7

Andy was uneasy about baring his upper body to the McCawley women, but they brooked no argument. He had bathed in a stock tank to wash off the dirt, grass, and other debris left by the dragging. He had also rinsed his clothing. His shirt and the upper part of his long underwear had been shredded beyond repair, but they still covered enough to meet the requirements of modesty.

The older woman dug out several thorns with a needle, then rubbed him with alcohol that set him afire. He ground his teeth and tried not to groan.

She said, "The more it burns, the more good it does. You lost some hide."

Andy feared the alcohol was burning away whatever skin the dragging had left him. He drew his arms in tightly against his ribs and squeezed his eyes shut until the worst had passed.

Juana McCawley said, "You have more thorns, but they are in too deep. They'll have to fester out in their own good time."

He was glad she did not intend to poke around anymore with the needle. He said, "I'm obliged to you, ma'am."

The daughter, Teresa, rubbed a soothing salve over the wasp stings. He enjoyed the careful touch of her fingers, a contrast to her mother's less than gentle treatment with the needle and disinfectant.

Big Jim McCawley fetched him a shirt and a suit of underwear. "Our Tony left these behind. They'll fit you better than mine would."

"Many thanks."

McCawley said, "Len tells me you talked to Jericho."

"Mostly it was him that did the talkin'."

"That's his way. He's not interested in what anybody else says. He'll either scare you to death or make you mad enough to chew up a horseshoe and spit it at him."

Andy could understand that Jericho's physical size would intimidate many, but he doubted that McCawley had any fear of him. McCawley was about as large as Jericho, and like Jericho he was all muscle. Either man looked capable of wrestling a bull to a standstill. If they ever came to blows they might tear up enough ground to plant a garden.

From what he had heard of Lupe Chavez, Andy thought he must be a large man too. He had to be if he lived up to the stories.

Neither Andy nor Len mentioned seeing McCawley's stepson with the Mexicans who had crossed the river in hot pursuit of Jericho's raiders. They had decided it might upset his mother and sister to know he was putting himself in harm's way.

Teresa asked Andy, "Where is the other Ranger, the one who was with you last time?"

"Farley Brackett? He broke off from us to follow a different set of tracks."

Self-consciously she said, "He seemed rather nice."

Andy blinked. "You sure you haven't got him mixed up with somebody else?" *Nice* was not a term he had ever considered in relation to Farley.

She said, "He's not exactly handsome, but he's not ugly either, even with that scar on his face. How did he get it?"

"He brought it home from the war. Somebody told me it came from a Yankee saber. I never asked him." Farley would probably have turned on him like a biting dog and told him to mind his own business.

She said, "I think he is a lonely man."

For good reason, Andy thought. Farley never let anybody get close to him.

She asked, "Has he ever been married?"

"I doubt he ever considered it."

She suggested, "Maybe he never met the right woman. Or maybe he doesn't like women." She phrased that more like a question than a statement.

Andy knew Farley liked women, though on his own terms. He had bought and paid for commercial affection in San Antonio, but this was not something Teresa would want to hear. Andy said, "He's just been too busy bein' a Ranger."

"Most Rangers do not remain Rangers forever, do they?"

Sooner or later Farley was sure to provoke the wrath of some officer and find himself dismissed from the force. But she would not want to hear that either. "Who knows what any of us are liable to do?"

She said, "I've never seen a really *old* Ranger."

That would be easy to explain, though he did not. Most eventually became too stove up, or they wearied of endless horseback travel and wanted to settle in one place. Or, as occasionally happened, they died in the line of duty.

He said, "I'll tell him you asked about him."

She reddened. "Oh no. Please don't do that." She left her chair and hurried from the room.

Her mother watched her go, then said, "It is not seemly for a young lady to express interest in a man."

Embarrassed, Andy said, "I was just tryin' to help. Ain't had much experience in matters such as this." Perhaps a good woman might smooth Farley's rough edges and make him easier to get along with. The Lord knew he needed help of some kind. On the other hand, any woman who would give Farley more than a minute's consideration was probably not in her right mind.

Mrs. McCawley smiled. "Some things you must leave alone. They will work themselves out if the Lord wishes them to."

Because it was late in the day, the McCawleys had little difficulty in persuading Andy and Len to spend the night before they started back to camp. Andy looked forward to a couple of kitchen-cooked meals. And he found it easy to look at Teresa McCawley, though the memory of Farley's sister Bethel intruded, giving him a disquieting sense of guilt.

After supper the three men sat on the front porch of the rock house. McCawley smoked a pipe in silence. Silence was one thing Len could not long abide. He asked, "How come you and Jericho to get crossways in the first place?"

McCawley took the pipe from his mouth and stared at its glowing bowl. "There was a time long before the big war that me and him rode together. We didn't have nothin'. We were both ambitious, wantin' to make somethin' of ourselves. But Jericho had a different notion of how to go about it. He saw people pushin' Mexicans off of their land and decided he could too. It was easy to say it was a patriotic thing to do since there'd been two wars with Mexico.

"I'd gone to work for Don Cipriano Chavez. He treated

me good, and I took a likin' to him. Jericho tried to run him off and grab his property like he'd done with some others, but the old man fought back. So Jericho had him killed. Juana's first husband too. He hounded the son, Lupe, till Lupe took refuge in Mexico. That's when I married Juana. Puttin' an American name on the land kept Jericho from pullin' his shenanigans at the courthouse. He's been a thorn in my side ever since. And me in his."

Andy said, "Looks like the law ought to do somethin'."

McCawley nodded. "It does. For the most part it looks away, or it sides with Jericho and them that think like him. It doesn't pay to lose a war, and the Mexicans have lost two."

Andy asked, "What about the Mexicans that were livin' here in Texas? Did they take a hand in the wars?"

"Maybe not directly, but most of them sympathized with Mexico. A lot of Americans claim that justifies takin' away their property. Many Mexicans still claim that everything south of the Nueces River belongs to Mexico. That makes Americans and their property fair game. People like Lupe Chavez figure they're only takin' back what belonged to them in the first place. Both sides believe they're in the right. Those of us who try to sit on the fence take fire from both directions."

Andy asked, "Do you see any answer?"

"Maybe someday, but wars last a long time. They're not over just because the cannons quit. They're over when nobody is left who remembers what the trouble was all about."

THE BULLET SOUNDED like an angry wasp as it passed between Andy and Len. The crack of a rifle shot followed in an instant. By instinct Andy ducked low on his horse's left side, opposite the source of the fire. Len shouted and set his mount into a hard run toward a little puff of white smoke rising behind a bush. Andy spurred hard to catch up with him.

They caught a Mexican trying desperately to reload a rifle. Andy leaped from the saddle and knocked him off his feet. The shooter fought, struggling to bring the rifle into position. Its bolt was jammed open. Andy wrested the weapon from his hands and hurled it away.

Mouth half full of dirt, the man shouted an angry string of muffled words. The only one Andy knew was *gringo*.

Len said, "Turn him over." He pulled the Mexican's hands together in front of him and snapped a pair of handcuffs on his wrists. The man saw the silver peso badge on Len's shirt and launched into another spasm of cursing. Andy caught the word *rinches*.

He asked, "Do you know what he's talkin' about?"

Len said, "Us, mainly. And he's upset over bein' a poor shot."

"What'll we do with him?"

"Take him to camp. The lieutenant'll have some questions for him."

"Reckon he's part of Lupe Chavez's bunch?"

"Could be. But there's oodles and gobs of bandits that don't belong to Lupe, just like there's a lot of Texas border jumpers that don't ride for Jericho. He may be one of those that got pushed off of their land. Killin' gringos helps them sleep better."

Andy looked around with some apprehension. "He might not be by himself."

Len said, "It's kind of like with rattlesnakes. Where there's one you'll sometimes find more."

Andy said, "I'll make a quick circle and find out." He rode out a little way while Len shouted at him to be careful. He saw no sign that anyone had been with the shooter, though he found the man's horse tied a short distance away. He led it back.

He motioned for the prisoner to mount. He cut a leather string from the man's saddle and tied the handcuffs to the big flat Mexican saddle horn. Anger in the prisoner's eyes began giving way to fear. He said something Andy did not understand.

Len said, "He's askin' what we're fixin' to do to him. I can't talk enough Mexican to give him an answer. About all I can say is *'Quién sabe?'* Who knows?"

Andy added that to his vocabulary. By now he had learned at least half a dozen usable words, not counting a few curses picked up here and there.

Riding alongside the Mexican, Andy was aware of the man's growing anxiety. His own initial resentment ebbed. He even began to feel a twinge of sympathy. "I believe he thinks we're goin' to shoot him."

Len said, "We ought to, but it's probably against some law or other. There's so many laws nowadays that a man can't do nothin', hardly."

By the time they approached the row of tents that made up the camp, the prisoner's head was bowed, his eyes closed. He mumbled to himself. Andy suspected he was saying a prayer.

They rode to the headquarters tent. The camp looked to be almost deserted except for the cook and a couple of Rangers standing at the mess tent. Sergeant Donahue emerged, gravely eyeing the prisoner. He asked, "What you got here?"

Len said, "He taken a shot at us. I swear I felt that bullet tickle the hairs growin' out of my ear."

Andy said, "We thought the lieutenant would have some questions for him."

"The lieutenant's been called to Austin. I'm in charge." Donahue motioned toward the headquarters tent. "Bring your prisoner in. I'll question him." The two Rangers had left the kitchen and ambled up to see what was going on. One of them was Mexican. The sergeant said, "Tanner, Pickard, you-all go on down to the mess and have Pablo fix you somethin' to eat. Me and Manuel will talk to your prisoner."

Manuel was the only Mexican Ranger in camp and one of only two or three Andy had seen anywhere. Manuel untied the leather string that bound the prisoner's handcuffs to the horn, then spoke sharply in Spanish. The man dismounted, casting a fearful look at the sergeant.

Donahue said, "I ain't real good at Mexican lingo. Manuel knows how to question a bandit."

It struck Andy that Manuel should have compassion because he and the prisoner were of the same blood, but Donahue dispelled that idea. He said, "Manuel hates bandits even worse than the rest of us do. He lost his family to them."

Andy turned that over in his mind. "Maybe he's *too* hostile."

"They may lie to him once, but they don't do it a second time. You-all go on like I said, and get you somethin' to eat. We'll take care of this, me and Manuel."

Manuel grasped the prisoner's shoulder and roughly pushed him into the tent. Donahue followed, closing the flap's opening behind him. Andy heard a clatter, then a solid thump, like a chair falling over and someone hitting the ground.

Len motioned. "It's none of our business from here on. Let's go eat."

"Sounds like they're knockin' him around."

"They're not treatin' him as rough as what he had in mind for us. He meant to see us both dead, remember?"

"I hate to see anybody mishandled."

"If you was to get caught by Mexican bandits, you figure they'd treat you like a pet? You know what your Comanche brothers did to people they captured. Like for instance your—"

Len broke off. Andy knew what he had been about to say—*like your mother*. The unexpected thought left him feeling cold.

He said, "I guess you're right. We'd better go eat." But he wondered if he would be able to.

Pablo saw them coming and lifted a blackened Dutch oven onto a bed of glowing coals. He dropped a generous quantity of lard in to melt as the bottom heated. "Pretty soon I fix you a good supper. You hungry, Andy?" He ignored Len.

Andy had lost his appetite, but it gradually returned as he smelled the aroma and listened to steaks sizzling in the boiling grease. Beef was plentiful. The Rangers had no compunctions about slaughtering cattle that strayed across the river from Mexico, even if sometimes they had to encourage the move.

Beans cooked for the noon meal had been reheated for supper and kept hot for anybody riding in late like Andy and Len. Andy sipped steaming coffee and tried to concentrate on the coming meal rather than what might be going on in the headquarters tent.

Len told Pablo about their trip, including their meeting with Jericho. He did not mention burning the windmill.

Pablo's mustache drooped more than usual. "That Jericho is *un mal hombre*. Very bad fellow."

Len shook his head. "I think me and Andy could've

whipped him. But he ain't on the fugitive list, so there wasn't no use."

Andy pictured Jericho in his mind. "I'm not all that sure we could've done it. He looked as big as a horse."

Len said, "The big ones take longer but fall harder."

Pablo announced that the steaks were done. *"Comida."* Andy and Len each got tin plates and dipped the meat from the boiling lard. They added a generous helping of beans and broke off chunks of cold flat bread left from the company's supper. Pablo pointed to a can of molasses. "Got plenty lick. Good with the bread."

Len said, "We'll finish up with that for *de*ssert." He lit into his supper with a vengeance. "The Ranger service feeds good when you're in camp. The hell of it is that we're gone most of the time and have to fix our own. Old Pablo's hard to beat." He looked up at Pablo. "Where'd you learn to cook so good?"

Pablo wiped his dark hands on a cloth apron that once had been a sugar sack. "I was one time a soldier. The officer, he gives me a pot and says I must cook. I know nothing of such things, but when an officer says do, you do."

Len asked, "When was that?"

"In the war against the *americanos*. Once I fight you. Now I cook your supper. Pretty good joke."

"As long as you don't put rat poison in the beans."

"I would not do that for such a good boy as Andy. But you?" Pablo shrugged as if in some doubt.

Andy carried his plate and utensils to a washtub and dropped them in. He had just poured a fresh cup of coffee when he heard a shout from the direction of the headquarters tent. Turning, he saw the Mexican prisoner running. The interrogator Manuel calmly stepped outside, leveled a rifle, and fired. The prisoner staggered and pitched forward on his face.

Andy spilled most of his coffee. Len simply stared, his mouth open.

Pablo did not appear surprised. He said, "He was dead already when he came. When Manuel finishes with the talking, it is left only to bury them. It is an old Mexican way, the *ley de fuga*."

Andy had heard the expression. It referred to shooting a prisoner trying to escape.

Len broke his silence. "Lieutenant Buckalew don't hold with such as that."

Andy said, "But he's not here. I'm bettin' they pushed the prisoner out of the tent and told him to run."

Len frowned. "Whatever you think, you'd best keep it to yourself. Donahue can make life tougher than a boot for them that ask questions. Anyway, you didn't see the prisoner start. You just saw him fall."

"Call it a Comanche hunch."

"It ain't somethin' you could swear to in front of a jury."

Andy had seen death before, but it still shook him to look it in the face, especially when it was sudden and unexpected. He walked up as Donahue knelt beside the dead man and examined a blood-rimmed hole in the back of his shirt.

Donahue said, "Caught him right between the shoulder blades. Damned if I'd want Manuel aimin' at me."

Andy felt a troublesome responsibility inasmuch as he and Len had brought the prisoner in. "Did you-all have to kill him?"

Donahue was surprised at being challenged. "Look, Private, he was runnin' away. He was just another Mexican bandit. There's plenty of them left, so it's a small loss to the world." He started to leave but turned for a few more words. "Since you're so concerned, you can take a shovel and dig a hole for him. You and Tanner." He pointed. "He ain't the first. You'll find a bandit graveyard yonderway about a hundred yards."

"Anybody goin' to read over him?"

"Hell no. It was the devil that sent him. The Lord doesn't want him."

Andy wondered how so many people seemed to know what the Lord wanted.

Len walked up in time to hear most of it. When Donahue was gone he said, "Looks like you talked us into a diggin' job."

Andy knew who would do most of the work.

Mounds indicated half a dozen unmarked graves. Whoever was buried there had simply vanished from the earth. Andy guessed that friends and kin still wondered what had become of them. He and Len took turns with the shovel, though Len's turns were shorter than Andy's. When the hole was dug they buried the blanket-wrapped prisoner without witnesses and without ceremony. Andy doubted that a minister or priest had ever visited this burying place or given it the sanction of a church.

He said, "Wonder what his name was?"

Len wiped his dirty hands on his trousers. "You probably couldn't spell it even if you had a board to carve it on."

They returned to the mess tent for coffee. Manuel stood at the edge of camp, smoking a cigarette and staring off into the gloom. Pablo saw Andy looking in Manuel's direction. He said, "He has much hate in his heart."

"The sergeant said bandits killed his family."

"His papa had a farm. Not big, you know, just a little farm, but the Spanish king gave it to his great-papa long time ago. Banditos come. They shoot Manuel, they kill his papa, his mama, they carry his sister across the river.

For a long time he looks, but never does he find her. So he kills bandits, and maybe sometimes he kills some who are not bandits. Many over there have tried to kill him, but some say he can never die. They say he is a son of the devil. The devil himself maybe."

Andy shivered. "Damned if he doesn't look like it."

Just before time for bed, Donahue came to the tent Andy shared with Len and others. He said, "Your horses need a day of rest. You and Tanner will stay around and stand horse guard tomorrow."

Andy noted that Donahue's concern was for the horses rather than the men. Guarding the company horses was usually easy duty but boresome. Most Rangers came to dread it. Andy had done his share on the San Saba.

Donahue added, "You can start tonight, Pickard. You'll stand the after-midnight watch."

"Yes, sir." Andy knew he would get little sleep before going on duty and none the rest of the night. He was paying for having questioned the sergeant.

Donahue gave Andy a long study, one eye almost closed. "I hear you was raised by the Indians."

Andy felt belligerence on the sergeant's part. "Till I was maybe eleven or twelve years old."

"I got no more use for Indians than I have for Meskins. I hope you ain't still got a bunch of Indian ideas in your head."

Defensively Andy said, "I don't scalp people, if that's what you mean. And I don't shoot them in the back."

"You better walk a real straight line, Pickard. I'll be watchin' you."

As Donahue walked away, Len said, "Talkin' too much can lead to trouble. You'd better learn to keep quiet, like me."

A raid was more likely here near the border than it had

been on the San Saba, so Andy fought the sleepiness that kept tugging at his eyelids after he went on duty. Out west it might not have mattered if he gave in to it so long as an officer did not catch him. Here it could lead to deadly consequences if either Texan or Mexican raiders decided to make a try for the Rangers' remuda. A man could get killed before he came fully awake. The ugly image of the dead prisoner kept rising before him.

He pictured what Rusty Shannon's reaction might have been had he seen what Andy had witnessed.

A vague figure moved in the night. A man walked among the horses, bridling one and saddling it. Andy challenged him. "Who are you?"

A voice said, "Manuel."

"What're you doin' out here afoot in the middle of the night?"

"I have business across the river. Sergeant Donahue, he knows."

Andy thought on what Pablo had told him. He shivered. "You already killed one today. Isn't that enough?"

"It will be enough when they are all dead." Manuel rode toward the river, disappearing like a malevolent ghost into the darkness.

Andy began to wonder if he had made a mistake in agreeing to come to this part of the country. Rangers— some, anyway—had a different view of duty here than they had to the north and the west. In retrospect, Rusty's farm looked better than he had realized when he left there.

8

arley Brackett rode in about noon, hunched in weariness. Andy was standing horse guard. Farley reined in beside him and declared with a tone of accusation, "You-all didn't wait for me."

"We figured you'd come on back to camp."

"I might've needed you if I'd had a little bad luck."

Andy suspected Farley had not returned to the appointed place either. This was his way of grabbing the offensive and keeping it. Andy refused to take the bait. "We figured you're man enough to take care of yourself."

"I am. Many a state policeman found that out to his regret." Farley frowned. "I wish you and Tanner hadn't rode off with the pack mule. I ain't et in two days. Damn a country where you can't stir up at least a squirrel or a prairie chicken. I came near shootin' a javelina hog."

A little spell of hunger might teach Farley humility, Andy thought. Farley had ridden away in his own direction without even mentioning that he might want the pack mule or at least some of what it carried. Andy saw no gain in pointing this out. Farley would come up with an answer.

Farley gave Andy's face closer attention. "You been in a fight?"

"Wasps. I lost." Most of the swelling had gone down.

Andy had thought it might no longer be noticeable, but Farley didn't miss much.

Farley snorted. "The country's full of bandits, and you waste time doin' battle with wasps."

Andy asked, "Where you been all this time?"

"I followed them cowboys plumb to Jericho's headquarters. That place is like a fort. The Spaniards that built it must've been awful scared of Indians."

"Len and me, we saw Jericho himself."

"So did I. He came in just before dark. He was damned mad about somethin'. I couldn't sneak up close enough to hear what his trouble was."

It might have been about a burned windmill. Andy chose not to tell about that. Farley would harp on it for a week. He said, "We got so close we could've counted his red whiskers if we'd wanted to."

Gruffly Farley said, "I got close enough to see what I went for, and I didn't let a few little wasps booger me away, neither." He shook his head. "Wasps! What are the Rangers comin' to?"

Andy flirted with the idea of putting a nest of wasps in Farley's bed, but he saw no way to do it without being stung again. He realized the notion was childish. Even so, it was pleasant to contemplate.

Farley turned toward camp. "I've been about to start gnawin' on my saddle strings. Has that Mexican Pablo called dinner yet?"

"Not that I've noticed." At mealtime the cook hammered on an iron rod bent into the shape of a triangle. The sound could reach for a mile.

Andy wanted to hear more about Jericho's headquarters, but asking questions would subject him to continued unpleasantness from Farley. He saw that a couple of the company horses had grazed far enough to be almost out of his sight. He trotted his mount around them, gently hazing them back toward the main remuda. The horses not in use were loosely herded during the day to allow them to graze freely but not to stray far enough that they could be picked off by an opportunistic thief. Every remuda seemed to have a few bunch quitters that preferred to be off by themselves. They had that in common with Farley Brackett.

Andy heard the dinner triangle, but he had to wait until someone came to relieve him. After a time Len showed up. He said, "Better go eat before Farley takes it all. Acts like it's the first meal he ever had."

Len could put away a prodigious amount of grub himself.

Most of the men had finished eating by the time Andy got there. Pablo stood at an iron stove. Its black smoke pipe extended out through a slit in the side of the tent. A young Mexican boy washed tin plates, cups, and utensils in a tub of soapy water. The boy was a prisoner being treated as a trusty. He had stolen a sack of sugar out of a Mexican store. Most border Rangers paid little attention to crimes by Mexicans against other Mexicans so long as they stopped short of murder. Even minor crimes against whites, by contrast, were treated as serious because it was thought they might lead to something worse if they were tolerated.

Sergeant Donahue's motto was, "Let them steal a chicken one day and they'll steal a cow the next."

Farley had finally eaten his fill. He sat facing Andy and cradled a cup of coffee in his hands. Sergeant Donahue was questioning him. "You say you saw Jericho's men brandin' cattle?"

"A steer herd, it was. Looked to me like they was puttin' a trail brand on them. Probably gettin' ready to drive them north to the railroad. I wasn't close enough to read the original brands."

Donahue nodded. "That connects with the report Manuel brought back from Mexico. Our spies told him Jericho is puttin' together a big trail herd, and the Chavez gang plans to capture it. They want to get even for that last sashay Jericho's men made across the river."

It was not a private's place to ask unnecessary questions. Andy assumed the sergeant intended for the Rangers to set up an unpleasant reception for Chavez's men.

Len was never bashful. If he wanted to know, he asked. "What's the chance we'll get Lupe Chavez hisself?"

Donahue seemed a little annoyed at Len's impertinence. Privates were supposed to listen, not speak. "Not good. We've never been able to catch him on this side of the river, just like we've never caught Jericho at anything that would stick against him."

Cutting off a chance for more questions, the sergeant strode toward the headquarters tent. He returned in a short time and said, "I'm takin' eight men with me on a special detail. We start in half an hour." He pointed to Andy and Len first, then nodded at Farley.

Len said, "I thought me and Andy was goin' to rest a little."

"You can rest when you get old. If you live that long. Now roll your blankets, then saddle up. I don't abide laggards."

SERGEANT DONAHUE DROPPED the men off singly at intervals. He said, "You'll each patrol your section along the river. Watch for Meskin raiders, but don't challenge them. When they cross, get word to the men on either side of you. That word will work its way up to me. We'll all join together and quietly follow them to Jericho's herd."

Len asked, "Hadn't we ought to stop them before they get there?"

The sergeant cut him a hard look. "Damn it, Tanner, you ask more questions than an old maid schoolteacher. Can't you just follow orders?"

"Always did. I like to know the reasons, is all."

"We're not doin' this to save Jericho's cattle. We're doin' it to cripple Lupe Chavez. I figure Jericho's men will whittle them Meskins down a right smart before we have to step in and pick up the leavin's."

"Jericho's apt to lose some men."

"If so, we can mark them off of the wanted list."

Donahue dropped Andy a few miles after he dropped Len. He left Andy with an admonition: "You'll ride downriver far enough to meet Tanner, then you'll turn and go back upriver till you meet Brackett. The bandits'll likely cross over in the dark, so hit the saddle as soon as it's light enough to see tracks. And don't let Tanner drag you into any long-winded conversations, or you're liable to miss somethin'."

Donahue had said no bandits were likely to cross the river in daylight, so Andy saw no harm in resting awhile. The sergeant might not approve, but what he did not know would not hurt him. Andy had raw bacon and jerked beef as well as some of Pablo's leftover biscuits. He ate a little, then stretched out beneath a mesquite.

He awakened to see the sun going down. He chewed a little more tough jerky while he took his time saddling his horse. Watching the riverbank for tracks, he moved downriver in an easy trot. Eventually he met Len coming toward him. Len dismounted and stretched his long legs.

Andy said, "I see that no outlaws have shot you yet."

"It's so quiet I could hear the sun bump as it went down. I think Donahue saved the most likely stretch of the river for himself."

"Are you spoilin' for a fight?"

"Jericho's men may not leave enough of them to give us a decent scrap."

Andy said, "It doesn't matter who gets them so long as they're got. It'll be justice if some of Jericho's bunch are got too. There's no saints on either side."

Riding back the way he had come, Andy could see little by the scant light of a quarter moon. He wished for bright moonlight but knew this kind of night would be a border jumper's preference. The darker the better.

He heard water splash and stopped abruptly. He made out the vague form of a man riding a burro across a wide, shallow stretch of the river. He drew his rifle but soon slipped it back into its scabbard. One man on a burro hardly constituted a raiding party. He could imagine many reasons for the crossing. The rider could be going to or from a sweetheart. He could have family on both sides. Or maybe he was just stealing a burro. Whatever his mission, it was not likely to be of concern to the Rangers. But seeing the lone man reminded Andy how easy it was to pass between the two nations. The boundary was too flimsy to be a challenge to anyone determined to cross over.

He rested again. Just before daybreak he heard a horse walking toward him from the west. He stepped quickly to where he had his mount staked and put his hand over its nose to prevent it from nickering. Not until the rider was almost upon him did he see clearly enough to recognize Farley from the way he sat in the saddle.

Andy said, "You're awful early. See anything?"

Farley exclaimed, "Damn. I didn't even see *you*. Don't you know you could get shot, surprisin' a man that way?"

"Shootin' me would've pleasured you, wouldn't it?" The question was not entirely in jest.

"It'd cause me a lot of aggravation, talkin' to all them lawyers. I'd rather just ignore you." Farley rolled and lighted a cigarette. "I take it you ain't seen anything either."

"Nothin' but a Mexican on a burro awhile after dark. Probably visitin' a woman."

"A good time of night for it. You ever had a sweetheart, Badger Boy?"

"Always been too busy."

"For a long while I've known you're sweet on my little sister. She could do better for herself." Farley turned his horse around and started back upriver. He shouted over his shoulder, "Go on back to sleep."

In early daylight Andy built a small fire. He impaled a chunk of fat bacon on the end of a stick and propped it securely over the low flames. He fetched river water in a tin can and added ground coffee. That he set atop the coals. It was a poor substitute for Pablo's cooking, but it would sustain him. He doubted that the sergeant had anything better. Few Rangers ran to fat.

The sergeant showed up about the middle of the afternoon, checking each man's position. He said gruffly, "I hope you ain't been asleep and let somethin' go by you."

Andy's answer was curt. "I've had my eyes open."

"Some people have their eyes open and still don't see past their shadow."

"Nothin' has crossed over except a couple of buzzards and a man on a burro."

Donahue gave him a hard study. "Maybe. I suppose if that loudmouth Tanner had found anything he'd be up here by now to tell you about it."

"I expect so."

"Tonight'll be another dark one. Get an early start in the mornin'. If you find that they crossed in your sector, fetch Tanner, then send word up the line to me. Each man will relay the message and then ride down to where you're waitin'."

"You don't want me and Len to start followin' the tracks?"

"No. Tanner'd be faunchin' around wantin' to fight. He'd likely spring the trap too early."

Andy's impatience got the best of him. He declared, "I can see that you don't think me and Tanner can do the job. Why did you bring us with you?"

"I can't always have my pick. I make do with what I've got. Sometimes it ain't much."

Andy's face warmed. Watching the sergeant ride away, he began thinking of comments he should have made in rebuttal. Such ideas usually came too late.

He rode downriver toward Len's solitary camp. Len was at the halfway point, waiting. He lay in the meager shade of a mesquite. Andy told him what the sergeant had said. "He said me and you aren't supposed to follow the tracks, just wait till everybody else gets there. He doesn't want us gettin' in a fight till everybody's ready."

Len said, "He doesn't know how good a fight we can put up by ourselves, me and you. We're as good as any he's got."

Andy voiced his doubt. "Donahue doesn't seem to like me much. I don't know why. He makes me wonder if I ought to be a Ranger at all."

"Leavin' the Rangers wouldn't get you away from people like him. You'll run into his kind wherever you go."

"I guess. I remember a Comanche warrior—" Andy

stopped himself before he spoke the name. He had never gotten past his Indian-taught reticence about using names of the deceased, at least those who were Comanche. For some reason that he did not understand, he had no such reservation in regard to white names.

Len asked, "You hungry?"

"I fixed a little breakfast, such as it was."

"I happened onto a fat young kid goat runnin' loose. He looked lost, so I declared him the property of the Rangers. Us two Rangers, anyway."

"Some people would call that stealin'."

"Looked like a stray to me. I didn't see nobody claimin' to own him. He probably swam across the river."

Andy doubted that. He also doubted that Len had made much of a search for the owner. But the goat had already been butchered. It hung by its hind legs from a tree limb. He said, "Whoever it belonged to, he'd probably call it a shameful waste to let that meat spoil."

After helping Len put away a good part of the kid, Andy made his way back to his own camp, then beyond to the point where he expected to meet Farley. Farley showed up after a time. He had a jug tied to the horn of his saddle. Andy asked him about it.

Farley said, "I found a Mexican comin' across the river with a mule load of this contraband. Ain't been no whiskey tax paid on it."

"Did you put him under arrest?"

"No, a workin' man has got to make a livin' whichever way he can. I just fined him one jug and let him go on his way."

"You're not a judge."

"He rode off happy as a pig in the sunshine. It was like I done him a favor by not shootin' him."

"Some favor. You swindled him out of that jug."

"He was breakin' the law. I had to do somethin'."

Trying to understand Farley's way of thinking could give Andy a headache. He said, "I'd best turn back. Sergeant says they're liable to come across tonight."

"See that you don't go to sleep in the saddle." Farley took a corncob stopper from the jug and tilted it over his arm without offering any to Andy.

GUADALUPE CHAVEZ TOOK a long drink of pulque and wiped his bushy black mustache with the back of his hand. He passed the bottle to his nephew. He said, "It would be my wish that you not go tonight, nephew. I had a bad dream about this."

Tony Villarreal tipped the bottle upward and grimaced at the burn of the raw liquor. "I had a dream too, but it was a good one. I welcome a chance to poke Jericho in the eye. Besides, you are sending some good men with me. Why do you worry about me but not about them?"

"They are not of my flesh and blood. You are."

Tony stood nearly a head taller than his uncle. Despite his fierce reputation, Lupe Chavez was small in stature, not much over five feet tall but still as wiry as a half-grown boy. Some of his facial features resembled Tony's mother's, though the harsh demands of an outlaw life made him look older than his actual years. His hair remained black as a crow's wing despite the furrows time and hardship had carved into his dark brown skin.

Tony said, "If God smiles on us I will bring you Jericho's ears."

"Be careful that you do not lose your own. Jericho may have the *rinches* on his side. They are gringos, but they can be terrible when their blood is hot."

"Their blood spills as easily as other men's."

"How would you know? How many have you killed?"

"None so far, but I look forward to the chance."

"You know that your stepfather is a friend to the *rinches.*"

Tony's face darkened. "I do not acknowledge any stepfather."

"But he is your mother's husband, and half of your sister's blood is his. It is gringo blood."

"Hers, not mine. If it were mine I would be willing to see half of it spilled to rid me of the taint."

"That is easy to say when you have not bled. But I have, and I found no satisfaction in it. I am satisfied only when I see the gringo bleed. He has caused all the problems of our people. He has murdered our kin and stolen our land and raised his own flag over it. I wish we could call down a pestilence that would cause him and all his kind to die in slow agony. I thought we had it once, in the time of the rebel Cheno Cortina."

"Uncle, perhaps you are the new Cortina."

"I could not polish his boots, nor those of my father. But I do what I can."

"And it is my pleasure to help you."

Chavez smiled. "You are a good boy. We may yet see a day when not a gringo remains south of the Nueces. This country belongs to the Mexicans. We will take it back when the time is right. But not you, not today."

Tony did not answer. No matter what Tío Lupe said, he was going.

As the evening light faded, Jericho Jackson held his fidgeting horse outside the corral and watched more than a dozen men saddling mounts. All were armed with a pistol and either a rifle or a shotgun.

Burt Hatton looked up at him, for Jericho stood taller and broader in the shoulders than any man who worked for him. Hatton asked, "You think Chavez will come tonight?"

"Tonight, tomorrow night, it don't matter. Gonzales told me they'll be comin', and we'll be layin' for them when they do."

Gonzales was a spy, useful because he would do anything for money. He played the role of a harmless, poverty-stricken *curandero,* a faith healer, and moved freely wherever information was to be gathered. His information was always for sale.

"I never trusted that sneakin' Meskin. He may be lyin' to you."

"He likes my money too much to take that chance. Besides, he knows I'd gut him like a catfish."

Hatton worried, "What about the boys holdin' the herd? They could get killed."

Jericho shrugged. "I've told them to hightail it at the first sign of trouble. Let the raiders have the cattle. They won't take them very far. Just when they think they're gettin' away, we'll hit them like a hailstorm. There'll be dead Mexicans layin' all over the place."

"And maybe a few of our boys."

"They're bein' paid to take the chance. If any of them lets some Mexican kill them it'll be because they wasn't good enough to earn their wages."

Hatton suspected that Jericho considered him as expendable as any of the other men. He resented that, though his loyalty to Jericho was equally shallow. It was simply bought and paid for like any other kind of merchandise. He said, "Maybe we'll be lucky and get Lupe Chavez."

Jericho shook his head. "He's too cagey to go out on these forays himself. He sends other people to take the risks. But maybe we'll catch his nephew, Jim McCawley's stepson. If we do, I don't want anybody killin' him. That's a pleasure I want to save for myself."

Jericho's grim eyes made Hatton feel cold. Jericho wanted to take revenge on Tony Villarreal for the death of his wife's nephew. Nobody had dared tell him the truth, that the boy had died in an abortive raid on a travelers' camp and not at the hands of Chavez's men. Hellfire and brimstone would rain down if Jericho ever found out.

Hatton made up his mind that he would not stay to see that day. At the first good opportunity he would gather up whatever belonged to him, and whatever else he could easily lay his hands on, then leave this part of the country. He could not escape into Mexico, for too many people knew him there and had knives sharpened and waiting for his throat. The word *California* had a nice ring to it.

Jericho said, "Let's try not to let none of them get away. I'd like to take a dozen dead Mexicans and pile them up for everybody to see, like McNelly done that time in Brownsville. Them people have got no respect for us, but they do respect force. I don't see why the Lord don't send down a plague to kill every one of them north of the Rio Grande, and maybe south for a hundred miles."

"They must've done somethin' awful to make you hate them so bad."

"They made me an orphan when I was just a bare-footed kid. Left me to root hog or die. Damn right I hate them. I been payin' them back ever since, and I ain't half done yet. I hope I can live to see the last of them gone."

9

A distant crackle of gunfire made Andy's heartbeat quicken. It came from the north, but he was unable to judge how far. A Ranger named Bill Hewitt pushed his horse into a run. Sergeant Donahue called him back.

"Hold up there. Don't get in a rush."

Hewitt protested, "The fightin' has started and we ain't in it."

"We'll get there in our own good time. Let them have at one another awhile."

"There's white men in trouble up there."

"And not a Sunday school teacher amongst them. It's no great loss if some of Jericho's outfit get dirt shoveled in their faces. They ain't much better than Meskins."

Andy had found the tracks shortly after daybreak. A dozen or so horsemen had crossed the river in the night between Andy's station and Farley's. He had hurried to let Farley know, then had backtracked to fetch Len while Farley sent word up the line. It had taken a couple of hours for all the Rangers to gather. Donahue had led them in an easy trot, following a trail so plain that a tenderfoot could not have missed it.

Andy understood Donahue's lack of haste. The sergeant was letting Jericho's men administer the bulk of the punishment and take some themselves. The Rangers would arrive in time to sweep up any remnants of the raiding party. Jericho's losses would cause no regret except in Jericho's camp.

Farley said, "With any luck, the Rangers will get most of the credit without it costin' us anything except some shells."

Andy asked, "What does it matter who gets the credit?"

"Wake up and think, Badger Boy. Donahue would sell his mother to get promoted to lieutenant. If the papers in San Antonio and Galveston get wind of this, he's liable to make it. And I'd bet my saddle and fixin's that he'll make sure they hear about it."

Though Andy had reservations about Donahue, it had not occurred to him that the sergeant might have planned this little campaign more to advance his career than to punish outlaws.

Farley said, "There ain't many people do things just from the goodness of their heart. Most of them look out for theirselves first. You'd better learn to do the same if you don't want to set your boots under a poor man's table all your life."

If this was true, Andy thought, perhaps headquarters in Austin would assign Donahue to some post where he would consider the adversaries to be worthy of his attention. He had only contempt for Mexican border jumpers.

Hewitt kept pushing out in front, eager to get into the fight. Len was but little behind him, pistol already in his hand. A growing cloud of dust indicated that gunfire had spooked the cattle into a stampede. Through the swirling of hoof-stirred earth Andy began to see horsemen circling about. They were too busy firing at one another to try to control the herd.

Donahue shouted, "Spread out. Shoot every Meskin you see."

Andy followed Len, wanting to keep him in sight because he feared the excitement might make Len careless. But in the dust and confusion he lost him.

A Mexican appeared, a white horseman in close pursuit. The fugitive's horse fell, spilling its rider. The man jumped to his feet and raised his hands, pleading. The pursuer rode within point-blank range and shot him between the eyes.

Andy felt choked. He blamed it on the dust.

Two hundred yards away he saw a white rider slump from the saddle, then struggle to rise from the ground. A Mexican leaned over the fallen man and put two more bullets into him. Before the Mexican could pull away, a Ranger shot him down.

Andy's stomach turned. Both sides were turning this into an orgy of killing.

Donahue was chasing a fugitive but pointed at another who was spurring eastward. He shouted, "There goes a Meskin. Don't just sit there, Pickard. Get the son of a bitch."

By reflex Andy set off in a long lope. Sensing someone behind him, he looked back and saw Farley twenty yards in the rear, trying to catch up. The runner's bay horse was long-legged and strong of wind. For a while it lengthened its lead. The chase stretched to one mile, then two. Andy began to doubt that he could overtake the raider. But gradually the bay weakened, its hide glistening with sweat, its mouth white with foam.

Someone else appeared behind Farley. He was neither Mexican nor Ranger, so Andy figured he was a Jericho man. Farley pointed a pistol at him, and the rider turned back.

Andy tried to aim at the fugitive, but uneven ground

made it impossible to hold the pistol steady. He shouted, "Stop or I'll shoot you."

The threat was hollow. Surely by this time the runner realized that if he was not shot now he would be shot soon after his capture. That was the fate of any raiders unfortunate enough to be run down.

The bay stumbled. Its rider tumbled to the ground, rolling up against a bush. Andy slid his horse to a stop and thrust the pistol toward the fugitive's face. "Raise your hands!"

He saw blood spread over the man's shirt front. As the raider looked toward him, recognition struck Andy like a fist to the jaw. This was Tony Villarreal.

The voice was weak but full of fight. "Go ahead, you damned *rinche*. If you're goin' to shoot me, do it."

Andy lowered the pistol, his mind in turmoil. He heard a horse coming up behind him. It was Farley's. He said, "Don't shoot him, Farley. This is Big Jim's stepson."

Farley said, "The hell you say. Looks to me like you've already shot him."

"Not me. Somebody did it before I saw him. How bad are you hit, Tony?"

Tony touched a hand to his ribs and drew it away, covered with blood. "What difference does it make? If you don't kill me, Jericho will. They're killin' everybody."

Dismounting, Andy turned to Farley. "Let's see what we can do for him. At least stop the bleedin'."

Farley did not leave the saddle immediately. "Ain't much we can do. He's a Mexican. Jericho's crowd'll finish him off."

"Not if we get him away from here."

"Where to? Not to the river. We'd run into some of

Jericho's men as sure as you're born. They might shoot him *and* us."

Andy jerked his head, motioning to the east. "We could take him to his folks. I don't think Jericho's outfit is apt to try for him if we can get him to Big Jim."

"Maybe not, but Donahue'll raise hell. Fire us both, more than likely."

"After what I've seen this mornin', bein' a Ranger doesn't shine all that bright anyhow."

Tony's face was pale from shock, but his raspy voice was still defiant. "I don't need help from no *rinches*. Catch my horse for me and I'll take care of myself."

Andy said, "You'd fall out of the saddle before you went two hundred yards. We ain't doin' this for you. We're doin' it for your folks. I don't see where we owe you a damned thing." He took off his neckerchief and wadded it. Sharply he said, "Hold that against the wound. Maybe it'll slow the bleedin' till we can get you out of Jericho's reach." He looked back, fearing he might see someone coming.

Farley brought up Tony's bay. "I doubt this horse has got many miles left in him."

Andy said, "If he quits, we'll ride double." He helped Tony up into the saddle. "Hang tight to the horn. I'll ride close by and try to catch you if you start to fall off."

Tony muttered, "I can take care of myself."

"You've done right poorly at it so far."

As Andy mounted, Farley moved around to the other side. He cautioned, "You must like trouble, Badger Boy. You're fixin' to get us into a mess of it."

"If you want to leave, go ahead. I can manage alone."

Farley shrugged. "It's always pleasured me to aggravate people I don't like. I don't like Donahue much, and I got no use at all for Jericho. Let's move before him or some of his gun toters come lookin' for this hotheaded idiot."

Tony rasped, "Go to hell."

Farley growled, "Some people have got no appreciation. They'd complain if they was hung with a brand-new rope."

Despite the risk that Tony's tired horse would give out completely, Andy held to a brisk pace for the first couple of miles. Then he slowed, for Tony was barely able to grasp the horn and stay in the saddle.

He said, "Maybe we'd better tie him on."

Farley said, "He could fall and get tangled in the rope. I seen a man drug to death once. It was a gut-grabbin' sight."

The mental image was disturbing. Andy said, "Tony, you'll just have to grit your teeth and hang on."

The young man made no response. Andy was not sure he was still able to comprehend.

Farley turned in the saddle and swore aloud. "I knew our luck wouldn't hold. Somebody's catchin' up to us."

Andy looked back, holding his breath. He saw two horsemen. "They're not Rangers. Must be some of Jericho's people."

Farley squinted. "People, hell, one of them is Jericho hisself, big as a barn door."

Andy started looking for a defensive position but saw nothing except low thorny brush and almost flat ground. "Poor place to stop and put up a fight."

Farley grunted. "Most of the fights I ever had was in poor places. Best we get down and stand behind our horses."

Andy and Farley both struggled to get Tony to the ground without letting him fall. Andy drew his rifle and propped it across the saddle.

The red-bearded man seemed too large even for the tall horse he rode. Jericho and another rider reined their sweating mounts to a stop. The other man said, "Told you he looked like Big Jim McCawley's kid. We like to've lost him."

Jericho smiled coldly at the sight of Tony, leaning against his saddle and holding on to keep from falling. "Well, he's caught now." He seemed to recognize Andy. "Thanks for catchin' him for us. I'll take charge of him now."

Andy said, "No, you won't. We've got him under arrest."

"I don't see no badges on you."

"They never issued us any, but we're Rangers just the same."

Jericho's mouth twisted as he considered the situation. Andy watched him warily. Jericho outweighed him by fifty or seventy-five pounds. He had an air like a bull ready to charge. If he had been one he would be pawing the ground.

Jericho said, "You've done your job. You can turn this renegade over to me and go on about your business."

"He *is* our business. He's our prisoner."

"You're a long ways from a jailhouse. Give him to me and he won't get away again, not now and not ever."

Andy said, "We've seen how you handled the others you've caught."

"There's just one way to treat a bandit: kill him where you find him. No judge, no lawyers, no jury that might turn him loose and let him do it again."

"Do you know who he is?"

"He's a nephew of Lupe Chavez."

"And he's Big Jim McCawley's stepson."

"Makes no difference. He's a bandit. It's open season on all of his kind."

Andy's rifle had been pointed upward, toward the sky. He lowered the muzzle so Jericho could look directly into it. Instinctively Jericho tried to draw to one side, but Andy let the front sight follow him. The rancher made a big target.

Andy said, "Now, sir, if you'll back off, we'll be on our way."

Jericho showed no sign of retreat. He said, "I never seen a Ranger that had two dollars in his pocket. I'll pay you a good price for him. What'll you take?"

"They ain't buyin' and sellin' people anymore. Didn't you ever hear of Abraham Lincoln?"

Jericho glowered. "They shot *him*."

Andy held firm. "You ain't gettin' our prisoner."

Jericho's mouth made contortions without producing any sound. At last he said, "I don't know where you figure on takin' him, but wherever it is, I don't think you'll get there." He jerked his head. "Come on, Baldy, before I let my temper make me kill a couple of Rangers."

Nobody spoke until Jericho and his companion were a hundred yards away. Farley took a deep breath. "You sure put the Indian sign on him. I guess it's all that Comanche in you."

"You heard what he said. He ain't given up." Andy turned to Tony. "Let's move while he's tryin' to figure out what to do next."

Andy helped Tony into the saddle. Tony touched his hand against the wound in his side. It came away with fresh red color. Andy said, "Still bleedin' a little. Keep pressin' my neckerchief against it."

Farley remarked, "That dirty neckerchief is liable to kill him if the bullet don't."

As they rode, Tony asked, "What he said about you bein' part Indian . . . is that a fact?"

"Depends on how you look at it. My folks were white, but the Comanches took me when I was a boy. Kept me a long time. Some of their teachin' has stuck with me."

"I've been raised white and Mexican both. I guess me and you have got somethin' in common."

Andy shook his head. "Damned little. I've never swum the Rio Grande to raid somebody's cattle."

"It's not just somebody, and it's not really about cattle. It's about Jericho Jackson. Tío Lupe and me, we won't stop till we've settled our score with him."

"Looks like he stopped you today. Most of the men who came with you appear to've got themselves killed."

"Too bad, but there's plenty more ready to rise up against him. He's already dead. He just don't know it yet."

Andy touched spurs to his horse's ribs. "He's about the livest-lookin' dead man I ever saw. And I'm bettin' he's trailin' behind us, just out of sight." He pointed in a north-easterly direction. "Seems to me that ought to be the right direction to Big Jim McCawley's."

Tony protested, "It's not his place. It's my mother's and Tío Lupe's. I don't want to go there."

"It's our only chance, poor as it is. Jericho would never let us get you to the river."

They traveled slowly because Tony had trouble staying astride. Andy had to reach across at times and hold him in the saddle. He kept looking back.

Farley said, "Ain't no use lookin' behind us. They ain't there anymore." He pointed. "They're alongside us, and it looks like Jericho has picked up a couple more men."

Jericho and three others were two hundred yards to the

left and working their way around in a slow lope to position themselves in front.

Farley spoke with a touch of sarcasm. "Well, Badger Boy, you got any ideas?"

"I can't think of a one."

Tony said, "Give me a gun. At least let me take him with me."

Farley said, "You bluffed him once, Andy. Maybe you can do it again."

"I wasn't bluffin'. I'd have shot him if I had to, and he knew it. I still will."

Jericho and his three riders stopped fifty yards away. They formed a line facing Andy, Farley, and Tony. Andy dismounted and helped Tony to the ground. He stood behind his horse, rifle again resting across the saddle.

Farley followed his lead. He said, "Maybe if we kill one or two, the others will figure out we're serious."

Andy said, "I don't like killin' a man if I don't have to." As the four began moving forward, he took careful aim and fired. A horse went down kicking.

Farley said ruefully, "But you've got no scruples against killin' a horse. I'd sooner kill a man."

"It's a poor choice either way." Andy levered another cartridge into the breech.

Jericho and his men stopped their advance. They appeared to be confused and quarreling. One rode away, his posture indicating that he had lost an argument. Jericho called after him angrily but to no avail. Jericho and the other remaining horseman dismounted.

Andy fired again, kicking up dirt between the two horses. Both jerked loose and ran. Farley took a shot, putting it just behind them. The horses broke into a full gallop, leaving the three men afoot. Andy could hear Jericho's voice, loud in rage.

He said, "They'll be a while runnin' those horses down. Let's circle around them and put some distance behind us."

Jericho fired a couple of futile shots as they cut to the south, then east again.

Farley muttered, "Keep shootin', Jericho. That'll just make the horses run faster."

Tony bent low over the saddle horn. Andy asked him, "You think you can make it the rest of the way?"

Tony ignored the question. He said accusingly, "You ought to've shot Jericho instead of the horse."

They had traveled most of a mile when Andy heard hoofbeats coming from the east. "Damn! I thought we'd left the trouble behind."

Shortly he saw two riders, one a large man on a big horse. Frustrated, he demanded, "How did Jericho get ahead of us again?"

Farley said, "Blink your eyes and take another look. That ain't Jericho, it's Big Jim McCawley."

Tony raised up, trying to see. "Tell that old gringo I don't need him."

Andy looked back. He saw Jericho and one horseman catching up but still three hundred yards away. "You'll never need him worse. Let's get to him before Jericho can get to us." He took hold of Tony's shoulder. "Hang on tight. We're goin' to lope up."

McCawley reached them first. He had already recognized his stepson. His eyes were wide with concern. "What's happened to Tony?"

Andy said, "He's got a bullet in him. If you hadn't come along, it was startin' to look like he might get some more. And us too."

Jericho paused to watch from fifty yards behind.

McCawley dismounted and stood beside Tony's horse.

"Let's take a look at you, son." Tony tried to pull away from him, declaring, "Don't call me son."

McCawley tore the bloody shirt open. He did not like what he saw. "We'd better get him to the house as quick as we can."

Andy said, "That's where we were tryin' to take him. Jericho had it in mind to stop us."

Tony argued, "I ain't goin' with you. I'm goin' to Tío Lupe."

Jericho moved closer, his hired man following with obvious reluctance. The Mexican who had arrived with McCawley pointed his rifle toward them. Jericho made a show of keeping his hands high. He halted a few feet from McCawley and his stepson.

"Jim," he said, "you came near losin' this boy of yours. If it hadn't been for these Rangers . . . You better break him of runnin' with your brother-in-law's renegades, or he's in for a damned short life."

Andy felt hair rise on the back of his neck. Animosity passed between the two big men like lightning coursing through stretched wire.

Jim McCawley spoke in the voice of a judge pronouncing a death sentence. "If you ever hurt any of my family again, you'd better have a grave dug and waitin' for you."

"There ain't no grave deep enough to hold Jericho Jackson." Jericho pulled his reins, backing his horse a couple of steps. "You keep that chili-eatin' kid away from everything that's mine. Else when I've taken care of the son, I'll come lookin' for the daddy."

"You'd better hope to God you don't find me."

Tony knotted a fist and leaned forward. "Kill him! Kill him while you've got the chance." He lost his balance. His father caught him and pushed him back into the saddle. "Easy, son, or you're liable to kill *yourself*."

Tony tried again to pull away. "I ain't your son. I don't have no gringo daddy."

The blood on his shirt had dried. Now it glistened again, fresh and red.

McCawley spoke in Spanish to the Mexican who had come with him. The Mexican rode in close to support Tony while McCawley remounted.

Jericho and his rider had pulled back but stopped thirty yards away. Andy could read Jericho's intentions from the way he sat, poised like a cat waiting to pounce. He said, "Might be a good idea if me and Farley was to ride with you, Mr. McCawley. Just in case."

"I'd be obliged. Even Jericho respects the Rangers."

"Not these Rangers, I'm afraid. But he'll respect the guns we're carryin'."

Tony still acted as if he might pull free and go his own way. His stepfather forcefully took hold of the reins and said, "It'll be good to get you away from your uncle Lupe for a while. Looks to me like he's poisoned your mind."

"Don't you say nothin' against Tío Lupe."

Farley told Andy, "I'm thinkin' Big Jim ought to've worn out a quirt on that boy's butt when he was young enough for it to've done some good. It's probably too late now."

Andy offered no argument.

10

Only two men had returned so far to the stone house where Guadalupe Chavez waited south of the Rio Grande. They had come separately, one with a bullet in his shoulder, the other walking and leading a bleeding horse. Both said it was unlikely anyone else was coming.

"It was a trap, Don Lupe," the wounded man said. "We found but four men with the cattle. They ran away. But the Jericho, he had other men hidden. They came down on us like a whirlwind."

"What of my nephew?" Chavez demanded, eyes afire with accusation. "Did you run away and leave Antonio?"

"I did not see him, but the Jericho's men were everywhere. They were killing everybody. We had no chance."

Chavez was more inclined to shoot the wounded man than to treat him. "You should have watched out for him. He is but a boy."

"He is a man, a man who should not have gone with us." The black eyes held accusation of their own. Chavez flinched at a pang of guilt. He had tried to talk Antonio into staying behind but had yielded to the young man's insistence. He should have held tough.

Chavez pointed to a much larger stone house. "Go to the women. Let them tend your wound."

"Yes, *patrón*." The man hesitated, holding a hand to

the bad shoulder. "Good men have died today. What do we do now?"

"I will tell you when the time comes. First I want to know what happened to my nephew. Send Gonzales to me."

Gonzales was an efficient spy. He could move about freely, appearing to be a ragged wood-gathering old peasant and no threat to anyone. To the contemptuous gringos he seemed beneath their notice, almost invisible. This worked to his advantage, for his ears were always open for information and his palms open for coin.

Gonzales appeared, his clothing tattered, his dusty feet protected only by *guaraches* so old that the leather was dry and twisted and black. His long gray mustache drooped like his shoulders. "You have work for me, *patrón*?"

"I want you to go across the river and see what has happened to my nephew. If he is dead, I want his body brought back here where he can be buried in hallowed ground with a priest to help his soul find its way to paradise. If he is alive I want to know where, so that I may send men to rescue him."

"This will be a dangerous business. The Jericho is killing every Mexican he sees."

"He will not waste a bullet on a worthless old man. He would not even stop to spit on you. I will pay well for the right information."

Gonzales nodded. Chavez had known he would respond to the prospect of liberal payment. His only concern was the man's greed. He suspected that Gonzales would be easily tempted. Should Chavez ever catch him dealing double, he would stake him down in an ant bed and let him consider the wages of perfidy while he died slowly, one bite at a time.

Gonzales said, "It is told on the other side that one of your men killed a nephew of the Jericho. For revenge he is resolved to kill a nephew of yours."

"Antonio?"

"Have you another?"

"Yes, but they are far away. Only Antonio has been with me. When were we said to have killed Jericho's nephew? I have heard nothing of this."

"I know nothing more, only what I have told you."

"Go then, and find Antonio. If he is alive, we must get him back. If he is dead . . . find out if Jericho has other nephews."

THE LEAD SLUG clanked heavily as Farley dropped it into a tin pan. He pressed a clean, folded cloth over the wound. Bleeding had started afresh as he probed. "I've treated many a wound like this, a couple of them in myself. Now, let's hope he don't take blood poisonin'. Been as many died that way as of the bullet itself."

Andy asked McCawley, "Don't you think you'd better take him to a doctor now?"

"The nearest one is a two-day ride from here."

Tony's mother said, "He'll get better care from his own family than from a busy town doctor."

Few small towns had a hospital. A doctor might keep a patient or two in his own home. More likely he would lodge patients in a boardinghouse and visit them as necessary or as time permitted.

Teresa said, "You're tired, Farley. I'll bandage him for you."

Andy noticed her use of Farley's first name. Propriety would call for her to say *Mr. Brackett*. He was aware that Farley had been watching the girl, trying not to be obvious about it. And several times Andy had noticed her dark eyes fixed on Farley until he looked her way. She would quickly transfer her attention elsewhere.

Farley stepped out onto the back porch to wash his hands in a basin. McCawley and Andy followed. The big man said, "I'm much obliged to you both. If it hadn't been for you, Tony would be dead."

Farley only grunted. Andy said, "We did what we could. I only wish we'd got to him sooner, before he was shot."

"You've made an enemy. Jericho doesn't forget, and he doesn't forgive. You bein' Rangers, he probably won't shoot you himself, but he may hire somebody that can't be connected to him."

Andy said, "I'm not sure we'll still be Rangers when we report back in. Sergeant Donahue doesn't forgive or forget much either."

"I'll go over his head. I know people in the Austin office."

Tony had resisted Farley's initial effort to treat him. He had insisted, "Get Tío Lupe. I want him to do it."

McCawley had argued that by the time Lupe Chavez could reach here, Tony would be dead. And Chavez would probably not be able to come in any case. On the Texas side of the river he had a price on his head large enough to tempt even some who sympathized with him.

Now Tony lay half conscious, senses dulled by several liberal doses of whiskey before the surgery began. Andy knew it would be poor taste to ask McCawley why his stepson seemed to resent him so much.

Farley had no such inhibitions. He said, "There must've been a hell of a bust-up between him and you. What did you do to him?"

McCawley seemed jarred by the question. "Nothin' except to be white. We were havin' a right smart of trouble with bandits, so I sent my family down to his uncle. Figured they'd be safer at Lupe's place in Mexico. I didn't figure on Lupe fillin' his head with so much hate for everything gringo. Juana and Teresa came home after that spell of trouble died down, but Tony stayed."

Farley said, "Maybe you should've gone and brought him whether he wanted to come or not."

"I wouldn't have gotten back across the river alive." McCawley's eyes were sad. "Some folks complain about discrimination against Mexicans, but the knife cuts both ways. There's blind people aplenty on either side."

All the windows had shutters that could be closed and barred from the inside, a holdover from earlier Spanish times when Indian raids had been a recurring challenge. McCawley saw to it that the window in Tony's room was shuttered so no one could see in and perhaps get a shot at him. He said, "If Jericho's dead set on killin' him, an open window would be too much temptation."

Andy said, "Do you think he'd be bold enough to come here?"

"If Jericho sets his mind to somethin', he'll walk through hell's fire to get it done. I'll be puttin' men on guard tonight."

Andy said, "You can figure on me and Farley."

Farley gave Andy a cautioning look that said to speak only for himself, but he assured McCawley, "I'll stand my share."

McCawley said, "I'd be obliged if somebody would stay in Tony's room tonight and make sure nobody sneaks in."

Or out, Andy thought. He would not be surprised if, despite his wound, Tony took a notion to slip out of the house and make for the border. He probably would not get far, but it would not be for lack of trying.

Tony's sister sat at his bedside when Andy and Farley returned to the room. Tony appeared to be asleep but restless. Teresa said quietly, "He's running some fever."

Farley laid his palm against the boy's forehead. "At least he won't be runnin' for the border tonight."

She said, "He wouldn't do that. Would he?"

"He might. He's got guts. Meanin' no offense, but it's too bad he ain't got good sense to match."

She said, "I'll admit he's a trial sometimes. But he is my brother. I'd hate to see more harm come to him."

Farley placed a hand on her shoulder. "It won't. Me and Badger Boy will see to that."

She reached up and touched his hand. "Badger Boy?"

"It's a long story. If you've got time maybe I'll tell it to you."

She smiled. "I have plenty of time."

Andy left the pair and walked out to the kitchen to see about getting a cup of coffee. He doubted that Farley's story would paint him in a good light.

Someone shouted outside, "Mr. McCawley. Riders comin'."

McCawley flung the door open and stepped out into the night. He shouted, "Don't anybody shoot unless we're shot at."

Rifle in hand, Andy joined McCawley at the front of the house. Farley came hurrying, pausing to blow out the lamp in the parlor. Andy said, "Don't seem likely that it'd be Jericho. Not bold and open like this."

McCawley said, "Anybody who can outguess Jericho ought to be able to outguess the weather and the cattle market too. I'd put him on my payroll." He shouted to the oncoming horsemen, "Who are you?"

The answer came in a familiar voice. "Sergeant Donahue, Texas Rangers. Is that you, Jim McCawley?"

"It is. You-all come in slow so I can get a look at you." McCawley lowered his rifle once he was satisfied that the visitors were indeed Rangers.

Andy counted five men including the sergeant. He was pleased to see that Len Tanner was among them. He had been concerned that Len might have charged into the fray with his usual recklessness and gotten himself hurt.

Donahue gave Andy and Farley a critical look. "Figured you two would be here. I talked to Jericho."

Andy acknowledged him with a nod.

Farley said, "I'd guess he hollered murder."

"Somethin' like that. Said you-all took a prisoner away from him."

Andy said, "It wasn't quite that way. He tried to take a prisoner away from us. We didn't let him."

Donahue's frown deepened. "You exceeded your authority."

"I always thought a Ranger is supposed to protect a prisoner and not let anybody take one from him."

"Jericho claimed you threatened to kill him."

Farley said, "All we done was tell him that if he didn't back away from our prisoner, we'd shoot out his liver and lights."

"You meant it, of course."

Farley replied, "It ain't my way to say somethin' unless I mean it." He glanced at Andy. "This Indian boy's neither. Folks don't always agree with us, but they seldom misunderstand what we tell them."

"Why did you bring your prisoner here instead of deliverin' him to camp?"

Andy said, "That was too far. He could've bled to death. Besides, we figured Jericho would gather up more men and head us off. He had blood in his eye."

"It was still there when I talked to him." Donahue

looked back at McCawley. "Jericho said it was your step-son. Have I your permission to go in and take a look at him?"

McCawley considered the question. "Just you. And understand that you're not takin' him when you go. He's too bad hurt to be moved."

Donahue stiffened. "I am an officer of the law. I do not accept conditions."

"You'll accept this one or you'll hear from my friends in Austin."

Donahue's mustache twitched in anger at this threat to go over his head. "Very well, but you should understand that I consider your boy a prisoner. I'll leave a guard. As soon as he's fit to travel, he'll be taken to jail."

McCawley yielded no ground. "We'll discuss that when the time comes." He motioned toward the door. "After you."

Len waited until Donahue and McCawley had gone inside. He moved up to Andy and said, "You-all have played hell with the sergeant's digestion. He wanted Jericho to get that boy. Said it would serve Big Jim McCawley right for marryin' a Mexican woman."

"I knew he had somethin' stuck in his craw."

"Ain't much he can do about the kid for now, but he'll chew on it. He'll have an awful stomachache by the time he gets back to camp."

Farley growled, "It'll be good for him."

Len shook his head. "But not for the rest of us."

Andy asked, "Were you with him when he talked to Jericho?"

"Yeah. Looks like Jericho's crew killed most of the Mexicans, but they took a pretty hard lickin' theirselves. He'll be shorthanded till he can rustle up some more men."

"So will Guadalupe Chavez. Maybe that'll put a stop to the raids around here for a while."

"Maybe." Len grinned. "But it was a pretty interestin' scrap while it lasted."

Donahue came out in no better mood than before. He was telling McCawley, "It wouldn't make no difference if you was the governor of Texas. An outlaw is an outlaw no matter who he belongs to."

McCawley asked, "Did anybody see him steal any cattle?"

"He was there."

"So were you. So were Jericho's men. Just bein' there doesn't prove anything."

"It'll be enough for a jury." Donahue jerked his bridle reins from the hands of a Ranger and jammed his foot into the stirrup. "I intend to see that he stands in front of a judge and jury that won't care about anything except him bein' Lupe Chavez's nephew."

Andy walked up as Donahue mounted. "Sergeant, you said you're leavin' a guard. Since he was our prisoner, I'd like to volunteer."

Donahue glared at him. "Permission denied. In fact, you and Brackett can consider yourselves unemployed. I am strikin' you from the roll as of now."

Farley protested. "On what grounds?"

"On the grounds that I don't trust either one of you any further than I can spit."

Farley said, "I got wages comin'."

"Take it up with Austin." Donahue pointed to the Ranger named Hewitt. "You'll stay here and be sure that boy doesn't set foot out of this house. Soon as he's able to ride, I'll send a detail to pick him up." Donahue looked back at Andy and Farley. "If you two have any belongings left in camp I'll send Private Tanner back here with them. If I ever see either of you again, I'll file charges on you for malfeasance."

Andy trembled with anger. He could not bring out the words he wanted to say.

Farley said them for him, a burst of profanity that would have done credit to a drunken mule skinner.

As the Rangers moved off, Len held back for a moment. "Sorry, Andy."

Andy shrugged. Nothing was left to say.

Farley grunted. "It may be a good thing anyhow. Have you ever seen an *old* Ranger?"

McCawley put his big hand on Andy's shoulder. It felt heavy as an anvil. "You've both got a job here with me if you want it. After a little coolin' off time . . . well, like I said, I've got friends in Austin."

RANGER HEWITT SEEMED unsure what his relationship with Andy and Farley should be, so he kept it formal. He said, "I'm sorry for what happened to you men, but I don't want it happenin' to me."

Andy tried to set him at ease. "We don't hold anything against you."

Farley added, "It ain't your fault you're workin' for a son of a bitch."

Hewitt said, "I'd ask for a transfer, but Donahue would probably fire me instead."

"You could hire out somewhere as a deputy sheriff. I hear most county deputies are paid better than Rangers," Andy suggested.

"But my daddy was a Ranger before the war. Died fightin' Indians. All I ever really wanted was to be a Ranger like him."

Farley said, "Then stay with it. Sooner or later Donahue is liable to bite himself like a rattlesnake. I don't see why the main office puts up with the likes of him."

Hewitt said, "You have to admit that he's pretty good at what he does. The trouble is that he knows it."

Andy nodded. "I can see why he's got his sights set on Lupe Chavez. I just can't see why he cozies up to the likes of Jericho Jackson."

Hewitt said, "You can't see it because you don't have a devious mind like his. He wanted Jericho to kill the McCawley boy because he knew it'd make Chavez mad enough to come shootin'. He wants Chavez and Jericho to hit like two freight trains rammin' together. With any luck they'd wipe each other out. Then Donahue would get credit for cleanin' up the border. He'd like to be known as another Leander McNelly."

Farley pointed out, "McNelly is dead, but Donahue looks so healthy it turns my stomach. I guess we shouldn't hope for too much in this world."

Next morning Andy watched as Jim McCawley prepared to walk out to the corrals. He said, "You haven't been in to see Tony this mornin'."

McCawley's expression was dark. "He talks to his mother and sister. He doesn't want to talk to me."

"I'm sorry."

"It's nothin' for you to trouble yourself about. It's between me and Tony . . . and Lupe Chavez."

Andy thought it best to change the subject. "I've been thinkin' about goin' back home to the Colorado River, but I'll stay awhile if you have a use for me. I don't know that I'm much of a cowboy, though. Never did much of that."

"I've already got enough cowboys. I'm afraid Jericho

hasn't given up on the notion of killin' Tony. I'd like you to stay around close and help watch out for him. Farley too, if he's of a mind to stay."

"I don't think Farley is in any hurry to leave." Andy had seen Farley in intense conversation with Teresa after breakfast. He added, "Jericho might not stop with Tony if he saw a chance to get you too."

McCawley filled a pipe with tobacco, tamped and lighted it. "There's no enemy quite as bitter as a friend who's turned against you. Jericho wanted this ranch so bad he'd sell his soul to the devil to get it. Lupe Chavez couldn't stop him, but I did."

"What's to keep him from slippin' up and shootin' you while you're out on horseback, workin' cattle?"

"I have some good men with me, white and Mexican both. And I've got eyes in the back of my head when it comes to Jericho. You watch out for Tony. I can take care of myself."

Andy hoped he was right. He watched with admiration as McCawley walked out toward the corrals. The man's stern determination reminded him of Rusty Shannon and Sheriff Tom Blessing. He had seen both stand tall in the face of severe adversity.

Ranger Hewitt came out of Tony's room. Andy asked, "How's the patient?"

Hewitt shrugged. "I'd just as well find me a shade tree and sleep all day. He's not in shape to go anywhere."

"I'm not worryin' too much right now about him leavin'. I'm worried about somebody comin' in after him."

Andy entered Tony's room. The young man lay on a cot, his face toward the wall. He did not acknowledge Andy's presence. He had lost a considerable amount of blood, and he still suffered from shock. Andy could imagine how much he must be hurting. A wound was usually more painful the second day than the first. Andy said, "Are you hurtin' too much to talk to Big Jim?"

Tony offered no answer.

Andy said, "He's worried about you. You're not bein' fair to him."

Tony did not look at him, but he murmured, "What the hell would you know about it?"

"All I know is that you're bein' an ungrateful young whelp and your family is too good for you."

"My real family is south of the river. I wish you'd taken me there instead of bringin' me to this place."

"If we'd tried, your mother and sister would be cryin' over you this mornin'. You'd be dead."

"You figure I owe you somethin'?"

"Not a thing except maybe to act like a human bein'. I'd give everything I own to have a family like yours."

Tony cursed. "Take them and be damned. Soon as I can I'm goin' back where I belong."

"If you can get past Jericho, and the Rangers, and me."

11

He appeared to be a ragged old Mexican beggar, riding up to the ranch house on a tired-looking burro the third day after the battle. The ancient saddle with its wide, flat horn appeared almost as large as the animal itself. The man presented no evident threat, but Andy looked him over for sign of a weapon. He saw none. The man spoke in Spanish. Andy did not understand him, so he beckoned to the McCawleys' middle-aged maid. She had stepped outside to shake crumbs from a tablecloth.

He told her, "I don't know what he wants."

She spoke to the old man in Spanish and listened to his reply. "He asks whose hacienda this is. I told him Señor Jaime McCawley is the *patrón*. He says he has heard that Señor McCawley is a generous man and kind to poor Mexicans."

"Tell him that right now Mr. McCawley is also a very suspicious man when it comes to strangers."

She and the gray-whiskered oldster conversed a bit more. She said, "He says he means no one harm, that he is simply a poor man on his way to see his son in San Antonio. He is hungry and wishes only for a little food. In return he is a *curandero,* a healer. He would work his magic on any here who may be sick."

"I doubt as his magic would help much on a gunshot

wound. And I wouldn't suppose he's got some kind of charm that would improve Tony's sour outlook."

"Many of our people put much faith in *curanderos*. They have powers no one else can understand."

Like Comanche medicine men, Andy thought. Logic told him the shamans' magic was useless, but he had seen strange things happen as a result of it. Sometimes logic did not work well either.

The maid said, "I will go and tell *la señora*."

"I wouldn't bother her." Andy found that he was talking to himself. The maid had hurried inside. Shortly, Juana and Teresa came out, the maid explaining to mother and daughter what the old man had said.

Big Jim's wife appeared intrigued. She asked something in Spanish. The man replied, "*Me llama Gonzales.*"

Andy took that to be his name, though the rest of the conversation went past him.

Teresa said, "Mama, these *curanderos* are fakers. There's nothing he can do for Tony."

Her mother said, "There are many things we do not understand, child. What is to be harmed if he takes a look? Just a look, that is all."

"Papa may not be pleased."

"There are things your papa does not know either. We have never turned the hungry away from our door. I see no harm in feeding the old fellow."

Andy felt uneasy, but it was not his place to argue with Mrs. McCawley. He said, "It might be a good idea to search him and make sure he's not packin' any iron."

Teresa told the old man what Andy had said. The *curandero* made no protest. He lifted his arms to demonstrate that he carried no gun. He had a skinning knife at his waist. He removed it and its belt, hanging them over the horn of his old saddle.

Mrs. McCawley said, "He is a stranger. There is no reason he would want to hurt Antonio."

Andy replied, "Right now any stranger will bear watchin'."

The old man seemed a stranger to water. Mrs. McCawley and the maid brought him a plate of beef and beans and a cup of coffee on the patio. He sat in the shade and devoured the food quickly without availing himself of a chance to wash his face and hands.

Teresa frowned. Quietly she told Andy, "These beggars all have some kind of story. If he is a true *curandero,* why does he not heal himself?" The old man had a swollen cut on his hand that he had said resulted from letting his knife slip while he butchered a fat goat.

Andy said, "Maybe he expects the dirt to heal it."

Teresa said, "I have a bad feeling about this man. Would you watch him?"

"I will." Andy suspected she would probably rather have asked Farley, but Farley and Hewitt were out at the corrals looking over some brood mares a couple of vaqueros had brought in to mate with McCawley's best stallion.

When he had eaten his fill, Gonzales asked to see the sick man. Mrs. McCawley led him to the room where Tony lay. He said his medicine would work better if everyone left. The two women withdrew, though Teresa's eyes begged Andy not to go. The old man frowned at him. Andy sat in a chair and said firmly, "I'm stayin'."

Tony seemed to brighten a little as Gonzales spoke quietly. Andy strained to hear, but it was a lost effort because he could not understand the language. Gonzales laid his hands on Tony and said words that Andy took to be some sort of incantation. He had witnessed similar performances by Comanche medicine men.

Tony had spoken little to anyone in the family, but he talked at length to the *curandero*. Afterward, though he said nothing to Andy, he appeared to have a stronger light in his eyes.

Maybe there's more to this magic stuff than most of us can see, Andy thought.

He stood at the front door, watching as the old man rode northward on the overburdened burro. Teresa joined him, a question in her eyes.

Andy said, "I don't see as he hurt anything. Maybe he did Tony some good, even if it's only in his head."

She replied, "These are strange times. You never know for certain who are your friends and who are your enemies."

"I guess he's just a harmless old—" Andy caught himself. He had been about to say *harmless old Mexican*. She might have taken that as an affront to her mother's side of the family. It was the sort of thing he would expect from Sergeant Donahue, and perhaps Farley. He completed the sentence. "Harmless old beggar."

She said, "It will take him a long time to reach San Antonio on that poor burro."

"Time doesn't matter much to a burro."

The next time Andy looked in, Tony was sitting up, a pillow propped behind him. It was the first time Andy had seen him that way. Tony nodded, saying nothing though he appeared at least civil. His attitude changed when his stepfather came in hot and dusty from working cattle and stopped to ask how he was. Tony turned his face to the wall and made no comment. Big Jim looked dejected.

Andy followed him out into the parlor. He said, "If it's any comfort to you, a while ago he seemed like he was feelin' better."

"Seein' me spoiled it, I suppose." McCawley went into the kitchen. He poured a glass of raw tequila and drank half of it in one swallow. "His uncle convinced him that I married his mother just so I could steal this ranch. But it was the only way I could keep Jericho and some others of his kind from gettin' their hands on it. Once these border troubles are behind us, I plan to sign every-thing over to Tony and his sister."

"Maybe you ought to tell him that."

"He'd want me to do it now. I'm afraid it's too early. The courthouse crowd would find a way to take it away from him, like they took so much away from old Don Cipriano and Lupe."

"They might do it anyway if anything happens to you."

"That's why I keep a crew of good men around me, so nothin' does."

Farley and Hewitt remained at the horse corrals until nearly time for supper. They proceeded to the patio to wash their hands and faces. Drying himself with a towel, Farley said, "We seen an old Mexican stop at the house this afternoon. What was he after?"

Andy explained that he claimed to be a *curandero,* and that he spent some time with Tony. That quickly caught McCawley's interest. He said, "Nobody told me."

Andy said, "Guess nobody felt like it was important. Mainly he just wanted to beg a meal, then be on his way to San Antonio."

Farley said, "San Antonio's north."

"That's the way he went."

Farley and Hewitt exchanged looks. Farley said, "For a little while. But after he traveled north for a ways, he took a turn to the west. Me and Hewitt seen him."

McCawley's jaw dropped. "West, toward Jericho's?"

Andy felt a stab of conscience. He realized he should not have allowed Gonzales into the house. "You reckon he was here to spy for Jericho?"

McCawley mulled over the question. "He might've been, but what could he find out that Jericho doesn't already know? That Tony is here? Jericho knows that. That we're keepin' a guard on him? Anybody with half a brain has to figure that we would."

Andy said, "He might've intended to do Tony harm, but I searched him for weapons before I let him come inside. I watched him all the time he was here."

"Did he say anything?"

"Not to where I could understand him. Most of it was sort of a chant."

"We could trail him," Farley offered.

McCawley shook his head. "We wouldn't likely catch up to him before dark. If he came here as a spy he probably won't stop till he gets to Jericho's place. Let's just be happy that there wasn't any harm done."

It nagged at Andy how the old man's visit had seemed to boost Tony's spirits. Maybe Tony believed in *curanderos,* or perhaps the old man had told him something. He returned to the door of Tony's room and looked inside. He wanted to ask what the visitor had said, but if it had been anything significant he knew Tony would not tell him. It was frustrating that he could not figure the old man's motives, though by now he was convinced that Gonzales had been up to no good.

BURT HATTON HESITANTLY entered the office that Jericho Jackson considered his private sanctuary from the frequent disturbances which plagued his life. He stood a moment, unsure of Jericho's reaction to the interruption, then tapped his knuckles against the doorjamb. He said, "That pet Mexican of yours is outside."

Jericho set down an account book he had been working on and flipped a stub pencil deep into the rolltop desk. It annoyed him that Hatton had entered unannounced and uninvited. "A little wait won't hurt him."

"He says he's just come from over at Big Jim's. Got word for you about that boy."

Jericho shoved the account book into a drawer and locked it. There was no telling when some of the help might decide to snoop, including Hatton. His finances were nobody's business but his own. "All right, damn it, I'll see him. But outside. I don't want him comin' in this house. He's liable to be carryin' lice."

It had been dark for an hour. Jericho lighted a lantern beneath the roof's narrow overhang and beckoned to Gonzales. The burro stood droop-headed where the old man had stopped him.

Jericho asked impatiently, "What you got for me, Gonzales?"

His knowledge of Spanish was limited. He knew Gonzales understood English, though the old man acknowledged it to few people. The appearance of ignorance served his purposes. Gonzales said, "I have done as you asked. I have seen the boy Antonio. He is in the house of his stepfather."

"Hell, I already knew that."

"He is stronger than his family thinks. He tells me he will soon get away. He wants to go back to his *tío* Guadalupe Chavez."

"I've figured he'd try. Him and Big Jim don't get along. When does he intend to go?"

"He says he thinks after two more days he is strong enough to ride. The McCawley and the women are to go to San Antonio. Among the vaqueros the boy has a friend who will bring his horse that night."

"Anybody watchin' him?"

Gonzales held up three twisted fingers. "*Rinches.* But they do not think he is strong enough to ride. He fools them. He has only to get out of the house while others sleep."

Jericho considered for a moment, then made a grim smile. "He won't go far. We'll get him as he leaves."

"It will be dark. He will be hard to see."

"Even if we lose him, he'll leave tracks. It's a long ways to the river. Come daylight we'll catch up to him."

"*Bueno.*" Gonzales extended his hand, palm up. Jericho dug several coins from his pocket. Gonzales counted them and looked pained. "What I have told you is worth much more."

"This is enough, you damned old bandit. You'll just get sloppy drunk on tequila. If I was you I'd buy me a young burro with it and feed that one to the hogs."

"But Señor Jericho . . ."

"Move along before I sic my dogs on you."

Looking as if he had bitten into a sour melon, Gonzales mounted the burro. His thin legs hung almost to the ground. He struck the burro across the hips with a rawhide quirt and cursed it as he rode southward.

Hatton said, "Kind of rough on the old reprobate, ain't you?"

"He'll take it. He likes my money too much not to. Anyway, I've got no respect for a man who betrays his own kind, even if his kind are Mexicans."

"How can you be sure he won't betray *you?*"

"He won't. He knows I'd skin him and nail his hide to the barn. I may do it anyway when I've finished with him. He leaves a stink wherever he goes."

THE OLD BURRO was still wet from swimming the river when Gonzales quirted him up to the stone house. A man walked out and confronted him, holding a rifle.

"I am Fermín Gonzales. I have come with news for Don Guadalupe Chavez."

The rifleman studied him with distrust. "I know who you are. Get down. Let me see if you are carrying a weapon."

Gonzales said, "Only this poor knife. It is so dull it will not cut hog fat."

The guard looked him over carefully anyway. Gonzales said, "I am but a poor man doing a service for my good friend Lupe. Why would I wish to do him harm?"

"Perhaps someone has paid you to. We know you come from the Texas side. You have been watched since before you rode into the river."

"It is good to see everyone so careful. One can never be certain who are friends."

"Or enemies." The guard said, "Wait. I will tell Don Lupe." He walked into the stone house. Shortly he returned, followed by Guadalupe Chavez.

Chavez's eyes were as distrustful as the guard's. His voice was sharp and without friendliness. "What have you for me, Gonzales?"

Normally it would be custom to invite a guest into the house and offer him something to drink. Chavez did not. Gonzales was aware of the slight, but he hid his resentment. A wise man does not bite the hand that may soon offer him money.

"I have seen your nephew Antonio."

Chavez's attitude changed abruptly to one of eagerness. "Where is he? Is he well?"

"He is in the house of his mother. He is not well."

"But he is alive?"

"Yes. He was shot by the Jericho's men. Some *rinches* took him to the hacienda McCawley. But he gains in strength. It is his intention to slip away and come back here to you."

"When?"

"If all goes well, he will leave in two nights." He explained about his ruse to get into the McCawley house and speak to Tony. He told of Tony's intention to escape. He said nothing about Jericho, for that would risk revealing that he was working both sides.

Chavez frowned. "It will be a long ride to the river. Do you think he is strong enough to endure it?"

"He thinks he will be. I am not so sure. It would be well if you met him and made certain. The *rinches* are sure to follow him."

A disturbing thought came to Chavez. "Do you think Jericho knows where he is?"

"How could he know? Unless, of course, there is a traitor somewhere."

"I wish I could send word to Antonio that we are coming to meet him."

"I can go back. They accept me as a *curandero*. I can tell them I have come with medicine for the boy." That offer, and the risk inherent in it, should be worth a larger payment, he thought.

"Do that. Tell him to come to the old adobe camp. He knows where it is. We will meet him and see him safely to the river."

"It will be done." Gonzales hesitated, staring at the ground. "I have expenses, Don Lupe."

"Of course. Wait while I go into the house." Chavez came back in a few minutes with a small leather bag that clinked as he placed it in Gonzales's hand. "You have done me a service."

"*Gracias, patrón.* May you live well and die a very old man."

Gonzales hefted the bag. He knew without counting that it did not come up to his expectations. Disappointed, he started to complain but thought better of it and turned away. Chavez would probably chastise him for being greedy, as Jericho had done, and pay him no more. He reined the burro toward the river.

Chavez watched until Gonzales was a couple of hundred yards away, then crooked his finger and beckoned to one of the pistoleros who had fought the gringos with him.

He said, "I have no trust in Gonzales. It was he who told me Jericho was gathering a herd. It was a trap. He has promised to go to the hacienda of Jaime McCawley. Follow him. If he rides in any other direction he has lied to me. Kill him."

"*Sí, patrón.* It will be done." The pistolero went to catch his horse.

Gonzales crossed the river, but once out of sight he turned eastward. He had no intention of returning to the McCawley ranch and delivering Chavez's message. The risk was too great, the reward too small.

He saw some possibility that Chavez and Jericho might collide in their search for Tony. Perhaps if they had been more generous he would favor one or the other. As it was, beyond the loss of their meager bribes he would feel satisfaction rather than grief if either or both of them died. He was acutely aware that the two men held him in contempt, though they were not so contemptuous that they would not use him.

This was a game that more than two could play. It would serve them right if he were the instrument of their mutual destruction.

He would follow the river down to Matamoros, where a man with money in his pocket could debauch himself on the sweet fruit of the vine, dance with lissome señoritas, and be young again while the money lasted. He felt younger already. He could hear the music playing in his head. He hummed along with it and for a while did not notice the horseman rapidly catching up from behind.

Awareness brought alarm, and he quirted the burro vigorously across both hips. It was of no use. The horseman pulled up beside him, a pistol in his hand. His eyes were those of a hawk swooping in for the kill.

Gonzales tried to cry for mercy, but his mouth and throat were dry. He heard the shot. He felt nothing when he hit the ground.

12

The sun broke over the eastern horizon as Big Jim McCawley helped his wife and daughter up into the buckboard. He turned back to Andy and said, "I hate to go, under the circumstances, but we've got to. I'm meetin' with a cattle buyer in San Antonio. Teresa needs books and things for teachin' when school takes up again. Tony seems to be comin' along all right. He just needs healin' time."

Andy said, "If anybody was fixin' to make a move against Tony, looks like they would've already done it. We'll keep a close watch over him."

Several of the ranch hands were going with the McCawleys to protect the family on the road. Travelers were beset from time to time by highwaymen who had no connection with either Jericho or Guadalupe Chavez. Andy, Farley, and Hewitt were staying.

Andy asked, "What do you want us to do if Sergeant Donahue sends for Tony?"

"How good are you at lyin'?"

"Never was much of a hand at it. The Comanches didn't have much use for a liar unless he was braggin' about a fight. They made allowances for that."

"Convince them that Tony is still too weak to be moved. We should be back in a few days. I know a good judge in San Antonio. I think I can get a court order to make Donahue leave him be."

That pleased Andy, though he wondered about the fairness of a legal system that would let a man of influence obtain favors unlikely to be available for the average poor citizen from the forks of the creek. He thought it probable that Donahue might know a judge or two himself.

The procession consisted of the buckboard, a wagon, and four horsemen. He watched it leave, then turned toward the house, where Farley and Hewitt stood beside the door.

In Andy's days at the ranch he had heard Tony say very little to anyone. He was surprised when Tony asked, "They gone?"

"They're just toppin' the hill. Why? Didn't they tell you good bye?" He let a little sarcasm creep into his voice.

"I'm glad Farley Brackett didn't go along. I don't like the way he keeps lookin' at my sister."

"Farley's got his faults, but he wouldn't harm a woman."

"My sister is half Mexican. He doesn't have much respect for Mexicans."

"She's also half gringo. Does that make you have any less respect for her?"

"That's different."

"Not much." Andy looked at a small bedside table where a cup of coffee was going cold. "Need anything?"

"I wish you'd open the shutters and let some air in here. It was awful warm all night."

"We've kept the shutters closed so nobody can slip up in the dark and shoot you through the window."

"But it's not night anymore. Nobody's goin' to try it in broad daylight."

"I guess not." Andy swung the shutters back and opened the window. "Me and Hewitt will be close by. Holler if you need anything."

"I just need lettin' alone."

That suited Andy. He had had about enough of Tony's sour attitude. He was tempted to saddle up and ride away, but he had given his word to Big Jim. He might go, however, when the McCawley family returned. They had plenty of help. They didn't really need him. And he had no obligations to the Rangers anymore. Sergeant Donahue had taken care of that.

Lately Andy had given considerable thought to Rusty Shannon and Alice. And Bethel Brackett. He did not feel at home in this hot and brushy borderland, so different in people, climate, and terrain from what he had known. He had been revisiting his old dream of settling down in a pleasant valley, perhaps in the hill country, somewhere along the San Saba or Llano rivers.

Idling had never suited him for long. He had a sense that time was a gift not to be wasted. Through the day he pitched in with a couple of Big Jim's Mexican hands in digging postholes for a new corral. He could keep an eye on the house while doing that. Physical exertion helped him sweat off some of his frustrations. The fatigue that came upon him toward the end of the day gave him a satisfying sense of accomplishment.

Despite his reassurances to McCawley, he felt a vague uneasiness as night came on.

Farley said, "I can't see what you're worried about. Ain't nobody made a try for the kid yet."

"Dark always worries me. You never know who or what might be out there in it."

At dusk Andy and Farley made a wide circle around

the house, walking to the edge of the brush and checking the outbuildings.

Farley said, "Like I told you, ain't nobody comin'. I'd bet my life on it."

"It's Tony's life we're bettin'."

Though he had seen nothing, Andy closed the shutters that covered Tony's window. Tony demanded, "Do you have to do that? I'll suffocate in here."

"Better than lettin' a Jericho man shoot you through the window. Maybe you'll think about this the next time you decide to pull a raid on somebody's cattle."

"I'll bet half of those cattle belonged to Tío Lupe in the first place."

"I'm not a judge. I'm just a Ranger. Or was. It's on account of you that I got fired."

Tony showed no remorse. "If you had any self-respect you wouldn't have been a Ranger anyway. The Rangers are a tool of the gringo land grabbers. They won't be satisfied till they've run all the Mexicans across the river." He scowled. "Who knows if they'll even stop there? I heard that to the day he died, Sam Houston was plottin' another invasion of Mexico."

"And I heard that the earth is flat, that if you go to the edge of it you'll fall off."

"Go ahead, make fun of what I'm tellin' you. You just haven't seen things from my side of the river. Someday some Mexican general will rise up and drive the gringos all the way north to San Antonio. Maybe farther."

Andy tried to think of an answer. "I guess you think that general might be your uncle Lupe?"

"Who knows? The strongest leaders we've ever had came up from the people. Like Father Hidalgo. He raised the cry for Mexican independence from Spain."

"As I heard it, they shot him."

"That was the Spanish. They were no better than the damned gringos. And we Mexicans beat them."

"And then the Texans beat you." Almost before Andy got it said, he wished he hadn't. He saw that he had touched a raw nerve.

Tony flushed. "You better watch out that when the stampede starts you don't get tromped in it." He turned his face toward the wall.

It was useless to argue with Tony. Andy felt foolish for trying. He went outside to be sure a proper guard had been set up. The face he saw at the front of the house was not the one he expected. He found a bronc rider whose name he remembered as Francisco.

Andy said, "I thought Toribio was standin' the first watch."

Francisco's grasp of English was tentative. He touched his hand to his stomach. "Toribio sick a little."

Andy remembered that Francisco had been in the house to visit Tony a couple or three times. Evidently their friendship went back a long way. "Well, you watch good. There may still be somebody lookin' to get at him."

"Good boy, Tony. I watch."

Andy had been sleeping on a cot in the hallway. An invader would have to go past him to get into Tony's room. Farley had spread his bedroll near the back door. Hewitt slept at the end of the hall nearest the front door. With guards inside and outside, Andy felt that Tony was well protected.

He did not remove his clothes, other than his boots. He would get up at least once in the night to check on the guards outside. The steady *tick-tock* of a tall grandfather clock in the nearby parlor slowly lulled him off to sleep.

He was jarred awake by gunshots from somewhere

outside. Flinging off the light blanket that covered him, he dashed into Tony's room. Though it was dark he saw that the shutters were open. Tony was not in his bed. Andy rushed to the open window and tried to see out into the darkness. He heard a horse running. Somewhere out there a man shouted angrily. More shots echoed back from the brush.

He bumped into Hewitt as both tried to go out the front door at the same time. He saw the guard Francisco standing, looking off southward in the direction from which the shots had come.

Andy demanded, "What's happened?"

Francisco turned. To Andy's surprise he was smiling. "Antonio . . . he get away."

"But how?"

"I bring horse for him so he goes to his uncle. Men in the brush shoot, but I think they no hit Antonio. He is gone *por allá,* for the river."

Farley came running up. "Damn kid. I didn't think he was in shape to climb out the window, much less to ride a horse."

Andy said, "Looks like he fooled us."

Francisco chuckled. "Fool everybody."

Andy was tempted to hit him, but he saw no gain in it beyond possibly venting a little of his frustration.

"Looks like Jericho's men were layin' for him." He heard more shots, farther away. "Sounds like they haven't caught him."

Francisco said, "Fast horse. Nobody catch."

Andy said, "Come on, we'd better see if we can help him."

Hewitt said, "We couldn't find an elephant out there in the dark."

"But we know he's headed south. He won't stop till he

gets to the river unless Jericho's men overtake him." He had no doubt that Jericho or his men had done the shooting. He would give odds that the angry voice he had heard belonged to Jericho himself. "Maybe we can cut his trail and catch up to him."

Andy went back for his boots. He trotted toward the barn, Hewitt and Farley close behind him. Hewitt fretted, "Donahue will have my hide for this."

Andy didn't give a damn about Donahue, but he felt that he had let Big Jim down.

They saddled and set out in a lope in the direction from which the last shots had come. The firing had stopped. That could mean Tony had eluded his enemies in the darkness, or it could mean . . . Andy did not want to think about that.

Hewitt said, "What I can't see is why Jericho is so hellbent on gettin' that kid. It's not like he's Lupe Chavez's right-hand man."

Andy replied, "It's somethin' about Jericho losin' a nephew. Even a man like him can have feelin's for his kin. He blames Chavez. Got a grudge against Big Jim too. Killin' Tony would give both men a kick in the teeth."

Patches of thick brush forced them to slow down to prevent thorns from injuring the horses. The men were not immune to them either. Andy heard Farley curse as an unseen mesquite branch slapped him across the face. "Damn near put my eyes out," Farley complained. "Every time I go somewhere with you, Badger Boy, somethin' happens to me."

The only saving grace was that Jericho's men were probably having the same trouble.

In the darkness and the brush it would be easy to lose the way and begin traveling in circles. Andy picked out a star he judged to be more or less due south. Whenever they had to skirt around an obstacle he kept reining back in the direction of the star. He paused from time to time to listen, but he heard no more shots, no hoofbeats. He was fairly sure they had not gotten ahead of Jericho's men. He hoped they had not ridden past Tony.

"At least they ain't caught him," he said. "We'd hear shootin' if they did."

They continued riding through the night, though without any solid indication that they were on the right track. Andy began to be plagued by doubts, which he thought best not to confess to Farley or Hewitt.

Just at daybreak he heard desultory gunfire in the distance. He reined up to listen. "It's at least three or four different guns. Sounds to me like Tony is makin' a stand."

Farley said, "He won't hold out long if they've got him bottled up in the brush."

Hewitt pushed past Andy and Farley. "I've got to protect my prisoner."

The two quickly caught up with him. Andy said, "He's not anybody's prisoner, not till we pry him loose from the hole he's in."

They almost rode upon the Jericho men before they realized how close they had come. Andy heard the hiss of a bullet passing by his ear and clipping into a tangle of mesquite limbs behind him. He drew his pistol and fired a couple of shots. He had little expectation of hitting something he could not see, but it might give the pursuers something extra to worry about.

Farley said, "Let's surround them."

Another bullet sang as it passed by. Andy realized it did not come from the Jericho crew. "Look out. Tony can't tell us from them." He shouted, "It's Andy. We're comin'."

Jericho's men did not seem talented at hitting moving

targets. They fired several ineffective shots as the three riders swung around them.

Andy saw that Tony's horse was down. Tony was lying behind it, pistol balanced across the saddle. Andy jumped to the ground. "Are you all right?"

Tony said crisply, "Hell no, I'm not all right. They shot my horse out from under me."

Andy saw blood on Tony's shirt and doubted it came from the horse. "Looks like they hit you."

Tony shook his head. "No, but the fall opened that wound up again. Been bleedin' some." His hand shook. "I can't hold my gun steady or I'd've gotten two or three of them by now."

"You ain't got a lick of sense or you wouldn't be out here in the first place. We're goin' to take you home."

"Like hell. You think you can get past them?" He nodded toward the Jericho men, less than a hundred yards away. "One of them rode off a while ago. I figure he went for reinforcements. The only direction we can go from here is south."

Andy realized he was right. They had caught Jericho's crew by surprise just now or they would not have gotten past them. They could not go back through or around them without heavy risk. He looked at Farley and Hewitt. "You-all ready for a swim?"

Hewitt said, "I'm still a Ranger. It's illegal for me to cross the river."

"Liable to be fatal if you don't."

"Since you put it that way . . ." Hewitt fired toward the men in the brush. "Just want them to know that we ain't gone to sleep."

Andy said, "Let's hoist Tony up into my saddle. I'll ride behind him."

Farley pointed out. "That means they'll have to shoot through you to get him. Are you sure he's worth it?"

"Probably not. But let's go."

Andy's horse fidgeted, made nervous by the shooting and the smell of blood. Tony was as weak as a sick colt. Andy and Hewitt struggled to get him into the saddle while Farley watched for the Jericho men to move. Andy swung up behind Tony. He said, "Hold tight to the horn so you don't slide off. One more fall just might put you under."

"It'll take more than that."

They moved into an easy lope. Shortly Farley shouted, "They're tryin' to go around us. We'd better whip up."

Andy looked back. He saw six riders, somewhat scattered but spurring hard. "How far is it to the river, Tony?"

"It's just ahead of us."

"Then we'd better give them a horse race. If they get in front of us, we'll never be able to go through them."

The ground seemed a blur as Andy and Farley and Hewitt pushed their mounts for all the speed they could get. But Andy's was handicapped by carrying the weight of two riders. Once the horse stumbled and went to its knees trying to jump over a bush. Andy almost lost his hold on Tony. The horse regained its feet, but it had lost some ground.

They hit the river still barely ahead of Jericho's men. Andy held tightly to Tony as the horse began thrashing, plunging through the water. This was not an ideal place to cross. The river had narrowed, but narrowing made it deeper.

The pursuers' aim was spoiled by the motion of their swimming horses.

Andy and the others broke out on the south bank and

resumed running. But Andy's hopes began to sink as he saw that they were going to lose the race. Jericho's riders were gaining rapidly. Gradually they maneuvered around to the front, fifty yards ahead. They stopped and faced about.

Andy brought his horse to a stop and slid off, reaching up to help Tony down.

The riders began firing at them. A bullet thumped against the cantle of Andy's saddle.

"Get behind the horse," he told Tony. That was difficult because the horse kept dancing about, trying to jerk the reins from Andy's hand and run away. "Then drop down low where they can't see you through the brush."

Farley said, "They don't have to see us to hit us."

"We don't have to make it easy for them." Andy raised up, trying to see a target. He saw a man moving around to the left. "Tryin' to flank us," he said.

Tony tried to aim. Andy took the pistol from his hand. "You can't hold steady enough to hit the side of a barn. Don't be wastin' shells. We'll need all we've got."

He fired at the flanker. He saw the man drop, then rise again and go hopping back toward the others.

Farley said, "Aim higher, Badger Boy. His leg is too far from his heart." He had his rifle. He leveled it, squeezed the trigger, and the man fell.

Hewitt said, "Good shootin'."

"I got a lot of practice back in the days of the state police. They learned to keep their distance."

For a while Jericho's men seemed confused and uncertain, unnerved by Farley's accurate shot. Every so often they would send a bullet whispering harmlessly in the general direction of the fugitives, who for the most part kept low.

Farley raised up a little, as if inviting a bullet. "Look yonder, up the river."

Andy had been concentrating his attention on their adversaries and had not paid attention to what was going on to the west. He saw at least a dozen horsemen loping alongside the river toward them. He asked Tony, "Some of your friends?"

Tony seemed to pick up strength. "That old *curandero* must've told Tío Lupe that I'd be comin'."

Andy frowned. "But I'm thinkin' he told Jericho too. That's why they were waitin' for you soon as you left the house. Looks like he lit the candle from both ends."

Jericho's men exchanged a few shots with the oncoming riders, then broke and ran for the river.

Tony looked up at Hewitt. "You're still a Ranger. Tío Lupe had rather shoot a Ranger than eat. I don't know if I'll be able to stop him."

Hewitt seemed to be measuring the distance between him and the Mexicans. "I'd best go report to Sergeant Donahue that his prisoner got away. I'll be lucky if he doesn't fire me."

Andy said, "Tell him it was all my fault. He'll believe that."

Hewitt left in a lope, riding eastward to avoid contact with either Jericho's men or the Mexicans. Andy was relieved to see that no one from either group chased after him. He figured Hewitt would cross over at some shallow point. "He's a pretty good sort," he said.

Farley nodded. "At least he doesn't talk your ears off like Len Tanner. If I was to ever be a Ranger again, I wouldn't mind havin' him with me."

Farley must be mellowing, Andy thought. Usually he had rather have a boil on his butt than to pay anybody a compliment. First Teresa McCawley, now Ranger Hewitt. After this, Andy would not be surprised to see the sun rise in the west.

The first of the Mexican horsemen reined up. Andy was strongly aware of several pistols aimed at him. He raised his hands to shoulder level and tried not to betray any anxiety. Some people fed on others' fear.

He had never seen Guadalupe Chavez, but he thought he had heard enough to recognize him on sight. He would have picked almost any of the others before he would have chosen the one who turned out to be Chavez. To Andy's surprise, he was anything but imposing. He was a small, thin man, not much more than five feet tall and weighing perhaps a hundred thirty. His fierce eyes were so dark that they appeared black. A heavy mustache gave his face a fearsome look that belied his size.

He pointed to Jericho's fleeing men and shouted an order in a voice far stronger than his physical stature would indicate. Most of his men set out in pursuit, spurring into the river.

Only then did he kneel to look at his nephew's wound. Andy could not understand the conversation, but he sensed anxiety in the older man's voice. The only word he could pick out was *rinche*.

Tony explained, "He thought I was shot again. I told him I would've been if you hadn't come after me."

Andy saw no softening in Chavez's malevolent glare. Chavez shifted to English. "You would take my nephew to the Rangers?"

Andy said, "No, we intended to take him back to his mother and stepdaddy."

"But you are Rangers, no?"

Andy said, "We used to be. We lost our job."

"Not good enough even to be a Ranger? Tell me why I should not shoot you."

Tony spoke again in Spanish. Andy sensed that he was defending them. He thought it best to let Tony do the talking. Chavez seemed unlikely to listen with patience to a gringo, especially a used-to-be Ranger.

Chavez's grim countenance softened a little. "Antonio says you are friends of his. You are not friends of mine, but maybe I don't kill you for a while yet."

Andy hardly considered himself and Tony to be friends, but he was not about to argue the point. He said hopefully, "Since Tony is safe now, me and Farley will go back and tell his folks what's happened."

Chavez narrowed his eyes. "Or maybe go and bring the *rinches*? I think you may be spies for them. I must think on whether I will shoot you or let you go."

Tony spoke again in Spanish. Andy looked at Farley, who was equally at a loss with the language. A pleading tone indicated that Tony was trying to dissuade his uncle. Chavez did not appear to be yielding much.

Gradually Chavez's riders began trailing back. Two rode over to look at the man Farley had shot. The others had left him behind. One shouted something to Chavez, who responded by making a slicing motion across his throat. The man leaned down from the saddle and fired once.

Chavez said, "He was not sure the gringo was dead. Now he is sure."

Andy flinched despite himself.

Farley said, "They do take their politics serious down here."

13

Chavez lighted a long black cheroot and stared up at Andy and Farley, his eyes unreadable. Though he was shorter than either man, he seemed taller to Andy. He held out his hand. "Your guns, please."

Farley hesitated. "I've got a sentimental attachment to my guns. I carried one of them all the way through the war. The other one I took off of a state policeman. He'd lost interest in it."

Andy cautioned, "You'd better give it to him, or he'll take it away from you the same way you got it." He forked over his own pistol to one of Chavez's lieutenants and nodded toward the rifle on his saddle. The man took it too. Farley then gave up. At Chavez's command a couple of his men helped Tony to his feet. Another led the unfortunate Jericho man's horse to Tony and carefully lifted him into the saddle. Chavez motioned for the Texans to get on their horses.

Tony slumped, weakened by the reopening of his wound, though the bleeding had stopped. He said, "Sorry, boys. When Tío Lupe gets his head set on somethin', it's hard to talk him out of it. But I'll keep workin' on him."

When Chavez was out of earshot Andy said, "From all the stories I've heard I thought he'd be a lot bigger, at least as large as Jericho or Jim McCawley. He reminds me of a banty rooster."

Farley replied, "A fightin' rooster. Santy Anna was a little man too, and look at all the hell he managed to cause."

The Chavez riders kept Andy and Farley hemmed up in the middle as they rode westward. It would have been foolhardy to try to run. They had nowhere to go except the river, and they would be cut down before their horses got their bellies wet. Andy tried to rationalize that Tony would soften his uncle's attitude, but he did not convince himself.

Farley muttered, "You've gotten us into a fix this time, Badger Boy."

"Me? I didn't do anything more than you did."

"But you're a jinx. Always was. Everything you get into causes me trouble. It's a wonder I'm not dead."

"You could've lit out with Hewitt."

"I wish I had. If we was still Rangers maybe Donahue would bring a rescue party and get us out of this. But as it is, I doubt he'll lift a finger. And it was you that got us fired."

Andy knew the futility of argument. For every answer he gave, Farley would come up with another complaint. He wondered how Teresa McCawley could see anything romantic about Farley. She would have a hard time gentling him if she managed to hook him, which she seemed to want to do. That was assuming he and Andy survived this scrape.

They came to a sprawling ranch headquarters, a mixture of stone and adobe buildings flanked by an expansive set of corrals built crudely but effectively of brush. It lay a mile or so south of the river. Smoke arose from several chimneys. The smell of burning wood reminded

Andy that he had not eaten since last night's supper. He thought it best not to say anything that might be taken for complaint. He suspected that Chavez had a low tolerance for complaint, nor would he be hesitant in imposing a penalty. He had scarcely blinked when one of his riders had shot the fallen Jericho man.

Chavez barked a series of orders to his followers. Most dismounted and took up defensive positions while the others led their horses into a corral.

Chavez said, "One never knows what the Jericho may do. Come. We go to my house. I will tell the women it is time for *comida*."

Andy hoped that meant something to eat.

Chavez led them to a large stone house built along the same old Spanish lines as the home of Big Jim McCawley. He motioned for them to dismount and signaled one of his men to lead the horses away. He walked to the hand-hewn front door and beckoned the Texans and his nephew inside.

Farley muttered, "Like a fly into a spider's web."

Andy said, "You better do a lot of listenin' and damned little talkin'."

Two women came to meet them. Both were relatively young, and one was obviously pregnant. Chavez put his arm around her. The motions of his free hand told Andy he was talking to the women about the boy's wound.

Tony explained, "An old woman lives here, a *curandera*. She will make me well."

Andy said, "I hope she's cleaner than that old man who came to see you at McCawley's."

"That old man was no real *curandero*. He was a spy for my uncle. I told him when I would get away. Tío Lupe and his men waited for me at the river, but because of the Jerichos I could not cross where they expected me. That is why they were late."

Andy said, "They weren't the only ones who knew what you figured on doin'. Jericho's crew was layin' for you."

Chavez broke in. "The old man was two times a spy, sometimes for me and sometimes for the Jericho. He will not spy again."

Andy considered the implication and took no comfort in it. Death meant little to either Chavez or Jericho so long as it was not theirs.

Chavez went to a rustic old wooden cabinet and took out a bottle of some kind. He poured a drink for Tony and one for himself. He did not offer any to Andy or Farley. Instead he pointed to a pair of straight chairs. "You will sit. My men watch outside. If you try to go I will not have to concern myself with you anymore."

Chavez put his nephew's arm around his shoulder and took him down a long hall. The women followed. Farley continued to stand. Andy said, "He told us to sit."

Farley said, "I don't do somethin' just because some Mexican tells me to."

"Might be a good idea this time."

Farley sat.

Andy looked about the room. Instinctively he sought any opening that might offer escape, though he knew he would be caught and probably shot the moment he stepped outside. The furnishings were generally of fine quality but showed age and wear. He guessed most went back to Spanish colonial times. The house itself certainly did. It bespoke a more prosperous period, when a don could afford to buy luxuries from Mexico City and even Spain.

Farley said, "Livin' pretty high for Mexicans."

"The old don was a big landowner on both sides of the

Rio Grande before the Americans came. I guess he believed in spendin' his money."

"I would too, if I had any."

"Your family still has a right smart of land. The carpetbaggers didn't steal all of it."

"It belongs to my mother and my sister, not to me." Farley's eyes widened a little. "Now that I think on it, the carpetbaggers did to us Bracketts what the Americans did to the Chavez family. But there were people here before the Chavezes. The Spanish did to the Indians what the Americans did to the Spanish and the Mexicans later. And what your Comanches did to the Apaches and any other Indians that got in their way. The same things keep happenin' over and over again. It's just the people that change."

Andy wanted to argue but recognized the truth in Farley's comment. "The trouble you stirred up with the carpetbaggers and the state police was like what Lupe Chavez does to Jericho and the other gringos."

"But I never hurt no honest citizens. Chavez don't make much distinction as long as they're gringo."

"He still looks on it like a war. Wars always hurt innocent people."

Farley frowned. "That ain't no reason to sympathize with him."

"But I do, sort of. It'd be simpler if I didn't. Then I wouldn't be pulled one way and another over what's right and what's wrong."

An old woman entered the house. She carried a small cotton bag. One of the younger women met her and escorted her down the hall. Andy reasoned that she was the *curandera* Tony had mentioned. He could hear a buzz of conversation from the direction of Tony's room.

Lupe Chavez returned, a satisfied look on his face. "All is well now. When the old woman speaks, heaven listens."

Andy said, "Wouldn't it be better to have a real doctor look at him?"

"Doña María is a doctor. She has not the papers from the university, but she knows things that are not written in the university's books."

Andy shrugged. He had little doubt that Tony would survive anyhow. He had been well on the way to healing before his fall reopened the wound. With a *curandera*'s attentions it might just take a little longer.

Chavez said, "You doubt, but there is much you gringos do not know."

Andy said, "I spent several years with the Comanches. They had their own version of the *curanderos*."

That piqued Chavez's interest. "You are not Indian."

"They tried to make one out of me. Came awful close."

Chavez demanded to know more. Andy told him how Comanche raiders had killed his mother and father and taken him to raise as one of their own. He had been well on his way to becoming a warrior when he fell back into the white man's world.

Chavez became more animated. "There was a time we had to fight the Indians. In the days of my grandfather they drove many of our people off of their land. But not him. He built this house to be a fort. Never did they break in. Neither will the Jericho. Neither will the *rinches*."

"They tell me Jericho's house is a lot like this one."

"Because my grandfathers built it to stand against the Indians. But it could not stand against the lawyers and the Yankee land grabbers. They fight with paper, not with guns. So many lawyers, so many papers."

"Me and Farley, we're not lawyers. There ain't nothin'

we can do to help you, and nothin' we can do to hurt you, either. I don't see any need in us stayin' here."

Chavez frowned. "I still do not know if you are spies for the *rinches*."

"We ain't. Even if we were, there's nothin' we could tell that would be of any use to them. They already know where this place is, and they'll pretty soon figure out that Tony is here. But they can't do anything about it. It's illegal for them to cross the border."

"It was illegal when the McNelly came with all his *rinches* across the river and invaded the Rancho Las Cuevas. He killed many men who were not bandits. He killed them only because they were Mexicans. Some were of my blood. My very own family."

Andy had heard stories about McNelly's bold raid in pursuit of bandits. It was claimed afterward that he hit the wrong ranch and killed several innocent men before he found his intended target. By then he was surrounded by Mexican soldiers and vaqueros. Only intervention by the U. S. Army extricated him and averted the annihilation of his command. Even so, he provoked an international incident that raised smoke all the way to Washington and Mexico City.

On the positive side, the border raids stopped for a while. Under the circumstances Andy did not think it prudent to mention that. All he said was, "I wasn't here. Neither was Farley."

"But you are *americanos*. You share the blame."

Andy was familiar with the concept of collective guilt, though he did not agree with it. To the Comanches, a wrong by one white was a wrong by all whites. Vengeance could be exacted upon any who came in handy.

Chavez said, "Poor Mexico. So far from God and so near to Texas."

The two younger women came up the hall. Chavez spoke, and both answered him at the same time. He turned to Andy and Farley. "We will eat now. Not even a gringo *rinche* is to be hungry in this house."

Andy took this as a hopeful sign that Chavez did not intend to shoot them, at least not for a while.

Chavez led them into a dining room, where the women began placing food on a large handmade table that had legs thick as fence posts. Its varnish had darkened with age and was worn through along the edges and much of the top. "You will sit."

He bowed his head and spoke a prayer. Andy found that inconsistent with the shooting of the wounded Jericho man, but he had never understood the flexible interpretations given religion by people who considered themselves civilized. It seemed they could find biblical justification for almost anything they chose to do.

Finished eating, Chavez said, "It is true that you wanted only to take Antonio back to his mother?"

Andy nodded. "And his stepfather. Big Jim has been awful worried about him."

"That man's name is not spoken in this house."

"Why? He's your sister's husband, and he raised Tony like he was his own."

"But he is not of our blood. The Jericho took our land with lawyers and a gun. The McCawley took it with a wedding. In the end it was all the same."

"You're wrong. Him and your sister love each other."

"That I do not believe. What he loves is the land. Our land."

Andy quit arguing. To anger Chavez might put Farley and himself in deeper jeopardy. He pushed his chair back from the table and said, "What now?"

"I am still thinking. You will stay while I decide." He

walked to the door and shouted to a vaquero who stood outside, watching the trail. "You will follow Porfirio. He will see that you go nowhere."

Porfirio was tall and lanky with dark eyes cold as January. He carried two pistols and a rifle, which he politely but firmly pointed toward a small stone outbuilding that had a front door but no windows. He motioned for them to enter, then closed the door behind them. Andy heard the clatter of a bar dropped into place.

He said, "Pretty dark in here."

Farley replied, "Kind of like our future."

"Don't give up. I believe Tony'll keep talkin' in our favor."

"He's not much more than a kid. You think Chavez will pay any attention to him?"

"Seems to me like these Mexicans put a lot of store in blood relations."

"Especially when you hurt one of them."

Andy's eyes accustomed themselves to the dark interior. He found a goatskin and spread it on the dirt floor, then stretched out on it. "After ridin' all night and finally gettin' my stomach full, I'm tired out."

"You may be fixin' to get a lot longer sleep than you figured on." Farley found a piece of canvas and made a bed of sorts. "Every time I try to do a good deed for somebody, I find myself in trouble all the way up to my chin."

Cracks in the stone wall and around the door admitted just enough light that Andy could guess at the sun's position. Just at dusk he heard a commotion outside: dogs barking, a babble of voices, several shouts of warning. He sat up, wondering if Rancho Chavez was being invaded by Rangers or perhaps Jericho's outfit. He heard no shots, however.

Andy went to the door and tried to peer out through the narrow space at its edge. "Can't see a thing."

Farley said, "If it's good news we'll hear about it eventually. If it's bad we'll hear sooner."

After a while Andy heard the bar being removed. Porfirio swung the door open and beckoned, giving a curt command. Andy and Farley both blinked, for even at dusk the light seemed bright after their confinement in near darkness. Porfirio pointed toward the house. *"A la casa."*

A buggy stood in front. Several vaqueros were gathered around it or were watching the front door. They appeared to be having a heated discussion.

One of Chavez's young women opened the door and motioned for Andy and Farley to enter.

Teresa McCawley shouted, "Farley! Are you all right?"

Teresa and her mother stood in the parlor. Teresa rushed to Farley and threw her arms around him. Farley looked surprised and confused, keeping his arms at his sides for a moment, then raising them to embrace the girl. "Ain't nothin' wrong with me," he said. "What's all the fuss about?"

For the first time Andy saw Big Jim McCawley over in a corner. He and Lupe Chavez were engaged in a silent staring match. It was not friendly.

McCawley asked, "You boys all right?"

Andy said, "We're fine. Been enjoyin' Mr. Chavez's hospitality. Kind of surprised to see you here."

"I'm surprised myself, but we had to come and see what happened to Tony. We had no idea we'd find you-all here too."

"Mr. Chavez insisted on us stayin'."

McCawley explained that one of the ranch hands had overtaken them on the San Antonio road with news of Tony's break. "Tony says he wouldn't have made it to the river if you-all hadn't come along at just the right time. I'm obliged to you. We all are."

Andy looked at Chavez, searching for any sign that he shared that gratitude. He said, "Me and Farley will escort you-all home when you're ready to go. You might run into some of the Jericho bunch." He looked to Chavez, half expecting to be contradicted.

In a cold manner Chavez told McCawley, "I offer you escort to the river. You will want to cross before dark. The women are welcome to stay as long as they wish."

Big Jim said stubbornly, "We'll all go together when my wife and daughter say so."

The two men stared hard at each other again until finally Chavez shrugged. "Naturally they will wish to stay with Antonio awhile. I do not like you, gringo, but you are safe under my roof."

"I've got a bedroll. I'll sleep outside and not contaminate your house."

Sternly Chavez said, "You stole our land by marrying my sister. So you will do the proper thing. You will sleep in a bed with the woman you married. She is your property now, just like our land."

Big Jim declared, "She's not property. Can't you get it through your wooden head that I married *her*, not your land?"

Juana McCawley's face flushed in anger. She lashed into her brother in rapid-fire Spanish that crackled like burning cedar. Andy did not understand the words, but their meaning was clear.

Chavez tried to stand up to her but finally slumped in surrender. He said, "I can defeat an army of *rinches* or the men of the Jericho. But I cannot stand against a determined woman."

Teresa held to Farley's arm. She launched a tirade of her own. Chavez shook his head sadly. "You also?"

"Yes, me too. Farley is my friend. You will not hold him any longer."

Chavez shrugged again. "You may all stay or you may all go. I wash my hands."

ANDY SPENT TWO uneasy days until the two women were certain Tony would recover. They gave up hope that he would consent to leave his uncle and return home with them. Big Jim assured them, "He's probably safer here anyway, south of the river. Jericho might try for him again if Tony was at our place."

Juana and Teresa said their good-byes to Tony. Big Jim stood behind them, sadness in his eyes. Tony had spoken to him but little, and only in a formal, standoffish manner. He pointedly avoided addressing him either by name or by any version of the word *father*.

Farley muttered, "That boy needs a good whippin' with a wet rope."

Andy said, "He just ain't finished growin' up yet. Maybe he'll get better."

"If he don't get himself killed before that. I'll say this for him, though, he'd poke a bear in the eye with a willow switch and then try to skin him."

Teresa kissed her brother and told him, "We'll be back to see you real soon." She looked hopefully at Farley. "You're coming with us, aren't you?" She added as an afterthought, "You and Andy?"

Farley seemed a little flustered. "If you want us to."

"I do."

As he and Andy mounted their horses, Farley said,

"You know how close we came to gettin' buried on this place?"

"The McCawleys saved our bacon. Them and Tony." He had to give Tony that much credit, at least.

Farley stole a glance at Teresa. "I swear that little girl gets to lookin' prettier all the time. If only she wasn't half Mexican."

"If it was me, I wouldn't let that make any difference."

"It oughtn't to, but it does."

Chavez sent an escort of vaqueros along to see the McCawley party safely to the river. None of the Chavez men would have dared molest them, but the region was infested by bandits over whom Chavez had no control. Several of McCawley's cowboys had camped on the north bank, waiting for their employer's return. They would pick up the escort duty. Andy and Farley were not really needed, but they had nowhere else in particular to go.

The procession crossed at a shallow ford. Chavez had sent a messenger to alert the McCawley crew, so the cowboys were waiting as the buggy and the horsemen pulled up out of the water. Andy's horse shook himself like a dog, startling the buggy team. McCawley had to draw hard on the lines.

Andy saw that the reception committee was more than the McCawley cowboys. Sergeant Donahue was there with several of his Rangers, including Hewitt. He touched the brim of his hat in deference to the women and told Big Jim, "From what folks say about you and Lupe Chavez, I wasn't sure you'd come back alive."

McCawley acknowledged him with a nod. "Folks say a lot of things that aren't true, Sergeant. Lupe and I are kinfolks, sort of."

"Some of the worst fights I ever saw was between kinfolks." Donahue turned a stern face toward Andy and

Farley. "Don't you two know that you had no legal right to go into Mexico?"

Andy said, "That was when we were Rangers, but we're just citizens now. You fired us."

"I sometimes say things in the heat of the moment that I do not mean."

"You hirin' us back?"

"I never took you from the rolls. The company is too far under strength."

Farley's eyes took on a calculating look. "Maybe you could see clear to give us a raise in pay."

"The pay scale is set by the state. I have nothin' to do with it."

"It was worth a try." Farley glanced at Andy. "What say, Badger Boy? Want to give the Rangers another chance?"

Andy was not sure what his reaction should be. He said, "I don't see where I've got anything better to do."

JERICHO JACKSON BRUSHED away the marks of the saddle from his favorite gray horse as it cooled down from the afternoon's riding. Working with his hands helped him relieve some of his tension. He fretted, "I don't know what's become of that old man Gonzales. I'd sure like him to tell me what's goin' on down at Chavez's."

Burt Hatton stuffed a wad of chewing tobacco into his mouth. "He probably took hisself up to Laredo and got drunk. You know these Meskins. Put a little money in their pocket and you won't see them again till they drink it all up. It takes twenty of them chili pickers to make a dozen."

"I'd give a thousand dollars to know what Chavez is up to."

Hatton said, "For a thousand dollars I'd go down there and ask him."

"Even if you got close enough to listen, you couldn't savvy what they said."

Jericho had not been among those who tried to ambush Tony as he left the McCawley house. Always leery of Big Jim McCawley, he had put Hatton in charge of that project. It had gone awry, as too often happened with Hatton. Jericho had come with the reinforcements who tried to stop Tony just short of the river, but he had been frustrated by the arrival of three Rangers.

For a time now Jericho had been on the lookout for a new lieutenant. When he found one he would send Hatton off on some mission likely to get him killed. The best thing to do with mistakes was to bury them.

Jericho said, "I can't help feelin' like that damned bandit is plottin' some kind of strike against me. He's bound to've figured out that we laid a trap for him with that herd of cattle. He'll be achin' to square up."

"Too bad we missed gettin' that nephew of his. At least we bloodied him up a little."

"All the more reason to wonder what Chavez may do next. I can't afford to leave here right now."

"Why would you want to?"

Jericho's eyes pinched. "That good woman of mine is still grievin' over her nephew. I been thinkin' about takin' her back to Missouri to spend some time amongst her kin. Maybe the change would ease her mind and set her to dwellin' on other things."

Jericho was about the strongest man Hatton had ever known, but he had one outstanding weakness in Hatton's view: he was excessively devoted to his wife. As unyielding as he might be to the men around him, he seemed almost subservient to her. Hatton believed women were emotionally unstable, so it was the man's responsibility to make the decisions. A woman's place was in the kitchen and the bedroom. She should keep her opinions to herself. That was little enough to ask if a man was expected to work and support her.

Hatton had been married once when he was young and foolish. He had left that nagging woman years ago and never looked back. He could not understand why Jericho bent backward to please his wife. Hatton would have told her to quit whining and get back to her knitting.

He knew that Jericho's fixation on avenging his nephew was prompted by his wife's grief even more than any of his own. Because of it, several Jericho men had died, and more might yet do so. Hatton would like to stop it, but he was boxed in. It might cost his life if he told Jericho who had really killed his nephew. He was not prepared to die for anybody, man or woman.

Jericho rubbed his red beard. "I've about made up my mind to hit Chavez before he can hit me again. I'll gather me a bunch of bold men, cross the river, and wipe out that Chavez outfit for good and all."

Hatton shook his head. "McNelly tried that once. Found himself up against a whole company of Meskin soldiers and come within an inch of gettin' slaughtered."

"Because he hit the wrong ranch and lost the element of surprise. By the time he got to where he meant to go in the first place, they were ready and waitin' for him. The way to handle Chavez would be to hit fast, hit hard, and leave nobody standin'."

Including some of us, Hatton thought. He did not relish being caught up in any such reckless venture. If need be, he could get along without Jericho. He had been skimming off some of the proceeds from cattle he had driven north for Jericho. He had a secret account salted away in a San Antonio bank. It would see him to a new life in some distant place beyond Jericho's reach.

He asked, "When you figure on doin' all this?"

"I don't see any reason to wait. Send out the word. We're hirin' fightin' men."

"Some of them will get theirselves killed."

"We won't have to pay the ones that don't come back."

14

Andy was trying to decide if he had made a mistake, remaining a Ranger. Sergeant Donahue's attitude toward him seemed no better than before. He realized he would not have been retained had Donahue not been too shorthanded to patrol the river properly. He sent Andy the farthest of all the Rangers, way upriver from the base camp. Given a pack mule to carry supplies, he had to set up his own rude camp west of Len Tanner's appointed area of responsibility. Every second day he rode east until he encountered Len, then turned back to the west.

He had cooked for himself before, but it made eating more a chore than a pleasure. He lost weight. Only his coffee had any appealing flavor. After a few days he became acquainted with several Mexicans who lived near the river. He communicated mostly with an improvised sign language. What he recalled of plains-Indian hand talk was of little use, for the Mexicans did not understand it any better than they understood his English. In spite of the language barrier he managed to arrange for a couple of the women to cook a meal for him each time he passed by, though it was costing him most of his meager Ranger salary.

His assignment was to watch for sign of any major

movements across the river from either direction. So far
he had seen none. After a time he was just going through
the motions, riding his appointed circuit as ordered but
expecting to find nothing. In his loneliness he found
himself spending more and more time visiting with res-
idents who farmed along the Rio Grande. He began
picking up fragments of Spanish. He found that some of
these people worked hard to scratch out a living from a
land that was grudging in yielding up its gifts. Others did
only as much as they had to. Some were cheerful; some
were moody, distrustful, and made little effort to com-
municate, especially with a Ranger. In short, they were
much the same as people he had known elsewhere, white,
red, or brown.

The one characteristic almost all had in common
was that they considered themselves to be Mexicans
rather than citizens of American Texas. To them the border was a political concept that they usually ignored. He
was conscious of small-scale smuggling in both directions, mainly of liquor and tobacco, horses and cattle. He
saw no significant harm in it so long as it did not involve
raiding and violence. Some small farmers worked land
and raised livestock on both sides of the river just as they
had done when Texas was part of Mexico and the boundary was only an imaginary line.

So what, he asked himself, if Austin or Mexico City
lost a little tariff revenue? Politicians could waste more
in a day than penny-ante smugglers might cost in six
months. If Donahue wanted such small-scale traffic
stopped, he would have to send somebody else.

One day as he paused at the river's edge to let his black
horse drink he saw two men approaching from the east,
one riding, one walking and leading a horse that limped.
He took them for local Mexicans until they came close

...uld see they were Americans, one tall, ...tall one, on horseback, raised a hand in ...round, sunburned face looked genial. Andy res... ...n kind.

"Hell of a thing," the man said, "havin' a horse come up lame way out in this nowhere country. My partner's gettin' footsore."

The shorter man was limping about as badly as his horse. His weary face was lined in misery.

The tall one said, "We been lookin' for somebody who might make a trade with us. A good horse for a lame one."

Andy replied, "Might be hard to come by without you're willin' to pay some boot."

The walker came up even with the man on horseback. He rubbed a dusty sleeve across his face and blinked the sting of sweat from his eyes. He had a scraggly beard of uncertain color, longer in some places than in others, like a garden with a spotty crop. He asked, "Do you know Jericho Jackson?"

Andy was instantly wary. "I've met the gentleman."

"Maybe you can tell us where his place is at. We're thinkin' we've come too far upriver."

Andy gave both men a long study. He saw nothing in their appearance that would brand them as criminals. Their clothing was dusty and worn, holes unpatched at the knees. They looked like any number of working trail hands he had seen. Everything about them bespoke short rations and low pay. But he had to distrust anyone looking for Jericho. "You've come farther than you had to. From here you'd travel north and bear a bit to the east."

"How will we know when we're on his land?"

"You won't have to find him. He'll find you, or his men will."

The tall man in the saddle said, "Sounds like who been lookin' for. Goin' to be hard to get there with a lame horse, though. I don't suppose you'd like to swap?"

"I don't suppose I would."

"You said we might need some boot. How's this?" So swiftly that Andy hardly saw the movement, the rider had a pistol in his hand. "Now, about that swap . . . we'd like it to be friendly."

His face no longer appeared genial.

Andy gauged his chances of successful resistance and knew they were next to none. Rusty had always told him there were times to fight and times to pull away. This was clearly no time to push his luck, not while he looked down the muzzle of a .44.

The man with the pistol said, "Before you get off, let's see you drop that six-shooter. Be real careful, or you could get a couple of holes in you that the good Lord didn't put there."

Andy considered warning them that he was a Ranger but thought better of it. The two might decide to take no chances with him if they knew. It would be easy to murder him and drag his body into the brush, where it might not be found for months, if at all. He eased the pistol from its holster and let it fall. The rifle was still in its scabbard, but he knew he had no chance to draw it. He dismounted and stepped away from the horse but held on to the reins. "It's not a good trade unless both parties are willin'."

"Me and Devlin are willin'. I reckon two out of three ought to be enough."

The limping man named Devlin removed the saddles from both horses and put his on Andy's mount. He took Andy's rifle and scabbard. "I wouldn't want you to back out on the deal and shoot us with this Winchester. Me and Barstow will cut cards later and see who gets it."

Barstow grinned. The genial look returned but seemed tainted now. "No hard feelin's, I hope. At least we're leavin' you your saddle and a horse to put it on. I hope you won't abuse him. He's gettin' some age on him, but that ankle will heal if you give it time."

The two men were laughing as they rode off to the north. Angry words welled up in Andy's throat and stayed there. He saw no use in saying them aloud when nobody could hear. He turned to examine the brown horse. He saw nothing special in its conformation to mark it as anything except a working ranch horse. The lameness was in the right leg. He lifted it, hoping the cause might be nothing more than a stone caught in the shoe. There was no stone. There was no shoe. The ankle appeared swollen.

"Looks like I'm not goin' to ride you anywhere," he said. He led the horse to the edge of the river to see if it would drink. It took several swallows, then raised its head, water dripping from chin and steel bits.

He was a couple of miles from his campsite. He had left the pack mule there, staked on a long rope to allow it to graze. He considered the mule, but it was not broken to ride. It would probably balk and refuse to move if he tried to get on it. Or else it would throw him off and kick him hard enough to break his ribs.

Perhaps when Andy did not meet Len at their usual rendezvous site he would come looking. Then again, he might decide Andy was simply late and get tired of waiting. Andy guessed that the sun was only a couple of hours short of setting. Chances were that the two horse thieves would stop and camp at dark, figuring they were safe. They might not appreciate how fast a determined man could walk.

They had not stripped his saddle of anything except the rifle, so he had his canteen and a chunk of bacon he had roasted but not finished at noon. He set off following the tracks. The thieves had taken the northeasterly direction he suggested. He was soon sweating. A southerly breeze found its way through his shirt and cooled him. At intervals he came across grazing cattle. Some shied away. Others, not used to seeing a man afoot, approached out of curiosity. A few even trotted alongside for short distances before they lost interest or he scared them off with a shout and a wave of his hat.

A coyote loped off a hundred yards, then turned to watch him. He had heard it said that coyotes could tell whether a man carried a firearm or not. He did not believe that, but he respected the Indian view of the coyote as trickster, a mischievous spirit always ready to foil the designs of men.

He stopped for short periods of rest, but impatience soon prodded him back to his feet. He wanted to go as far as possible before darkness. Though he intended to keep traveling after nightfall, following the tracks would be more difficult, perhaps impossible. Then he would have to depend upon his sense of direction. The two seemed to be traveling as straight a line as the uneven terrain allowed.

The stars indicated that it was somewhere around midnight when he spotted the faint glow of a dying campfire a little west of his line of travel. He indulged a moment in self-congratulation for managing to stay so close to the trail after darkness made him give up looking for it.

He hoped to catch the two asleep. He did not want to

confront them in daylight with no weapon better than a mesquite club.

He moved carefully toward the glow, listening for any sound that might indicate someone was still awake. He heard nothing but distant night birds and the humming of nocturnal insects seeking to mate. He almost stumbled into the two horses. One snorted and pulled against the stake rope that held it. Andy sank to his knees and waited for a reaction from the sleeping men. He heard nothing.

He found the saddles. One of the thieves had buckled Andy's scabbard to his own rig. He quietly slid the rifle free. He tried not to look into the remnant of the fire because it compromised his vision in the darkness. He located the two men, both wrapped in their blankets asleep. He saw a gun belt rolled up and lying by one man's head. Gingerly he drew the pistol from it and stuck it in his own holster, which the thieves had not bothered to take. He moved to the side of the other man. He too had a pistol in a belt, and a second lying beside his head. Andy assumed that was his own. He retrieved both and retreated to the smoldering fire.

To one side of it he found a can in which the men had boiled coffee. Some of it remained, but it was cold. He set the can on the coals to reheat it.

He could have awakened the men then but preferred not to take a chance with them in the dark. He sat on the ground, sipping the bitterly strong coffee and waiting for daylight.

They might have been trail hands, but if so they had given up the drover's habit of rising before dawn. The sun was breaking free before Barstow yawned and laid his blanket aside. He blinked and stretched his arms, then became aware of Andy sitting there watching him. He froze.

Andy said, "Sleepin' kind of late, aren't you? I heard a rooster crow somewhere an hour ago."

Devlin flung his blanket aside and grabbed for his six-shooter. He came up with an empty holster. Andy waved a pistol at him. "It's over here."

Both men stared at him in shock. Barstow slowly raised his hands. Devlin followed, his jaw sagging.

Barstow turned angrily on his partner. "Told you we ought to've taken turns standin' watch last night."

Devlin's tone was accusatory. "Mister, I didn't believe you'd be so mean as to follow us on a lame horse."

"I didn't. I walked."

"Walked?" The two looked as if such a foreign idea had never entered their heads.

Andy said, "I get the notion you two ain't been at this outlaw business long. You're not very good at it."

Barstow said, "We got awful tired of herdin' cattle for beans and bacon. We thought there must be an easier way to make a livin'. We heard Jericho Jackson was lookin' for men who can handle theirselves and that he pays good."

"Whoever told you that should've also told you life can be short over at Jericho's. He's bad about gettin' men killed."

"Couldn't be any more dangerous than swimmin' cattle over a river when it's runnin' high."

"With Jericho you're liable to be crossin' stolen cattle over the Rio Grande with a bunch of mad Mexicans grabbin' at your shirttails. But I'm savin' you from that. I'm puttin' you under arrest."

"Arrest?" Barstow demanded.

"I forgot to tell you. I'm a Ranger."

Barstow turned on Devlin. "Damned if you ain't fooled around and got us in trouble again. It's easy, you said. Just swap horses, you said. If you hadn't been careless you never would've got yours lame in the first place."

"I couldn't help it. I didn't know he was so clumsy. He looked pretty good in the dark."

Andy surmised that Devlin had stolen that horse just as he had taken Andy's. He said, "I'm takin' mine back. You-all can switch around, one walkin' and one ridin'."

Devlin complained, "But I got blisters on my feet."

"The wages of sin. You-all get busy and fix us some breakfast. No use in startin' out on an empty stomach."

The meager meal consisted of coffee, bacon, and some dried-out bread the two had brought from somewhere. Done but hardly satisfied, Andy said, "Roll up your blankets and let's be movin'."

Devlin's stirrups were set a little short, but it would take time to unlace the leathers and retie them for Andy's longer legs. It was too far to go back for his own saddle. He hoped nobody would make off with it before he could get back to reclaim it.

Devlin complained constantly about his sore feet until Andy made Barstow change places with him. Then Devlin complained that Barstow's horse had a rough gait that shook his innards all the way up to his teeth. He reminded Andy a little of Farley Brackett.

Barstow trudged along, starting to sweat though the morning was only moderately warm. He argued, "Ranger, we ain't really done anybody harm. You got your horse back. We ain't robbed no bank or nothin'. Can't you see your way clear to just turn us loose? We'll take up our old jobs drivin' cattle and go to church every chance we get."

Andy said, "I know an old preacher man named Webb. He says that the church house is half empty as long as everything goes along smooth. But when there's trouble, people start comin' to meetin'. You two were all set to join Jericho's bunch of renegades. Now you're ready to sing in the choir."

"We'd been drinkin'. We're sober now, and things look different."

"Yeah. This time *I'm* holdin' the gun."

"I hear tell that the penitentiary is already over-crowded. I'd hate for us to make it worse."

Andy wondered how long the conversion would last when nobody was pointing a gun at the pair of would-be bad men. "It'll be up to a judge and jury to decide about that."

"Think how much a trial will cost the taxpayers."

Andy thought back on the prisoner he had seen shot in the Ranger camp. "Be glad it was me that caught you. Some Rangers wouldn't bother with a trial. Bullets come cheaper than lawyers."

Barstow shut up for a while, but Devlin kept whining.

Andy saw three horsemen approaching in a slow lope. He could not tell immediately whether they were Texan or Mexican, but instinct told him they were trouble. He drew his pistol and laid it across his lap.

Barstow said, "I hope them ain't some of your quick-trigger Rangers."

Devlin quit whining. His eyes were apprehensive. "We're your prisoners. You got to protect us."

Andy said, "They're not Rangers, at least none that I know. I'll bet they're Jericho hands."

The three reined up so close that Andy could have reached out and touched the one who by his manner appeared to be in charge. The leader demanded, "Who are you people? Don't you know you're on Jericho's road?"

It was not much of a road. It was more like a cow trail. Andy sized up the three and quickly decided they were not the kind he would lend money to. Like Andy, the leader held a pistol in his lap. The other two gripped rifles.

Andy said, "I'm Andy Pickard. I'm a Ranger. These men are my prisoners."

"I'm Orville Mapes, and your name don't mean a thing to me." He studied Barstow and Devlin. "These men ain't part of Jericho's outfit. What did they do?"

"They stole a horse. Mine."

Barstow spoke up with hope. "We was on our way to see Mr. Jericho Jackson about a job."

Mapes mused, "And you stole a Ranger's horse? Jericho ain't goin' to figure you're real smart."

"We didn't know he was a Ranger."

Devlin said, "If we had, we'd have shot him right off."

Mapes looked again at Andy. "Ranger or not, you've got no authority on Jericho's land without he gives you permission."

"Rangers don't have to ask for anybody's permission. They can go anywhere they decide to."

"Not on Jericho's property. I think you'd better hand me that six-shooter."

Andy knew he could not shoot his way out with three men at close range. He would be dead before the echo faded. He gave up the pistol and his rifle. They also confiscated the weapons he had taken from Barstow and Devlin.

Barstow asked, "What about us? You're goin' to turn us loose, ain't you?"

Mapes said, "I'm takin' you to Jericho. He'll decide what to do with you."

Barstow tried to speak with confidence. "He's just the man we wanted to see." A wavering in his voice betrayed doubt.

"Maybe. Then again, there's people who've seen him and wished they hadn't." Mapes jerked his head at Andy. "You-all seem to be short a horse. I don't suppose you'd object to this man ridin' double with you?"

His tone indicated that it was a command rather than a question. Andy saw no point in replying. He took his left foot out of the stirrup to allow Barstow to swing into position behind the saddle. The horse humped up a little, not liking the extra burden. Andy wished he would pitch Barstow off, but the horse settled down.

As they rode, Barstow continued pressing the case that he and Devlin could provide useful service on Jericho's crew. Mapes looked straight ahead and seemed to pay little attention.

Their conversion had been shorter than some of Preacher Webb's sermons, Andy thought.

At first he was surprised to see that Jericho's head-quarters looked much like those of Lupe Chavez and Big Jim McCawley. On reflection he recalled that all had been built at about the same time and by the same people, the forebears of Don Cipriano Chavez. Designed for defense against hostile Indians, Jericho's place would still be a formidable fortress. Andy would not like to have to lead a charge against it.

Mapes pointed them toward an adobe barn backed by an extensive layout of corrals, much like Big Jim's. "We'll all wait out here till Jericho sees fit to come and look you over."

One of the men with him asked, "Why not take them up to the main house instead of troublin' Jericho to come to the barn?"

"Nobody goes up to the main house unless it's with Jericho's say-so," Mapes said. "He doesn't like his missus seein' the kind of men he associates with."

"You mean us?"

"If you was married to a pretty little woman from Kansas City, you wouldn't want her puttin' up with this grimy bunch."

Barstow asked anxiously, "What happens to us?"

"Who knows? He may decide to hire you, or he may decide to shoot you. With him you never know."

Devlin suggested, "Maybe we ought to've written him a letter before we came."

Andy wondered if he could write.

Mapes herded Andy and the two thieves into a corner of the barn. He said, "You-all had just as well sit. I'll go up and tell Jericho you're here. He'll get around to you in his own good time."

Andy sat on the dirt floor. Mapes left his two helpers to watch. One leaned against a saddle rack and spun the cylinder of his pistol. The other propped himself against the doorjamb and aimed his rifle casually at supposed targets outside. Andy compared their faces with those of Barstow and Devlin. They had a hard-bitten, determined look. They might at one time have been working cowhands, but now they fitted Andy's conception of hired pistoleros who would commit any crime if the pay was right.

He asked Barstow, "Think you-all have got it in you to qualify for a bunch like that?"

Barstow seemed too troubled to answer. Devlin stared apprehensively at the two Jericho men but tried to sound confident. "You're the one that needs to worry, Ranger. I doubt as they've got any patience for lawmen here. They're liable to cut off your ears and send them to Austin."

Barstow growled, "Shut up, Devlin. You may give them ideas about what to do with me and you."

Jericho seemed in no hurry to see his visitors. Andy waited in the barn for more than an hour before he saw a shadow fall across the threshold. Jericho's broad shoulders almost blocked the door. He walked halfway across the room and waited while his eyes adjusted to the poor light. Andy and the two thieves stood up. Jericho looked first at Barstow and Devlin, then at Andy. His eyes brightened with recognition.

"I've already made your acquaintance, Ranger. You had that boy Antonio. I wanted him, but you wouldn't let me have him."

He had seen Andy once before that, but Andy thought it prudent not to remind him of the day when one of his windmill towers had mysteriously burned down. Andy said, "It's against Ranger policy to turn a prisoner over for lynchin'."

"I wasn't goin' to lynch him. He'd have gotten a fair trial. We have our own court to try thieves and killers and trespassers."

"A kangaroo court."

"Nobody has ever appealed a rulin'."

"Maybe they haven't lived long enough."

Jericho's face darkened. "Don't be tryin' my patience. I don't have enough of it to waste."

As long as his blood was up, Andy decided to keep pushing. "They say you're runnin' a haven here for men in trouble with the law."

"Call it a sanctuary. The Mexicans hit somebody, then run to sanctuary on the other side of the river. You Rangers can't touch them there. I say if it works for them, it ought to work for me. I'm runnin' a sanctuary of my own here. I don't want the Rangers messin' with it."

"But you're in Texas. Lupe Chavez ain't."

"I'll say this for you, Ranger, you've got guts to come on my ranch and try to lecture me like that."

"I'm just sayin' what I think."

Jericho rubbed a big hand across his chin, squeezing his red-bearded face into a grotesque shape. "And most men in your place would've let me have that kid. Was you really prepared to die protectin' him?"

"I don't know. I never had to make that decision. Big Jim McCawley came along just in time."

The name brought a wistful look from Jericho. "Big Jim. You know, me and him used to be friends a long time ago, before he fell in with the Mexicans."

"But you still wanted to kill his son."

"Stepson. The boy ain't of his blood."

Jericho turned belligerently on Barstow and Devlin. "What about you two? What's your excuse for trespassin' where you wasn't asked?"

Devlin pleaded, "Me and Barstow came here hopin' we could work for you. We ain't got no truck with the Rangers."

"Work for me?" Jericho snorted. "What could you do?"

Devlin said eagerly, "We stole the Ranger's horse."

"And got caught. Damned little recommendation."

Barstow said, "We learn easy. Just tell us what to do and we'll do it."

Jericho beckoned to Mapes. "Take these two to Burt Hatton. If he can find a use for them, they can stay. If he can't . . ." He did not finish. Andy knew by the apprehension in the two men's faces that they were finishing the sentence for him in their minds.

Jericho turned his attention to Andy. "I've never been friends with the Rangers, but maybe it's time I tried to be. I can see where they might be of use to me."

"It's our job to enforce the law. We're not supposed to play favorites."

"I'd just ask you to lean a little in my direction in case a dispute was to come up. Most of my trouble has been with Mexican border jumpers, so that oughtn't to be hard for you to do. They're illegal anyway, the minute they set foot on the Texas side of the river."

"I'm just a private. Even the camp cook doesn't ask my opinion about anything."

Jericho asked Andy's name, and Andy told him. Jericho said, "I don't suppose you're a married man, Pickard?"

"I haven't had time for such as that."

"Any prospects?"

"Maybe, if I was to ask her. But it wouldn't be much of a life for her, bein' married to a Ranger who's always movin' around from one camp to another."

"You'll get tired of that sooner or later. Every man ought to get married. Havin' a wife gives you somethin' to come home for instead of spendin' all your time with the likes of the men you've seen around here."

Andy was surprised to hear that kind of talk from a man everyone branded as an unredeemed outlaw. It did not fit the image he had built in his mind. Lupe Chavez had not fit his preconceived notion, either. Both men aroused doubts about the validity of public opinion.

Jericho said, "Havin' a good woman can be the salvation of a man. I'd have you come down and meet mine, but she's not in a mood for company right now. She never could have any children herself, so she took her nephew under her wing after her sister died. Some of the Chavez gang killed him a while back."

"Sorry."

"I've had to watch that good woman grieve herself half

to death. That's why I've wanted to get my hands on Chavez's nephew. I want Lupe to know how it feels."

"Would it make your wife feel better to know Tony's mother was grievin' the same way she does?"

"*I'd* feel better. Blood for blood. An eye for an eye."

Andy asked, "Is that why you're so dead set against Mexicans?"

"My feelin' about Mexicans goes back a lot further than that. It goes all the way back to when Texas fought for independence from Mexico."

"You're not old enough to've been in that fight."

"I'm old enough to remember it, though. I remember seein' my daddy take his rifle down from over the mantel and ride off to join the rebellion. Mexican soldiers caught him and stood him against a wall. Shot him down like a dog.

"My mother put me on a mule. We started runnin' for the Louisiana border to get away from Santy Anna's army. It was rainy and cold, and we bogged in mud plumb to our knees. She taken pneumonia and died. Left me all by myself, just a shirttail young'un. Damn near starved to death before I learned to take whatever I needed, however I had to. Lie, steal, whatever it took. I've been at war against Mexicans ever since."

Andy could think of a few arguments, but he knew they would not make a dent against so deep a hatred.

Jericho said, "I suppose you've got an old mother somewhere, puttin' a lamp in the window every night, waitin' for you to come home."

"Indians killed my mother. I was so little I can't hardly remember her."

He thought he saw a flicker of sympathy in Jericho's eyes, though it was gone as soon as the man blinked.

Jericho said, "Too bad. I still remember mine, twenty

times a day. My wife looks a lot like her." He quickly changed the subject. "I suppose you're anxious to get back to your company."

"I was figurin' to turn in those two horse thieves, but I guess you're goin' to keep them and put them to work."

"I'll leave that up to my foreman, Burt Hatton. He'll escort you off of my ranch."

"I can find my own way."

"He'll see to it that nobody gives you any trouble. He'll have your horse waitin' for you at the corner corral." Jericho pointed. "And you tell your fellow Rangers that if I ever want any of you on my place again, I'll send for you."

Irony edged into Andy's voice. "Sergeant Donahue will appreciate hearin' that."

Jericho went out the door. Andy followed. After being in the dark barn so long, the bright sun hurt his eyes. When his vision cleared, he saw three men and four horses at the corner corral. Two of the men were Barstow and Devlin. Andy did not recognize the third until he reached the gate. Jericho had disappeared.

Andy said, "I know you."

Burt Hatton said, "And I know you."

This was the man who had led the nighttime attack on Andy, Len, and Farley as they rode south from San Antonio to join the Ranger company on the river.

Andy said, "The night you-all tried to hit us, we suspected you belonged to Jericho's outfit."

The man did not reply.

Andy said, "We heard somebody holler like he was shot. Was he?"

Hatton growled, "Get on your horse. We're takin' you away from here."

"I can go by myself."

"Jericho wants to be sure you're gone. You can go peaceful or we can tie you in the saddle." He poked the muzzle of a pistol in Andy's direction for emphasis.

Andy said, "I believe that six-shooter's mine."

"You'll get it when I'm ready. Or you'll get what's in it."

Devlin was holding a paint horse with a huge Mexican brand across most of its left hip. It had undoubtedly come from across the river, probably on some dark night. Though Indians fancied paints for their unusual coloring, Rusty had taught Andy to regard them with suspicion until they proved themselves. Andy said to Devlin, "Looks like they gave you a new saddle, and a horse to put under it."

Devlin said, "He ain't as good as your black. I'm thinkin' about another swap."

"You'd have to shoot me first."

"I've been thinkin' about that too."

Hatton snapped, "Come on, I got other things to do."

Andy followed him out the gate, the other men riding behind. They took a southeasterly course, in the general direction of the Ranger company's camp. Andy doubted that Hatton intended to go all the way there. He simply wanted to be sure Andy got off to a good start.

They rode for about an hour. Hatton pointed to a thicket of mesquite and catclaw. "Over there."

Andy saw no sense in riding into a thicket, but he looked into the muzzle of Hatton's pistol and decided against asking questions.

Hatton reined up just at the edge of the thicket. A javelina sow and four pigs snorted and went clattering into the brush. Their backs bristled and their short legs moved in a blur. Hatton beckoned for Barstow and Devlin to come closer. "Jericho left it up to me to decide if you boys have got a job. You want it bad enough to earn it?"

Both men nodded. Barstow said, "Just tell us what to do."

"I want you to prove yourselves. I want you to shoot this Ranger."

Barstow's mouth dropped open. Devlin looked as if he had just swallowed a scorpion. Barstow said, "You mean kill him?"

"Here and now."

Andy felt helpless and cold. Hatton's eyes were grim, leaving no doubt that he meant what he said. Barstow and Devlin appeared to be near panic. Barstow's voice was strained. "I ain't never shot a man. I can't do it in cold blood."

Hatton scowled. "I figured you two for counterfeit as soon as I saw you. You'll shoot him or I'll shoot all three of you. You'll make a good meal for those javelinas."

Hands trembling, Devlin drew his pistol.

Hatton said, "Steady down. You're as liable to hit your horse as to hit that Ranger."

Devlin held the pistol in both hands. It continued to waver.

Hatton cursed. "I told Jericho that neither one of you is worth the rope it'd take to hang you with."

Barstow bent down and came up with a rifle. "I reckon we rate a little higher than that." He swung the muzzle toward Andy.

Andy's mouth felt as if it were full of cotton.

Barstow moved the rifle a little farther. It pointed at Hatton.

Hatton demanded, "What're you doin'?"

Barstow was sweating as if it were the Fourth of July. "Never kill a Ranger. If you do, the rest of them will come after you. They never forget, and they won't give up till you're hangin' off of a tree limb or shot full of holes."

Hatton declared, "I'll have your heads on a pike."

Devlin trembled. "For God's sake, Barstow."

Andy took advantage of the moment to push his horse forward and grab Hatton's pistol with both hands. They wrestled. Hatton squeezed off one shot toward the thicket. A javelina squealed. Andy managed to twist the weapon free.

Hatton wheeled his horse around and spurred away, bent low over the horn of the saddle to present a poor target. Barstow took one shot but was too nervous to hit him.

Devlin complained, "You spilt it now, Barstow. We'll never get a job with Jericho."

"It's a damned poor job that says you got to kill somebody in cold blood, and him lookin' at you the whole time. There ain't enough money between here and San Antonio . . ."

Andy slowly regained his composure. "Thanks, Barstow. For a minute I felt like an angel landed on my shoulder."

Barstow was still sweating. He lowered the rifle. "If there's any angels around here, they're lost." He looked puzzled. "I was afraid Jericho wouldn't hire us, but I didn't expect he'd send his foreman out here to kill us."

Andy said, "I believe Hatton did that on his own." Killing Andy would have eliminated one witness to the attack on him, Len, and Farley. "And even if you had shot me, he'd have killed both of you and left us all lyin' here for the hogs. Dead men don't testify."

Barstow removed his hat and rubbed his sleeve over a face dripping with sweat. "Workin' cattle gets to lookin' better all the time. Maybe we can get our old jobs back."

Devlin said nothing. He was too busy losing his breakfast.

Barstow asked Andy, "You goin' to turn us in for stealin' your horse?"

"I would've, but you saved my life. I owe you a chance to get yours straightened out."

Barstow said, "Me and Devlin was just lookin' for a little more excitement than we been havin'. I think we've had enough of it to last us a long time."

"If I was you-all, I'd take a wide swing around Jericho's country, then head north . . . way north."

"That's what we'll do. And if I ever get arrested again it'll be for singin' too loud in church."

Andy watched them ride off in an easterly direction, then he turned southward. He wanted to recover his own saddle. This one, which had belonged to Devlin, could be traded to one of the poor Mexican farmers who had been selling him food down by the river. Devlin's horse, if it got over its lameness and didn't turn up on a list of stolen property, would give him an extra mount so he could alternate and always have one resting.

All in all, he had come out a little ahead on what had seemed to be a stroke of bad luck. He hoped that someday he might see Burt Hatton again under circumstances more in his own favor.

He had also seen another side of Jericho Jackson, a side that left him conflicted. Things had appeared much simpler when he'd seen Jericho simply as a cold and calculating land-grabbing outlaw. He did not know how to handle this unexpected complexity.

BURT HATTON ENTERED the outside door to the room Jericho used as an office. He was seldom asked into the main part of the house. Jericho was strict about insulating his wife from the ranch help. Hatton's shirt was torn. A long red scratch marred his cheek.

Jericho looked up from his ledger book. "What happened to you?"

Hatton delayed his answer. "Mind if I get me a drink?" Jericho nodded, and Hatton went to a cabinet where he knew the whiskey was kept. He poured a small glass half full and swallowed it with a sense of urgency. "Horse cold-jawed on me. Ran through the brush."

Jericho often had a feeling that Hatton said only what he thought his boss wanted to hear, but the story was plausible enough. No man worth his salt worked in the brush country without taking scars and getting thorns embedded in his hide. "Did you set the Ranger safely on his way?"

"Last I seen of him he was headed south."

"Good. I'd like to have a friend or two in the Ranger camp when the bullets fly again."

"I don't think you'd better count on him for a friend. We oughtn't to have let him get off of this place alive. We'll have trouble with him yet."

"Dead Rangers are bad for business. What about them two cowhands? Did you put them to work?"

Hatton frowned. "I sent them on their way. They didn't have enough sand in their craw for our kind of business."

"Too bad. We'll need all the help we can get when we make our big push on Lupe Chavez."

Hatton poured another drink. "And when is that to be?"

"I don't know yet, but it'll come. It'll be like the battle of the Alamo all over again, only this time it'll end different."

Hatton had a worried look. "Maybe we ought to leave

Chavez alone. You've got more land already than you can rightly see after. What do you want with land in Mexico?"

"This is about more than land. It's an old fight that never got settled. And there's the business about my wife's nephew. Lupe has got to pay for that."

"Maybe I was wrong about them Meskin outlaws that killed him. Maybe they wasn't Lupe's men after all."

Jericho's brow furrowed. "You scared, Burt?"

"Not scared. Just thinkin' about the men that might get killed."

"They're bein' well paid for it."

"There's some things money ain't enough for."

"Money can buy anything. You just have to be willin' to pay the price."

15

Len Tanner was at Andy's makeshift campsite when Andy rode in. "Where you been?" the lanky Ranger demanded. "I found your saddle where you left it. Been worried that some Mexican bandits might've drug you off and cut out your gizzard."

"I've been up to Jericho's."

"What in the hell for?"

"Gettin' another saddle." He waited for Len's puzzled expression to come to full flower, then explained about the horse thieves and Jericho's men taking the three of them to headquarters.

Len said, "It's a wonder Jericho didn't shoot you."

"The funny thing is that I got along right decent with him. He wasn't what I expected. I never once saw him breathe fire."

"You never saw no halo around his head, neither. He's a bad hombre."

"So everybody says. It's odd, but he reminded me of Lupe Chavez. Neither one of them has any idea how much they think alike. They just look at things from opposite sides of the river."

"They'd both cut your throat in a minute. But right now you'd better report to Sergeant Donahue before *he* cuts your throat. He suspicions that you swum the river to join up with Lupe Chavez."

"What would make him think that?"

"You took up for that boy Tony. You helped him get back to his uncle."

"I'd have done that for a lost pup. And I did it for the McCawleys, not for Lupe Chavez."

"Donahue ain't goin' to see the difference. As far as he's concerned they're all Mexicans, even Big Jim."

Andy said, "I'll go downriver and report to him. First, though, I'm hungry. Want to help me scare up some wood for a fire?"

While they ate, Len told Andy that the river had been quiet. "Ain't been sign of any raiders crossin' that we could see. Just the usual traffic. A few farmers, kinfolks passin' back and forth. I picked up a lame horse wanderin' around here. Don't know who he belongs to."

Andy said, "One of those horse thieves had him. I guess he's mine if we don't find out who he was stolen from."

They rode down the river past Len's camp. Halfway to the next Rangers' post they came upon Sergeant Donahue riding the line. Len said, "Here's your stray, Sergeant."

Donahue gave Andy a look that for a culprit would mean five years in prison. "Absent without leave. What's your excuse, Private Pickard?" He bore down on the word *private*.

"It wasn't by my choice," Andy said. He repeated what he had told Len about the horse thieves and being escorted to meet Jericho.

Curiosity erased Donahue's scowl. "I've never seen Jericho's headquarters. Not many Rangers have ever been there."

Andy gave him a rough description. "It looks a lot like the McCawley ranch, and Lupe Chavez's."

"I've never seen Chavez's either, but I'd sure like an excuse to go there and give them Meskins a good whippin', the way McNelly did." His eyes brightened at the thought. "By the way, what about them two horse thieves?"

Andy shrugged. "The last I saw of them they were headed in the direction of Canada." He thought it best not to divulge that he had made no effort to stop their going. He had probably broken some unbreakable Ranger rule.

Donahue said, "You should have pulled the trigger on them. Nothin' cures a thief better than a forty-five slug."

"I figured on bringin' them in as prisoners."

"Chances are fifty-fifty that some judge would turn them loose, and they'd go right back to what they were doin'. Death is pretty damned permanent."

"I'll try to remember that."

Donahue nodded, satisfied. "Since your goin' was not voluntary, I'll reconsider filin' charges. But consider yourself on probation."

Andy had considered himself on probation ever since Donahue took temporary command of the company. He asked hopefully, "Any word on when Lieutenant Buckalew will be back?"

"None. I think they may have found somethin' else for him to do. I'm lookin' to be advanced to lieutenant any time now. Maybe even captain."

"That'd be nice." Saying so put a sour taste in Andy's mouth.

Donahue said, "Go back to patrollin' your section of the river. I expect you're about out of supplies?"

"Pretty near."

"I'll send a pack mule out tomorrow with coffee and sugar and salt. As for meat, I see lots of cattle and hogs runnin' loose."

"They all belong to somebody."

"Meskins. If they holler, tell them this is a tax they owe for us keepin' them safe."

Safe. Andy considered the irony. These people along the river were subject not only to banditry from both sides but to harassment by those Rangers who considered every Mexican suspect. The few American settlers were not much better off, for they were particular targets of Mexican outlaws still trying to avenge Santa Anna's defeat.

At times Andy thought seriously about giving this part of Texas back to the horned toads, the scorpions, and the sharp-toothed javelinas. They had a prior claim.

Donahue turned downriver, and Andy proceeded upriver. He found the lame horse contentedly grazing in the river's grassy floodplain. The limp was less pronounced. Andy tossed a loop around the animal's neck and led him to his makeshift camp. He found his saddle hanging from a tree limb so wild animals would not gnaw on it. Len's work, he guessed. Now Andy had two horses and two saddles. He was coming up in the world.

An old man crossed at a shallow point, urging a burro along with a willow switch. He saw Andy and veered away. Andy had seen the old man and the burro before, and the old man knew Andy to be a Ranger. Everybody up and down this stretch of the Rio Grande did. It would be a long time before these river people trusted the Rangers, Andy thought. And some Rangers would never come to trust the people who lived along the river. The gulf between the two cultures was too wide to bridge, at least for now.

A trail led northward from this shallow crossing. Andy saw a procession coming from the north. He counted four men on horseback. A buggy trailed behind, carrying two women. As it came closer he saw that they were Juana and Teresa McCawley. One of the horsemen was Big Jim. The others were some of his cowboys.

Andy rode out to meet them. The riders drew guns, then put them away as they recognized him. He suspected he knew their mission before they told him. "Headin' down to see Tony?" he asked McCawley.

"We haven't heard a thing about him since we were down here the last time. The womenfolks are worried."

"I always figure if it's bad news you'll hear about it soon enough. Since I haven't heard anything, I'll bet Tony is all right." He tipped his hat to the two women.

Mrs. McCawley said, "You look thin, Andy."

"Eatin' my own fixin's, ma'am. Nobody would ever hire me as a cook."

"If you'll come up and spend a few days with us, we'll put some weight back on you."

"It'd pleasure me, ma'am, but I don't see as I can."

Teresa asked, "Have you seen Farley?"

"Now and again. He's closer to the main camp, so he slips down there and gets himself a decent meal when he knows the sergeant's not around."

Mrs. McCawley said, "It isn't far from here to my brother Lupe's ranch. He knows you now, so you could go over there when you get hungry."

"He might not like havin' a Ranger show up. Anyway, it's illegal for me to cross the river."

She frowned. "It's too bad people have to draw boundaries. There was a time when the river made no difference."

McCawley drew up beside Andy. "The trail has been unusually quiet. I've heard that Jericho has been hirin' a lot of men, but we didn't run into any. Not them or hardly anybody else. Makes me wonder."

"I had a visit with him. Maybe he's reformed."

"I wish I could believe that, but I know him too well. He has a hunger that can't be satisfied. Most people get drunk on whiskey. He gets drunk on acquisition."

Andy watched Big Jim and the buggy go into the river. The cowboys remained behind.

Andy asked one, "You-all aren't goin' to stay with them all the way?"

A cowboy replied, "Big Jim said we wouldn't be welcome down there. He feels like they'll be safe enough since the womenfolk are kin to Chavez."

Andy feared McCawley might be stretching his luck in view of Chavez's dislike for him. Perhaps Chavez would not raise a hand against his sister's husband, but some of his followers might not be so reluctant. The McCawleys were almost out of sight when several riders came up from the south and met them. They halted briefly, then went on, escorted by what Andy assumed must be Chavez men. He saw no sign of hostility. Soon the procession moved beyond his view, hidden by the brush.

Andy asked the cowboy, "You-all goin' to stay and watch till they come back?"

"No, they figure to be there for several days. We'll come back to meet them when it's time."

Andy considered. "Maybe things'll stay quiet for a while. Chavez wouldn't seem likely to set up any raids while his kin are there. He wouldn't want his sister to see him as a bandit. She thinks of him as a hero."

The cowboy said, "I've got a cousin who steals horses, but I keep tellin' myself he's not a thief. He just knows how to get them cheap."

LEN WAS WAITING at the rendezvous point where he usually met Andy. He said, "Got orders from Sergeant Donahue. He says for everybody to gather their stuff and go back to the main camp."

"Does he think the raids are over with?"

"He ain't one to explain why he does things. He's generally got a reason whether it's a good one or not."

The change suited Andy. His stomach had complained for days about his shortcomings as a cook. Maybe now he could get a few solid meals. "I'll be along as soon as I can. Meet you at your camp."

"I'll see if I can catch a couple of fish while I'm waitin'." Len had grown up on a river. Fishing was second nature to him.

Andy said, "If a fat little shoat was to wander by with no earmarks on him, that'd suit me better than fish."

"I ain't even seen a javelina lately."

It was almost dark when they rode into the main camp. Len suggested they report to the camp cook first. The sergeant could wait. Pablo bade them welcome and gave Andy a pitying look. He said, "Pretty soon you get so thin the wind carries you away. You better take two plates."

When they carried their food to a wooden table, Farley came over. He said nothing in greeting but came right to the point. "Seen anything of the McCawleys?"

Andy knew which McCawley Farley was really interested in. "Several days ago. They went over to Lupe Chavez's to see about Tony."

"To Chavez's?" Farley looked as if Andy had struck him. "And they ain't come back?"

"Not unless it was today, after I left."

"From what I hear, there's fixin' to be bad trouble down there. They're liable to get caught in the middle of it."

Disturbed, Andy put down his fork. "What kind of trouble?"

"The sergeant ain't talkin' but some of the boys say he's pulled all of us back so we won't get in Jericho's way.

His spies have told him Jericho's fixin' to hit Chavez like Sam Houston hit Santy Anna."

Andy found the idea hard to accept. "And Donahue figures to just let it happen? The Rangers are supposed to try and stop that kind of thing."

"Donahue's been chompin' at the bit, wantin' to go down there and do it hisself. But the law don't allow it, so he's standin' back and lettin' Jericho do it for him."

"Jericho's pulled raids over there before."

"Not like this. He's been hirin' men anywhere he can get them. They don't have to be cowboys. They've just got to be ready and willin' to use a gun."

Len listened gravely. "Maybe it's just as well to let the thing get settled for once and for all. It's been brewin' a long time."

Farley said, "But once the shootin' starts, a bullet won't care who's in the line of fire. Women, kids . . . that girl of McCawley's"

Andy tried to rationalize. "Chavez is nobody's fool. Maybe he's already got wind of what's comin'."

"He's not God. He can't know everything. His people will be outnumbered. They won't stand a snowball's chance in hell."

Andy wrestled with his conscience. The simplest course would be to remain neutral and let things play out on their own. The conflict was inevitable. The only question was when and where. It was not his business. He had no kin in the fight. Nobody could fault him if he could do nothing about it.

Well, there was one thing he could do. He could carry a warning to Chavez. At the least he could try to get the McCawleys out of harm's way before the attack. He felt he owed them that. But to do so would violate his orders and the prohibition against Rangers crossing the river.

He did not ponder long. He rose from the table, leaving his supper half eaten. "Tell the sergeant I've just resigned."

That would take care of the legalities.

Len spilled half a cup of coffee. "What're you fixin' to do?"

"If I don't tell you, you won't have to lie to him."

Farley smacked the palm of his hand upon the table. "You're thinkin' the same thing I am. I'm goin' with you."

"Every time we ride together, you get yourself hurt and then blame me for it. You'd risk it for Lupe Chavez?"

"To hell with Chavez. I'm thinkin' about the McCawleys."

"One McCawley, anyway. Are you forgettin' she's a Mexican?"

Farley said, "She's just half." He told Len, "Tell the sergeant I resigned too." He hurried to saddle his horse. Andy had to hustle to catch up with him.

Both horses had been ridden during the day, so Andy had to caution Farley to slow down. "We can't help anybody if we kill these horses."

Farley reluctantly pulled down to a brisk trot. "First shallow crossin' we come to, we better take it. The sergeant can't stop us if we're on the other side."

"Good idea," Andy said. Farley still had the wily instincts cultivated during his long hide-and-seek relationship with the state police after the war. They put the horses into the river half a mile farther on.

Stopping on the south bank to let the animals rest, Andy saw several riders moving at an easy lope on the other side. He sensed that they were Rangers. "Donahue didn't waste much time comin' after us."

"We've rained on his barbecue. He's figured on Jericho wipin' out Lupe Chavez and his whole outfit. The border would quieten down after that, and Donahue could claim the credit."

"And get a promotion."

Farley said, "I've got no use for Chavez, and Jericho ain't any better. The border would be better off without them. But I'd hate for somethin' to happen to the McCawleys."

"Especially Teresa."

Farley did not respond.

They skirted along the Rio Grande. The terrain and thorny vegetation were similar to that on the Texas side. The sandy soil was the same, the air the same, but Andy had an uneasy sense of being an unwelcome intruder, treading on forbidden ground. A couple of hundred yards made a tremendous difference.

Farley had the same reaction. He said, "I feel like a carpetbagger at a Confederate reunion. We're a couple of gringos on the wrong side of the river. Targets for any Mexicans that come along."

Andy still saw Rangers riding along the northern bank. "Better here than over there. Donahue could probably chew up an iron bar and spit it at us."

He pondered the incongruity of his being on this mission with Farley. He had ridden with the dour Ranger before but always because he had been obliged to do so. Neither he nor Farley had ever pretended to like each other. At best their relationship had been one of forced tolerance.

He knew Farley was correct about the risk. The hostile feeling here against Americans in general and Texans in particular ran strong. A man could be killed for nothing more than being light-skinned and blue-eyed, just as on the other side some had been murdered for no better reason than that their faces were dark. Unreasoning hatred was not confined to one race.

Darkness overtook them. Farley said, "This part of the country ain't overrun with landmarks, even in the daylight. In the dark, how're we goin' to know when we reach the road to Chavez's place?"

"I think I'll recognize it."

"Think? Thinkin' ain't knowin'."

"If you've got a better idea, tell me about it."

They rode most of the night, stopping once to rest the horses. Andy tried to sleep but could not. His skin prickled with anxiety. For all he knew, this might be the day Jericho planned to attack. However, daylight brought no sign of invasion, no distant gunfire. He said, "Looks like we'll make it in time."

Five armed horsemen suddenly appeared like apparitions out of the brush and confronted them face to face. A strong voice demanded, *"Quién es?"*

Andy raised his hands. "Friends. *Amigos.*" He chilled at the sight of five guns pointed toward him and Farley. He hoped somebody spoke English, for under his current stress he could not muster a dozen words in Spanish. "We've got a message for Lupe Chavez."

One of the men demanded, "What message?"

Andy tried to think of the Spanish word for *danger.* *"Pel . . . pel . . ."* The rest would not come to him. "We've come to bring warnin'. Jericho's fixin' to invade him."

He feared the meaning was not getting across. The men talked quietly among themselves. Andy had a troubling sense that some advocated shooting him and Farley here and now. Their undisguised hostility told him it would take but little to tip the scales in that direction.

A tall, thin man began to dominate the conversation.

Andy recognized him as Porfirio, who had held him and Farley at the Chavez place. So far as he remembered, Porfirio had not spoken English, but he seemed to be swaying the other four away from the notion of killing.

After several minutes of talk Porfirio motioned with the muzzle of his pistol. *"Vámanos."*

Andy said, "I suppose that means we're goin'."

Farley replied, "But where? To Chavez's, or to hell?"

They angled southwestward. In a while Andy saw the buildings he knew were the headquarters of the Chavez ranch. "I hope they'll believe us."

Farley said, "Even if they don't, Jericho's got to ride over me to get to the McCawleys. I ain't lettin' that girl and her mother be hurt because Lupe Chavez is too thickheaded to listen."

Andy thought Farley should know a lot about thickheadedness. He had about the hardest head of anyone Andy knew.

They rode up to the wide front door of the sprawling stone house. Porfirio dismounted and raised his hand. *"Esperen."*

He banged a heavy door knocker twice before a heavyset maid appeared, cautiously peering out through a narrow opening. He spoke quietly, and she admitted him inside. Andy looked at the other men who had brought him and Farley here. Their grim faces told him not to move.

Shortly Porfirio returned. Lupe Chavez stood in the open doorway, picking his teeth. They gleamed a brilliant white against the heavy black mustache and the dark brown of his face. Andy hoped for a sign of welcome but saw none. Chavez said, "You know *rinches* are not welcome. What brings you to my door?"

Andy said, "We've come to warn you about Jericho."

Farley put in, "He's fixin' to hit you like a hailstorm. If he can, he'll kill everybody here."

Chavez shrugged his thin shoulders. "He has come before. He has not found us easy to kill."

Andy argued, "From what we hear, he's raised enough fightin' men to do the job this time."

"He drove us out of Texas. Does he think now he can also drive us out of Mexico?" Chavez dismissed the notion with an oath that did not need translation. "He will leave here with his guts dragging on the ground, if he leaves here at all."

The mental image was graphic but not reassuring.

Farley asked, "Are the McCawleys still here?"

"They are."

"Do what you want to about Jericho, but I'm takin' those womenfolks away." Farley looked at Andy and corrected himself. "*We're* takin' them out, me and Andy."

Anger flared in Chavez's eyes. "You will not come to my house and tell me what I must do. It is for me to decide."

Farley flared back. "Then you'd better decide right."

Big Jim McCawley came out and stood a few feet away from Chavez. He reacted with surprise upon seeing Andy and Farley. "What's all this row? Aren't you-all too far south for Rangers?"

Andy said, "We're not Rangers now, we're just citizens. We're tryin' to tell Lupe Chavez that Jericho is comin' to settle old scores, and bringin' plenty of men with him. Things are fixin' to get woolly around here."

Farley interjected, "We come to tell you to gather up your womenfolks and take them away."

McCawley said, "I've never run from Jericho."

Andy said, "This is one time you'd better."

Chavez dismissed the idea with a wave of his hand. "We are not rabbits, to run from a pack of hounds."

"Even hounds run when somethin' bigger is after them."

Chavez asked McCawley, "Should I listen to these *rinches*? I do not want to look foolish."

Andy said, "Better to look foolish and alive than be layin' here dead."

No friendship existed between McCawley and Chavez, but they quickly came to a mutual agreement in the face of a common threat. Chavez said, "It is not that I have fear of Jericho, but I am a cautious man. I will send the women and children away." He gave an order to Porfirio. Porfirio relayed it to his companions, who quickly scattered.

Chavez turned back to Andy and Farley. His eyes narrowed in threat. "If you are playing me false and the Jericho does not come . . ."

Soon several wagons and a couple of buggies began picking up excited women and children at the clutter of stone and adobe houses that made up the Chavez headquarters. A vaquero drew McCawley's buggy up to the door of the Chavez home. The maid and two younger women came out, followed by McCawley's wife and daughter. Tony appeared, pale and thin, still hunched over from the effects of his wound.

Juana McCawley told her husband, "Tony says he will not go."

Tony said, "I want you to take my mother and sister away."

McCawley said, "We'll all go. You too."

"No, I will stay and stand beside my uncle. You and these Rangers do not belong. This is not a gringo fight."

Juana told her husband, "I will stay with my son, but I want you to take Teresa away from here."

McCawley held firm. "Go off and leave you? You know me better than that. I'll send Teresa with the other women, but I'm stayin' with you and Tony."

Teresa placed her hands on her hips. "My place is with family. If you stay, I stay." She looked at Farley. "You will be here, won't you? If you are here I will not be afraid."

Farley said, "I think you're all playin' the fool. I was figurin' on takin' you out of here."

"You would have to drag me."

Some of the wagons were already leaving, carrying refugees to a safer place. Andy made one more attempt to persuade the McCawley women. "We rode all this way to see that you get out of danger."

Juana said, "You brought warning. That is enough. Jericho will not take this place by surprise. Now you should go, the three of you." She touched her husband's hand. "As Tony said, this is not a gringo fight."

McCawley's face colored. "I've always hated that word *gringo*. I've never answered to it, and I don't now."

She retreated. "I say it only to make you go."

"Not without you two. And Tony." He bent forward and tapped a forefinger against Tony's chest. "Your uncle didn't raise you. I did. Like me or hate me, I'm the only father you've got."

Tony did not budge. "I'm stayin'."

McCawley shrugged. "Then I guess we all will."

Farley looked at Teresa. "I still think you ought to go. But if you don't, I don't either." He glanced back at Andy.

Andy said, "I'm not leavin' by myself."

After most of the women and children were gone, Chavez sent Porfirio to the river to watch for sign of

Jericho. He sent other riders to rouse the neighbors. As the day wore on, men from nearby ranches drifted in to augment Chavez's limited force. Whatever endangered Chavez endangered them all.

Chavez was too busy to pay attention to Andy and Farley until far into the afternoon. He seemed then to notice them for the first time. "You are still here? I thought you *rinches* were long ago gone. I do not need you."

Andy said, "We're not here for you. We stayed because of the McCawleys."

"Then stay close to them. Let no harm come to my sister and her daughter and I will try to forget that you are gringos like the Jericho."

Late in the afternoon Big Jim McCawley came to sit beside Andy and Farley in front of the big house. He carried a rifle and wore a pistol on his hip. "I guess this outfit is as ready as it'll ever be. Lupe has set up a heavy ring for defense. He would've made a good general in the big war."

Andy said, "The trouble with defense is that you have to stand and take whatever comes at you. You don't carry the fight to the enemy."

"You see somethin' you'd change?"

"I might try a little Comanche strategy. They used to set up decoys to draw the enemy in. Then they'd swoop down from both sides."

"A flankin' maneuver?"

"I guess that's what you'd call it. Instead of lettin' the enemy surprise you, you surprise him."

McCawley thought it over. "I'll talk to Lupe. He might not like it if he knew you thought of it, so I won't tell him that."

McCawley returned after a time. Andy knew by the satisfied look on his face that he had been successful.

McCawley said, "I just led him along a little at a time till he came up with the rest of it himself. Now he thinks it was his own idea."

Andy asked, "Did you ever think about goin' into politics?"

16

Jericho heard a laugh from somewhere behind him in the blackness. He looked back angrily. "Burt, go tell them to keep quiet. This won't work worth a damn if we don't catch Chavez by surprise."

Hatton rode only as far as the first half dozen men behind him. He told them to pass the word back for silence. They were within half a mile of the river. Though predawn darkness and the brush still shielded them from view, sounds could carry to the other side.

Jericho had counted thirty-seven men when they left headquarters. So far as he knew none had had a change of heart and turned back. He had taken the precaution of telling the newly hired hands that they would be paid after the mission was completed, not before. He was by necessity dealing with a class of men in whom he felt little faith. Honor was a stranger to most of them. Some would accept his money, then disappear. He did not even trust Burt Hatton, his next in command. He had purposely delayed paying Hatton all the money due him. He had a strong feeling the man's loyalty was so shallow it had to be bought anew over and over in the form of wages.

Hatton returned, grumbling. "I got a bad feelin' about this."

Jericho was in no mood to listen to Hatton's recitation

of misgivings. "You've had bad feelin's as long as I've known you. This'll be over so quick that we won't even break a sweat."

"You never know where the Meskin soldiers are at from one day to the next. Somebody's liable to fetch them, like they done that time to McNelly."

"We have to see to it that nobody gets away. Then they won't tell the soldiers anything."

Jericho could see that he had not calmed Hatton's fears, but it didn't matter much: Hatton had little choice but to go along. "Once this is over, Burt, we won't have to put up with Chavez anymore. Him and his bunch won't keep nippin' at us like a bunch of heel flies."

"You ever see a firin' squad, Jericho? I did once, down at Matamoros." He shivered. "Them soldiers stood two poor fellers up against a gate and shot them. The blood spilled like water."

"We'll finish up and be back across the river before they can even blow a bugle."

THE SUN DROPPED low, then set without sign of intruders. Porfirio sent back word from the river that he had seen no activity on the other side. Andy began to sense restlessness in the men stationed around the house. They had been primed for a fight, and no fight had come.

Farley expressed a thought that Andy had considered but rejected. "Reckon Sergeant Donahue's reports were exaggerated?"

"Nobody said exactly when Jericho was comin'. They just said that he would."

"If he don't pretty soon, you'll see things start comin' unraveled. A lot of the neighbors will start wantin' to go home and do their milkin'."

"Ain't likely he'd come in the night. Neither side could see their targets in the dark."

"When we fought the Yankees it seemed to me like the best time to attack was at first light. It generally caught them half asleep."

After dark Andy heard several men ride off to the west. Several more rode east.

Farley said, "They're desertin' already."

Andy said, "I don't think so. I believe Chavez has sent them off to wait out of sight. When Jericho strikes, they'll come in on the flanks."

"Sounds like Confederate military tactics."

"Or Comanche."

"Makes sense. Most of these Mexicans are more Indian than Spanish. If Lupe Chavez would shave off that mustache I'd take him for a Comanche."

The night was long and restless. Despite his fatigue from yesterday's ride, Andy found it difficult to sleep. He would doze, then awaken abruptly in a sweat, thinking the attack had begun. He realized he had been dreaming. He and Farley had taken a position behind a three-foot adobe wall that ran parallel to the front of the house.

Farley grumbled, "I don't see how you can sleep."

"I can't, much."

"I keep thinkin' about that little girl in there. If anything was to happen to her . . ."

"Those walls are thick. Ain't likely any bullets will go through."

"But what if Jericho managed to break into the house? The walls wouldn't help much."

"We have to stop him before he gets that far."

The stars began fading in the east, and several roosters crowed. Andy's nerves began to tingle. Farley had finally gone to sleep. Andy started to wake him, then changed his mind. Farley would wake up quickly enough if Jericho came.

Lupe Chavez emerged from the house and walked around his defense perimeter, cautioning the men to stay low and avoid being seen as the morning light improved. He came at length to Andy and Farley. "You are still here? I thought you might slip away in the night."

Andy said, "We told you we were stayin'." He repeated what he had told Chavez the day before: "We're not here for you. We're here for the McCawleys."

Chavez turned a disapproving gaze upon Farley. "Especially my niece, I think."

Farley said nothing.

Chavez sniffed. "Young women can be foolish. She should look to someone better than a gringo *rinche*."

Farley declared, "Show me somebody better."

Porfirio galloped in from the north and shouted for Chavez. Andy could not understand the words, but he understood the excited look and the way Porfirio pointed as he reported to his *jefe*.

Farley had dozed again. Andy shook him. The Ranger was suddenly awake and alert, his rifle ready.

Andy pulled the skin at the corners of his eyes, trying to sharpen the image. He thought he saw movement to the north, toward the river, but he could not be sure.

Farley thumbed back the hammer of his gun. To Andy the click sounded as loud as a gunshot.

McCawley came out of the house and took up a position beside them. Andy asked, "What about your womenfolks?"

"Tony's inside with them. He's standin' at a window."

Andy saw a rifle balanced upon a windowsill.

The sun had not yet broken over the horizon, but the predawn light was enough that now he could clearly see

movement to the north. Jericho's horsemen had fanned
out in a line over a space of more than a hundred yards.

Chavez gave an order in Spanish. McCawley said,
"He's tellin' everybody to keep down. Let Jericho think
he's caught us asleep. And he would have if you-all hadn't
brought warnin'."

Andy rough-counted the riders. He saw around forty.
"There's more of them than there is of us."

The Jericho men were within fifty yards of the Chavez
defense line when a defender raised up. A Jericho rider
fired at him. Andy heard Jericho shout, "Pour it on them."

The invaders spurred into a run, coming on like a
whirlwind.

The defenders began rising, taking aim at the mass of
horsemen coming at them. Gunfire crackled all around
Andy. Riders pitched from their saddles. Horses fell,
some struggling to regain their feet, some lying on the
ground and kicking. To Andy's left a defender screamed
and went down.

McCawley staggered backward, a bullet in his leg.
Andy ran to help him, easing him to the ground.

He heard a curse. Farley held a hand to his side. Blood
oozed out between his fingers. The impact had knocked
the breath out of him. He gasped, trying to get air back
into his lungs. Andy started toward him, but Farley waved
him away and pointed in the direction of Jericho's men.

Powder smoke rose like a patchy fog, hiding many of
the adversaries from one another. Andy was sparing with
his ammunition. He fired only when he could see something to aim at. Bullets smacked into the adobe wall or
whispered past his ears to sing off the stone wall of the
house behind him. The incessant firing made his ears
throb with pain.

The attackers came near breaching the defense line,

then wavered. He heard a shout in a voice he thought was Jericho's. The invaders began pulling back, shocked and badly bruised by the determined defense.

About now, Andy thought, Jericho must be wondering what could have gone so wrong with his plan. Ordinarily so large a force should have overrun this ranch in a matter of minutes. They should have swept through the buildings with relative ease, cutting down the inhabitants before they had time to mount any creditable defense. Jericho was probably cursing, asking himself if he had a spy in his ranks.

The invaders took cover wherever they could find it, behind corrals, behind outbuildings, in the fringes of brush. They began a desultory firing. The defenders fired back. None of the shooting now was doing much damage to either side so far as Andy could see. He knelt over McCawley, pressing a handkerchief against the wound to slow the blood. He then went to Farley, but Farley refused help. He had regained enough breath to say, "It ain't that much."

Andy heard a drumming of hooves from the east, then from the west. The flankers were coming in, attacking Jericho's men from both sides. Many invaders hit the saddle and beat a fast retreat toward the river. Andy could hear Jericho's angry voice calling for them to come back and fight. Shortly he was left with only a handful of men unable or unwilling to quit the scene. They were well concealed but not in a position to carry the fight forward.

The shooting died away. Neither side offered many visible targets. An uneasy quiet fell over the contested ground.

Lupe Chavez raised up a little, looking over the wall. He cupped his hands around his mouth and shouted,

"You, Jericho, you give up now? You bring with you too many cowards. They run like rabbits."

Jericho answered, "You don't see *me* runnin'. I come to settle things with you, Lupe. I ain't leavin' till I do."

"You are welcome to stay. I give you six feet of ground. It will be all your own."

"You damned chili picker, you ain't seen the day you can put me under."

The two men went quiet for a bit. Andy returned to McCawley. "I'll help you into the house."

McCawley put up no argument. Andy got the rancher's arm around his shoulder and boosted him up onto his feet. He half carried, half dragged him to the door. Juana opened it and cried out in alarm. The two women helped Andy bring McCawley into the house. They laid him upon the floor, well below the windows through which a bullet might reach him.

Tony looked down on his stepfather, his face softening. "He ain't goin' to die, is he?"

Juana said, "You have struck him in the heart, but the bullet did not. Do you just stand there, or do you help?"

Tony went to his knees. "I'll help." He ripped his stepfather's bloody pants leg open with a knife blade.

Andy went back outside, where only an occasional wild shot was being fired. Crouching, he returned to Farley, on his knees behind the wall, his shirt off and wadded up, pressed against his side. He did not give Andy time to ask questions. He said, "I told you, Badger Boy. This happens every time I'm with you."

"I'm not the one that shot you."

"No, but I'll bet they was aimin' at you instead of me. You're the damndest jinx I ever saw."

"I'll help you into the house."

"It ain't so much. Clipped my ribs is all. Might've cracked one, the way it feels."

Andy's patience was strained. "Don't be so stubborn. Teresa will patch you up, her and her mother."

Mention of Teresa had a positive effect on Farley. "All right, but soon as I can I'm goin' as far from you as I can get. A hundred, two hundred miles. Maybe more."

Teresa gasped as Andy brought Farley in. She appeared even more concerned over Farley than over her father. Andy tried to explain that the wound was not all that serious, but he saw that Farley was enjoying her attention. He went back outside.

For a while all was quiet. The shooting had stopped. Andy was sure the remnant of invaders remained, though they were well hidden.

He heard Jericho call again: "Chavez, you still there?"

"I am here, *diablo Tejano*. What you want now?"

"I got a proposition for you. We can make a deal."

"You came here to kill me, and now you want to deal? You got no cards."

"I have one. I'm bettin' I've got more guts than you do."

Indignant, Chavez stood up to his full height, just a little over five feet. He shook his fist. "I got plenty guts, gringo."

"Then let it come down to just me and you. We step out into the open, both of us. Best man wins. Either way, everybody else goes free."

"It would not be an even fight. You are a bigger target than me."

"Maybe I'm a better shot. It'll be easy to find out."

Chavez hesitated. "Why should I do this? You are in a trap. When you try to get away my men will kill you."

"I thought you wanted that pleasure for yourself. When it's over everybody will say you were too much of a coward to face me."

Chavez bristled. "I am not a coward."

"Then show me."

Chavez shouted in Spanish. Andy assumed it was an order for everyone to stay put, to take no part. Jericho shouted for his men to keep hands off. "This is between me and Chavez. Whichever way it goes, everybody else rides out of here peaceful. You hear me, Burt?" He paused, looking around. "Burt?"

Burt Hatton was not there. Andy wondered if he had been shot or if he had fled.

Jericho stepped out from behind a small shed, carrying a rifle. He walked toward the wall. Porfirio handed Chavez a rifle, then stood back as Chavez went out through an opening and stood waiting. Jericho walked to within twenty feet of him, then stopped.

Chavez said, "A long time we have been enemies, Jericho. But never did you come against me like this. For why now?"

"Some of your bandits murdered my wife's nephew. It was like she'd lost a son. I couldn't stand still for that."

"I know nothing of it."

"I had it in mind to kill your nephew in return, but it's better this way. I'd rather kill you."

"If you can, gringo. If you can."

For what seemed several minutes the two men stood glaring, taking each other's measure, each waiting for the other to move. When it happened it was so fast that Andy could not tell which man moved first. Two shots sounded as one. Chavez staggered, eyes stricken as he dropped his rifle and clasped both dark hands against his stomach.

He tried to speak, but no sound came except a groan. His knees buckled. He went down on one shoulder.

Jericho's left arm hung at his side, shattered. Blood soaked a torn sleeve and dripped from his fingers. He swayed like a tree about to fall.

Porfirio moved toward him, fury in his eyes, but Chavez called to him in a weak voice. Porfirio dropped on his knees beside his fallen leader. The language was Spanish, but Andy surmised that Chavez was telling him to let Jericho go.

Tony hurried out and knelt beside his uncle. Quiet words passed between them. Tony looked at Jericho with hatred and seemed about to move against him. Chavez grasped Tony's sleeve and stopped him. A deal was a deal.

Chavez coughed and went limp. Tony folded his uncle's hands across his chest and pulled his fallen sombrero over the still face. He pushed to his feet, his eyes profoundly sad. "You'd better go, Jericho. I can't hold Uncle Lupe's people back very long. I may not be able to hold myself."

Jericho looked toward Andy. "What about you, Ranger? You got somethin' to say?"

"I ain't a Ranger anymore, but I expect there'll be Rangers waitin' for you at the river." He did not know what the Rangers could do about Jericho, however. His invasion of Mexico had not been a violation of Texas law.

One of Jericho's men took his boss's good arm and led him away.

Several of the Chavez men stood over their fallen *jefe* and removed their hats. One made the sign of the cross. Porfirio said something in a low voice. Three men carefully lifted Chavez and carried him toward the house.

Andy walked up to Tony. "I guess you're the boss here now. What comes next?"

The thought seemed to take Tony by surprise. "I don't know. I'll need time to think it through. I wish Uncle Lupe hadn't made that deal with Jericho. If we don't kill him now, we'll have to reckon with him sometime later on."

"He took a whippin' he won't get over any time soon. And that arm is bleedin' bad. He might not make it home."

"If he does, bein' crippled may just make him meaner."

Andy watched Jericho ride away with a few of his followers. The rancher was hunched over, in obvious pain.

Andy said, "This didn't have to be. It happened because of two hardheaded men. Either one of them could have stopped it years ago."

Tony said, "No, they couldn't. It wasn't just them. It was the Alamo and San Jacinto and the Mexican War. I was able to pick sides, but most people never got a choice. Their side was picked for them the day they were born— American or Mexican."

"You're some of both. Maybe you can help bring all this to some kind of settlement."

Tony shook his head. "It'll take a lot of time and a lot of funerals before that happens. I picked the Mexican side. I can't turn my back on it. I can't help my belly firin' up every time I see a gringo push some Mexican around. I want to kill him and all the blue-eyed gringos around him."

"What about Big Jim? He put up a good fight on your uncle's side, and he got himself bloodied for it."

"He's still a gringo. I'd like to forget that, but I can't. Every time I look at him, I'll remember what the gringos did to us."

"But a lot of Americans took abuse from Mexicans too. Remember Santa Anna? Remember the Alamo and Goliad?"

Tony looked at ground darkened by the blood of Guadalupe Chavez. "We remember what we want to remember, and we forget whatever makes us ashamed. There won't be peace on the river until no one is left who remembers these times."

JERICHO JACKSON'S ARM was afire. The pain brought blinding tears to his eyes. He turned his head, trying not to let Jesse Wilkes see them.

Wilkes said, "We better stop and do somethin'. You're bleedin' plumb to death."

Jericho felt drained of strength, but he did not want to stop before they crossed the river. He realized he stood a good chance of not reaching it at all. "Tie it off so it won't bleed so much," he said. "It's way too far to a doctor, but I know where there's a *curandero*. He'll fix me up till I can get to somebody better."

Wilkes tore a sleeve from his own shirt and wrapped it tightly above the wound. "Maybe that'll slow it down a little. In the war I seen doctors saw off arms that didn't look as bad as yours."

Jericho grunted. Wilkes was almost as pessimistic as Burt Hatton had always been. "Got any idea what happened to Burt?"

Jericho could see that Wilkes wanted to speak but was hesitant. He demanded, "Tell me somethin'."

Grudgingly Wilkes said, "I hate to say this, but I seen Burt turn his horse around and run for the river right after the first shots was fired. He wasn't in favor of this raid in the first place."

"Damned coward." Jericho tried to spit, but his mouth was too dry. "I've always suspicioned that he didn't put up much fight the time Lupe Chavez's bandits killed my wife's nephew. I wouldn't be surprised if he turned and ran then just like he did today."

Wilkes seemed to be summoning courage. Reluctantly he said, "Burt lied to you about that fight. He said he'd kill any of us who ever told you the straight of it."

"He ain't here now. Tell me."

Stumbling over the words, Wilkes managed to say, "It wasn't none of Chavez's men. What happened was, we came onto three travelers, and Burt wanted their horses. Thought they might be carryin' money too. Said we could rob them on the quiet and lay the blame on Mexican bandits. And we wouldn't have to divvy up any of it with you. He figured on jumpin' them after dark and takin' them by surprise. They surprised us instead. We didn't know it then, but it turned out they was Rangers."

A building anger almost made Jericho forget the pain. "He told it a lot different."

"He didn't know but what you might shoot him—and maybe us too—if you found out he got the boy killed on a fool stunt like that. It was a lot easier to drop the blame on Lupe Chavez."

Jericho slammed the palm of his good hand against his leg. "The lyin' son of a bitch! The main reason for this raid was to get even with Lupe for killin' that boy. And now you tell me it wasn't even his bunch that done it."

Wilkes hung his head. "I ought to've told you a long time ago."

"Yes, you should. But get me back to the ranch. If Burt is there, it'll pleasure me to shoot him between the eyes."

Approaching the river, he saw strangers waiting on the

north bank. They were Rangers, he guessed, and they appeared to have taken several of his men into custody.

Jericho said, "I can't see clear enough to tell if Burt Hatton is amongst them."

"I don't think he is."

"Maybe he went upriver and crossed where there ain't no Rangers. We'll do the same."

Wilkes argued, "Them Rangers might be able to do somethin' about your bad arm."

"To hell with the arm. We're goin' after Burt. If I start to fall off, you grab me. I ain't stoppin' till I catch him."

BURT HATTON REINED up and studied the Jericho headquarters. The place looked deserted. All able-bodied men who could handle a gun had gone on the raid. He had known as soon as the opening volleys were fired that the expedition was a failure. The surprise Jericho had counted on had gone sour somehow. Chavez had been ready with a lethal defense.

The early fire cut down several men on either side of him. Hatton quickly decided he did not intend to join them and die for someone else's folly. Jericho had allowed his hatred for Chavez to trump his judgment. Hatton had turned his horse around and quirted it most of the way through the brush and the sand to the river. Just in time he spotted a party of men waiting on the other side and guessed that they were Rangers. He rode farther west and crossed at another shallow point.

Now he surveyed the Jericho headquarters. He did not know if Jericho had survived, but chances were that he had. The boss had always enjoyed better luck than any two men were entitled to. Hatton sometimes suspected he had made a pact with the devil.

Well, Jericho would not put Burt Hatton in harm's way ever again. Hatton intended to gather up what belonged to him, plus some that didn't but should, and hunt for greener grass. The farther from Jericho, the better.

If he was lucky, he thought, no one would be in the house except Jericho's citified wife. Hatton had always resented her because Jericho thought she was too good to associate with the common hands. That old black maid of hers would probably be there too, but she was harmless. She was likely to do nothing except holler. The two might give him a little sass, but he did not expect them to offer any physical resistance. Chances were they would cower in a corner and cry.

He tied his horse outside. He started to push through the outside door into Jericho's office, but he changed his mind. That was the way he had always entered because Jericho did not want him venturing into the rest of the house where that pampered woman might have to look at him. This time Jericho was not here to make him go in like a servant. By God, he would go in the front like white folks should.

He shoved the door open and waited a moment, letting his eyes adjust from sunlight to the darkened interior. Hearing a gasp, he turned. Jericho's wife stared at him, her mouth open in surprise. Hatton had never studied her closely before. He found her skinny and frail-looking. He wondered what Jericho had ever seen in her. He could buy the favors of better-looking women in any town for the change in his pocket.

She demanded, "What are you doing here? Where is my husband?"

"Maybe in heaven, maybe in hell."

Her hands were clasped at her flat breasts. "He's dead?"

"A bunch of them are. I don't know about him. Things was a lot worse than we expected, so I lit a shuck."

Her face tightened in anger. "You are a coward, sir."

"If I wasn't, I'd be gettin' dirt shoveled in my face. Them Meskins are damned good shots." He made his way from the parlor to Jericho's office at the end of a corridor. He knelt in front of the safe and exercised his fingers.

He had never opened the safe before. Jericho allowed no one to touch it. But he had watched Jericho many times, and he had made a mental note of the combination in case a situation like this might arise.

Mrs. Jackson followed him, the black maid just behind her. She demanded, "What are you doing at that safe?"

"I'm fixin' to open it."

"Why?"

"It's got money in it. I ain't leavin' here with my pockets empty. I've spent too much of my life that way."

He turned the knob one way and the other, trying to remember the sequence of numbers. He missed once, but on his second try he swung the door open. Inside was a metal box in which he had watched Jericho place large sums of money from time to time. He did not bother to count. He could do that later, when he was well away from here. He rifled through the papers and ledgers to be sure he was not overlooking any currency. Satisfied, he tucked the box under his arm and rose to his feet.

Mrs. Jackson gripped a pistol with both hands. It was a big Navy Colt, heavy enough that she had trouble holding it steady. "You are not going to rob my husband," she said. "Put that back."

Instead, he threw the box at her and jumped aside as she pulled the trigger. The explosion shook the room.

Smoke blossomed around her. Before she could thumb the hammer back he grabbed the warm barrel and twisted the weapon from her small hands. He raised it and swung it down hard, striking the top of her head and slanting down the side of her face. She dropped like a sack of corn.

The black woman screamed and came at him with a poker from the fireplace. He deflected the blow with his left arm and pointed the pistol into her face. "Back away, Mammy, or you'll be a dead nigger."

The maid dropped to her knees beside the unconscious woman. "Miz Jackson. Wake up, Miz Jackson."

Hatton retrieved the metal box and backed toward the door, still carrying the Navy Colt. He said, "When she wakes up, tell her I didn't come here to do that. But I don't stand for anybody pointin' a gun at me—man, woman, or child."

He tied the box to his saddle, patted it as he might a dog, then mounted and rode north in an easy trot. He whistled an old tune he had heard in a San Antonio dance hall.

A day that had gotten off to a miserable start had completely changed complexion. It looked now like a sunny day in spring. All it needed was a rainbow.

JERICHO'S ARM HUNG stiffly at his side. Every heartbeat sent pain drumming through his body as he rode up to his stone house. Jesse Wilkes had been obliged several times to hold him and keep him from falling. His head ached, and he felt fever rising. Before long he was going to be sick as a calf with the yellow scours.

"Help me into the house, Jesse. I don't want to fall down in front of her."

He had always tried to let his wife see nothing but strength and purpose from him. He hated the thought of her seeing him in this deplorable condition. He had sent one of his riders to fetch a *curandero,* but it would be a couple of hours at best before the healer could get here. Tomorrow he would have Wilkes start with him to San Antonio, where an honest-to-God medical doctor could tend to that arm.

Wilkes opened the door, then supported Jericho as he crossed the threshold. They stopped abruptly just inside. Jericho's wife lay on a divan. A cloth covered most of her face, but not so completely that he did not see a deep bruise across her jaw.

"What the hell? Did she fall?"

The maid burst into tears. "It was a man done it, that man you call Hatton. He was takin' money out of your safe, and she tried to stop him."

Staggering, Jericho made his way to his wife's side. She appeared to be only half conscious, but she recognized his voice. Her fingers closed weakly over his hand. She murmured, "Jericho? Is that you, Jericho?"

"It's me. I'm home." Jericho lifted her hand and kissed it, then turned back to the maid. "How long since Burt left here?"

"Not long. I ain't kept track of the time."

"Which direction did he go?"

"I was too busy to watch him leave, but it sounded like he went north."

Jericho said, "Wilkes, help me back to my horse. We'll catch him if we have to trail him plumb to San Antonio."

"Jericho, you ain't in no condition. If you don't take care of that arm, it's liable to kill you."

"Damn it, I didn't ask you, I *told* you. If the Lord decides to take me, that's all right. We all got to go sometime. But I want to see Burt Hatton go ahead of me. Hand me that shotgun from over the mantel."

"Like as not he's got a rifle. He may not let you get close enough to use a shotgun."

"I'll get close. I don't think I can hold a rifle steady, but that scattergun will get him."

"You may not live that long."

"Ain't nobody ever killed me yet. It'll take a better man than Burt Hatton to do it."

HATTON HAD PUT several miles behind him. The day's excitement had drained him. He knew he had to keep going, because if Jericho had survived the shooting at the Chavez ranch he might have reached home by now. Hatton wondered which would anger Jericho more, his wife's injury or the safe with its money box gone. It was a cinch that if Jericho was alive and on his feet he would sooner or later follow Hatton's trail.

But Hatton was in dire need of a drink. He could have taken a bottle from Jericho's house if he had thought of it, but his mind had been too involved with grabbing the money and getting away. His path would carry him by a crossroads general store that dealt in groceries, cheap whiskey, and sometimes destitute young Mexican women desperate to make a living any way they could. He saw the place ahead, a flat and ugly structure built of pickets and plastered to keep the wind and rain out.

It was his intention simply to buy a bottle and drink while he rode. But once he was inside, the metal box pressed firmly under his left arm, he decided to linger long enough to savor one drink at leisure. Then he could ride on. The first drink led to a second. By that time a slender young woman had sidled up to him at the rough plank bar and put an arm around his waist. He did not understand much she said, but imagination filled in the gaps. He poured a drink for her and another for himself. His fear of Jericho began to fade as the whiskey and the woman's big brown eyes warmed his blood. The bottle was more than half empty when he grabbed it by the neck and followed her through the rear of the store. She led him into a small picket shack in the back.

He lost sense of time. He swung his legs down from the bed and knocked over the empty bottle. His head felt light, and the room did slow circles around him. He tried to pull his britches on but had trouble keeping both feet from going into the same pants leg. The woman had to help him. He knew she had dipped into the metal box. He did not know how much she took out of it, and at the moment that did not matter. It came back to him that the box was Jericho's, and that Jericho was sure to come looking for it. He buttoned his shirt wrong but left it that way. He strapped his gun belt around his waist, part of the shirttail hanging over it.

The woman was rubbing against him and making what he surmised was love talk in Spanish, but he was feeling an urgency to move on. His fear of Jericho began to penetrate the fog raised by whiskey and lust.

He said, "*Adiós,* sweet thing," and staggered out the door into the daylight. His heart took a leap as his bleary eyes discovered two men standing there. They were Jericho and Jesse Wilkes. The metal box fell from his hands and burst open on the ground. Paper currency began blowing away.

Jericho carried a shotgun under his right arm. His left arm hung stiffly at his side. The sleeve was the rusty red of dried blood, and in the center it glistened with blood still fresh. The voice was not what he was accustomed to from Jericho. It was a little man's voice, strained and weak, but the words crackled with hate. "Burt Hatton, you are a woman beater, a thief, and a liar."

Hatton saw the muzzle of the shotgun coming up. He drew his pistol and squeezed off one shot before the blast slammed him back against the picket wall. As he slumped to the ground he heard a woman's scream from inside the shack. A green bill drifted in front of him. By reflex he reached out, but his fingers were too weak to grasp it. The wind carried it away.

17

Andy stood beside his horse and looked back toward the Chavez house. He had tried to help Farley saddle up, but Farley had stubbornly waved him away though his face was twisted in pain. He managed to saddle his horse by himself.

Teresa stood just outside the front door, watching.

Andy said, "She doesn't want you to go."

Farley did not reply. He went about tightening the cinch, mumbling under his breath.

Andy said, "That wound is liable to get infected. Why don't you stay here and let them take care of it for you till you're sure it's goin' to heal all right?"

"Why don't you mind your own business, Badger Boy?"

"Personally, I don't care one way or the other. But that girl has got feelin's for you, and it's hurtin' her to see you go. I think you've got the same feelin's for her."

"What if I do? What kind of life would people let us have together, me white, her Mexican? Half, anyway."

"I'll bet Big Jim and his wife had some doubts too, at first. But it looks to me like they've done pretty good together."

"I ain't Big Jim."

"No, you sure ain't." Andy felt a flicker of resentment,

seeing the sad-eyed girl watching from the house. "If you was, you wouldn't worry about what other people say. You'd only think about what *you* want, you and her."

Farley groaned as he pulled himself into the saddle. His hand went to his side, pressing against the wrapping that bound his ribs. "If we hurry up, maybe we can catch Jericho before he crosses the river."

"What for? We're not Rangers anymore. What Jericho does is none of our business."

Farley grimaced. "It just rubs me raw thinkin' about what he done here today. There's been people killed and a good many more shot up on his account. He ought to be called to answer for it."

"He took a bullet. Wouldn't surprise me if he loses that arm."

"It ain't that I got any sympathy for Lupe Chavez. I don't. But he's dead, and Jericho's still alive. Everybody would be better off if they was both dead. Maybe the border would finally settle down."

The border would not settle that easily, Andy thought. Two people, even those as powerful as Jericho and Chavez, would not make that much difference.

Andy had seen Jericho ride away with one of his men. Jericho had appeared to be in a bad way. He said, "Like as not the Rangers will pick him up as soon as he crosses the river."

"What can they do to him? Any law he broke was on this side of the river, not in Texas."

Andy admitted with regret, "You're probably right."

Before the house faded from sight, Farley shifted in the saddle and looked back. Andy suggested, "It's not very far. You could still turn around."

"I've made up my mind."

They rode in silence most of the way to the river. As

they approached it Andy could see horsemen on the far side. He guessed there might be thirty or more. "Some of them are Rangers. Looks like they've been pickin' up Jericho's men as they cross over."

Farley drew rein. "I expect Sergeant Donahue is with them. Looks like we're in trouble, me and you."

"Might be. We left word that we'd resigned before we went over, but he didn't accept that the last time I did it."

Farley appeared to wrestle with his conscience. Finally he said, "Go on by yourself if you want to. I'm turnin' back."

"Thought you'd made up your mind."

"It's *my* mind. I can change it if I want to."

Andy smiled. "Just be sure you don't ever say or do anything to hurt her, even if she is a Mexican."

"Just half," Farley said. He turned and started back toward the Chavez headquarters.

Andy watched until Farley was out of sight, then put his horse into the river. Len Tanner rode to the water's edge to meet him as he came out. "Awful glad to see you, Andy. I was afraid you might've got yourself shot in the big doin's over there."

"They tried, but they missed."

"Was it Farley that I seen turn back? I hope he didn't get his grouchy self wounded." His tone of voice indicated that he wished otherwise.

"Once in the side and once in the heart. The one in the heart is a wound he's apt to carry the rest of his life."

Len understood and shook his head in disbelief. "Well, I'll swun. After all the things he said."

Andy saw Sergeant Donahue riding toward them. "What has Donahue been sayin'?"

"About you, nothin' that falls easy on the ears. But

about today, he's grinnin' like a possum. He's sure this is fixin' to earn him a promotion."

"I don't see Jericho in that bunch."

"Ain't much he can do about Jericho anyway, seein' as everything he done was in Mexico. But he's got most of Jericho's men, the ones that made it back across the river. He's holdin' them till we can check all of them against the fugitive list. The ones Jericho didn't lose on the other side of the river, he's apt to lose over here."

Donahue stopped his horse and gave Andy a hostile study. "You're under arrest, Private Pickard. In goin' across the river you violated a direct order."

"I resigned before I went."

"That resignation was not delivered directly to me. I do not recognize it." He looked past Andy. "Where is Private Brackett?"

"He's stayin' over there for a while. He got himself wounded."

Donahue said, "Serves him right. What about Jericho? He has not crossed."

"He left before we did. Had a few men with him. They probably saw the Rangers waitin' and decided to find a quiet place farther up the river."

Donahue frowned. "Then he's probably on his way back to his stronghold."

"He looked like one arm was shot to pieces. I'm guessin' he headed for home to get it taken care of."

"You've been to his headquarters before. I want you to guide me there."

"But I'm under arrest. And I'm not a Ranger anymore."

Donahue snorted impatiently. "I told you I do not accept your resignation. But take me to Jericho's and I will consider you no longer a Ranger."

"What about that arrest business?"

"I'll drop the charges."

"If we find Jericho I don't see much you can do about him. Not legally."

"I just want him to know that he's not the cock of the walk around here anymore. I'm goin' to tell him the Rangers can go anywhere they want to. From now on Jericho's road is open to the public."

Donahue did not wait to see if Andy would accept. He called, "Tanner, I want you and Bill Hewitt. You are goin' with me and Pickard."

IT STRUCK ANDY again how similar Jericho's stone house was to those of Lupe Chavez and Big Jim McCawley. He saw a man sitting on a bench at the edge of a colorful flower bed, just to the right of the front door. The man watched the Rangers' approach but made no move to get away. He sat until they were within stone-throwing distance, then stood up to wait for them.

Donahue demanded, "Who are you?"

"Name's Jesse Wilkes."

"We've come to see Jericho Jackson."

Wilkes jerked his thumb toward the door. "Inside."

Donahue dismounted and said, "Hewitt, disarm him, then stay out here and watch him. We do not want any interference."

Wilkes said with glum resignation, "Ain't nobody fixin' to interfere with you. Just go ahead in."

Pistol in hand, Donahue motioned for Andy to open the door. "I'll be right behind you."

Andy felt a momentary queasiness about going in first. If Jericho was waiting with a drawn weapon, Andy would take the first bullet. Donahue was using him for a shield.

He blinked, for coming in from the sunshine made the

room appear dark the first moment. He saw two women standing in the parlor, facing him. One was black. The other was white, a tall, thin woman Andy knew must be Jericho's wife. He saw a deep bruise on her swollen face.

. Donahue stepped out from behind him. "We've come to talk to Jericho Jackson. Where's he at?"

Mrs. Jackson remained silent but pointed down a dark hall. She led the way. Donahue said, "Pickard, Tanner, you-all stick close to me. No tellin' what Jericho's reaction may be."

Mrs. Jackson stopped at an open door and motioned for the Rangers to go inside. Andy saw Jericho Jackson lying on a bed. A candle burned on a stand beside him. Beside the candle lay a Bible.

Andy did not have to move closer to see that Jericho was dead. He turned toward the woman. The grief in her eyes told him to ask her no questions.

Donahue's eagerness was gone. Soberly he said, "You men can bear witness that the fugitive is deceased." He puzzled, "But how could a wounded arm have killed him?"

Mrs. Jackson summoned enough voice to say, "Ask Wilkes."

Outside, Wilkes explained that he and Jericho had followed a man named Burt Hatton. Andy recognized the name. Though Jericho had blasted Hatton with a shotgun, Hatton had managed to put a bullet through Jericho's lung.

Wilkes said, "Wasn't nothin' anybody could do for him except bring him home to his woman. I done that. Now, if you-all have got no further business with me, I'll see to his buryin'."

Donahue said, "Somebody else will have to do that.

You'll be goin' with us. We'll want to check you against our fugitive list."

Mrs. Jackson had come out to stand beside the door. Andy asked her, "You goin' to be all right, ma'am?"

She shook her head. "No, but I'll get by. I still have a home back in Missouri."

Donahue asked, "What do you figure to do with this ranch and everything that belonged to your husband?"

"I've not had time to give it thought. I'll probably sell what was legally his. As for that which was not, I'll try to find who rightfully owns it."

Donahue frowned. "Be careful who you let have it. This is a white man's country now."

She stiffened. "The kind of outlaw white trash my husband surrounded himself with? He tried to shield me, but I am not blind. I was always aware of his shortcomings. Where I can, I'll make amends."

Donahue warned, "You could be askin' for trouble."

"If trouble comes, I'll call on the Rangers." She went into the house and closed the door.

Donahue cursed under his breath. "She'd better not call on *me*. Be damned if I'll answer."

Andy said, "If you don't, you may have to hunt for honest work."

THEY RETURNED TO the main camp, where the Jericho men had been escorted for screening to determine which of them might be wanted somewhere. Len had searched his fugitive list and found Jesse Wilkes was sought on a murder charge. Several others held in the camp had already been identified as well.

Sergeant Donahue was jubilant. "This will look great

in the newspapers. I can see the headline: BIG CLEANUP ON THE BORDER."

Then he saw something else, and he froze to attention. Major Jones of Austin walked out of the headquarters tent and beckoned. "Sergeant, I want to see you."

Flustered, Donahue made a halfhearted salute. "You've come just in time, Major. We've done a good piece of work here."

"So I see."

"We've broken up two of the worst bandit gangs on the border, one on each side of the river. The people of Texas can be proud of my Rangers."

"Well and good, but I think the adjutant general will want to know why you didn't do it sooner."

Donahue blinked. "What do you mean?"

"I am given to understand you had advance word that Jericho was gathering a hard crew for that invasion. You stood by without making any effort to interfere. If these men are wanted today, they were wanted then. Why didn't you round them up before they went into Mexico?"

"Nobody's ever invaded Jericho's little kingdom."

"You had good reason to do so. All you lacked was the will."

Donahue slumped. "At least Chavez and Jericho are both dead. The country is well rid of them."

Jones nodded. "True. But many others are dead too, white men and Mexicans both. You will have a chance to explain all that in Austin. Perhaps the adjutant general will see fit to keep you in the rank of sergeant. Or he may suggest that you seek employment elsewhere."

The major turned and walked away, leaving Donahue standing with his head down.

Andy waited until the major went back into the tent,

then followed him. He said, "Sir, I've already tried twice to turn in my resignation. What do I have to do to get it accepted?"

The major stared in surprise. "You can't mean you want to leave the force."

"I think I've been a Ranger about long enough. The time has come for me to try my hand at somethin' else."

Jones's voice was regretful. "I can handle the resignation for you. But are you sure?"

"I've thought on it a lot. I'm sure."

Outside, Len Tanner put his hand on Andy's shoulder. "I'm goin' to miss you."

"And I'll miss you. Don't you ever consider quittin' too?"

"Nope. Never had so much fun in my life." He gripped Andy's hand so hard that it hurt. "Tell Rusty and them I said howdy."

ANDY'S HEARTBEAT PICKED up as he saw Rusty Shannon's double cabin ahead. He had grown to manhood here. He felt that he was home, though he knew he would not stay for long. He looked over the fields, expecting to see Rusty working there, but in this he was disappointed. He rode up to the cabin, dismounted, and shouted, "Anybody home?"

Alice Shannon stepped out onto the dog run that separated the two sections of the cabin. She shaded her eyes and called, "Andy? Can that be you?"

"Sure is. You got anything to eat?"

"If I don't, I'll fix somethin'." She hurried out to meet him. As her apron flared in the wind he noticed that her stomach was extended. He hugged her but took care not to squeeze too hard.

He said, "Looks like pretty soon there's goin' to be another mouth to feed around here."

"Two of them if you're stayin'."

"I just came for a little visit. Wanted to be sure the two of you are all right. I can see that *you* are. How's Rusty?"

"Fine. He's tickled over the prospect of bein' a daddy. He went over to Shanty's. Ought to be home pretty soon. Come in and have some coffee. We'll eat supper when Rusty gets back."

Andy heard a rattle of trace chains and looked toward the road. He saw Rusty's wagon. "I'll wait out here for Rusty." He frowned, trying to think of a delicate way to ask her. Finding none, he blurted, "Last time I was here you were still wonderin' if the reason Rusty married you was because you reminded him of Josie."

"Josie will always be with him. I don't try to take her place. But I've made my own place with him now." She touched her stomach and smiled. "The baby and me." She went back into the cabin.

Rusty hauled the mule team to a stop and jumped down from the wagon, wrapping the reins around the brake. He rushed up to pump Andy's hand. "Thought you were way down on the border. Are you on leave?"

"No, I'm not a Ranger anymore. I decided it's time to find out just where I belong."

"You've got a place right here as long as you want it."

"No, this is yours and Alice's. And however many little Shannons may come along. I've thought a lot about that country out west, along the Llano and the San Saba. I took a likin' to it while I was stationed there."

"It's a pretty country. But it's a long ways from here."

"Everything around here is settled up. That's a new country. Lots of room to grow in."

"Not by yourself. You'll need somebody to help you,

somebody to come home to of a night. It took me a while to realize that myself, but I know it now." He looked toward the house, where smoke rose from the kitchen chimney. "I didn't realize how lonesome this place used to be till I brought Alice to share it with me."

Andy looked at the ground. "Seen Bethel Brackett lately?"

"Saw her in town a few days ago. She's prettier than ever."

"Anybody courtin' her?"

"If they're tryin', they're not gettin' anywhere. First thing she did was ask me all about you. She hadn't heard from you in a long time."

"I ain't much hand at writin' letters." He glanced at the house. "Reckon Alice would take it badly of me if I was to skip supper and go on over to see Bethel?"

Rusty grinned. "She'd think it's the smartest thing you've ever done."

Andy moved quickly into the saddle. "I may not be back tonight." He spurred the horse into a long trot. He looked behind him once. Rusty and Alice stood in the yard, arms around each other. Alice waved.

Andy put the horse into a gallop.

The sun was going down as he reined up in front of the Brackett house. He yelled, "Bethel! Are you in there?"

He heard a cry from inside. She stepped out onto the porch, then hurried down the steps. She skipped toward him with outstretched arms as he swung from the saddle. When they broke apart he asked, "Ever been out west to the hill country?"

"Never have."

"How would you like to go?"

She hugged him again, hard. "Just tell me when we're leavin'."

HARD
TRAIL TO
FOLLOW

Dedicated to two retired Texas Ranger friends,
Joaquin Jackson and Bob Favor

1

Andy Pickard knew that sooner or later he might have to whip his future brother-in-law.

He had sensed Farley Brackett's dark presence before he saw him, sitting on a roan horse where the rows ended almost at the bank of the Colorado River. Farley's erect posture in the saddle indicated that he was not in a good humor. He seldom was.

Andy had walked a thousand miles up and down this fallow field, guiding a plow point through the mellow earth and staring at the rump end of a brown mule. At least, it seemed like a thousand miles. He leaned back to exert pressure on the leather reins tied together and looped behind his neck. The mule stopped in its tracks, always more willing to answer to "Whoa" than to "Giddyup." It slumped immediately into a position of rest, flicking long ears to ward off a bothersome horsefly. Andy slipped a red bandanna from his neck and wiped his sweaty face while he waited to hear the latest complaint.

Farley's voice was laced with sarcasm. "What's that you're leavin' behind you, a furrow or a snake track?"

Farley's attitude grated like a boil on Andy's backside. The furrow was not as straight as it should be, but he had never claimed he was a good farmer. He tried to match

Farley's sarcasm. "A crooked row don't mean a thing to a cornstalk. It'll grow just the same."

"You ought to've stuck to bein' a Ranger. You'll never make a farmer if you live to be a hundred and six."

"I'd gladly swap you this mule for that roan. You can push the plow awhile, and I can laze around over the country like a property owner."

Farley had spent little time behind a plow, leaving that to Andy and a couple of black laborers. As a prospective Brackett-in-law, it looked as if Andy was about to marry into a life long on hard work and short on appreciation, at least from Farley.

Farley said, "If it wasn't for Bethel, I'd fire you."

"If it wasn't for her, I'd've done quit."

He had thought a lot about leaving. Were it not for Bethel, he would have put this farm behind him months ago. He felt sure the Texas Rangers would be pleased to take him back. They had tried to persuade him not to re-sign in the first place. The things a man would do for a woman . . .

It was a big farm and a good one, something to take strong pride in if he had been born with hands that fit a plow handle. But of late he had revisited an old dream of going back west, perhaps to the hill country where he had spent a long stretch with the Rangers. It was still but sparsely settled. Land was easy to come by in com-parison to this well-populated region of southeastern Texas. Some country out there was so far from the state land office in Austin that a man could squat on it free, at least for a few years, until he could build up his net worth. Another possibility was the rolling plains far to the north-west. There he had friends who would ride to hell's rimrock with him if necessary. They had done it more than once.

When Bethel had accepted his marriage proposal, the couple planned such a move. She had been as eager as he was. Then her mother fell ill and deeded the farm to her son and daughter in anticipation of death. The wedding and other plans were deferred because Bethel was reluctant to leave her dying mother. This was home. She had grown up here. Her father was buried in this ground, and it was likely that her mother soon would be. Now that Bethel owned half interest in the place, she no longer discussed leaving.

That her cross-grained brother shared ownership was Andy's hard luck.

At the time, Farley was recuperating from a wound suffered in Ranger service on the border, so Andy had agreed to stay and help. He worked for foreman's wages, hopeful that Bethel would sooner or later come back around to his way of thinking. Lately that hope was wearing thin.

Farley seemed now to have recovered from the latest of many injuries, major and minor, to which he seemed especially prone. He had reverted to the same cranky misfit he had been before. Andy told him, "We'd get the plantin' done faster if you'd pitch in and help. You could take the east field."

Farley shook his head. "Can't. Got to go to town and get some stuff for Teresa."

"Write me a list, and I'll go in your place," Andy said.

"I ain't sure you can read any better than you can plow a straight row. Never did see an Indian that could be taught how to farm."

There he goes with that Indian thing again, Andy thought. He was not an Indian, but Comanches had captured him when he was a small boy and kept him several years. Farley harbored a strong dislike for Indians.

Frequently he threw Andy's old Comanche name up to him. "You're lettin' that mule get almost as lazy as you are, Badger Boy. Him and you had better get back to work."

Andy prided himself on being able to get along with most people, but for years his relationship with Farley Brackett had swung back and forth between uneasy tolerance and outright hostility. Necessity had forced them to ride together as Rangers. Andy's betrothal to Farley's sister had joined them again, however reluctantly, on the Brackett farm. He had wanted to show her he could be a responsible husband and settle down to the tranquil life of a farmer. By now he had concluded that it would never be tranquil so long as he had to deal with Farley.

Turning the mule around, he roughly pushed the plow point into the ground and started another row. Farley was still talking, but Andy let the words drift away unanswered on the wind. He was saying a few words of his own.

He had often wondered why a woman so pretty and so gentle in nature should be saddled with such a brother. He tried to take into account that Farley had endured hardships enough to sour any man. He bore a war scar on his face and hidden scars deep within. His brothers had died fighting the Yankees. He and Bethel had lost their father to partisan violence that continued after the war. Farley had made himself a scourge to Union Reconstruction authorities and to state police who tried to enforce their edicts. His wildness had been both asset and liability during his later service as a Ranger.

Andy had long tried to accord him the benefit of the doubt. He realized Farley had abundant reason for being angry at most of the world, but sympathetic understanding was hard to maintain when he made himself so damned disagreeable.

The sun sank behind clouds low in the west, turning them to orange flame. The last few rows were no straighter than those before, but the hell with it. Farley could do them over if he was dissatisfied. Andy wearily laid the plow on its side and unhitched the mule. The lagging animal picked up new energy when it realized it was going to the barn for feed and rest.

Andy laid up the leather harness in the barn and fed the mule in a trough hewn from the trunk of a tree. Farley was brushing the roan. He offered no conversation, but his eyes smoldered. Anything Andy said would draw a barbed response, so he kept his silence. His feet dragged in fatigue as he walked toward the big house Bethel's father had built in prosperous times before war tore his family apart. Bethel waited on the front porch, youthful and slender and pretty enough to make a man want to hug her to death. She stood on tiptoes and invited a kiss. "You're tired," she said. "You should've quit earlier."

Looking into her welcoming eyes, he felt warm as sunshine. He embraced her so hard she gasped for breath. He said, "Didn't want to waste any daylight."

That was something he had often heard Rusty Shannon say. Rusty had more or less adopted him after his return from life with the Indians. He had managed to keep his patience during Andy's difficult adjustment to the white man's road. Though Rusty had carried a gun many years in the Ranger service, he had remained a farmer at heart, content now to work his own land a few miles from here. Andy had hoped he might be able to do the same, but now he dreaded the thought of following a mule up and down these fields the rest of his life. He had never lost the Comanche instinct for freedom, for drifting with the seasons and yearning to see the yonder side of the hill.

Bethel said, "You'll feel better when you've washed up. Teresa and me will have supper ready pretty soon. Have you seen Farley?"

"Seen and heard him. He's out at the barn."

Bethel caught the sarcasm. "I wish you'd find a way to get along with him. He's had a hellish life. And he *is* my brother."

"That's hard to forget. He keeps remindin' me that I'm just a hired hand, and you're the only reason he lets me stay here."

"You're a lot more than a hired hand. What's mine is yours, or will be when we're married."

"Ain't nothin' really mine here except a couple of horses. Your old daddy built this place. I didn't."

Bethel's eyes pinched. "Get ready for supper."

Bethel's father had made a modest fortune steamboating on the Brazos River before buying a large block of land and turning it into a prosperous farm. Carpetbaggers had stolen half of it after the war, but it was still a substantial enterprise.

Andy had barely finished drying his face on a towel when Farley stalked onto the back porch, pitched Andy's wash water into the yard, and poured a fresh panful from a bucket. He said, "Badger Boy, about what I said out yonder . . ."

Andy hoped he was on the verge of an apology, but he should have known better. Farley said, "I meant every damned word of it."

Andy's face burned. No appropriate retort came to him. He clenched his teeth and went back into the house.

Teresa Brackett was placing food on the long dining table that had once served a large family. She smiled, but her dark eyes betrayed uneasiness. New to the family, she had become painfully aware of the strained relationship between her husband and Andy. She took pains to speak gently, trying to make up for Farley's abrasiveness.

"There will come a better day," she said.

It couldn't get much worse, he thought. He had too much respect for her feelings to say it aloud.

In the past, Farley had often voiced a prejudice against Mexicans, but despite himself he had fallen in love with Teresa, the half-Mexican daughter of a border rancher. If there was anything consistent about Farley, it was his inconsistency. Now and again he acted almost human, but he usually got over it before it could become a habit.

Andy suspected that Teresa was already with child, though nothing had been said. It had been only a few months since she and Farley had married. If she delivered a son, the poor kid was in for a hard upbringing, Andy thought. Farley would work him like a mule.

Damned if I want to be around here to see it, he thought.

Farley's boots clomped heavily as he entered the dining room. He dropped into a chair at the head of the table, reaching immediately for a steaming biscuit without waiting for the two women to seat themselves. He quickly dropped it onto his plate and blew on his burned fingers. Teresa placed her hand on his shoulder for a fleeting moment. Farley's only response was a curt "You ought to've told me it was so hot."

She seated herself in a corner chair that gave her a view of his profile. She said just as curtly, "You should've known. It came right out of the oven."

Andy took satisfaction from her retort. Teresa was not letting Farley run over her. She had some snap, that little olive-skinned woman. It would serve Farley right if she bit his head off.

Teresa asked, "Did you bring me the things I asked for?"

Farley speared a slice of roast beef with his fork and plopped it into his plate. "Never quite got to town. Lost too much time makin' sure Andy didn't plow that field crossways."

Bethel's voice had the same snap as Teresa's. "He works harder than anybody around here."

"I could do better with my eyes shut."

Andy withheld comment, though he pictured himself shutting Farley's eyes with his fists. The image brought him pleasure.

Bethel said, "Teresa, you and me will go to town together tomorrow, and you can pick out just what you want. When it comes to buying something for a woman, Farley has no more taste than a one-eyed burro."

Farley snorted. "I had pretty good taste when it came to pickin' a wife. Better than you've got in pickin' a husband."

Andy said, "I don't think either one of them has won a jackpot."

Farley asked about his mother. Bethel said she did not feel strong enough to come to the table. She would take her supper in bed. Farley ate the rest of his meal in silence, then shoved his plate away. "You women may hear a rumor in town tomorrow, so I'd just as well tell you now."

Bethel tensed. "Tell us what?"

"I've been askin' around for opinions. I've about decided to run for sheriff."

Disturbed, Andy let his fork drop noisily upon the table. "Against Tom Blessing? But he's held that office for years."

"Too many years. Tom's gettin' to be an old man. He's

earned the right to sit and rock on his front porch. The county needs a younger man to take over that job. I'm also thinkin' of the salary and the rewards. We could stand some more cash income on this place. It's a long time between crops."

Andy had not thought of Tom as an old man, though he had grandchildren old enough to help him on his farm. He argued, "Me and you have both worked with Tom on Ranger business. He's a good man, and he's given this community a lot more than he ever got from it."

"It's time he had a chance to rest." Farley's brow furrowed, his eyes boring into Andy's. "You ain't goin' to oppose me on this, are you?"

Andy did not waste much time thinking about it. "I will if Tom runs for reelection."

Farley's face colored, the scar on his cheek darker than the rest. "For somebody who's anglin' to be part of this family, you show damned little loyalty."

"I've known Tom Blessing a lot longer than I've known you. He's been a friend to me and Rusty and everybody else around here."

Farley pushed his chair back. "Bethel, you could've had any man you wanted. Why in the hell did you pick *him*?"

Bethel spoke a couple of sharp words, then choked off the rest as Farley got up and left the room. She turned her gaze to Andy. He saw silent rebuke in her narrowed eyes.

He said, "He asked me, so I told him. If he didn't want an honest answer, he oughtn't to've asked me."

"You've got to give him more time. You just don't understand him." Bethel sounded hurt.

"But I do. I understand him too damned well."

Teresa looked down at her plate, her face flushed.

Andy saw that further discussion would lead to an even more heated argument. He stood away from the table. "I'd best let the air clear a little." He walked out onto the front porch. Farley stood there, smoking a newly rolled cigarette. His angry gaze touched Andy, but he said nothing. Andy went on to the barn, where a tack room had been converted into small but comfortable sleeping quarters for him. The arrangement had originally been meant to be temporary, until he and Bethel married. There were times, like now, when he wondered if they would ever stand before a preacher.

He sat on a hay bale and began sharpening a hoe to give his hands something to do. A shadow fell against the door. Bethel stood there, frowning at him. She asked, "Are you in a mood to talk?"

Andy laid the hoe aside. It had not really needed sharpening anyway. "I'm always in a mood to talk to you. But if it's about your brother, I doubt there's any use. He's what he is, and I'm what I am. I don't see either one of us changin'."

"You could if you'd both have patience."

"I *had* patience, once. Farley has worn it down to a nub."

"This farm has been a heavy load for him. He's never had this kind of responsibility before. Once he knows he can handle it, maybe he'll settle down and be easier to get along with."

"He's *never* been easy to get along with. If it wasn't for you, I'd've already quit tryin'."

"Try a little longer. We don't want our marriage to start with you and my brother fighting over every little thing that comes up."

"He's the one you should talk to. It's him that's always raisin' hell about somethin'."

She shook her head. "It looks like I can't talk to either one of you." She left the barn, leaving Andy wondering if he could have said something differently. He didn't know what it might be.

LATE THE NEXT afternoon he was slipping the harness from the mule when he saw two riders approaching the barn. He tensed until he realized neither was Farley. He didn't know anybody who would willingly ride with Farley anyway. His future brother-in-law was not adept at making friends. Andy's spirit lifted as he recognized Rusty Shannon. Beside him rode Sheriff Tom Blessing, still straight-backed in the saddle despite his years, and broad-shouldered as a blacksmith. In fact, he *was* a blacksmith, and a farmer, and a carpenter as well as a peace officer. He could do just about anything he put his mind and hands to. Serious, self-sufficient men like him had brought Texas up from the struggling, poverty days of the republic to where it was today.

They dismounted, and Andy eagerly shook hands with both men. He considered them the best friends he had, along with a Ranger named Len Tanner and an old black farmer named Shanty.

Rusty's hair remained the same dull reddish color as when Andy had first seen him, though it had begun to show strands of gray. His years as a farmer had given him a muscular build and calloused hands. His eyes were still as keen as during the many years he had been a Ranger. They took in the whole farmstead in a sweeping glance. If anything had been amiss, he would have seen it.

He said, "Been a while since you've been over to visit with me and Alice, or to play with the young'un."

Andy nodded in regret. "I've been meanin' to, but workin' this farm has been like swimmin' in water over my head." He removed the last of the harness and slapped the mule on the rump. It moved eagerly toward the feed trough. "You-all come on up to the house. The women-folks keep the coffeepot on, and they'll have supper ready directly."

Tom asked uneasily, "You reckon Farley's there?"

"I expect so. He's got a habit of quittin' early. New wife, you know."

Rusty said, "We don't care to run into Farley, not just yet. We've come to ask you if it's a fact that he's fixin' to run for sheriff."

Andy looked upon Rusty as a foster brother and Tom as something of a foster father. He studied the older man with misgivings. "That's what he told me. I tried to talk him out of it, but I'd just as well argue with a fence-post."

Tom asked, "Is he mad at me about somethin'?"

"No more than at anybody else. He doesn't need a reason to get mad. It comes on him natural, like rheumatism."

Tom's eyes showed concern. "I've been sheriff a long time. I hadn't thought about puttin' away my badge."

"Anybody who knows Farley is goin' to think hard before they vote for him. He's not a man they'd want to have authority over them. Especially packin' a gun."

Rusty said, "That's what I've been tellin' you, Tom. You've got lots of friends. How many has Farley got?"

Andy said, "You could crowd them all into a small outhouse and have room left for a plow horse."

Tom frowned in thought while Rusty and Andy continued to present their case. Rusty said, "If you was to quit, that'd leave the county in Farley's hands. You wouldn't want to do that to the folks who've always supported you."

Andy said, "I've put up with Farley a long time, and I guarantee that there ain't no pleasure in it."

Tom said, "I suppose you're right."

Andy said, "Sure we're right. You've been here since they dug the river, and we need you. Everybody needs you."

The sheriff unconsciously rubbed his hand over the badge on his vest. "I'll talk it over with the missus."

Andy said, "I'd bet you a box of cigars that she'll tell you to give Farley the lickin' of his life."

Tom seemed almost convinced.

Rusty said, "That's settled." He gave Andy a critical study. "Speakin' of Farley, I've wondered why you've stayed on here like a hired hand, puttin' up with his ill temper. There's other things you could do instead."

"But I'd have to leave Bethel. She's tied down here till her mother either gets well or dies."

Rusty did not appear satisfied with the answer. "If she's really the woman for you, she'll understand. If she's not, she won't. Should you change your mind, you're always welcome over at my place. I can find plenty for you to do."

Tom said, "Same goes for me. I could use a better deputy. The county judge saddled me with a sleepy-eyed kid who doesn't know which end of the broom to sweep with. You'd be natural for the job on account of your Ranger service."

Andy said, "I'll keep it in mind. You're sure about not stayin' for supper?"

Tom said, "I need to go back to town. I've got a bad

one locked up, waitin' for the Rangers to come and get him."

Andy asked, "Anybody I'd know?"

"Name's Luther Cordell. Him and his bunch held up a bank over in Galveston. Wounded the banker." Tom's eyes went hopeful. "I'd like to hire you as a special deputy to help me watch Cordell till they take him off of my hands."

Andy did not consider long. "I've got too much responsibility here."

Tom turned toward his horse. "It never hurts to ask."

Andy watched both men remount. He said, "Tom, don't you be worryin' none about Farley. He couldn't win that election if he was runnin' against a dead man."

"I'm just worried about the cost of electioneerin'. Cigars don't come cheap."

As the two men rode away, a black farmhand came out of the cowshed carrying a bucket of fresh milk in each hand. Andy asked, "Want me to tote one of them up to the big house for you, Tobe?"

"I'd be obliged, Mr. Andy." The black workers called him *Mister,* though they used his given name. Tobe handed over one of the buckets. "That old brindle cow ain't givin' milk like she ought to. I'm afraid if Mr. Farley sees the bucket ain't full, he'll accuse me of quittin' too quick."

"I'll tell him she's dryin' up. She'll freshen when she has her calf."

It pleased him that some things were beyond Farley's control, like the succession of the seasons and life cycles of the animals.

Farley sat in a rocking chair on the porch. He did not even glance at the milk bucket. His voice was sharp.

"I seen Tom Blessing and Rusty out there talkin' to you. What did they want?"

Andy considered not telling him anything, but he decided perversely that Farley needed more to worry about. "They asked me if you're really figurin' to run for sheriff. I told them you are."

"What did they say?"

"Tom thought about quittin' at the end of this term." Andy waited for Farley's satisfied smile, then added, "Me and Rusty talked him out of it. We told him he'll win the race right handy."

Farley's smile vanished like the blowing out of a lamp. "Damn you, Badger Boy." He jumped up so quickly that the chair tipped and almost turned over on its side. One rocker thumped solidly upon the porch as it came back down.

Andy saw the fist but could not dodge it. He staggered backward, dropping the bucket. Milk splashed across the porch and spilled down the steps. For a moment Andy saw only sparkling lights. Then Farley's scarred face showed through them. Andy swung at it with all the force he could bring to bear. Farley fell back against the rocking chair, knocking it over with a loud clatter. Farley bawled in rage and rushed at Andy, swinging his fists like a windmill. One drove breath from Andy's lungs, but he managed to land a fist solidly against Farley's nose. Blood ran down Farley's lips and off his chin.

Andy heard a woman's anguished cry. He did not know whether it came from Bethel or Teresa. He struck Farley again and saw his brother-in-law sprawl backward on the porch.

Both young women stepped between them. Bethel

grabbed Andy's arms. Farley struggled to gain his feet. Teresa knelt over him, pushing against his shoulders to keep him down. Bethel scolded, "Back off, Andy. What do you think you're doing?"

Andy fought for breath. "Tryin' to show your brother . . . there's some things I won't take."

"But he's not a well man. That wound—"

"That wound is all healed up. He just leans on it like it was a crutch."

Teresa scolded her husband with the same sharpness Bethel had used. "Fighting like a schoolboy. Look at you, your face all bloody. Who struck first? No, don't tell me. I don't want to know."

Bethel said, "It makes no difference who struck first. It takes two to make a fight. Either one of you could have backed off."

Andy said, "I've been backin' off too long. I'm tired of it."

Bethel's eyes cut him like a blade. "And maybe you're tired of me, too."

Andy sobered quickly under the lash of her anger. "You know better than that. But some things get to be more than a man can stand still for."

Teresa let Farley get to his feet. He swayed like a cornstalk in the wind. She took his arm and led him toward the door. She said, "We're going out to the back porch and wash your face. Look at your knuckles, all skinned and bleeding."

Farley submitted to her will but gave Andy a smoldering glance before going inside. "This ain't over with."

Bethel forcibly guided Andy backward into the rocking chair. Her voice still crackled. "What am I going to do with you?"

"What are you goin' to do with your brother?"

Shaking her head, she went to the door. She paused long enough to say, "Give Farley time to get washed, then you come in and do the same. We'll have supper on the table pretty soon."

Andy was too angry to eat.

FIGHTING WAS MORE strenuous than plowing. By bedtime he was sore in muscles he did not know he had. He had skipped supper, fearing that anything he ate would probably come back up. Anyway, he did not care to sit at the same table as Farley. His stomach still churned after his temper had cooled. He sat rocking on the porch, listening to night birds chirping in the live-oak trees. He wished his life could be as simple as theirs seemed to be.

Bethel came out and sat on the edge of the porch, near enough for him to touch. He did not try, for he sensed that she was still provoked at him. The two sat in silence, close together, yet far apart. He wanted to speak to her, to say something that might quiet her overcharged emotions, but he could think of nothing that would not sound hollow. He had no intention of backing down.

Finally she said, "Maybe it'd be better if you left here awhile."

That surprised him, but he knew it should not. "Been thinkin' the same thing. I don't want to go by myself, though. I'd want you to go with me."

"You know I can't. There's Mother, and there's Farley."

"Yes, there's Farley. There'll always be Farley." Andy wished he could keep the sharpness from his voice, but he was not good at hiding what he felt.

"What can we do, then?"

"Nothin' much we *can* do. We're boxed into a corner. Farley's not fixin' to change, and I can't abide him ridin' me all the time. Looks like I'd best do what you said and leave."

She reached up and took his hands. "I didn't mean what I said. I don't want you to go."

"But you don't want me to stay either. If I do, there's bound to be another fight. Maybe several. Looks like there's no choice for me, but you've got one. You can go with me."

"You know the answer to that."

Andy felt an ache deep inside. "Then don't set a place for me at the breakfast table. I'll be gone by daylight."

She arose and sat in his lap, her arms around him. He felt her tears wet against his cheek. She whispered, "I love you, Andy."

"And I love you. But . . ." There was no point in repeating what he had already said. Though regret slashed him like a knife, he realized that neither could back away. Each had taken a stand. Pride demanded that both stay with it.

2

Neither Rusty nor Alice Shannon had made any comment about the bruise on Andy's cheek or the cut on his chin, but they must have seen them. Andy watched Alice rocking her baby boy in a cradle on the Shannon cabin's open dog run, where a gentle breeze toyed with the corner of the infant's blanket. Rusty and Andy sat on a hand-hewn bench against the log wall. Idly whittling on a stick and dropping thin shavings on the ground, Rusty said, "Old Shanty made that cradle. Said he built it to last for at least a dozen young'uns. Looks like me and Alice have got our work cut out for us." He glanced up at her with a shy grin.

Smiling, Alice scolded gently, "Rusty! We don't talk about such as that."

The smile caused Andy a fresh ache, for it was like Bethel's. He covered up by saying, "I've been too busy to go over and see about Shanty. How's he doin'?"

Shanty was a black farmer who had inherited a small piece of land between Rusty's place and the settlement.

Rusty said, "Pretty good, for his age. I go over and help him now and again when somethin' heavy comes up. And to make sure old Fowler Gaskin doesn't steal him blind. Shanty ain't forgotten that he was once a slave. He won't hardly speak up for himself against a white man. Not even a sorry reprobate like Fowler."

Gaskin was another neighbor. Any time he dropped by a farm, it behooved the owner to count his chickens and inventory his toolshed. He believed in the adage that God helps those who help themselves, and he frequently helped himself to whatever was not nailed down.

Andy said, "Ain't it about time Fowler died of old age?"

"I've been hopin' a rattlesnake might bite him, but I suppose they recognize their kin."

Frowning, Alice said, "He's a nasty old man. He hates Rusty and me."

Rusty explained, "He came borrowin' one day when he knew I was gone. He thought Alice would be easy to buffalo, but she tickled his ribs with the muzzle of a shotgun. He ain't been back."

Andy said, "If you'd shot him, no jury around here would convict you."

Rusty replied, "You never shoot a buzzard close to the house. It stinks too much." He abruptly changed the subject. "Now that you've left the Brackett farm, what're you goin' to do, Andy?"

"I don't know for sure. Been wantin' to go back out to the hill country, get me a place and run some cattle. I've saved up a little from my Ranger wages and what I earned on the farm, but it's not enough. I've thought about goin' up to the rollin' plains and seein' if the Monahan family could use some help. Maybe in a year or two . . ."

"You're welcome to stay here with us. I'll pay you for your help. That cabin we built for you once is still in good shape. Been usin' it for storage."

Andy knew Rusty's gesture was made out of kindness, not out of real need for help. "You've already got three mouths to feed. And there'll be more as time goes by."

Andy looked up at Alice. She said nothing, but he knew her need for that money was greater than his own. She had one baby, and there would be more. He said, "Thanks, Rusty, but I already owe you more than I could ever pay. You took me in and finished raisin' me even when my own kin turned their backs on me for my Indian ways."

"That's why I want to help. I've got a lot invested in you."

"I need to make my own way. Besides, I'm not like you. I can't see spendin' the rest of my life followin' a plow. I'd be miserable at it, and I'd make everybody around me miserable. Especially Bethel. It's better I leave her than to make her unhappy tryin' to be somethin' I'm not."

"Everybody has got to find his own road. Looks like you're meant to travel yours on horseback."

Andy nodded. "I can't help bein' what I am."

"Then live the way that fits you. There ain't money enough in the world to pay for spendin' your life at somethin' that makes you miserable." Rusty paused in his whittling. "You heard Tom say he could use another deputy."

"I appreciate his offer, but I need to get farther away, where I won't keep runnin' into Farley."

"There's always the Rangers."

"I've thought about that. I remember some good times with them, but I also remember how much blood I saw. A little of it was mine."

Rusty took a big slice from the stick he was whittling. "Well, if you ever need a place to come back to for a while, it's here."

Leading a pack mule, Andy rode to Shanty York's. A lanky, baying hound greeted him a couple of hundred yards out and escorted him in, announcing him all the way. Andy found the old man taking his ease in an ancient rocking chair beneath a brush arbor beside his one-room cabin. Andy had helped build that cabin after a mob of night riders had burned the original, trying to drive Shanty off his land. Shanty shouted at the dog, "Fowler, hush up that noise."

He was a small man, his shoulders hunched under the weight of his years. Though he addressed most white people as *Mister,* he had known Andy from the time he fell back into white hands after his years with the Comanches. Word by word, he had helped the lost and frightened boy to remember the native tongue he had almost forgotten.

"Andy! How do, boy," Shanty said, walking out and extending a wrinkled hand. To him, Andy was still a boy, though he was far into his twenties. "Been a while since you come to see this old wore-out bag of bones."

Andy said, "You know how it is for a farmer, always more to do than there's hours in the day."

Shanty studied Andy's pack mule with a critical eye. "Looks like you're fixin' to travel." He phrased it as a comment, but it was a question in disguise.

"Might be."

The old man looked thin enough for the sun to shine through him. Andy said, "You don't appear to've been eatin' regular."

"It was a long winter. Vittles got short. But I'll be pickin' stuff out of my garden patch pretty soon."

Shanty led Andy back to the shade. He motioned toward the rocking chair, but Andy took a bench instead.

HARD TRAIL TO FOLLOW   307

The old man studied him quietly, as if he were reading everything that was on Andy's mind. He said, "I'm just a wore-out farmer. Nobody ever comes to me for advice because if it was any good, I'd've took it myself and be better off."

Andy realized that Shanty was hinting for him to ask. He said, "Your advice has always been good enough for me."

"I been wonderin' how long it'd be before you and Mr. Farley come to a partin' of the ways. I hope there wasn't no shootin'."

Andy had not told him about their fight, but the bruise and cut spoke for themselves. Andy flexed a sore hand. "No shots fired. Just a little discussion."

"You love that girl enough to fight for her?"

"I did. That's how I came by these marks."

Shanty became pensive. "I had me a girl once, when I was young back in slave times. Trouble was, the field boss wanted her, too. He was bigger than an ox and meaner than a boar hog, but I fought him just the same."

"Whip him?"

"No, he gave me the beatin' of my life. But my girl felt sorry for me, and we jumped over the broomstick together. We had us a good life till they sold her down the river." Old memories brought sadness to his eyes. "Never seen her again, nor our child neither."

Andy wished he had something comforting to say, but nothing came. Feeling that his visit had only served to stir up painful old feelings for Shanty, he turned down an invitation to stay. Shanty had little enough for himself, much less food to share. Andy gave as an excuse that he needed to get on into town. He took the road that veered off to the river. He had gone but a mile or so when he heard a sudden snorting and shuffling of tiny hooves just ahead. Brush crackled as half a dozen wild hogs broke out of its cover.

Once this had been prime country for a deer hunter, but most of the larger wildlife had been killed out or driven farther away as the area settled up. Feral hogs, descended from strays lost by early farmers, still ranged along the river, unmarked and unclaimed. People around here routinely killed them for meat, but this was something Shanty could not or would not do. He feared someone would claim ownership and put up a holler. A few among his neighbors still resented that he was a black landowner and felt he was not entitled to share in the land's bounty. One was Fowler Gaskin.

Andy dropped the rope that led the pack animal. He drew his pistol and spurred his horse into a run, circling to get in front of the fleeing animals. He brought the horse to a quick stop, leaned down, and aimed almost point-blank at a fat shoat.

Squealing, it stumbled but did not fall immediately. It ran beneath Andy's horse, setting it into a nervous frenzy and forcing Andy to pull hard on the reins. The wounded pig followed the others for several yards before it went down. When he brought his mount under control, Andy rode up close and put another bullet behind the pig's ear to make certain.

The horse's nervousness was compounded by the smell of blood and gunpowder. Andy waited until the other hogs had clattered off out of sight before he rode back to pick up the pack animal. He looked in all directions before he dismounted. Now and again wild hogs went on the offensive. They could do serious damage, especially boars with long tusks. He gutted the shoat, then lifted it up onto the pack animal. The mule resisted the new burden.

"Hold still, damn it," Andy said as he tied the pig into place. "You'll carry it if I have to kill you."

He rode back to Shanty's and reined up in front of a small smokehouse behind the cabin. He said, "Look what I found a little ways down the river."

Shanty worried, "I hope it wasn't wearin' no mark. Somebody might come lookin' for a piece of my hide."

"No mark. If anybody asks you about it, tell them to come talk to me."

Once they finished cutting up the shoat, Andy said, "Better nail your smokehouse door shut. Fowler Gaskin may come callin'."

The hound whimpered and begged until Shanty fed him a strip of fat. Andy said, "Did I hear you call that dog Fowler?"

"They's some resemblance. Fool dog is always nosin' around where he's got no business, and he'll steal if you take your eyes off of him. If I had the heart to do it, I'd shoot him."

"The man, or the dog?"

"The dog. It's the Lord's business what happens to the man. I always pray for them that torments me. I pray that the Lord will turn Mr. Gaskin from his sinnin' ways and help him find peace when he gets to heaven."

"The sooner he leaves on that trip, the better. Except I doubt heaven is anxious to see him. He's more apt to go the other direction."

"The Lord must have some purpose for the wicked, or else he wouldn't have made so many of them." The dog showed continued interest in the pig. Shanty shooed it away, though it did not retreat far. "Late as it is, you'd just as well stay and share supper with me. After all, you brung the meat."

The sun was already half-hidden behind timber to the west. Andy said, "I guess there's no need ridin' to town in the dark."

Shanty smiled. "We'll have us a time, talkin' about the good old days."

"They weren't all good."

"We don't have to talk about the bad ones. They's past and gone."

"Not all of them."

Andy saw no purpose in burdening Shanty with his problems, but the old man saw through his evasion. He said, "Maybe if you'd try again, you and that little woman could patch things up."

"I didn't say I was leavin' her."

"You got a powerful lot of stuff tied on that pack mule."

"I'm not goin' for good. At least, I don't mean to be. I've just got to put some miles between me and Farley Brackett for a while. Else they'll be huntin' one of us down for a killin'."

"Good Book says to turn the other cheek."

"I tried that. I only got two."

The cabin was too small for Andy to sleep on the floor, and he declined an offer of Shanty's cot. He spread his blankets beneath the brush arbor, but he did not go to sleep at first. He kept seeing Bethel and hearing her voice. He was tempted to get up and go back to her. But he kept hearing and seeing Farley Brackett, too. And he kept feeling his hands cramp on the plow handles.

Sometime during the night the hound's barking awakened him. Andy thought some varmint was probably after Shanty's chickens, a fox maybe, or a coon. He lifted the pistol from the holster lying by his head. He discerned

that the dog was near the chicken house, telling the news
in full voice. In the moonlight Andy saw the outline of a
man fumbling with the door that led in to the roosts. He
doubted it was Shanty.

"What you doin' out there?" he shouted.

Startled, the man froze for a second, then hunched
over and set off in a run. His movement reminded Andy
of a spider. Almost certain who it was, Andy squeezed
off one shot into the air. In a moment he heard a horse
galloping away. The direction told him he had identified
the man correctly.

Shanty came out of the cabin barefoot and in his
underwear. "What kind of a varmint was it, Andy?"

"A two-legged one by the name of Fowler Gaskin. Figured on havin' him a chicken dinner."

"I reckon his cupboard is most as empty as mine. He
comes borrowin' from time to time, in the dark. He's got
eyes like a cat."

"Or a skunk." Andy's initial anger drained slowly as
he contemplated the scare he had given the old scoundrel. "He's liable to have to wash his britches when he
gets home."

Shanty said, "The only time his clothes gets washed
is when he gets caught in the rain."

SHERIFF TOM BLESSING listened with a poorly disguised
smile as Andy told about the nocturnal prowler. "Sounds
like Fowler, all right. Did he get away with anything?"

"I didn't give him the chance."

"Best I could do is charge him with trespass, and you'd
have to prove it was really him. Even if he'd got away
with a chicken, Shanty'd have to prove it was his. Nobody
brands chickens."

"Fowler could have plenty of meat without havin' to steal it. He could go out and hunt wild hogs if he wasn't too low-down lazy."

"Shanty would say that the Lord puts people like Fowler here to test our religion, same as he gives us flies and ticks and scorpions." Tom shrugged off the subject. "I hope you've come to ask me about that deputy job."

"No. It'd be somethin' to do for a while, but I need to get farther away."

"It'd look tame compared to the time you spent with the Rangers, and it'd pay about as well. I'd be pleased for you to sleep in the jailhouse if you ain't particular about the company."

Andy was weakening. "Couldn't be worse than Farley."

Tom frowned. "You ain't met my newest guest. Come and let me introduce you to Luther Cordell."

The jail had only a few small cells, for this was mostly a law-abiding farm community. Hunched on the edge of a steel cot, Cordell reminded Andy of a large, shaggy bear. He looked like a tramp who might have hopped from a boxcar and tumbled down the grade. His shirt was dirty and frayed at the cuffs, one elbow out. His trousers were streaked with the grime of hard travel. His hair was tangled, and his face had not felt razor or comb in weeks. A dark beard obscured most of his facial features. However, Andy was drawn by the intensity of the man's eyes. They were like large black buttons that seemed to look through Andy and focus beyond him.

Tom said, "You'd think a man that robs banks could dress better and get himself a haircut."

Cordell's voice was like a dry cowhide dragged over gravel. "Can't afford to. I invested most of my money in whiskey and sweet-smellin' women. What went with the rest of it, I don't know. Just frittered it away, I suppose."

Tom said, "When the Rangers come for you, the state'll give you a haircut and a brand-new set of clothes."

"That'll be nice. It ain't often anybody gives me anything without I persuade them first."

"At the point of a gun?"

"That cuts down on conversation. Most people talk too much." Cordell's gaze drifted to Andy. "That's a likely lookin' young feller. What's he in for?"

Tom said, "He's an old friend of mine. I'm tryin' to talk him into bein' a deputy."

"He couldn't be sorrier than the one you've got. A lot of the time he snores so loud I can't even talk to myself. You'd best get a better guard if you don't want me to sneak out of here."

Andy imagined how it would be to fight hand to hand with Cordell. The man must outweigh him by fifty pounds, most of it muscle and bone. Very little was fat. Cordell was larger than the sheriff and appeared solid as an oak.

Andy said, "I hope you didn't have to fight with him, Tom."

"No, caught him by blind luck. I rode out to talk to Fowler Gaskin about a complaint. Cordell and Fowler had emptied a bottle together and was both sleepin' it off. Took him without a struggle."

Cordell grumbled, "I've always been cursed by a streak of kindness. I felt sorry for that poor old man and shared my whiskey with him."

Tom said, "We know that *poor old man*. He would've stole it off of you if he could. Folks around here quit feelin' sorry for Fowler Gaskin a long time ago."

"I'll remember that the next time my kind streak starts actin' up." Cordell belched. "Damn beans. You need a new cook as much as you need a new deputy. Next jail I'm in, I hope it'll serve better groceries."

"I eat the same grub when I can't go home."

"You get paid for it."

"Not enough. But at least this jail is new. Our old jail burned down."

"I may set a match to this one, too, when I leave."

Tom said, "You're not goin' anyplace, not till the Rangers come for you."

"At least I like the company here. For a sheriff, you're a pretty good feller."

Tom led Andy back out of hearing range. He said, "I like Cordell in spite of myself. He's more pleasure to talk to than most of the people I lock up in here. I just wish he wasn't a bank robber."

Tom himself was one of the most likable men Andy had ever known. He probably gave away half of his salary to people he saw in need.

Andy said, "Everybody has got some weakness. I guess Cordell's is banks. But you don't need me to help you guard him. An elephant couldn't bust out of here. They built this jail stout enough to stand up under a Galveston hurricane."

"He's busted out of others. Got a reputation for bein' hard to keep in a coop." Tom rummaged in a desk drawer and brought out a badge. "I wish you'd take this." He handed it to Andy. Tarnished, it said *City of San Antonio*. Andy figured the county was saving money by reusing what someone else had discarded.

"Sorry, Tom." He handed back the badge.

Tom argued, "I'd see to it that the commissioners'

court treats you right when it comes to pay. I've got a little dirt on most of them."

Andy said, "I appreciate the offer just the same."

"I done it for me more than for you. I ain't spent a night at the farm since I've had Cordell behind these bars. He talks pleasant, but I know he's slippery."

"Not too slippery for you to catch him."

"He was drunk."

A skinny young man with sleepy eyes walked through the door. He seemed momentarily startled at seeing the sheriff. "Tom. I wasn't gone but just a minute. Thought I heard a noise and stepped out to see."

Tom retorted, "That was your snorin'." To Andy he said, "This is Speck Munson. Speck, meet Andy Pickard. I was just offerin' him a job as a deputy."

Munson's thin face fell. "Does this mean I'm fired?"

"Not yet, but it means I'm thinkin' about it, so watch you don't aggravate me. Looks like Cordell's slop jar needs emptyin'."

Munson said a reluctant "Yes, sir" and fetched a set of keys from the sheriff's desk. He walked to Cordell's cell door.

Tom demanded, "What the hell do you think you're doin'?"

"You told me to empty the slop jar."

"Not till you've handcuffed him. I've told you a dozen times. Make him slip his hands through the bars first."

Cordell extended his arms, one hand on either side of a bar. Munson locked the handcuffs over his wrists, securing the prisoner to the cell door.

Tom muttered to Andy, "See the kind of help I been gettin'?"

"He's not used to workin' with men of Cordell's caliber."

"He just ain't used to *workin'*."

Andy watched Munson carry the jar, holding it at arm's length and turning his head away from the smell. Munson complained, "Tom, we're feedin' him way too much."

He returned in a while. He locked the cell door, then unlocked the handcuffs. Cordell faked a quick grab at him through the bars. Munson jumped as if a rattlesnake had struck. He dropped the cuffs.

Cordell's black eyes danced with laughter. "Like to've got you that time."

Munson was shaking as he laid the cuffs on Tom's desk. Tom said, "He's baitin' you for fun, but maybe that'll teach you to keep both eyes open. When he sees a real chance, he won't be funnin'."

Andy said, "When I was a Ranger, I used to study criminals and try to decide what makes them that way."

"Ever figure it out?"

"Never did."

"Some people are natural sons of bitches from the day they're born. Others learn it along the way. As far as we know, Cordell has never killed anybody. He probably carried flowers home to his mama."

Andy leaned against the bars across the aisle from Cordell and gave the man a long, silent study. Cordell stood it for a while, but Andy's staring finally got to him. He asked, "What's so interestin'?"

"You. I was wonderin' what you'd look like with a shave and a haircut and the dirt washed off."

Cordell grunted. "I've got a face that'd break a mirror. I keep it covered up with whiskers so as to not shock the public."

Andy spent the night on a hard cot in an empty cell. It would have cost him four bits to sleep in the wagon yard, a privilege he denied himself but allowed for his horse and pack mule. Tom had a cot near the jail's front door, but his sleepy eyes indicated that he had not slept much. He took out his pocket watch and frowned at it. "High time Speck was here to take over and let us go for some breakfast."

It was a while before Speck Munson showed up at the door, carrying a tray with the prisoner's morning meal.

Tom said, "I was about to send out a posse for you."

"The rooster slept late."

The smell of coffee made Andy realize he was hungry. "Still takin' your meals across the street?"

Tom nodded. "When I have to stay in town of a night. Once I get Cordell off of my hands, I'm goin' out to the farm and stayin' for a week. I intend to debauch myself on my wife's peach preserves."

"Maybe it's time you *did* retire. You could stay out there from now on."

"Don't think it ain't been on my mind, but I don't like leavin' the office in Farley Brackett's hands. I ain't sure he's the man for it."

Andy could not argue that point.

The restaurant's biscuits had been baked an hour or more already and kept in a warming oven long enough to dry them out. The eggs were burned along the edges, and the bacon had been fried to tastelessness. The kitchen badly needed a woman's influence. Andy pitied Tom, having to put up with this day after day.

He had finished his eggs and was sipping his bitter black coffee when a farmer rushed into the restaurant. "Sheriff, somethin' don't look right over at the jailhouse."

Tom was instantly on his feet. "What?"

"I seen a man go in the door. Another is waitin' outside

with some horses. Acts nervous, like he's standin' watch."

Tom exclaimed, "Speck wasn't supposed to let anybody in there." He was out the door before Andy could free himself from the table. He started to run after Tom but realized he had left his pistol in his bedroll to avoid carrying it into the jail. He sprinted to the wagon yard, past a startled hostler, and found his saddle on a rack where he had left it. He jerked his rifle from its scabbard and set off in a fast trot.

He heard gunfire from inside the jail. Two men burst through the door. One he recognized instantly as Cordell. The other man snapped a quick shot at Andy, kicking up dust. Andy dropped to one knee and brought up the rifle. He sighted on Cordell, but a horseman hurried up, leading two riderless mounts. He moved in the way of Andy's bullet and almost fell from the saddle before regaining his balance. Cordell shouted something Andy could not understand. The three set their mounts into a hard run, rounding the corner of the jail, putting it between themselves and Andy. He had no chance for another shot.

Holding his breath, Andy rushed into the jail. Speck Munson lay curled in a heap, an ugly bruise on the side of his head. In the center of the room, Tom was sprawled on his stomach, a pool of blood spreading around him. Calling his name in a choking voice, Andy grasped the sheriff's shoulder and turned him over. A bullet had nicked the badge on its way in.

Tom was in a bad way.

The wooden floor shook as other men came pounding into the room, shouting questions. Andy did not look up at them. Tears blinded him, burning his eyes.

"Damn it, Tom," he murmured. "Damn it."

The wagon-yard hostler said, "I'll go for the doctor."

Andy tried to get a grip on his surging emotions. "I'm goin' after Cordell and whoever's with him."

Several men indicated they intended to join him. Andy said, "Anybody who wants to go with me, meet me at the wagon yard."

He picked up his rifle and rushed out to saddle his horse.

3

Luther Cordell should have been grateful for his release, but instead he showed a crackling anger. "Damn you, Milt, you didn't have to shoot that sheriff. You could've just clubbed him like you done the deputy."

Milt Hayward was a large man like Cordell, broad shoulders hunched a little, his heavy-featured face flushed in defensive response. "He was blockin' the door. I didn't have all day to make up my mind. How come you didn't holler about me shootin' that Galveston banker?"

"You nicked him just enough to make him mad. Anyway, nobody's goin' to miss a banker much, or a lawyer. But kill a lawman and you've got every Ranger and two-bit local sheriff in the state gettin' a rope ready for you. For all three of us."

Irony edged Milt's voice. "Maybe you want to go back and apologize."

"I doubt them folks are in a listenin' frame of mind." Cordell turned to the kid who trailed behind them. "How bad are you hit, Buster?"

Buster Jones wasn't his real name, but it served as a convenient substitute for the name his mother had given him. He was bent over his saddlehorn, arms tight against his body as if holding in the pain. "Not bad enough for you-all to go off and leave me."

"Only a rattlesnake would do that. Hang on till we're in the clear. Then we'll stop and look at that wound."

They pushed their horses hard, bent on putting as much distance behind them as possible in the first minutes. They had little chance to hide their tracks, but they were on a well-beaten trail where the dirt was soft. Perhaps their tracks would be hard to differentiate from the many others already there.

They had covered three miles. Cordell saw nobody coming up behind them. "We better stop and take care of Buster."

Milt objected, "Them people are bound to be after us by now. That kid'll get us caught sure as hell."

"The kid didn't need to've got shot at all. It was a hare-brained idea, breakin' me out. You know I always manage to bust loose by myself. I was just bidin' time till that sleepy-headed deputy got careless."

"Then you'd've snuck back and dug up the bank money. You'd've kept it all for yourself and cut me plumb out."

Cordell grunted. "You don't trust me much."

"I ain't trusted anybody since I was six, and my old daddy whipped me with the buckle end of his belt. Soon as I get my share, I'm gone. Then you can ride to hell and out the far side as far as I'm concerned."

Cordell had never understood the greed that led a man to put money ahead of loyalty to those who rode with him. In this case he attributed it to a poor upbringing. Milt's sour manner kept him from cultivating friends. Associates in crime, but not friends.

Got weaned from his mama's milk too early, Cordell thought. *Probably brought up on poke salad and clabber.*

They stopped in the shade of a live-oak tree. Cordell and Buster dismounted. Milt remained in the saddle, where he had a better view of their back trail. Buster was a freckle-faced, gap-toothed kid of nineteen or twenty with a better upbringing than Milt's. The wound was low in his shoulder. A little farther over and the bullet would have hit him in the heart.

His face was drained from shock, making his freckles stand out like speckles of brown paint. His voice was anxious. "Is it goin' to hurt much, Luther?"

"Naw, I got a touch lighter than ary woman's." He opened Buster's shirt and pulled it down off his shoulder. He poked around the wound while Buster flinched and made hissing sounds. Cordell said, "Bullet's still in there, and it looks like it busted the bone. This ain't the time or place to try and dig it out. Wisht I had some whiskey to pour in that hole."

Milt reached in his saddlebag. He pitched a pint bottle to Cordell. "I paid dear for this stuff. Don't waste it."

"I won't." Cordell took a long drink and handed it to Buster so he could do the same. "This might smart a little," he said, and poured most of the remaining whiskey into the wound. Buster shouted loudly enough to be heard back in town. The bottle was nearly empty when Cordell pitched it back. Milt looked as if he had just bitten into a buzzard's supper. "Damn you, Luther, I told you this stuff was hard to come by."

Taking a sweat-stained silk neckerchief from his neck, Cordell tied it around Buster's shoulder and under his arm. "I ain't one to shovel out a lot of advice, boy, but this ought to make you think about findin' a better way to make a livin'."

Buster groaned.

Cordell continued the lecture. "For every night I've slept in a bed, I've laid on the ground a hundred times. Right now I ain't got twenty dollars in my pocket, hardly. You-all busted in before I finished breakfast, and I ain't likely to get dinner or supper either. Yes, sir, this kind of life has sure been good to me. I'd trade it in a minute for forty acres and a mule."

Milt demanded, "Are we goin' to talk all day, or are we travelin'?"

Cordell frowned. "Nobody likes a grouch."

"And I don't like the idea of a rope necktie. Let's go pick up that money and get the hell away from here."

Cordell's goal was a badly deteriorated log cabin that appeared almost ready to slump to the ground. Pressed by a posse, the three had split up after visiting the bank in Galveston. Cordell had been carrying the money. The day had been late and the clouds threatening rain the evening he had come across the cabin by chance. He had confronted a wizened old man who called himself Gaskin. At first he had all the charm of a snake with its rattles pinched off, but he had softened when Cordell offered to share a bottle of whiskey in return for a night's shelter from the rain.

While Gaskin was immersed in whiskey, Cordell had hidden his saddlebags in the bottom of the old man's woodbox, along with the proceeds from his latest venture into banking. He had figured on being up and gone the next morning before Gaskin woke up.

That farmer sheriff ought to have been out feeding his chickens or plowing his field. Instead, he had shown up while Cordell was fighting the worst hangover he had suffered in a long time. He had no chance to retrieve the bags or find a better hiding place. Perhaps Gaskin had not discovered them yet. The old reprobate had struck Cordell as one who did not cook much for himself but lived mostly on whiskey and tobacco. Maybe he had not dug out enough firewood yet to expose the treasure.

He said, "Ain't nobody but an old man where I left the

saddlebags. I doubt he'll give us much trouble. Even if he does, Milt, I don't want you shootin' him. One man today is enough."

"What have you got to bitch about? We broke you out of jail."

"I kind of liked that sheriff. Them people back there thought a right smart of him, too."

"Maybe he ain't dead."

"You'd better be prayin' that he's not."

"I tried prayin' when I was a young'un. Nobody answered. Get me my share of that money and I won't need God or the devil either one."

Getting shed of Milt could not come soon enough for Cordell. The last thing a man needed in this line of business was to ride with such a reckless misfit. The only reason they were together was that he thought he needed someone with more maturity than Buster. But Milt had not grown up; he had just grown older.

As best Cordell remembered, Gaskin's shack should be a little way ahead. He had purposely avoided describing the place or the man for fear that Milt would decide to try taking all the money. That would be three times better than a one-third cut.

Milt shouted a curse. "Damn the luck, here they come!"

Cordell twisted in the saddle. He saw seven or eight riders a few hundred yards behind, pushing hard to catch up. For a moment he considered making a try for the bank loot in spite of the odds. He gave up the notion with reluctance. "We can't stop for that money now."

Buster lagged behind. Milt cursed again. "We'd've had time if you hadn't farted around patchin' up that kid. He's goin' to die anyway. I can tell by lookin' at him. I say we go off and leave him."

"You don't quit a partner."

"You do when it's your neck. I ain't gettin' hung for him nor anybody else." Milt broke away and turned south, quirting his horse at every stride.

Cordell ground his teeth in frustration but decided Milt's desertion was probably for the best. Cordell had had to do most of the thinking for this outfit anyway. And Milt's defection meant a larger split for himself. "Hang on tight, Buster. We'll head for the river. Maybe we can lose them in the brush."

He heard a pistol shot from behind. *Some chuckle-headed farmer,* he thought, *wasting lead.* The range was too great for accuracy, but the sound encouraged him to spur harder. Somebody back there might have a rifle and the presence of mind to dismount and take good aim. Firing from a running horse was about as useless as teats on a boar hog. He had run from enough hastily formed citizen posses to know that most gave up when they found themselves getting far from home. With a little luck he and Buster should outlast this one.

They reached the river at a point where the timber was thick, heavily choked with underbrush. He considered swimming across, but the river looked wide and deep. The pursuers might catch up while the horses were swimming. He and Buster would be easy targets. Chances were, he thought, that the posse would expect him to keep going west, upriver, the direction he had been running. He cut back to the east, into the heaviest underbrush he could find. He helped Buster down from the saddle and held his hands over the two horses' noses to keep them from nickering at those of the posse.

Buster groaned. Cordell said, "Quiet. Don't even breathe heavy."

He could see little through the brush, but he heard the riders talking, shouting, crashing through the thick undergrowth. For a time they seemed to be coming toward Cordell and Buster, then they turned away. Cordell had had no chance to conceal the trail. He hoped there was not a good tracker in the bunch.

He whispered, "Sounds like they're goin' off from us, but we'd better stay put for a while. How you makin' out?"

Buster was not making out well at all. Ashen-faced and trembling, he whimpered, "Oh, God, I didn't know it'd hurt like this." Cordell knew that sometimes a bullet could do a lot of damage even without striking a vital spot. Shock alone could kill.

He had nearly ten thousand dollars hidden away, and right now there was not a thing it could do to help this boy.

ANDY WAS ANGRY with himself. Many people assumed that because of the years he had lived among the Comanches, he should be a good tracker. The men who rode with him had tacitly delegated the tracking to him. The truth was that he had no particular skill at it. He had known Indians who could track an eagle's flight across the water, but that knack had always eluded him. Farley Brackett had once told him he couldn't track an elephant through a cornfield.

He could no longer find the trail of the fugitives. He had seen where one split off. A couple of possemen followed those tracks. Andy and three others tried to follow the two men who had remained together. Andy lost the trail when it led into timber along the river.

He said, "Too much vegetation. And hogs've rooted through here. They've torn up the ground."

Joe Yates was a blacksmith by trade, not a lawman. He had hurriedly saddled a horse he had just shod and had not even taken time to hunt for his hat. Sweat rolled down from the top of his balding head. He suggested, "Maybe somebody livin' around here saw them."

Andy had a nagging feeling that the fugitives were close by, but these thickets could hide the elephant Farley had talked about. He said, "Shanty York's cabin is a little ways up yonder. He might be able to tell us somethin'."

Yates said, "That darky's gettin' so old he probably can't tell a horse from a cow at thirty yards."

"There's a lot of life in him yet."

Shanty came out of the cabin, pressing one hand against the small of his back to lessen the pain of his rheumatism. He listened to Andy's description of the men, then shook his head. "I done all my doin' in the cool of the mornin'. Been laid up since dinner with this misery along my ribs. Ain't seen nobody."

Andy was disappointed but not surprised. It stood to reason that Cordell would avoid dwellings where somebody might see him. Andy said, "If they come around, tell them what they want to hear and give them whatever they want. They're too dangerous for you to mess with."

"I'll be meek as a lamb. I already inherited my piece of the earth. I aim to keep livin' on it as long as the Lord lets me."

Riding away, Yates said, "How would he know about the meek inheritin' the earth? That's out of the Bible. He can't read."

"I doubt there's a page in the Book that somebody like old Preacher Webb ain't read to him. He don't forget much."

Biscuits Vanderpool operated the restaurant where Andy had almost had breakfast. He had been squirming for a while, a sign that the saddle was chapping his rump. He said, "My horse is about give out. And I got to get back and start fixin' supper for my customers."

Andy looked toward the lowering sun and shrugged. "I reckon we've all run our horses farther than we ought to. I'll make a fresh start in the mornin' and see if I can cut their trail someplace."

Yates said, "You're not a Ranger anymore. You've got no authority to arrest anybody."

"A six-shooter has authority of its own, and any citizen can make an arrest."

"Think you have a chance of catchin' them?"

"Not much. They'll likely be halfway across the next county before daylight."

Vanderpool said, "That's what the telegraph is for. I expect by now the word has gone out to every lawman in a hundred miles."

The telegraph had become a valuable asset to law enforcement. Andy had read about a new gadget supposed to allow people actually to talk to someone miles away instead of sending out written messages by code. He would have to see one to believe it. There had to be a limit to how many more new things inventors could think up. There wasn't room for them, and most people couldn't afford them anyway.

Even in the heat of the chase, there had seldom been a minute that he had not thought about Tom Blessing. Now, returning to town empty-handed, he could think of little else. "I feel like I've let Tom down."

Yates said, "It wasn't any more your responsibility than it was ours. Ain't none of us really lawmen."

"Tom tried to hire me as a deputy. Maybe if I'd agreed, things would've turned out different."

Vanderpool said, "A man can drive himself crazy thinkin' about what might have been. You've got to live with what was and is."

4

ordell moved nearer to the edge of the thicket so he could observe the open ground beyond. He saw horsemen a couple of times, probably part of the posse that had chased him. Not until dusk did he help Buster onto his horse and venture out of the brush. Even then he held close to it in case they had to make a hasty retreat. After riding a mile or so he saw a cabin. At first he thought it might be Gaskin's, but he realized that the old man's place was farther from the river.

No telling who lives there, he thought, *but I've got no choice.* Buster stood a strong chance of dying on him if they kept riding. He drew back into the timber as he saw four horsemen leave the cabin. He watched tensely, hoping they had not seen him. The men kept riding in the general direction of town. He expelled a pent-up breath. That had been too close.

He saw a positive side, however. What better place to seek refuge than where the posse had just been?

He said, "Hang on, Buster. Maybe we can pass the night here, at least."

It was a simple one-room log cabin, with a smokehouse, chicken house, a couple of log corrals, and a long shed off to one side. A garden showed evidence of hard work, its rows neatly hoed. Plants of several kinds were showing themselves, though none were yet mature enough to yield.

Cordell had always respected good farmers, though boyhood on a hardscrabble Louisiana cotton farm had left him looking for a life without all that sweat and heavy lifting. He had thought there must be an easier way to make a living. There might be, but this was not it. That old cotton farm looked a lot better in hindsight.

Smoke rose from the rock chimney, a sign somebody was fixing supper. The thought made his stomach rumble. A dog came out, wagging its tail and barking a greeting. Cordell drew a pistol he had grabbed as he left the jail. It was not his own, but with the other offenses he had committed, theft of a firearm seemed no more than a misdemeanor. He hollered, "Hello the house."

The door opened inward. An old black man peered out. He said, "You-all a little late. The rest of the posse done been and gone."

A darky! Cordell grimaced in disappointment. He had assumed from the well-kept appearance of the place that its owner was white. "This your farm?" he asked, doubting that it was.

"Yes, sir. It ain't a whole lot, but it's mine."

Cordell briefly considered moving on, but Buster badly needed to stop. He asked, "You got a name?"

"Yes, sir, it's Shanty. Shanty York."

"Me and the boy here, we need shelter for the night. And somethin' to eat."

He thought he saw realization come into the old man's eyes. The posse had probably described the fugitives enough that he recognized the pair. Shanty said, "They's just the two of you?"

"Just us. You got anybody else in there with you?"

"Ain't nobody here but me." Despite obvious misgivings, the old man opened the door wider. "You-all come on in. I'll put your horses in the pen yonder."

"I'll take care of them myself." It struck him that Shanty might get on one of the horses and run after the posse.

Cordell was strong, known to bend horseshoes. He eased Buster down from the saddle by himself. "The boy's hurt. Help me get him inside."

Shanty looked too frail to be of much help, but he lent what support he could. "All I got is that old cot yonder."

"That'll have to do. Find me some clean cloth in place of this dirty neckerchief. Got any whiskey?"

"No, sir, I don't hold with it."

"I thought all darkies loved whiskey."

"Not this one. A man never knows when his time might come. I don't want Saint Peter to smell whiskey on my breath."

"I wasn't thinkin' about drinkin' it. I need to wash Buster's wound, then see if I can dig the bullet out."

"I got somethin' the doctor give me a while back when I cut myself with the carvin' knife." Shanty fetched a dark bottle from an open cupboard shelf. Cordell pulled Buster's shirt down and removed the bloodied neckerchief with which he had wrapped the wound. The bullet hole was red and inflamed around the edges. Buster cried out as the disinfectant set fire to him. Cordell had to hold him down.

Shanty said, "Looks bad."

"He needs a doctor."

"There's Dr. Smith in town. I could go fetch him."

"And fetch the law while you're at it? You know who we are, don't you?"

Shanty was hesitant in answering. "I figure you're

the ones Andy and them are lookin' for. They say you-all shot Sheriff Blessing. I wisht you hadn't. He's a fine man."

Shanty had a small fire going. Cordell opened the blade of his pocketknife and held it over the flames until the burning was too much for him to stand. He smelled the hair singe on the back of his hand. "You hold him down the best you can." To Buster he said, "Grit your teeth. This ain't goin' to be no Saturday-night dance."

Buster cried out as Cordell probed for the bullet. The boy lunged forward, almost breaking free of Shanty's weak grip. Sweat broke out on Cordell's forehead and ran down to sting his eyes. Buster continued to cry. Blood welled up and spilled from the wound.

Shanty said, "You ain't no doctor. You're fixin' to kill him."

Cordell withdrew the blade. His hands were trembling. He realized he was doing more harm than good. He wiped a sleeve across his forehead and felt his throat tighten. "You're right. This ain't no good." In helpless frustration he threw the open knife across the room and clenched his fists.

Shanty stanched the blood flow with a folded cloth. He said, "That bullet'll kill him if it stays in there. You'd ought to take him to Dr. Smith."

Cordell snapped, "I can't do it, old man, don't you see? They're liable to hang him." He immediately regretted the outburst. None of this was Shanty's fault. It was Milt's, and it was Cordell's for allowing himself to be caught and jailed like a Saturday-night drunk. He could not fault Buster, for the kid was too green to have realized the possible consequences.

Shanty said, "Maybe they wouldn't hang him, not if he wasn't the one done the shootin'."

Cordell rubbed a huge, bloody hand across his whiskered face. "God, if I could just turn back the time. I ought to've made him go home, even if I'd had to take a whip to him."

"Boys his age can be mighty willful. Might be he'd've just gone off with somebody else and done the same thing."

"But he didn't. He went with *me*."

Carefully Shanty wrapped Buster's wound.

Cordell said, "We didn't mean for nobody to get hurt. The fool that did the shootin' ain't with us no more." He wondered why he felt compelled to explain anything to an old black man who was almost certainly at the bottom of the community's social ladder. "Did they say the sheriff is dead?"

"No, sir, all they knowed was that he was hurt plenty bad. He might've gone to glory by now, though."

"That sure would be tough luck for me." Without consciously willing it, Cordell reached up and touched his throat. He imagined the feel of a rope around it. "Are you a prayin' man, Shanty?"

"I thank the Lord every mornin' that I can wake up and get out of bed."

"Him and me ain't well acquainted. I hope you'll pray for that sheriff. And this boy, too."

"Done done it. But I'll do it some more."

They left Buster lying on the cot. Shanty fried up some pork. Buster could not eat, so Cordell finished it. The old man's wrinkled black hands shook with nervousness. Cordell assured him, "We don't mean you no harm. We'll be gone come daylight."

"You're goin' on, then? With the boy in this shape?"

"Nothin' else we can do."

Cordell figured Shanty was likely to take advantage of

any opportunity to get out of the cabin and run. He spread a blanket on the floor against the door so Shanty could not slip out. He dozed off and on but did not let himself fall into deep sleep. In dawn's pale light Buster's wound looked worse.

Cordell asked him, "Think you'll be able to ride today?"

Buster nodded. His voice was so weak that Cordell heard the sound, but not the words. He said, "We've got to move. Somebody's liable to show up."

Shanty said, "He don't look like he's got much breath left in him. He'd ought to stay here."

It crossed Cordell's mind that the old man might be thinking of a potential reward. But he reconsidered, for Shanty seemed genuinely concerned. Cordell stepped through the door and looked into the sunrise. He saw no one. "I believe you mean well, but there's too many people lookin' for us that don't have good intentions. Soon as we've et some breakfast, me and Buster will be on our way."

He saddled the horses and led them to the cabin. He helped Buster to his feet, but the youth could not stand alone. He slumped back onto the cot.

Shanty said, "He'll die if you make him ride."

"Them people from town are liable to kill him if he doesn't."

Shanty argued, "I don't think so. They're good folks, most of them. Leave him here with me. Soon's you've got away, I'll go and fetch the doctor."

Cordell was slow in making up his mind. Either choice tore at his conscience. To keep riding might kill Buster. On the other hand, angry posses had been known to exact summary justice at the end of a rope. Cordell had had a couple of close calls of that sort himself. Buster was too young to have his life snatched away from him in such a sudden and brutal manner. He had not had time to sample many of the world's pleasures. So far as Cordell knew, the boy had not even known the wonder of being with a warm and willing girl.

Guilt lay heavy on Cordell's conscience. He had seen something of his own younger self in the misguided kid. After the first time he had reluctantly allowed Buster to go along on a foray, it had been increasingly easy to keep saying yes.

Staring down into the fevered face, he made his decision. "I'll leave him with you for now, but don't send for the doctor yet. I'll be back."

"If the posse comes again, they'll see his horse. Everybody knows I ain't got one."

"I'll lead him down to the river and stake him on grass where nobody is apt to spot him."

Mounted, Cordell took the second horse's reins. To Shanty he said, "You're a good and decent man. I wish I had some money to give you, but I don't right now."

"You don't owe me nothin'. I just don't want to think about that boy dyin' out on the trail. It ain't a fit way to meet his maker."

Cordell turned in the saddle. "One last thing. Do you know an old man named Gaskin?"

"Yes, sir, I'm afraid I know the gentleman."

"Whichaway is his place from here?"

Shanty pointed. "Was I you, I'd pass him by."

"How come?"

"I was taught not to speak bad about folks, but Mr. Gaskin is a sinful man. If he thought there was any reward out on you, he'd turn you in for two dollars."

"Would *you* turn me in? Or Buster?"

"If they was to come right out and ask me, I couldn't

lie. It'd be against the Book. But if they don't ask me, I don't see where I got to tell them anything."

"That's good enough."

As Cordell rode away, it crossed his mind that once he got hold of that money, he ought to leave Shanty a few dollars for his trouble. Sure, the old man *was* black, and black folks were used to working for nothing. Cordell had been brought up to believe that was what they were put on this earth for. But he appreciated the old man's kindness toward Buster.

EVEN AFTER LEAVING Shanty's cabin, he continued to wrestle with his conscience. He had been forced to choose between two equally onerous actions. He unsaddled Buster's horse and staked him on a long rope in the timber by the river. He hung the bridle on a branch where he could retrieve it after he recovered his hidden money. He would prefer to stay in the timber where he could not be seen, but much of the land was open, either in pasture or in plowed fields. He had to trust to luck. On occasion it had been known to let him down, as when Sheriff Blessing had caught him handicapped by a hangover.

In a while he saw the cabin. It was as he remembered it, making a last stand against inevitable collapse. He stopped two hundred yards away and scrutinized the place for a while. He saw no movement, no smoke coming from the chimney. He did not see Gaskin working in his field or the neglected little weed patch that passed for a garden. Even this late in the morning, there was a chance he was still asleep. Cordell doubted that he often watched the sun rise.

He checked the back side of the cabin on the slim chance that Gaskin might be at his woodpile, chopping fuel for the fireplace. He was not. If he was here at all, he must be inside. Cordell tied his horse well clear of the cabin in case it should fall down while he was here. It looked as if all it needed was a strong west wind.

He walked around to the front, grasped the wooden door handle, and pushed. The door dragged the floor. Pistol in his hand, he quickly stepped inside.

Gaskin was not there. Cordell saw several pieces of firewood lying where they had carelessly been dropped on the floor. He took three long strides toward the woodbox and stopped cold. The box was almost empty. The saddlebags were gone.

His first reaction was stunned disbelief. Trembling with a rising anger, he picked up a piece of firewood and hurled it through the glass window. Though he was alone, he shouted, "You miserable thievin' son of a bitch. You've stolen my money!"

It did not seem fair, after all the risk he had endured to take that money, the days he had spent in jail, the wound Buster had suffered in freeing him, only to have a low-down, sneaking thief steal it all.

He tore the cabin apart in a desperate search, thinking Gaskin might have hidden the loot somewhere inside. It was a futile effort.

His indignation gradually cooled enough that he could think with some rationality. He asked himself what a miserable reprobate like Gaskin might likely do first if he suddenly came into such a windfall. He would go to town, of course. He would start spending it the same way Cordell had intended to when he had traveled far enough to feel safe, on good Kentucky whiskey and fiddle music and sweet-smelling women.

He had seldom felt so frustrated. He had partially destroyed Gaskin's cabin in a search that turned up nothing. He found a shovel and dug in several likely places where the ground looked to have been disturbed. It was a fruitless effort. He considered burning the place out of spite, but the money might still be there, hidden too well for him to find it. Its ashes would do him no good.

He considered the possibility that Gaskin had taken it with him to town, though that would be risky. The farmer had not struck him as being particularly smart, but maybe the old rascal had sense enough to understand that the law would take the money away from him. That being so, he had probably left most of it hidden. It must be around here somewhere.

Cordell could not risk going to town to search for Gaskin. He decided his best choice, though a poor one, was to hide out and wait for Gaskin to return home. If he could get his hands on the old fart, he would turn him inside out until he got his money back. Then he just might break him into little pieces and leave him for the wild hogs he had seen ranging along the river.

He felt a heavy weight of responsibilty for Buster. He should not have left him in the hands of a poor, old darky who had little to offer except good intentions, but he had seen no better choice. It was Cordell's intention, when he recovered his money, to take him far from here, perhaps back to the home from which he had come. They would hide out in some thinly populated area while Buster recuperated. This region along the lower Colorado River was among the oldest settled parts of the state. Anywhere a man turned, there were people—too many people—and they showed little tolerance for those in Cordell's chosen occupation.

Off to the southwest stretched a considerable thicket where Cordell thought he could hide while keeping an eye out for Gaskin's return. He had no provisions. He had

not wanted to take the little that Shanty had, and he
found nothing in Gaskin's cabin beyond some coffee
and tobacco and moonshine whiskey. Gaskin had several
chickens, which evidently had to scratch for their living.
He managed to catch one and tie its legs together while
it squawked and flapped its wings. It would taste good
tonight, roasted over a hidden campfire, with some moonshine to help it go down.

ANDY KNOCKED ON the doctor's front door, dreading
what he might be told. The doctor's wife parted a lace
curtain and peered out through the oval glass. She did
not immediately recognize him.

"I'm Andy Pickard, ma'am. I've come to ask about
Tom."

Her solemn expression did not ease his anxiety. She
swung the door inward and said, "Dr. Smith can tell you
better than I can. Come on in."

A strong medicine smell assaulted Andy as he entered.
The woman motioned toward a chair. Andy sat but was
too nervous to remain seated long. He stood up, turning
his hat around and around as he stared out the window.
Shortly the doctor came into the room, wiping his wet
hands on a towel. His white apron was spotted with
blood. He smelled of medicinal alcohol. His expression
was as solemn as his wife's.

Andy asked, "How's Tom?"

"Hanging on by a toenail. He's a tough old rooster. He
has more scars on his hide than a fighting bull. But I'm
afraid he doesn't have much chance."

Andy looked away. His eyes burned as if they had sand
in them.

The doctor frowned. "I don't suppose you had any luck chasing the ones who did this to him."

"They got clean away."

"Maybe not. Judge Tompkins has been on the telegraph. They can't outrun that."

Mention of the judge gave Andy a new thought. "The judge ought to have the authority to appoint deputies, shouldn't he?"

"There is one deputy already, Speck Munson. But I had to give him a sedative. His head is swollen, and he took a deep cut across his temple. He won't be of use to anybody for a day or two."

He wasn't of much use before, Andy thought. "Did Speck tell you what happened?"

"He could not talk much except to say that a big man walked in and surprised him, struck him with a gun barrel. He knew nothing that happened afterward."

Andy said, "It's clear that they released Luther Cordell and shot Tom as he rushed in. But I think I managed to wound one of them. He may be layin' dead out there someplace."

"A temporary improvement at best. There always seem to be adequate replacements for those of his ilk who fall by the wayside."

Andy asked, "Could I see Tom before I go?"

"You won't be able to ask him any questions."

"I'd just like to see him."

The doctor ushered Andy into a back room. He found Rusty there, face grim. Rusty seemed to want to say something, but nothing came. Alice sat beside Mrs. Blessing, holding her hand. The two had been close since Alice had nursed the older woman through a long illness.

Anger gripped Andy as he looked down upon the

sheriff, lying with all but his pale face covered by a sheet. He said, "We've got to do somethin' about this."

Rusty nodded but said nothing.

The doctor gave Andy an intense study. "Perhaps you are the one to do it."

"Maybe I am. I'll talk to the judge."

"Tell him you have my backing for anything you intend to do. Tom Blessing has been a friend of mine for a long time."

"He's been a friend of everybody."

GRAY-HAIRED JUDGE TOMPKINS sat with his heavy horsehide chair turned at an angle from his rolltop desk. He stared solemnly out the window, his mind carrying him somewhere far away. The sound of Andy's boots thumping on the pine floor startled him. The chair groaned under his weight as he swiveled it around. "I didn't know you'd come in, Pickard. I was just thinking about Tom."

"Me, too. That's what I came to talk to you about."

"I understand your posse returned with nothing to show for their trouble."

"The spirits must've been lookin' the other way, but we're not through. Tom said yesterday that he wanted to make me a deputy. I turned him down. I wish now I'd taken him up."

The judge's eyes narrowed. "We can fix that. I could deputize you." He took a cigar from a box on his desk and offered it to Andy. Andy declined. Tompkins bit the end from it and stared absently at it for a minute. "But you know that being a deputy in this county would give you no jurisdiction if you pursued a man beyond the county line."

Andy repeated what he had told Yates, that a pistol carried authority of its own.

The judge said, "But should you arrest a man outside of your jurisdiction, it could cause the case to be thrown out of court."

"Even if the man is guilty?"

"That is one unfortunate effect of Texas law. It is often honored more in the breach than in the enforcement, but given an accomplished defense attorney . . ." He left the rest for Andy to ponder.

Andy's mouth twisted as he considered the unfairness of an acquittal based on a technicality.

The judge continued, "You may not have considered another possibility. You have been a Ranger. You know that Rangers are not encumbered by county lines." He gave Andy a moment to think about it. "I believe I have enough influence in Austin to get your Ranger commission reinstated."

Andy's spine tingled. "You'd do that?"

"With the greatest of pleasure. I'll compose a wire right now, with your consent, of course."

"You've got it, Judge. I didn't think I'd ever care to be a Ranger again. But for Tom's sake, I'm ready and rarin' to go."

It occurred to Andy that Bethel might not approve. She had been pleased when he took his leave of the Rangers. He hoped she would understand. But if she didn't . . . well, she had endured many disappointments in the past. One more should not prove too heavy a burden.

The judge said, "Consider yourself a temporary deputy sheriff till we hear from the Rangers. That way you'll have official sanction for whatever you do, at least within county lines."

"That'll be helpful."

"You won't have to carry the full weight alone. I've sent for another man. I'm going to appoint him interim sheriff pending an election."

Andy had a sinking feeling. "Who?"

"Farley Brackett. He has had years of experience as a Ranger, and he has already filed for election as sheriff."

Andy felt as if half the air had gone out of his lungs. He considered backing out of his agreement. The last thing he wanted was close association with Farley, especially in a subordinate position.

He hoped his Ranger appointment came quickly.

He asked, "Have you got the authority to appoint a sheriff?"

"I have to have approval by the commissioners' court, but that is just a formality. They'll do what I tell them. I have something on every one of them."

Andy had heard the same thing from Tom.

The county clerk walked past the door, saw the judge, and turned back. His bow tie hanging loose and his shirttail partly out, he was laughing to himself as he entered the room.

The judge said, "Drinkin' a little early, aren't you, Bud?"

"Just one," the clerk said. "There wasn't any business in my office anyway. And I'm glad I went, because I saw something I wouldn't expect to see again in a hundred years."

The judge nodded. "And you're busting a gut to tell us about it."

"It's old Fowler Gaskin. I don't know where he got it, but he's waving a handful of money around and drinking it up as fast as he can raise a glass."

Andy's jaw dropped. "You're sure it was Fowler?"

"Nobody else looks like Fowler Gaskin."

Andy said, "Fowler never had ten dollars at one time in his life. Wherever he got it, it's a cinch he didn't break a sweat earnin' it."

It took but a moment for Andy to put the pieces together. "Tom arrested Luther Cordell out at Fowler's place. Cordell didn't have but a few dollars on him, and yet he had just robbed a bank. I'm bettin' he hid his loot somewhere at Fowler's place, and Fowler found it."

The judge saw the logic. "We'd better go talk to him."

"The damned old fool will get his head blown off. Cordell will be lookin' for that money. If he doesn't find it, he'll be lookin' for Fowler."

Tompkins said, "Perhaps we should let him. Fowler Gaskin's funeral would be regarded as community betterment."

"As much as I'd like to be one of Fowler's pallbearers, we can't just stand back and allow it to happen."

"No, but one can wish."

They walked together to the saloon. It was regarded as a social center for men of the town and countryside, a respectable place where many a bale of cotton had been sold, many a mule traded, a place where even a preacher could feel at ease, sort of. Sermons had been delivered here by itinerant ministers who had no church. The proprietor seemed pleased to see the judge walk through the door. A tall, angular man dressed in black, he looked more like an undertaker than a bartender. He was a deacon, known for delivering short but pointed sermons to patrons he thought had stayed too long.

He jerked a thumb toward the old man slumped at a table in the corner. "Judge, can you put Gaskin under arrest or somethin'? I won't sell him any more whiskey, but he won't leave. Says he'll sit there till he's sober, and then I'll have no excuse for not bringin' him a fresh bottle. I hate to just take him by the seat of the britches and throw him out. He's so spindly he's liable to break."

The judge gave Gaskin a moment's frowning study. "Fowler Gaskin, as county judge I am ordering that you be placed under arrest on a charge of being drunk and disorderly. Andy, please take him in hand."

Gaskin was too light in weight to put up an effective struggle against a husky young man in his twenties. Especially drunk. Andy said, "For a long time now I've wanted to do that."

Gaskin tried to focus his gaze, but it wavered between Andy and the judge. "Arrest me? I ain't broke no laws. I've paid good cash money for my drinks." He pulled a handful of bills from his pocket to demonstrate. "You got no call to arrest a man that's got money."

"Where did you get it?" Andy asked.

"From the Lord Hisself. Who else would've put it right there in my cabin? He takes pity on the poor and downtrodden. Ain't but few men been trod down on more than me."

"The Lord didn't have anything to do with that money. It was taken in a Galveston bank robbery."

"I found it in my cabin, right where the good Lord put it. He does work in mysterious ways."

"Do you think He intended for you to spend it on whiskey?"

"He didn't leave no instructions. He must like a little drink hisself, or why would He have put whiskey on this earth?"

Andy wrested the money from Gaskin's hands and counted while the old man spewed profanity against him and the judge and all others within hearing. The tally was far short of the amount supposed to have been taken in the robbery. Surely Gaskin hadn't been in town long enough to drink up so much. "Where's the rest of it, Fowler?"

Gaskin spat on the floor. "I hid it to where there can't nobody find it but me. Ain't no use you goin' to look."

"Maybe you're too drunk to see the mess you're in. You remember the feller you were drinkin' with, the one Tom Blessing arrested at your place?"

"Nice feller, he was. Shared his whiskey like a true Christian."

"Some Christian. He's back on the loose and no doubt lookin' for his money. He'd skin you alive to make you tell where it is, and then hang you on a meat hook in your own smokehouse."

Gaskin's clouded mind seemed unable to grasp the full reality. "He can't afford to kill me as long as I'm the only one who knows where that money's at."

"No, but he could break you up piece by piece. An arm first, and then a leg, and then the other arm. He could start whittlin' on your ears, and maybe your privates. How long do you think you could keep a secret?"

"He wouldn't come back, not after bustin' out of jail. He's long gone." The old man rubbed his red-rimmed eyes. "You just want to steal my money for yourself. That's what it is, you're a damned thief."

"Cordell will turn this country upside down. Safest place for you right now is in jail."

Gaskin took a couple of steps backward. "I'm an innocent man. I ain't stole nothin' from nobody."

"Jail is the one place where Cordell can't come lookin'. Tell me where you hid the money and I'll put it in there, too, for safekeepin'."

"No, sir, I ain't tellin' nobody. That money's mine."

"You're a damn fool, Fowler. But you always were."

5

Andy was only vaguely familiar with Tom's office, but he remembered seeing the sheriff put the keys in the desk's bottom drawer. He placed Gaskin in an inside cell that had no window through which anyone could see him from outside. He considered it unlikely that Cordell posed any real threat to Gaskin so long as he was locked in. If Cordell wanted to break into the jail, that would be fine with Andy. It would save having to go out and hunt for him.

Only one other prisoner was in jail. He had become too rowdy on moonshine and raised a ruckus in the street. Tom would probably have turned him loose by now were he able. Andy decided to release him so he would have one less problem. The bleary-eyed farmhand shuffled to the office, dragging his feet. Andy gave him back his personal belongings, but the prisoner kept waiting expectantly. He said, "Sheriff Tom always gave me a dollar or two to help me on my way."

He had claimed he slept through the jailbreak and Tom's being shot. That had been an obvious lie. He simply did not want to become involved in any repercussions. Andy said, "I'll help you on your way, all right. With a swift kick."

"Just thought I'd ask." The man left, but not in good

grace. Andy shouted an admonition that he not be found drunk in this town again anytime soon.

He did not want to leave the jail untended so long as Gaskin was in it. He did not even risk crossing the street to order supper at the restaurant. Biscuits Vanderpool took it upon himself to walk over and ask what Andy would like to have. Andy chose beefsteak, gravy, biscuits, and coffee. "As for Fowler Gaskin," he said, "anything you can scrape up will be better than what he's used to."

Gaskin hollered from his cell, "By God, I'm a taxpayer, and I deserve a good supper."

Andy doubted that Gaskin had ever coughed up enough taxes to pay for a pot of beans. "All right, bring him whatever you bring me, but we're not goin' to fatten him up at county expense."

Rusty came to the jail after Vanderpool returned. They visited about the weather and crop prospects but avoided discussing what lay heaviest on their minds. They quickly ran out of talk, and Rusty left to look in again on Tom.

Andy lay on the same hard bunk that Tom had pointed him to. The front door was locked and reinforced by a heavy bar. Only dynamite would break it down. Andy did not sleep much, partly because of Gaskin's snoring and partly because his mind would not shut down. He kept seeing Tom in his uneasy dreams.

He had just finished eating the breakfast the restaurant operator had brought over when Speck Munson walked in. His head was bandaged, and he looked to be in pain. He said, "I'm reportin' for work, if I'm still hired."

"I guess you're hired until somebody tells you otherwise. If you're worried about it, you could ask the judge."

"Long as he doesn't tell me otherwise, I won't bring it

up." Speck looked ashamed. "I suppose everybody blames me for what happened."

They probably did, but Andy thought the young man looked miserable enough already. Perhaps the experience had taught him something. "I suppose it happened so fast that you didn't have time to do anything."

Munson nodded, wincing as the movement brought pain. "I barely seen the man that hit me. He was a bad-lookin' one, and big as a barn."

"How do you know if you barely saw him?"

"It don't take long to see mean, and he was mean to the bone."

"Did you hear Cordell call him by name?"

"I thought he said *milk,* but that ain't no name."

Munson collapsed into a chair. Andy knew that in his condition he could not be trusted with responsibility. He said, "Maybe you'd better go home and get some more rest."

"Better if I stay here and make a hand. Maybe the judge won't fire me if he sees me at work." Before long Speck was asleep in the chair.

He was probably still feeling effects of the sedative the doctor had administered. Andy hoped Judge Tompkins would not walk in and see Speck in this condition, but that hope fell by the wayside. Speck was the first thing Tompkins saw as he walked through the door. He said, "Doesn't that boy do anything but sleep?"

Defensively Andy said, "It's the doctor's pills, I think."

"He never was right for this job. I had Tom hire him because the boy needed a regular paycheck. But it wouldn't be right to fire him so soon after he's been injured in the line of duty. I'll wait until he's well."

"He'll still need a paycheck."

"A plow is more fitting for him than a badge. I'll give

him a job on my farm. Have you seen Farley Brackett yet?"

The name made Andy frown. "He hasn't been in."

"He's due. And I got a wire back from Austin. They're taking your Ranger application under advisement, so you'll have to remain a deputy for a while."

It was a disappointment, but Andy shrugged it off.

The judge said, "A Ranger was on his way here to pick up Cordell and take him back to Galveston. Maybe he can stay and help you. If you have to cross over the county line, you can let him make the official arrest."

"Did they say who they sent?"

"No name. Till we hear about your reinstatement, you should keep the deputy's badge."

"I never had one."

The judge rummaged in a desk drawer and came up with the same San Antonio city badge that Tom had offered. He gave it a quick glance and said, "It's the man behind it that counts. Nobody is going to read the inscription anyway. Especially if you are holding a gun on him."

The judge turned toward the door. "I'm going over to see about Tom. Want to go with me?"

"I sure do." Andy awakened Speck and told him to keep the door locked. Then Andy and Tompkins walked to the doctor's house. The doctor's wife met them at the door. Her grim expression told them what neither wanted to ask. Andy heard Mrs. Blessing sobbing in the back room. He and the judge exchanged worried glances. The doctor met them, shaking his gray head.

"I am sorry. Tom just passed."

Mrs. Blessing sat in a chair against Tom's bed, one arm lying across her husband's still form. Alice stood over her, trying to comfort her but unable to speak. Rusty stood on the other side of the bed, looking as if he had been kicked in the stomach. "Tom's gone," he said.

Andy could not reply. He turned away and crushed his hat in his hands.

Farley Brackett was waiting outside the jail when Andy and the judge returned, both badly shaken. Obeying orders, Munson had refused to let him in. Farley grumbled to the judge, "If I was the sheriff, the first thing I'd do would be to fire that dumb kid."

The judge said, "He just did what I told him to." He gave Farley the news about Tom. Farley's peevish expression shifted quickly to one of exaggerated sadness. He said, "That sure is too bad. We'll miss old Tom."

Andy suspected Farley was not grieving all that much. Tom's passing gave him a better chance to take over this office permanently in the special election that was certain to come.

Speck was up and giving the jail a listless sweeping that left no visible effect. He went off by himself and cried when told about Tom.

Tompkins administered the oath to Farley. Farley said, "Judge, I promise you I'll get the skunk that shot Tom. We all owe a big debt to that good man for the years he's served the citizens of this county."

Andy did not comment. He knew that anything he said would be bitter. Tom was not yet an hour dead, and Farley was already settling into his job.

Farley had noticed Andy's badge. He said, "I gather that I'm in charge now. Andy's got to take orders from me, right?"

The judge was momentarily surprised by the antagonistic looks that passed between Andy and Farley. He had known nothing of their conflict. He considered for a moment. "Yes, but I would expect that authority to be used judiciously." He paused, then sprang one more surprise on Farley. "Pickard's deputy status is only temporary. I have asked that he be reinstated as a Ranger. When that happens, I would consider his authority to be paramount."

Farley's face fell.

Speck had listened in puzzlement. He understood nothing of this. He asked, "What do you fellers think we ought to do now?"

Andy answered quickly, before Farley had a chance to consider. "I think the sheriff should stay and watch the jail in case Cordell tries to get at Fowler Gaskin and make him tell where he hid the money. Farley'll need help, so you'd better stay with him, Speck. Cordell has probably already been to Fowler's place huntin' for his money, but I'll go out there in case he's still hangin' around, waitin' for Fowler."

The judge voiced approval, leaving Farley no room for argument.

Farley complained, "I don't even know what Cordell looks like."

Andy said, "Speck can tell you. He saw a lot of him while he was in this jail."

Speck said, "I'd like to see him back in here again. I'd keep him in leg-irons and make him empty his own slop jar."

ANDY SAW THAT Cordell had already made a thorough search of Gaskin's cabin. The place looked even more chaotic than he had seen it before. Pots, pans, and plates were scattered across the floor, the shelves emptied. The cot and the woodbox were turned upside down. Several stones had been chiseled out of the fireplace. The wooden floor had been pried up in several places.

He recognized the possibility that Cordell had found the money and fled with it. In that case he was probably already out of the county. But Andy thought it equally possible that Cordell had not found it. Though lazy and shiftless, Gaskin was crafty as a coyote. He was unlikely to have hidden his treasure where it would easily be found. More probably he had secreted it so well that a searcher would have to make a pact with the devil to find it.

Cordell seemed the man to make such a pact.

After a perfunctory search around the outside of the cabin, Andy reasoned that Cordell had done it before him. Any further searching would be a waste of time. He decided to return to town.

At the jail, Farley looked him over with critical eyes. "You don't look to be packin' any money, so I don't reckon you found it. And Cordell has given you the slip. Ain't no tellin' where he's got to by now."

Arguing with Farley would only get Andy's blood stirred up. Instead, he agreed. "He tore Fowler's cabin half to pieces. I don't know if he found the money or not."

"You didn't trail him?"

"You know I'm not much good at trackin'."

"That's the gospel truth. All those years with the Comanches, and you didn't learn a damned thing."

Andy turned to Speck. "Has Fowler given you any trouble?"

"Cussed me up one side and down the other is all. Keeps sayin' he didn't steal anything and he don't belong in here."

"Bad as I hate to say so, he's probably right. All we've got on Fowler is that he was drunk and disorderly. We can't even prove it was bank money he was spendin'. The judge'll probably tell us to turn him loose in the mornin'."

Farley said, "That's too bad. It's warmed my heart, seein' that old sneak sittin' behind the bars."

Andy was tempted to comment about Farley's warm heart but passed up the opportunity. "You can sit up tonight and watch him if you want to. Me and Speck can use the sleep."

Andy heard Gaskin's raspy voice calling his name. The old man's knotted hands clasped the bars so tightly that the knuckles were white. He demanded, "You been out to my place?"

"Just came back."

"Find anything?"

Andy decided the old sneak needed something to worry about. "Somebody tore your cabin to pieces and dug holes everywhere."

Gaskin's face fell. "You ain't lyin'? He dug all around?"

"You could plant a garden."

For a moment Andy thought Gaskin was going to cry. He sank back onto his bunk and buried his face in his hands. "That money is rightfully mine. I found it."

"Finders don't always get to be keepers. At least you were rich for a little while." Andy turned away from the cell, leaving Gaskin to ponder the fickle nature of fate.

Gaskin called after him, "Maybe he gave up and left."

"Maybe."

Farley muttered, "Soon as we turn him loose, he'll hightail it home to see if the money's still where he hid it."

Andy said, "I doubt that it is. Cordell has likely got it and gone." He did not entirely believe that, but he did not want Farley to second-guess a half-baked idea he had been toying with.

Farley said, "You enjoy torturin' the old man. Must be the Indian in you, Badger Boy."

Speck didn't get it. "What's this about Indians? There ain't no Indians around here anymore. Are there?"

Farley said, "Get Andy to tell you the story of his life. But not where I've got to listen to it."

GASKIN ATE BUT little supper and only dabbled at his breakfast the next morning. He trembled with anxiety. "Ain't you-all ever goin' to let me out of here?" he demanded.

Andy said, "I'll talk to the judge when he gets to his office."

"Tell him I'm figurin' on suin' the county for false arrest. Time my lawyer gets through wringin' you-all out, I'm liable to own the courthouse."

Andy knew Gaskin had no lawyer. He had dodged lawyers and courthouses all his life. They meant nothing to him but aggravation.

Andy said, "Better eat your breakfast. If the judge turns you loose, you'll have to survive on your own cookin'." It was a wonder the old man had not poisoned himself years ago.

The judge reluctantly agreed that they had little reason to hold the prisoner. "My preference would be to let him sit there and rot, but we can't keep feeding him at the county's expense. If he would just commit a murder or something else worthwhile, we could turn him over to the state."

Andy carried the ring of keys to Gaskin's cell. "Gather up your stuff, Fowler. You'll find your mule at the wagon yard."

"I ain't payin' no feed bill. I didn't tell you-all to put him up over there."

"Just go, Fowler."

Andy stood at the door and watched Gaskin hurrying across the square on wobbly legs. Farley moved up beside Andy and growled, "Once I'm full sheriff, there'll be some changes made. I'd let that old scoundrel stay in jail till he put roots down through the floor."

"That wouldn't be accordin' to law."

"Some law you've got to make up as you go along."

Farley went back into the office and began rummaging in the drawers of Tom's desk. He found a sheaf of Wanted notices and began to study them. He smiled to himself. Andy guessed he was imagining himself catching all those criminals single-handed.

Andy remained in the doorway until he saw Gaskin riding up the street, quirting his rawboned mule. The mule flinched at the sting but did not pick up the pace. Gaskin disappeared on the wagon trail that led off in the general direction of his farm. Andy looked back to make sure Farley was not watching him, then walked to the wagon yard and saddled his bay horse. He did not want Farley going along, for one man stood a good chance of staying out of Gaskin's sight. Two men would double the likelihood of his spotting whoever followed. Andy hung back out of sight, sure where the old man was going. He did not close the distance between them until he neared Gaskin's shack. He stopped in a stand of trees where he could watch without being seen.

Gaskin was still applying the quirt with little effect. The old mule had no speed left. Gaskin was so eager that he jumped off a hundred feet short of his cabin and ran the rest of the way in the wobbly gait dictated by his stiff joints. He attacked the woodpile in back, hurling firewood aside. He picked up a shovel that was lying nearby and drove its point into the ground where the wood had been. He was so engrossed in his frantic digging that he did not see Andy ride up behind him. Andy watched him drop to his knees. With a glad shout, Gaskin pulled a set of saddlebags out of the hole. He opened them anxiously and yelped again in joy.

Andy dismounted and walked up unnoticed until he said, "I'll take those, Fowler."

Gaskin turned so quickly that he almost fell. He clutched the saddlebags to his thin chest. His eyes were desperate. "These are mine. I found them, and they're mine."

"You know that money was taken from a bank. It's got to go back."

"Like hell." Gaskin turned to run. Andy grappled with him, trying to wrest the bags from his hands. He jerked them loose but was off balance and stumbled. With a curse, Gaskin picked up a large chunk of wood and struck Andy across the head. Andy's hat sailed away. His knees buckled as Gaskin yanked the bags from his hands and shouted in triumph.

A gravelly voice said, "Don't be in such a hurry, old man. That's my property you've got your grubby hands on."

On his knees, Andy looked up through a painful haze. The black-bearded Cordell seemed to sway back and forth. The pistol in his hand looked like a cannon. Gaskin froze, clutching the bags as if they were a baby.

Cordell said, "I'd let you-all fight it out, but I'm afraid one or both of you might get killed. Naturally they'd blame me. They always do." He extended his free hand to Gaskin. "Gimme."

Gaskin backed away, frantically holding on to the bags. Cordell touched the muzzle of his pistol to the old man's Adam's apple. "I said gimme."

Gaskin yielded them up and went to his knees, sobbing. "They're mine. You got no right."

"Go rob your own bank. Any fool can do it. Just show them a gun to let them know' you're serious, and they'll empty out the vault." Cordell turned to Andy, relieving him of the pistol on his hip. Andy had been too stunned to draw it. "I remember you from the jailhouse. I don't remember you wearin' a badge then."

Andy's head throbbed. "Damn you, you killed one of the best men that ever lived."

"Wasn't me. The man that done it has took off to Mexico or someplace. Mexico looks pretty good to me, too, now." Cordell balanced the saddlebags over his free arm. "Let me have that cartridge belt. And just so you don't get a notion to follow too quick, I'm takin' your horse and that mule yonder. You-all stay put and don't get in another fight. I won't be here to bust it up."

Cordell mounted a horse he had tied at the side of the cabin and rode up beside Andy's, taking the reins. "I don't want to be accused of horse thievin'. I ain't that low. I'll leave your horse and mule down the trail a ways." He rode southward. The lagging mule limited his speed, pulling back on the reins and stubbornly refusing to move beyond a trot.

Andy said grittily, "If I was him, I'd shoot that mule."

Gaskin said, "If I had my shotgun, I'd shoot *you*."

Andy ran his hand across the place where Gaskin had struck him. It burned. He felt the stickiness of blood. His head ached as if a hatchet were sunk in it to the handle. "Fowler, you like to've brained me."

"I intended to. First time in my life I ever had any real money, and you caused that thief to get away with it."

"He was layin' for you to come back. He'd've taken it whether I was here or not."

Gaskin gave Andy another sound cursing, then went into his cabin. Andy heard him cry out in rage. Gaskin staggered back outside, trembling. "He wrecked my house. Tore up everything."

The place was a wreck long before Cordell came along, Andy thought. He tried to muster a little sympathy for Gaskin, but it was not there. He said, "You ought to set fire to it and start over."

"You always hated me," Gaskin whined, "you and Rusty Shannon and all the rest of them. You got no Christian feelin's for a poor man."

Gaskin didn't have to be a poor man. He owned the makings of a good little farm. All it needed was a competent farmer, somebody who would work at it and keep leaving fresh footprints from one end to the other. Gaskin raised just enough corn to put bread on his table and make moonshine whiskey in a still down by the creek. Andy found it hard to imagine Gaskin putting out the energy to move part of his woodpile, dig a hole to hide the saddlebags, then cover them up with firewood. Only money or whiskey would provide that much motivation.

For a moment Andy pictured what he could do with this place if it were his. The thought was fleeting. The last thing he wanted was to spend the rest of his life in this older and heavily settled part of Texas, tied to a plow, though it was what Bethel wished him to do. Memory carried him back to the western hills and the rolling plains. Someday, some way . . .

Two riders approached from the direction of town. As his vision gradually improved, Andy discerned that they were Farley and Speck. He dreaded hearing what Farley would say. He took the initiative by declaring, "I didn't ask you-all to follow me."

Farley said, "No, but you should've let me in on what you were up to. I could've told you you couldn't handle the situation by yourself. Now Cordell's got the money and gone *por allá*. You'll go back to town draggin' an empty sack and lookin' like a fool." He made no effort to hide his satisfaction. "But maybe with a little luck I'll be able to pick up the pieces."

Farley did not mention Speck. Andy guessed he hoped to catch Cordell and grab some glory for himself. He said, "That's all right. I'm not runnin' for sheriff."

Farley examined the hole where Gaskin had retrieved the saddlebags. "So this is where the money was at."

Andy's eyes were still blurry, but perhaps Farley and Speck could follow the fleeing outlaw. He pointed in the direction Cordell had taken. "He hasn't been gone long. Took my horse so I couldn't follow after him."

Farley said, "You never was much of a farmer, and you ain't much of a deputy either. I swear, I don't know what you're good for, Badger Boy. Come on, Speck, let's go catch the man that Andy let get away."

They moved off in a lope.

Andy was angrier at himself than at Farley. He shouldn't have let Cordell sneak up and get the upper hand on him. It wouldn't have happened if he hadn't been wrestling with Gaskin. The old fossil wasn't worth all this grief.

Gaskin complained, "You caused me to lose my money, and on account of you I lost my mule, too."

"That mule probably didn't like it here anyway. I sure wouldn't." Large chunks had been chewed from wooden fence planks near the barn, a sign the mule had been starved for nutrients. It had to subsist on whatever native grass it could find and dry roughage that was more straw than hay. "I ought to arrest you for cruelty to an animal."

"You're hell-bent on arrestin' people. Maybe if you hadn't put me in jail, I wouldn't've lost my money."

"If you hadn't been in jail, Cordell would've caught you by yourself and nailed your hide to the cabin door."

Andy went to Gaskin's well and turned the windlass to bring up a bucket of water. He drank his fill, then poured the rest over his throbbing head. "You've got good water here, Fowler. You'd be better off if you drank more of this and less of that moonshine."

"I'll have all the whiskey I want when I get through suin' you and the county. You'll be workin' for me the rest of your life."

"You're makin' my head hurt, Fowler. Shut the hell up."

Andy considered setting out afoot for town, but he feared he did not have enough strength to get there. Besides, Farley and Speck would likely return for him sooner or later, with or without Cordell. He sat down to rest on a bench at the front of the cabin. Gaskin went inside and began rattling things around in an attempt to straighten up his damaged dwelling. Andy felt that he deserved no help, so he offered none. Gaskin kept up a constant monologue, cursing Andy and Cordell and anyone else he considered responsible for keeping him poor all his life. Every misfortune that had befallen him since childhood was someone else's fault.

It was near dark when Farley and Speck returned, leading Andy's horse and the mule. Andy's pistol and cartridge belt hung from the saddlehorn where Cordell had left them. Farley said, "You're luckier than you deserve to be, Badger Boy. He left these where we would find them. He's an honest man, for a thief."

Cordell had probably been glad to be rid of the lagging mule, Andy thought. Farley and Speck had obviously not caught up with the outlaw. "Why didn't you trail him?" Andy asked sarcastically, knowing that Farley was no better tracker than he.

Farley said, "It was like he just left the ground and flew away. Them tracks stopped dead at the edge of a creek. We couldn't find where they came out." He shook his head. "Damned poor Ranger you are, messin' around and lettin' him escape."

Andy shrugged. "When you start campaignin', you can tell everybody it was all my fault. Things would've been different if you'd been full sheriff."

He mounted his bay horse and started toward town. Maybe by tomorrow his head would stop hurting.

6

Cordell had dodged a lot of lawmen in his time. He knew how. He was confident they would not expect him to turn back toward town, so that was what he did. He entered the creek and followed it downstream several hundred yards. He felt that the two horsemen he had seen trailing after him would decide he was most likely to go upstream, for his best hope of escape lay to the west. Leaving the creek, he saw no sign of pursuit. He indulged in a moment of pride for his ability to outwit the law. He speculated that perhaps in some previous life he had been a coyote. He had that devious animal's instincts.

He stayed within cover and observed Shanty's cabin for some time before he ventured into the open. He found Buster's bridle where he had left it hanging in a tree. The saddle lay across a shoulder-high branch, out of the wild hogs' reach. Buster's horse grazed where he had been staked near the edge of the river. Cordell saddled and led him to the cabin. Shanty's mule followed, braying.

Shanty came out and shaded his eyes with his hand, calling to his dog to hush up. Cordell asked him, "How's my boy? He doin' any better?"

Shanty frowned. "He's still feverish and hurtin' a right smart. Can't get him to take no nourishment."

Cordell nodded. "I'm obliged to you for seein' after him. Been anybody snoopin' around?"

"Ain't been a soul come by. Ain't many folks bothers with old Shanty."

"I'm fixin' to take him off of your hands."

Shanty was dubious. "He ought not to be ridin'."

"Wisht I could leave him longer, but there's folks in town that's anxious to see me and Buster. We ain't anxious to see them."

In the cabin, Cordell laid the palm of his hand against the wounded man's forehead. Shanty had been right. Buster was fevered more than before. Cordell said, "Ain't you ready to get out of bed and do some travelin'? Layin' around saps a man's strength."

Buster raised up on one elbow, his face twisting in pain. "I been worried . . . you wouldn't come back."

"You ought to know I wouldn't go off and leave a pardner, not when I owe him his split. I got our property back."

Buster was wearing his trousers but not his shirt and boots. Shanty brought him the shirt. He had washed the blood from it and had done a fair job of patching the hole where the bullet had gone in. He said, "I been tellin' your friend he ought to go on and let you stay here."

Buster begged, "Don't leave me. I'm afraid."

"I ain't leavin' you. Soon as it's safe, I'll get you to a sure-enough doctor. He'll fix you up better than you was before."

Cordell knew it was likely that his description had been sent out in all directions. His black beard and shaggy hair would give him away to anybody who was paying attention. He asked, "Shanty, you got some scissors and a razor? I'd like to get rid of this briar patch. I wouldn't be surprised to see a sparrow come flyin' out of it."

He trimmed off most of the beard with the scissors, then lathered and shaved the rest. He was surprised by the clean face that looked back at him from Shanty's cracked mirror. He had not seen it in a long time, but then, neither had anyone else. Years ago, women had told him he was handsome. He doubted they would say that now. His jaw seemed more square than he remembered, and the face showed lines that reminded him of an irrigation ditch. The beard had probably been an improvement.

I've gotten ugly as hell, he thought. But a man did not have to be good-looking so long as he had money.

"I'd better shed some of this long hair, too."

Shanty said, "I ain't no barber, but I'll see what I can do."

When he finished with the scissors, there seemed to be enough hair and beard on the floor to stuff a pillow. Cordell surveyed the results in the mirror. "You're right, you ain't no barber, but it sure changes my looks. We'd better be travelin', boy."

He helped Buster to his feet and supported him through the door. He gave him a boost up into the saddle. "Think you can hang on?"

"I ain't goin' to fall off." Buster steadied himself on the saddle horn. "We owe Shanty somethin'."

Cordell reached into a saddlebag and drew out several bills.

Shanty shook his head. "I ain't askin' for money. The Lord'd be ashamed of me if I didn't do all I could for a sick boy."

"This is just for the vittles me and Buster ate. And you're apt to need a new razor. I think I ruined yours." Cordell thrust the money into Shanty's hand and climbed into the saddle. "Don't worry about the Lord. He'll smile on you for what you've done."

Shanty nodded gravely. "He already has. I just hope He smiles on that boy."

"You might not want to watch us leave. If anybody asks, you can tell them it sounded like we rode south."

Cordell headed west. Buster trailed behind him, cramped in pain. Cordell regretted the necessity, but they had to keep moving. The law might not be alone in looking for them. Milt Hayward might be looking, too. It would be his style to ambush and kill the two of them, then take the money, all of it.

STILL HURTING, ANDY had no patience for listening to Farley run him down. He trailed behind Farley and Speck as they rode into town at dusk and reined up at the jail. Speck volunteered, "I'll take the horses over to the wagon yard."

That suited Andy. More than anything else, he wanted to get to his bunk and lie down. It would feel good despite being hard as stone. He staggered inside and made his way toward the open cell in which he had slept before.

He heard a familiar voice. "Looks like you hunters came home without no quail."

A long, lanky figure unwound from the chair at the sheriff's desk.

Andy caught a quick breath. "Len? Len Tanner?"

"If you was lookin' for Sam Houston, he died. I come in his place."

Andy gladly grasped the Ranger's hand. For a man who seemed too thin to cast a shadow, Len had a grip like a blacksmith. Andy winced.

Len saw the mark on Andy's head. "Looks like somebody went and pistol-whipped you. Cordell?"

"I'm ashamed to say it was Fowler Gaskin. Hit me with a chunk of firewood."

"Ain't that old buzzard dead yet? I thought by now somebody would've put him out of his misery." Len addressed Farley for the first time and without enthusiasm. "I see you ain't got no handsomer. Ain't that little Mexican woman of yours run you off yet?"

"Half-Mexican," Farley corrected him. "Nobody's been run off except Badger Boy."

Andy would explain to Len some other time. He asked, "How come you're here?"

Len said, "Captain sent me to pick up Cordell and take him back. Seein' as he's not in the jailhouse, and you didn't bring him in, I have to figure he's on the loose."

Andy could only nod.

Len took a small book from his pocket and flipped through its pages. Andy recognized it as a Ranger's fugitive list. He had carried one himself during his time of service. Len said, "There was three of them hit that bank. Except for Cordell, we don't have enough description to find the other two in here."

Andy said, "Speck told us Cordell called out a name that sounded like *milk*."

"That don't make a lick of sense."

"It's all we've got. What about the kid that was with them?"

"Cordell probably picked him up somewhere along the way. There ain't no tellin' who he might be."

"I hit him as he was bringin' the horses up, but he managed to ride away."

No kid had been with Cordell at Gaskin's place. Andy wondered. Perhaps he had died of his wound, or perhaps Cordell had found some place to leave him. He told Len briefly about his encounter at Gaskin's. "He said it was his partner that shot Tom. I don't know whether to believe him or not."

"Cordell has got most of a page in the fugitive book. I'd put my money on him unless I heard otherwise."

Andy's voice coarsened with anger. "Whichever one pulled the trigger, they're all guilty. I'm afraid by mornin' they'll be out of the county. I've got no legal authority to go farther than that."

"Yes, you do. Judge Tompkins told me he got a wire from the state office. They approved your reinstatement. You're a Ranger again."

Farley had listened with a frown. He said, "That won't set well with Bethel. Maybe now she'll come to her senses and look for a better man."

Farley would be eager to help her do that. Andy said, "I hope she understands. But even if she doesn't, I've got to do all I can to catch the people that killed Tom."

Len said, "Damned shame about that. He was as square a man as I ever knew." He moved toward the door. "I'm about ready for some supper. Ain't et a bite since noon. The state of Texas is buyin'."

Andy removed the badge Judge Tompkins had given him. "I won't need this anymore." He handed it over to Farley.

Farley grunted, glancing at the lettering. "You'd think this county could afford its own badges." He started to pin it to his shirt but changed his mind. "I wonder where Tom's is."

Andy said, "They'll bury it with him."

"I'd rather have my own anyway." Farley tossed the deputy badge at the desk and missed. He did not stoop to pick it up.

Andy went to supper with Len, but Farley stayed back. He said, "I'll eat later. I don't aim to have Tanner talk both of my ears off."

Len had a reputation for conversation that stopped only when he went to sleep, and not always then. It had driven Farley to distraction when they worked together as Rangers.

Rusty Shannon entered the restaurant while Andy and Len awaited their supper. Face grim, he howdied and shook hands with Len but had little to say. Andy asked about Mrs. Blessing.

Rusty said, "Alice is with her. So are several of her neighbors. Doc Smith gave her somethin' to make her sleep." His face twisted in grief. "I've got to stay here and help with the funeral. Len, you and Andy go and get them."

Andy hoped everyone would understand why he could not stay for the funeral. "We'll get them," he promised, "if we have to follow them to the moon."

Len pondered. "I wasn't authorized to go on a chase. They just told me to get Cordell and take him to Galveston. Maybe we can catch him before the main office starts worryin' about me not showin' up."

Next morning, Andy, Len, and Farley left Speck in charge of the jail. Leading a pack mule with supplies enough for several days, they were at Gaskin's cabin a while after daylight. Len had talked all the way, recounting what he had been doing since he, Andy, and Farley had served together on the Rio Grande.

The old man met them at the door, in his underwear. His droopy eyes said he was still half-asleep. He growled, "I hope you-all are here to help me straighten up my place. It's your fault it's in this shape."

Len said, "It's been in this shape ever since I first saw

it." He had spent a lot of time at Rusty Shannon's between Ranger missions, so he had known Gaskin for years.

Squinting hard, Gaskin recognized Len. "Old Never Hush. You still a Ranger?"

"It's all I know to be."

"I hope you're half as good at Rangerin' as you are at jawin'."

Len said, "I don't say nothin' that ain't gospel truth. That's more than I can say for some folks."

Andy pointed in the direction Cordell had taken in leaving. Len studied the trail and gave Farley a critical look. "Don't you know better than to mess up a fugitive's tracks? I can't tell what's yours and what was left by Cordell."

Farley was defensive. "We're wastin' time here. I can show you where me and Speck lost the trail."

They pushed into an easy lope until they came to a creek. Farley said, "Here's where we found Andy's horse and Gaskin's mule. Cordell rode in, but he never rode out."

Len said, "He must've, unless he drowned. Did you follow the creek upstream?"

"A couple of miles. You wouldn't think he could come out without leavin' sign, but I guess he did."

"How far did you ride downstream?"

"A couple hundred yards. He wouldn't have gone that way. It'd take him back toward town."

"That's just what he might figure you'd figure, so like as not he figured to fool you. Let's go downstream."

They traveled more than two miles before Len found where Cordell had left the creek. He gave Farley a grin that silently said, *I told you.* He rode out onto the bank, pausing to study the tracks. "I see a cabin."

Andy was suddenly fearful. "That's Shanty's place.

I hope he didn't hurt that old man." He put his horse into a long trot.

Len caught up with him. "Cordell might steal the pennies from a dead man's eyes, but I doubt he'd hurt a harmless old darky. Probably just lookin' for somethin' to eat."

"Shanty wouldn't have much to spare. It was a hard winter."

The tracks led almost directly to Shanty's, though they detoured to a thicket. They indicated that Cordell had paused there, probably watching to be sure no outsiders were around.

Shanty was near the shed, feeding grain to his small flock of chickens. He tossed handfuls onto the ground and called, "Chickie, chickie," while they pecked around his feet. He did not hear the horses until they were close by. They startled him.

Andy called anxiously, "Are you all right?"

Shanty stared in surprised silence before greeting his company. He usually glowed when anyone came to visit. He seemed ill at ease. "Andy, Mr. Farley, Mr. Len."

Andy said, "We been trailin' a wanted man. Tracks show he came this way. Have you seen anybody?"

Shanty was hesitant. "What name does he go by?"

"He answers to Cordell."

"There was a feller come by here. That might've been his name. Yes, I believe it was."

"Was he alone?"

"A young feller come with him."

Andy was puzzled by Shanty's slowness to answer. He said, "Maybe Cordell made you promise not to tell us anything, but your word to an outlaw don't count. Tom Blessing is dead on account of them."

"I didn't know Mr. Tom had died." Shanty removed his

hat and bowed his head. Reluctantly he said, "The boy had a bullet in him. I done what I could for him. Mr. Cordell, he was gone a long time, then he come back for the boy. Took him away yesterday."

"The boy . . . what was his name?"

"Buster was all I heard. I told Mr. Cordell that he'd ought to leave him because the boy was awful weak. Looked fair to die. But he said there was folks in town might hang him on account of Sheriff Tom. He seemed like too nice a boy to get hung."

Farley said drily, "But not too nice to hold up a bank."

Len asked, "Which way did they go when they left?"

"Can't rightly say. Mr. Cordell told me to go inside and not watch them. Could've gone any whichaway."

Farley said accusingly, "Helpin' them makes you an accessory. You could go to jail for that."

Andy tried to put words in Shanty's mouth to counter what Farley said. "Cordell held a gun on you, didn't he? I doubt he gave you any choice."

Shanty said, "When I seen how bad off that boy was, I couldn't say no. Like the Book says, you never know when an angel may come to your door unawares."

Farley said, "If you'd been a better shot, Badger Boy, he *would've* been an angel."

Shanty said, "The Book says thou shalt not kill. Been a time or two I was tempted, but the Lord stayed my hand." He turned to look toward his cabin. "I expect they'll be buryin' Mr. Tom today. I better put on my go-to-meetin' clothes." His voice broke. "An awful good man, he was. A real friend to me."

A few in town might resent a black man's presence at the funeral, but they would not say anything aloud. His friends far outnumbered them.

Len rode a wide circle around the cabin and came

back. He pointed west. "Tracks of two horses lead off yonderway."

Shanty said, "Mr. Cordell left me some money, but I can't rightfully spend it. I wish you'd give it back to them it belongs to."

Andy said, "How do you know that what he gave you was stolen? He might've won it in a card game. You ought to go to town and buy you some groceries with it."

"Them groceries would go sour in my mouth."

"Then hide it away till we come back. We'll put it with what we take from Cordell when we catch him."

Farley snorted. "*When?* Sure of yourself, ain't you, Badger Boy?"

"We'll get him. Maybe today, maybe tomorrow, maybe next week. Somebody's got to pay for Tom."

The trail was plain for a while, then became increasingly difficult to follow. Cordell had sought out places where the ground was hard or gravelly. Farley complained, "He's gainin' time. We'll lose him."

Andy's voice had a barb in it. "That wouldn't help your campaign much, would it?"

Farley flushed. "I wasn't thinkin' about the campaign."

Andy felt certain he was.

At length Farley drew up and took a sweeping look at the ground ahead. "The county line is around here somewhere." They were not on a road, where there might have been a marker. "That bein' the case, I'm at the end of my jurisdiction."

Andy asked, "You're fixin' to turn back?"

"I hate to, I purely do, but I've got to think of my responsibility as actin' sheriff of this county. Folks will expect me to be where they can reach me if I'm needed."

Andy let his sarcasm show. "Besides, if we catch

Cordell outside of the county, it'll be the Rangers that get the credit."

"I never gave a minute's thought to who gets the credit."

Len offered Farley a graceful way out. "There's no tellin' how long we may be gone, and that boy Speck didn't strike me as bein' real peart."

Farley sounded reluctant but looked relieved. "Right. I wish I could go on with you, but I've got a duty here."

Len nodded solemnly. "I'm glad you see it my way."

Farley turned back in the direction of town. Len said, "I'm glad to be shed of his gripin'. I couldn't hardly get a word in edgeways."

Andy waited until Farley was well beyond earshot before he expressed his doubts. "Cordell has tried several times to make us lose his trail. He'll do it sooner or later. Probably sooner."

"All we can do is try our best."

"He's liable to spend that money before we catch him."

Len shrugged. "I don't lay awake at night worryin' about some Yankee bank. I'm mainly interested in gettin' Cordell a room and bed at the state hotel in Huntsville." Len saw several distinct tracks. He dismounted to observe them closely. "One of the horses has got an odd-shaped hoof, like his foot was twisted a little."

Andy squatted on his heels and studied the track. He was not sure he would be able to distinguish it if he saw it again, mixed up with other tracks. His Indian training had some gaps in it.

7

Long hours in the saddle had worn heavily on Buster. Only his uncertain grip on the horn kept him from sliding off. The kid's horse followed Cordell's, for Buster was too weak to offer guidance. Frequently Cordell had to stop and let Buster catch up. Much of the time the kid appeared to be only half-conscious. Cordell saw a small crossroads village ahead. He needed no reminder that the two had had nothing to eat since leaving Shanty's cabin.

He said, "I don't see no telegraph line, so maybe they ain't heard about us yet. I'll leave you in that grove of trees yonder while I go in and get us somethin' to eat. Might buy me a change of clothes, too. Like as not they've put out a description on what I'm wearin'."

He knew he looked different without the beard and long hair, but his frayed homespun cotton shirt was of a kind not widely seen anymore since most men had begun turning toward store-bought clothes. It might spark recognition in someone who had a sharp eye and memory for detail. Another reason for not taking Buster, aside from the boy's weak condition, was that the notices likely described two or even three men, one of them wounded. Alone, perhaps Cordell would not draw attention.

The village probably did not rate a place on any map.

He saw one saloon, a general store, and a blacksmith shop. A small church sat off to itself far enough that it should not distract from business at the saloon. Wind lifted dust from a street pounded into powder by hooves and wagon wheels. He had to summon willpower to ride by the saloon without stopping. The fewer people who saw him, the better. Saloons produced more idle gossip than a barbershop.

The general store offered a variety of smells ranging from dried fruit to leather goods to kerosene, but no whiskey. He found only the paunchy, graying proprietor and a woman customer, who wistfully fingered a bolt of blue dress material. The proprietor called, "I'll be with you shortly, sir. Please feel free to look around while I wait on Mrs. Jones. You might find something you want."

At another time and in another place Cordell might have wanted Mrs. Jones. She was a pleasant-looking woman, possibly in her early thirties. He had always found the ladies attractive. At one time he had considered eighteen properly young. Now as his own age advanced, he was more tolerant of extra years and experience. Eighteen seemed barely out of the cradle.

He removed his hat and bowed from the waist as she glanced at him. She gave him the merest hint of a smile and quickly turned her blue eyes away. He knew it was only an acknowledgment of his courtesy. Lacking any reason to believe otherwise, he had to assume she was a churchgoing woman, a devoted wife and mother.

Bittersweet memories came in a rush, and for a moment he was caught up in a sobering sense of loss, of opportunities not taken, of happiness wasted. He felt envy for the man, whoever he might be, lucky enough to have this woman for his wife.

She said to the proprietor, "The material is pretty, but it'll have to wait, Mr. Arnold. Perhaps the crops will be better this year."

Cordell thought of the bank money, some in his pocket, the rest in his saddlebags. He was tempted to buy the bolt of cloth for the lady, but he knew pride would not allow her to accept such a gift, not even from a friend, much less from a stranger.

He watched her go out the door. "Fine-looking woman," he said.

Arnold nodded, looking over the glasses perched halfway down his nose. "For now, but a few more years of slaving on that farm and she'll be wrinkled and gray. It happens to all of them."

"Pity." Cordell thought of prairie bluebonnets, beautiful in the spring but too soon dry and wilted. He turned to the selection of groceries. "I'm needin' some coffee, some flour, some bacon." He watched the proprietor strain to reach canned sardines on a high shelf, then place them on the counter along with canned tomatoes. Cordell fished dry crackers out of a barrel. He thought of Buster. "A little candy, too."

Arnold took a pencil from its resting place over his ear and pushed his glasses up higher on his nose. As he jotted down the prices, he asked, "Anything else?"

Cordell selected an ordinary blue work shirt that would not attract attention and a pair of plain cotton trousers. With those, he thought, he would pass anywhere as a farmer.

Arnold said casually, "I don't believe I've seen you before."

Cordell was unsure whether that was innocent curiosity or if the storekeeper might have heard something. He said, "I've got kin a little ways east of here. I don't want them seein' me in these wore-out clothes. They'll think I've come beggin'."

Arnold said, "I can understand how they might. The only time I ever see or hear from most of my kin is when they want somethin'."

"Ain't it a fact?" Cordell considered a moment before saying in the most offhand manner he could, "I've been travelin' and ain't heard much news. Anything happenin' that I might've missed?"

"Not around here, but east of here there was a jail-break. Sheriff got killed."

Cordell had feared the sheriff would die, but this was the first time he had heard confirmation. If the folks back there had been keen to capture him before, they would be far more determined now. "They catch whoever done it?"

"The laws are out lookin'. They say there was three of them to start with. One split off. The other two was a big man with a black beard and a young man carryin' a bullet wound. You might keep an eye out for them. They're liable to be dangerous."

"Them kind always are." Cordell had left his pistol and cartridge belt with Buster to avoid arousing suspicion. Most farmers didn't pack iron, not in this settled country. "Maybe I ought to've brought a gun with me, just in case."

"Best thing is to not let them get that close. Leave them to the law. That's what we pay them for."

They probably don't pay the law half enough, Cordell thought. Years ago he had considered becoming a lawman, but he had decided being on the other side of the fence paid better. Long, hungry days on the run had often given him reason to regret that decision. Even now he would quit if he thought he could. But too many people had long memories.

Cordell paid for his purchases. Arnold said, "I keep a pistol under the counter. If they come in here, I'll shoot to kill."

That was the attitude most people would take, Cordell thought. He felt a chill.

The smart thing would be to leave Buster to fare the best he could and get far away as fast as his horse could travel. For a moment he considered that option. It was what Milt had done. But Cordell lived by a different code. He was ashamed that he had entertained the thought for even a moment. One did not abandon a friend, not if he considered himself a man.

He left the village in the same direction in which he had come in. Once out of sight he circled back to the grove where he had left Buster. He found the kid lying quietly, half-asleep or half-unconscious. It was hard to tell which. Cordell set about building a small fire. He saw no water nearby, so coffee would have to wait. Creeks were plentiful in this eastern part of Texas. Surely they would come across one somewhere, and they could camp for the night. For now, a can of tomatoes would take care of thirst. At the moment, he wanted to stop the growling of his stomach. He fried up some bacon in a little skillet he had bought.

He grunted to himself as he considered the irony of his situation. He had saddlebags full of money but could spend little of it without arousing suspicion. By some people's standards he was at this moment a wealthy man, yet he was half-starved and had nothing to eat except fat bacon, some canned sardines, and a few crackers. Besides that, he had a near-helpless kid on his hands.

It was a great life, being an outlaw.

He would give everything he owned, from the bank money down to his horse and saddle, if he could go back twenty-odd years and start over. It would be cheap at any price.

He watched as Buster's eyes fluttered, then came open. He speared a thick strip of bacon on the point of his knife and extended it toward his young companion. "Careful. It might burn you, but it'll give you the strength to keep ridin' a little longer."

Buster took the bacon and made a valiant effort toward eating it. He gave up after a minute and shook his head in futility. "We got to keep ridin'? Toward what?"

"To where it'll be safe for you to rest. Try again. You've got to eat if you're ever goin' to get well."

Buster finally managed to get the bacon down and drink juice from the tomato can. The fever had left him badly dehydrated. He lay back, exhausted.

Cordell said regretfully, "I wish we could stay here, but there's a chance that store man will add up somethin' besides the bill. We got to keep travelin' awhile longer."

Buster groaned as Cordell lifted him into the saddle.

After a few more miles they made a dry camp. Next morning they were traveling by the time the sun came up. By noon Buster was talking out of his head, and his horse was beginning to limp a little. Soon after they had stolen it, Cordell had noticed that it had a misshapen foot, as if it had been injured at some time.

He watched dark clouds building in the east, and before long he could smell rain in the wind. He saw a house surrounded by trees and decided to make an appeal to human kindness on Buster's behalf. It had worked with Shanty. Maybe it would work here. If it didn't, he could employ persuasion with the help of Samuel Colt.

Close up, he could see that one window was broken out, and the roof needed attention. A dead garden out back indicated that no one had lived here in a while, though a field to the south had growing corn. Somebody was farming the land. The place had probably been bought by a neighbor trying to expand his own acreage. It was becoming harder and harder for small farmers to survive. They had to get larger or get out.

"Buster," he said, "I thought lady luck had turned her back on us, but it looks like she's smilin' again."

Buster did not reply. Cordell wondered if he even heard.

RIDING INTO TOWN with Len, Andy saw a wizened, gray-haired man seated on a bench in front of a store, idly whittling a piece of pine. Around him on the porch and beyond lay the shavings and dried and drying brown remnants of chewing tobacco. A little of it ran down his stubbled chin. He reminded Andy of Fowler Gaskin.

Andy asked, "Mister, have you seen anything of two men—a big one and a young one? They'd be ridin' a bay horse and a dun."

The idler gave Andy a dour look and spat a stream of spittle, part of which reached the street. The rest fell on the stained porch. "Stranger, half the horses that pass this way are bays, and duns ain't exactly scarce. If you'll look up the street, you'll see several of both. Take your pick."

Len said, "We're not funnin'. We're Rangers."

The man spat again. "That ain't much recommendation. Some of the sorriest people I ever knowed was Rangers." His face turned belligerent, and he pointed at Len. "I know you, Tanner. You helped lie me into the pen once. Said I'd been stealin' hogs."

"You was."

"The puny evidence you had wouldn't've held water if you hadn't brought in a pet judge."

Andy figured that even if the old man had seen Cordell and Buster, he would lie about it. "Come on, Len. Some people you just can't talk to." He moved toward the courthouse.

Len said, "We caught that old rapscallion dead to rights. It's hard to make friends of people after you've throwed them in jail. They take it personal."

Andy almost tripped on a spittoon that sat beside the door of the sheriff's office. Above it was a small sign: *Spit before you enter.*

The sheriff sat at his desk, laboriously writing with a pen that scratched as it inked a message on a white sheet of paper. He looked up with a frown as if he resented being disturbed. The pen rolled halfway across his desk, leaving a black trail. His voice was far from cordial. "Rangers. I can tell by lookin' at you."

Andy had discovered that a few law officers were jealous of the Rangers. They shouldn't be, he thought, for chances were that they were better paid than Rangers. They just didn't have the reputation or the aura that seemed to follow Rangers whether justified or not.

Sheriff Shively was a dyspeptic-looking sort with a bald head and a prickly attitude. He drew a whiskey bottle out of a drawer and took a swallow, then put it back without offering it to the visitors. He listened impatiently as Andy explained their business, then growled, "Damn Rangers always waltz in here actin' like they've just come from the right hand of God, and they know everything. Now I suspect you're fixin' to ask me for help."

Len said, "Me and Andy don't claim to know it all. Just a little here and there."

"If you Rangers were half the lawmen you claim to be, that outlaw never would've broke out of jail. In fact, you'd've shot him when you caught him, and he wouldn't've made it to jail to start with. Shoot first is my motto. Saves time and taxpayer expense."

Peeved at Shively's attitude, Andy did not bother to explain that no Ranger had been on hand when either the arrest or the break took place. Len did, however, in full detail. "Seein' as it was a sheriff like yourself that was shot, I'd think you'd want to give us all the help you can."

"I knew Tom Blessing. To my way of thinkin' he was too easy on criminals. That's what got him killed. A smart lick across the head with a gun barrel is my way of keepin' them quiet. And if they raise a ruckus, shoot them. No pettifoggin' lawyer can bail them out of the graveyard." Shively narrowed his eyes in speculation. "If I was to help you catch them, who gets the reward?"

Andy's face warmed with indignation. About now a true Comanche would be swinging his war club. But Len shrugged off any such feelings. He said, "We ought to be able to work out somethin' that'd suit everybody."

The sheriff's calculating look indicated that he was mentally counting the dollars. "Tell me what you want me to do. I'll decide if I want to do it or not."

Len said, "You know the people that belong here. Take a look at any strangers and see if they fit the description of Luther Cordell and the young feller that was with him. Me and Andy can make the arrest."

"I'll do my own arrestin', damn it. What makes you think they're here?"

Andy said, "They was headed in this direction when we lost their trail. They might've kept on goin', but there's a chance they've decided to lay up on account of one bein' wounded."

Shively muttered to himself. "I'll do some askin' around. But I don't need no Rangers gettin' in my way. I'll do this myself."

Andy was strongly inclined to tell Shively off and leave, but Len gripped Andy's arm in silent admonition. Len said, "They may not be easy to arrest. We're here to take that job off of your hands."

The sheriff scalded the pair with his eyes. "If I want you, I'll holler. Go set yourselves down at the Lone Star Bar and wait. It always looked to me like settin' is what Rangers are best at."

A quiet deputy with nervous eyes and the beginning of a beer belly waited until Shively had gone down the hall before he spoke. "Don't pay too much mind to the way Homer talks. He's been sour on the Rangers ever since the time he spent three hard days huntin' a horse thief. Two Rangers was just loafin' in a barroom when the man come ridin' up on this stolen pony. They grabbed him before he could swaller his drink. Got a reward from the man that lost the horse. They didn't give none of it to Homer."

Andy said, "He wasn't entitled. He didn't make the arrest."

"But he'd spent three days on the hunt, while they hadn't broke a sweat. A thing like that would naturally gall a man."

"Maybe so," Andy said, "but it don't alter my first opinion, that Homer Shively is a poor excuse for a law-man."

The deputy shrugged. "I get paid to do what he tells me. Homer will still be here when you're gone, and so will I. At least till next election. He's made a lot of people sore at him, so folks may not vote for him again."

Andy said, "Even so, we don't want to take a chance on him makin' a mistake and lettin' Cordell get away."

Andy and Len made an effort to follow Shively as he dropped in at one saloon after another as well as the barbershop and two general stores, making inquiry, giving a thorough looking over to most of the men he encountered. It became monotonous.

Finally, however, Shively devoted his attention to a man sitting in a dark rear corner of a barroom, nursing a whiskey bottle already reduced by more than half. He was a large man with a beard.

Shively approached him with pistol drawn. "All right, you, stand up and raise your hands."

The man's red-veined eyes had trouble focusing on the sheriff. He made no move to comply.

Shively repeated, "Stand up, damn you. Keep them hands where I can see them." He poked the pistol in the stranger's direction.

The man's voice was belligerent. "You ain't no general, and I ain't no soldier. Who the hell are you to be givin' me orders?"

"I'm the county sheriff, and you're under arrest for murder."

Andy saw that this man was not Cordell. He said, "Shively—"

Before he could say more, Shively brought the barrel of his pistol down on the stranger's head. The man fell across the table, tipping it over. The bottle crashed to the floor.

Andy flared. "Damn it, Shively, I tried to tell you. That is not Cordell."

Shively gave him a look of disbelief. "He's a big man with a beard. He fits the description."

"I saw Cordell close enough to know this isn't him. I hope you haven't busted this man's skull."

"He oughtn't to've sassed me. It was his own fault, not showin' respect to the badge."

"He was probably too drunk to see it."

Shively turned to his deputy. "Get somebody to help you drag him over to the jail. We'll charge him with bein' drunk and disorderly."

Andy wanted to knock Shively all the way back to the wall, but he restrained himself. Though justified, such an action would probably set off a legal confrontation between state and county jurisdictions and lead to no end of paperwork. Andy dreaded paperwork.

Len took Andy's arm and pulled him aside. "Maybe he had the right idea about us takin' a sit-down in some pleasant place. We can wait and see what he finds out."

"I don't understand how he ever got elected sheriff."

Shively heard the comment and turned angrily. "There used to be a lot of lawbreakin' riffraff in this county. The citizens got tired of it and wanted a man who would get tough. That's me. I give this kind of trash no quarter."

Sometimes the line between lawbreaker and lawbringer was too thin to define, Andy thought.

He had never developed any particular liking for liquor. He took a beer but sipped it so slowly that the glass was only half-empty after Len had finished two shots of whiskey. Len said, "Everything in this world can't be just like we'd want it. You was about to get in a tangle that I wasn't sure you could win."

"He's got a good whippin' comin' to him."

"And he'll get it sooner or later, but it ain't our place to do it. Right now we've got more important business."

Andy felt uneasy about wasting time when Cordell might be using it to get farther away. "Maybe we ought to go see if Shively has pistol-whipped anybody else," he suggested.

Len showed no sign that the whiskey had affected him. For such a skinny man, he had long demonstrated that he could put away a prodigious amount of food. He seemed to have the same high tolerance for whiskey. He said, "We'd better. He looks slippery as hog grease."

They found that Shively and his deputy had left town. The hostler at the stables said, "I told him I'd seen a couple of strangers out at the old Graham place. A big man and a smaller one. Him and his deputy rode out of here like they'd been turpentined."

While Andy and Len quickly saddled their horses, the hostler gave them directions. "Neighbor named Wilson bought the farm after old man Graham died. It's a good house. Roof don't leak, hardly."

Riding in an easy lope that would not overtax the horses, Andy said, "If it's really Cordell, he's apt to shoot Shively's head off."

Len asked, "Then what are we hurryin' for? We ought to give him time to do it."

"What happens to Shively doesn't worry me, but the idea of losin' Cordell bothers me a lot."

They could see what they took to be the Graham house a mile or so ahead. They heard a distant rattle of gunfire. Excitement prickled Andy's skin. He said, "We'd better whip up."

They pushed their horses hard across the remaining distance. As they approached the house, they saw two men standing and two men flat on the ground. Andy halfway hoped Shively was one of those lying still, but he saw that the sheriff and his deputy remained on their feet.

Len declared in surprise, "I'll be damned! They got Cordell."

Hearing the oncoming horses, Shively whirled around, pointing his pistol toward the Rangers. Andy instinctively dropped low over the saddle horn. The sheriff might shoot first and check identities later. Shively lowered the weapon when he recognized the two. As Andy and Len reined to a stop, Shively said with pride, "Told you I didn't need no Rangers to help me. Looks like that reward is all mine."

Andy thought he should be pleased that Cordell was dead, regardless of who killed him, but he was not. "Maybe," he said.

The larger of the dead men was lying facedown. Andy dismounted and studied him for a minute, then turned him over. He felt his stomach draw into a knot. "This isn't Cordell."

Shively's chin dropped. "What do you mean it ain't Cordell? He's a big man, like you said. And he's got a beard like you said. You tryin' to slicker me out of my reward?"

"Cordell's beard was as black as a crow's wing. This one is brown, with some gray in it."

Shively began to sweat. "Then why did he draw a gun on us as we rode up?"

"What gun? I don't see one."

Andy went to look at the young man, whose lifeless eyes stared up at the bright blue sky. He had seen Cordell's companion only at considerable distance. This boy appeared somewhat heavier, though he could not be sure of that. He said, "If this is the right man, he ought to have at least two bullet holes in him. One of them was mine." Andy knelt. "I don't see a gun on him either."

Sweat rolled down Shively's reddening face. "I swear they was both armed and fixin' to shoot at us. They must've hid those guns."

Andy turned to the deputy. "Did you see them aim at you?"

The deputy trembled. "Homer said they was. I was busy duckin'."

"They never fired a shot, did they?"

The deputy did not answer, but his silence told Andy all he needed to know. Furious, he faced Shively. "You wanted so bad for it to be Cordell that you shot first and didn't ask any questions. You just killed two innocent men."

Shively stammered, "How . . . how do we know they're innocent? It's just your word that this ain't Cordell."

Andy heard hoofbeats. Turning, he saw a middle-aged farmer in overalls, riding up on a mule. The man gave Shively a quick glance and demanded, "What's happened here, Sheriff? I heard shootin'." His gaze dropped to the men on the ground. "Oh my God! George!"

He slipped down from the mule's back and dropped to his knees beside the larger of the two dead men. "Who shot him?"

Shively wiped a sleeve over his sweaty face. "You know him, Wilson?"

"My brother-in-law, George Blaine. I let him move in here to work this farm on shares. That's his boy Adam yonder." He repeated, "Who shot them?"

Shively took a step backward. "It was all a misunderstandin'. An accident. I thought they was a pair of outlaws."

"And you shot them down like dogs?" Fire leaped into Wilson's eyes. "If I had a gun, I'd kill you." He advanced on the sheriff, his fists clenched.

Shively pointed his pistol at the farmer. "Stand back, Wilson. I'll shoot you if I have to."

Andy grabbed Shively's hand and forced the pistol down, then roughly twisted it from the sheriff's grasp. "You've already killed two unarmed men and pistol-whipped another. How many more mistakes do you want to make in one day?"

Wilson demanded, "Who are you?"

Andy said, "We're Rangers. We got here too late."

Wilson's shoulders slumped. He looked again at the two men on the ground. "My wife'll near die when I tell her. She set a lot of store in her brother. That boy, too." He turned a furious gaze back upon Shively. "Since you're Rangers, I want you to arrest him for murder. He's lorded it over this county too long."

Shively's voice was hollow. "I was just tryin' to do my duty. Anybody can make a mistake."

Len said sarcastically, "And that reward never entered your mind. Me and Andy are placin' you under arrest."

Shively's voice seemed about to break. "I thought it was them. Swear to God I did."

Andy told the deputy, "You'd better stay here with the bodies. We'll send help from town."

The deputy looked queasy, but he made no protest.

Wilson declared, "You'd better not let Shively out on bail. If I see him on the street, he's a dead man."

Andy considered placing Wilson under arrest, too, for safety, but perhaps the farmer would cool down once the initial shock subsided.

They presented Shively to the county judge, who agreed that the sheriff belonged in jail for his own good as well as for justice. He said, "He's made too many enemies. Without that badge to protect him, he's a walking target."

With the sheriff in jail and the deputy still out at the farm, Andy and Len were the only lawmen in town. Andy said, "Len, you better go get you some supper while I watch the jail. I'll eat when you get back."

Len was gone long enough to have eaten two suppers. Darkness had come by the time he returned. His expression was grave. He said, "There's a lot of ugly talk goin' around. This old wooden jail looks too flimsy to stand up against a mob."

Len's uneasiness was contagious. Andy said, "We'd better slip him out of town before things come to a head."

Len said, "You need to keep huntin' Cordell. I'll take Shively back east to the next county seat and send a wire to Austin."

Andy was reluctant, but right now Cordell was more important to him than Shively. "I'll miss havin' you with me, Len."

"You've ridden by yourself many a time, and you know your job. Besides, I'm gettin' to where I can't remember which stories I've told you and which I ain't."

"I don't mind hearin' them twice. Sometimes they're different in the second tellin'."

"I've got a creative memory."

Andy stood watch while Len brought his horse around behind the jail, leading a second for Shively. Len said, "Watch out for yourself, Badger Boy. Don't take no chances with Cordell."

Andy felt an emptiness as Len and the deposed sheriff disappeared into the darkness. He took no offense when Len called him Badger Boy. It was a different matter when Farley Brackett did it.

Andy freed the prisoner Shively had arrested in the saloon. The man was obviously hurting. Andy gave him the bottle he had seen Shively take from a desk drawer. "Don't drink it all at one time," he said.

The judge came around after a while, worried about the possibility of mob violence. Andy showed him the empty cell and explained Len's mission. The judge nodded approval. "You've already done what I was about to recommend."

Andy asked, "What do you reckon'll happen to Shively?"

"He'll stand trial before twelve good men and true, who will probably decide he deserves a stretch in the state pen at Huntsville. He'll find a number of men he sent there. They'll be glad to see him." The judge grimaced, pondering the mental image. "Now, I don't think you and I want to hang around here and face those men when they come. It could be unpleasant. I suggest that we leave the jailhouse door open for their convenience and repair to the Lone Star Bar for a quiet drink."

Andy said, "Just one beer."

After a day like this one, a beer would be worth its weight in silver.

8

The remnants of a woodpile lay scattered out back. Cordell hurried in with an armload and went back out to fetch more before it got wet. He whittled shavings from a piece of broken chair to get a fire started. Buster seemed to alternate between chills and fever.

Cordell rolled Buster's blanket out on the floor near the fire. He said, "You'll feel better when I get some warm food into you."

A damp, cold wind ushered in the rain. Cordell felt a chill. He pulled Buster's blanket up to cover the boy's shoulders. "Can't have you catchin' pneumonia on top of your other troubles."

He stoked the fire in an effort to heat the room better. He brought in more wood, though it was wet now. Stacked near the fire, it might dry before he had to use it. He made coffee and fried some bacon, but Buster showed little interest in it or even in the candy Cordell had bought. He lay listless, his face hot to the touch. He occasionally murmured words Cordell could not decipher.

"Damn it, kid," Cordell said, "don't you go and die on me."

The last thing he wanted to see was visitors, but there they were, a man and a woman in a wagon. They drew up near the door. The woman climbed down and hurried into the house, out of the rain. The man drove the wagon around back. He unhooked the horses and hurriedly led them to a shed where Cordell had placed his and Buster's.

The woman was surprised and a little frightened to see Cordell. He would guess her to be a farm wife in her thirties. "We didn't know anybody was here," she said, keeping her distance. She shivered, her clothing wet.

Cordell said, "We mean you no harm, ma'am. Get over close to the fire and warm yourself. Me and the boy were just passin' by and came in out of the rain."

She complied, holding her arms tightly against her body. "A spring rain can be awfully cold."

"Yes, ma'am. Sure can."

The man entered the house with obvious apprehension. He gave Cordell an uneasy study. "I was surprised when I saw two horses in the shed. Been a while since anybody lived in this house. We tried to get here before the rain started."

"Live around here, do you?" Cordell asked.

"A few miles farther on. We didn't figure on the rain. Our name is Archer. I'm Daniel. My wife is Patience." Hesitantly he extended his hand, and Cordell took it.

The woman had glanced at Buster when she entered. Now she gave him a closer look. "I thought he was just sleeping. But now I see that he's sick."

"Got himself hurt, ma'am," Cordell said.

"Has he been to a doctor?"

"We ain't been anywhere close to one."

The man knelt beside Buster and pulled the cover back. "Burnin' up with fever. What happened to him?"

Cordell let his hand ease down toward the pistol on his hip, then caught himself. He saw no sign of a gun on this couple. They were farmers, and no immediate threat. "Got himself shot."

Archer said, "I'd better not ask you how."

"I'd as soon you didn't."

Archer's expression indicated that he was making a pretty good guess.

The woman gasped. Her hand went up to her mouth. "You two are outlaws."

"There's some would call me that, but this boy ain't one, not at heart. He just let himself get misled."

"By who?"

"Mainly me. I was raised better, but somewhere along the way I turned left when I ought to've turned right. I'm mortally ashamed for lettin' this boy follow me down the same road."

Mrs. Archer said, "I think you're the man we've heard about. They say you killed a sheriff."

"I've never killed anybody in my life, except maybe in the war, and I ain't even sure about that."

Archer's face was grim. "Looks to me like the boy's dyin'. He needs a doctor real bad."

"If I take him to one, he faces a stretch in the pen—or worse."

The woman had gotten past her fear. Severely she said, "I think he'd rather take his chances with the law than to lie here and die in this miserable old house."

"I just don't see what I can do."

Archer glanced at his wife. "There's somethin' *we* can do. Patience and me, we can take him to town in the wagon and let you go on by yourself. You could be a good many miles on your way before the law knows anything about it."

Cordell could not understand these people. They were willing to help without even asking about payment. "You could get in trouble."

Mrs. Archer said, "We're all human beings. Anyway, the sheriff is a friend of ours."

Cordell turned to the door, working his way through a tangle of misgivings. Reluctantly he said, "You've got a deal. I'll harness that team back up for you." Hurrying outside, he saw that the rain had slackened. He hitched the team to the wagon, then saddled his horse. He decided to leave Buster's here. Buster wouldn't need him.

He carried the boy to the wagon and placed him in its bed, making sure the blanket was wrapped tightly around him. The Archers followed him out. Cordell extracted a handful of bills from a saddlebag. "This is for your trouble."

Archer shook his head, and his wife frowned disapproval. "We're not doin' this for money," Archer said.

"Then why?"

The woman said, "It's plain to see that you're not a churchgoing man. If you don't know, there's no way we can explain. You'd better be on your way, Mr. Cordell, if you intend to stay ahead of the law."

Cordell was taken aback by the use of his name. He had not told them what it was. That damned telegraph! A man couldn't ride fast enough or far enough anymore to get ahead of it.

He watched the wagon move away into a light mist that lingered after the rain had waned. He told himself this was the best thing for Buster. Maybe the law had enough mercy that it wouldn't hang a green kid, though he probably faced a stretch in Huntsville. At least he would have a chance for a better life once he served his time. Maybe he would stay on a straight road from then on, as Cordell wished *he* had.

But what if Buster didn't live? Archer had said he

looked to be dying. Cordell tried to deny it to himself, but deep in his soul he knew Archer was right. It might already be too late for a doctor to save the kid. Cordell could leave here now and get away from the law, but he would never get away from Buster. He would always wonder: did the boy make it, or did he not?

Aw hell! he thought. *I never did have the sense God gave a jackrabbit.*

He set his horse into a lope to catch up to the wagon.

The Archers both looked back over their shoulders. Cordell rode up even with them. They asked no questions, and he offered no explanation. At length Archer said, "You're takin' a big chance. From what we hear, the law is lookin' for you all the way to Austin and San Antonio."

"Life is like a poker game. Sometimes you hold a good hand, and sometimes you don't. You play them as they're dealt and hope for gambler's luck."

Mrs. Archer said, "Or pray for providence to intervene."

It was midway between midnight and dawn when they reached town. Archer pulled the wagon to a stop in front of a house. A wooden sign was attached to the front gate, though Cordell could not read it in the dark. Archer knocked on the door hard enough that Cordell feared he might wake up half the town. Soon a moving lamp cast a dim light through the front window. The door opened. Out came a smallish man in long underwear, unbuttoned trousers, and no shirt. He extended the lamp toward Archer's face.

Archer said, "It's an emergency, Doctor."

"It always is when folks come in the middle of the night." The doctor carried the lamp to the wagon and peered at the blanket-wrapped figure. "Anybody I know?"

"I doubt it. The kid has got a bullet in him. He's far gone."

Cordell dismounted and lifted Buster from the wagon bed. The doctor motioned toward the house, and Cordell followed him to a back room. The doctor said, "Put him down on the bed. I'll have a look at him." He apologized to Mrs. Archer for being half-dressed. "Hold the lamp, would you, Mr. Archer?" He folded the blanket back, opened Buster's shirt, and gazed with disbelief at the wound. He demanded, "Who the hell put this bandage on him?"

Cordell said apologetically, "It's all I had."

"Damned poor job." The old bandage was stiff with dried blood. He stripped it away and said, "I hope the bullet was taken out, at least."

Cordell said, "I tried. Couldn't get it."

"How long has it been in there?"

Cordell counted. "Four days, I think. Maybe five. I lost track."

Angrily the doctor said, "You let him languish to the point of death, then expect me to save him? He should have seen a doctor right away. That bullet has poisoned his blood."

Cordell had sensed it but had denied it to himself. "What chance has he got?"

"There's no point in lying to you. I doubt that God himself could bring him back."

Cordell slumped into a wooden chair. His throat was constricted, and his eyes burned. Must be that smoky lamp, he thought.

The doctor's tone softened. "Is he your son?"

Cordell shook his head. "I wouldn't have led my son into a mess like this. And I shouldn't have let that boy get into it, either. I'd give anything . . ." He broke off.

Mrs. Archer's eyes showed pity. "Maybe you'd better get away while you can. We'll stay here with him. He won't die alone."

"No, I'll stay. I won't blame you if you send for the law."

Archer said, "We won't do that till the boy is gone. Even then, we'll try to give you a little time."

"Why?"

"It's plain to see that you did what you could for him, except gettin' him to a doctor. A lot of men in your situation would've gone off and left him."

"I ain't so noble that it didn't cross my mind."

Patience Archer said, "That's the first step toward redemption, facing temptation without giving in to it."

"I'm afraid I'm beyond redemption."

"No man is beyond redemption until he draws his last breath."

Buster called out weakly, "Cordell. Where are you?"

Cordell left the chair and gripped Buster's hand. "I'm here. I wasn't goin' anyplace without you."

"Cordell, am I dyin'?"

Cordell swallowed, trying to think of an answer he could give without lying. He saw none. "No, kid, you're goin' to be all right."

"I heard the doctor." Buster began to weep. "I don't want to die."

Cordell was too badly choked to say anything.

Buster pleaded, "Don't tell my mother . . . I don't want her . . . to know what I done."

Cordell wanted to speak but nothing came.

Buster murmured, "God, it hurts so bad."

He drifted into sleep. Head bowed, Mrs. Archer began to pray in a whisper. She reached out to her husband, taking his hand, then reached toward Cordell. He was uncertain what was expected of him, but he bowed his head as she had and took her hand while she continued her prayer. He could not remember the last time he had heard someone pray. Though confused and ashamed for his shortcomings, he took warmth from the compassion of these strangers.

Buster slipped so quietly into death that Cordell was not sure just when the passage came. The doctor covered Buster's face with the blanket, then moved toward the window. "Sunup," he said to Cordell. "The sheriff will open his office in a little while. I'll have to tell him. If you're going to leave, you'd better get started."

Cordell struggled for control of his voice. "I'm obliged to you, ma'am, for the prayer. It's been so long since I've talked to the Lord, I guess I've forgotten how. And I'm afraid He's forgotten about me."

She said, "He never forgets anyone. If it's any comfort, your young friend is now in His care."

"It's better care than I gave him." Cordell laid his hand on the blanket that covered Buster. "I'm thankin' you both. You done more than anybody like me had a right to expect." He turned toward the doctor. "I'm leavin' you some money. I wish you'd see that he gets a decent burial with a preacher to read over him. And get him a proper headstone."

"Anything you want put on it?"

"Just that his real name was David Jackson. And that he was a good boy." Cordell blinked his burning eyes. "I've got to let his mother know somehow. I can't just let her wonder what ever became of him."

"You heard what he said."

"I can tell a good story when I have to. He was shot

tryin' to protect some folks from a robber. If any of his family ever comes askin', I hope you won't tell them different."

The rising sun caught Cordell squarely in the eyes as he walked outside. It brought tears.

Riding away from town in an easy lope that he hoped would not overtax a horse already tired, Cordell felt as if a hundred-pound weight had settled in the bottom of his stomach. He kept seeing Buster's fevered face and rehashing the things he might have done differently. He had had more than one chance to take Buster to a doctor. He had told himself he held back out of fear that the boy might be hanged. Now he wondered if that had been the real reason. Maybe his stronger fear had been for himself.

It changed nothing to brood over past mistakes, but he could not help it. If thirty lashes across his back would relieve him of his guilt, he would welcome them.

He slowed to a trot to ease the stress on his horse, but he looked back often, half expecting to see someone catching up. The ground was still wet from the rain, and his tracks were more visible because of it. He would be easy to trail. He looked for a well-traveled road where his tracks might be lost among others, though this meant more people would see him. The old notices would describe him as heavily bearded and wearing different clothes, but the Archers and the doctor were sure to give the authorities a more current picture of him.

He came to a road perpendicular to the westerly direction he had been traveling. It had seen some traffic since the rain. Two freight wagons approached from the left. He turned to the right, two hundred yards ahead of the wagons, hoping the hooves and the iron rims would obliterate his tracks or at least cause confusion and lost time to anyone trying to follow.

He sensed that they might be Rangers, hard men to shake loose from. In the wild days of Reconstruction after the war, the Rangers had been disbanded. A unionist government had organized an alternative, a state police force. Most of these men could not find their butt with both hands. For someone of Cordell's persuasion, those had been good times.

Late in the morning he saw a farmer in a distant field, working two mules to a plow, and envied him. The farmer didn't have an ill-starred kid weighing heavily on his conscience. He had probably left a comfortable house at sunup after his wife fixed him a good breakfast and perhaps a lunch to carry with him to the field. Tonight he could go home to a hot supper—maybe even pie or cake—and share a soft bed with his woman. If he ever felt compelled to look back over his shoulder, as Cordell was doing, it would only be in hope that he would see a good rain coming over the horizon.

Cordell could not remember the last time he had enjoyed pie or cake, much less a woman.

We harvest what we plant, he thought. *Sometimes wheat, sometimes weeds. Looks like all I've sowed is weeds.*

LEN'S NEVER-ENDING TALK had made the miles seem shorter. Sometimes Andy paid little attention to the words, but it had been comforting to hear the constant rise and fall of Len's voice and know he was not alone. He was alone now, and since leaving town he had seen nobody except a couple of farmers.

A house lay just off to his right. He decided to go ask a few questions. Though he had found no trail he could be certain was Cordell's, his instincts told him he was traveling in the right direction.

A window was broken out, and a few shingles were gone from the roof. The place was obviously vacant. He had a gut feeling that he should check it anyway. His Comanche hunches had a hair-raising way of being correct from time to time. A vacant house would be a good place for the fugitives to lay up.

Even if he saw Cordell, he was not certain he would recognize him. The times he had seen the man, a thick beard had covered most of his face. He might look different if he shaved it off. But a shave would not change the eyes, and Andy remembered the eagle sharpness of Cordell's.

Horse and wagon tracks were plain in the drying mud. Someone had been here recently. Dismounting, Andy looked closely at the horse tracks. He did not see the twisted hoofprint Len had shown him earlier.

A dun horse nickered and ambled out from behind the old house, curious about Andy's mount. Andy felt a tingle of excitement. This could be one of those he saw at the jailbreak. He circled around to look at the tracks the horse left. He recognized the print and drew the rifle from beneath his leg. Cordell might be in that house.

Andy's mouth went dry. He tied his horse and approached from the front, crouching to make a more difficult target. He jumped up on the small front porch and threw his back against the wall in case someone came out shooting. Nobody did. He rushed through the door, holding his pistol at a level that would take a man in the brisket. The worn pine floor creaked under the weight of his boots. He saw no one. The place was as dead as an Indian graveyard.

He saw dried mud on the floor and coals in the fireplace, still warm. He was certain the fugitives had been here, but they had been on horseback. Andy wondered about the fresh wagon tracks. One of the men was wounded. It could be that the wagon had carried him away. That would explain why his horse was still here.

Cordell had probably kidnapped whoever had happened along in the wagon. Perhaps he had killed them. He had not had time to go far. Andy hurried out toward his tied horse. The horse and wagon tracks headed westward. *Even I ought to be able to follow those,* he thought.

Cordell had the devil's own luck, but maybe this time his luck was running out.

Andy had ridden for an hour or so when he met two freight wagons coming eastward. He signaled for the lead driver to stop. The bewhiskered man first gave him a quizzical look and seemed disinclined to obey. Andy wished he had a badge to show him, but the state had not yet seen fit to issue them to the Rangers. Len had had a silversmith make his from a Mexican peso. He had paid for it himself.

"I'm a Ranger," Andy shouted. "Pull up."

The driver sawed on the lines and brought his team to a halt. "We don't stop these wagons for just anybody," he said. "I couldn't tell you was the law."

"Did you meet a wagon along the way?"

"Just one. There was a farmer and his wife on the seat and a sick man layin' behind them. They said they was takin' him to town."

"Anybody else with them?"

"Big feller on horseback. Are they charged with somethin'?"

"Two of them are. They killed a sheriff."

The driver hunched his shoulders as if he had taken a

chill. "Glad we didn't have nothin' they'd want. That big man had a dark look about him. He may not be took easy."

"I'll take him."

"Maybe. Maybe not." The driver shook his head. "It's no wonder they've buried so many of you Rangers."

Andy said, "They ain't goin' to bury this one anytime soon."

Though he burned to break into a run, he held to a moderate pace. He did not want to be set afoot, leading a wrung-out mount.

Darkness caught him soon after he left the teamsters. Clouds obscured the stars and moon. It was about to get as dark as the inside of a tar barrel. He wanted to keep riding, but he knew he was likely to lose the tracks. Moreover, he had pushed his horse hard. At least, he knew his quarry was headed for town.

He staked his mount and the pack mule. He made coffee over a small fire and tried to content himself with a strip of beef jerky. It was like chewing a dry cowhide. The only flavor came from the pepper and salt applied in the drying. To him, jerky was the next thing to nothing. But when he had nothing else to eat, jerky had its compensations.

About the middle of the next morning, the wagon tracks led him within sight of town. There they were lost amid a multitude of newer tracks. He had been here before and remembered that the town was a county seat. He saw its courthouse from half a mile away, its cupola reaching far above its second floor. From a quarter mile, Andy heard the loud strike of its clock. He recalled having been here as witness in a trial. Court had to stop and wait while the bell shook the building and made more racket than three lawyers yelling at the same time.

This was a typical farming town for its part of south-central Texas, a cotton gin standing alone and silent at the edge of the settlement. Last year's crop had been ginned, and this year's harvest was months away. Andy's fingers itched as he remembered how the dry hulls scratched when he pulled the bolls. It was another reason he had no wish to spend his life as a farmer.

He wished Len were here, though neither would know just where to start looking. He could imagine Len asking, "Ain't there some Indian spirit you can call up?"

Perhaps he could, if he could talk to a Comanche medicine man. But they were long since gone, either dead or exiled to Indian Territory. Still, he reasoned, if those people were bringing the wounded man to town, they would be looking for a medicine man, a white one.

At a loading dock on the side of a general store, a clerk wearing a tie and an apron was loading groceries into a wagon. Andy rode up to him and asked, "You got a doctor in this town?"

The clerk pointed. "Doc Satterwhite, down the street yonder on the opposite side. He's pretty good if you're not too sick."

"Much obliged."

He found the house by a sign on the yard gate. He doubted that Cordell was still there, but if he was, he would flush like a quail.

If Len were here, one could take the front door, the other the back. As it was, Andy walked up to the front door and knocked. He dropped his hand to his pistol and held his breath until a woman peered at him through a curtain. She swung the door open. Andy took a quick look inside before he moved. He saw nothing in the front room that caused alarm. He could hear a child whining and a mother's soothing voice in a back room.

The woman at the door asked, "What can we do for you?"

"I'm a Ranger, ma'am. Did somebody bring a wounded man in here last night?"

"Yes, the Archers from out on Branch Creek."

"Is he still here?"

"I'm sorry to say that he is not."

Andy heard a man's voice in the next room. "Excuse me, Mrs. Johnson. I'll be right back." A middle-aged, little man with a carefully trimmed mustache and goatee came out into the front parlor. "I'm Dr. Satterwhite. I heard you ask about a wounded man. Friend of yours?"

"He's a fugitive. I've been trailin' him and an older man for several days."

The doctor frowned. "I did what I could, but it was already too late. It always hurts to see a young man die in such a miserable way. Whoever put that bullet in him has no reason to be proud of himself."

Andy felt as if the doctor had hit him with a sledge. "It was me," he admitted. "I aimed at somebody else, but the wrong man got in the way."

The doctor's severe countenance softened as he recognized Andy's regret. "It should not have been a fatal wound. He could have lived if he had received proper attention early enough."

"I reckon we were pressin' him and Cordell too hard."

"Cordell?" the doctor said. "That's the name the sheriff and the Archers used. The sheriff said he's a bad one."

Andy said, "Bad enough."

"Funny thing, though, for a bad man. He wept when that boy died. You'd have thought he had lost his own son. He left money for a decent Christian burial and asked me to buy a headstone."

"Did he give you a name? All we know is that the boy was called Buster."

"I wrote it down. It was David Jackson."

"Did Cordell mention where he came from?"

"No. I heard the boy beg him not to let his mother know how he died. Cordell promised."

Andy considered for a moment. "The people that brought Jackson in . . . I hope Cordell didn't do them any harm."

"Quite the contrary. He thanked them for their help. Mrs. Archer told me he even tried to give them money, but they wouldn't take it."

"Odd. Most outlaws aren't much on givin' money away. But I guess he didn't put much work into gettin' it."

The doctor said, "On the contrary again, I'd say he paid a high price."

The sheriff was a portly man named Mitchell, well into middle age and walking with heavy dependence on a cane. He explained that he had suffered a broken leg a few months ago, trying to stop a runaway team of mules. He said, "I halfway been expectin' you. A wire from your state office said you might come along lookin' for Luther Cordell. They asked me to lend you any assistance."

Andy said, "A wounded kid was brought to town last night. Cordell was with him."

"I know. I talked to the Archers. They said he left about daylight. Everybody was careful not to watch which way he went. I've sent two deputies out to try and pick up his trail, but I don't hope for much. Too many roads leadin' out of here, and too much traffic."

Mitchell related the description the Archers had given. Andy was not surprised to learn that Cordell had shaved off his beard and cut his hair. Mitchell said, "Mrs. Archer told me she was scared of him at first, but she got over it when she saw how upset he was about that boy. Said a man couldn't be all bad if he had them kind of feelin's."

"Didn't seem like he had much feelin' for Tom Blessing."

"It's hard to understand the criminal class. They ain't hooked up the same as me and you."

Andy said, "I'd just as well wait and see if your deputies find anything. I could use a good meal anyway."

Mitchell opened a desk drawer and offered a drink. Andy demurred. Mitchell took a swallow and almost choked.

"Prime moonshine," he said. "A cousin of mine makes it."

Andy said, "That's illegal, isn't it?"

"There's good laws, and there's bad laws. I don't enforce the bad ones. A man ought to be able to do what he wants to with his own corn crop." Mitchell dismissed the subject. "Hadn't you better take a look at the body? Confirm that this David Jackson is the man you shot?"

"I only saw him at some distance, but I'll go see."

They walked over to the undertaker's. The kid lay covered in a coffin balanced across two sawhorses. The undertaker was finishing a wooden lid. He stopped to uncover the face.

Though Andy had not had a good look at Jackson, he studied the peaceful features and knew instinctively that this was the rider he had shot. Regret settled over him like a shroud. "He's nothin' but a kid."

Mitchell said, "You acted in the line of duty."

"He's no less dead."

"I've killed a couple of men that needed it real bad, but they still laid heavy on my conscience. You have to look at it as part of your job. When you wear the badge, you take what comes with it."

Andy tried for consolation. "I guess if I hadn't shot him, somebody else would've. He was marked when he took up with the wrong kind of company." He felt a rising of anger against Cordell. "What kind of a man would lead an innocent kid into a life that was likely to get him killed?"

Mitchell suggested, "Maybe he never was all that innocent. Some of the worst criminals I ever saw was preachers' sons."

The undertaker said, "Brother Jones will preach the funeral at two o'clock up at the burying ground. The Archers said they'll be there." He looked like a preacher himself.

Mitchell said, "Even an outlaw kid deserves a few mourners. I'll go."

Andy covered Buster's face. "Me, too. I owe him that much. And I'd like to talk to the Archers."

Standing beside the open grave, Bible in his hand, the minister delivered a fervent preachment against young men taking the wrong road in life. Andy was the only young man present to hear it. The gathering was small, just the sheriff, the Archers, and a few townspeople who came mostly out of curiosity, or perhaps for lack of anything better to do. The brief ceremony closed with each person dropping a handful of sand into the grave. It made a soft, whispering sound, falling upon the pine lid of the plain coffin.

The Archers were grim-faced as they turned away. Andy hurried to catch up to them. He identified himself as a Ranger and said, "I'd like you to tell me anything you can about Cordell."

The man and his wife glanced at one another before Archer answered, "We don't know much to tell you. We only saw him for a little while. It was not the kind of situation that calls for a lot of talk."

"What did he look like?"

Archer described him as large, muscular, clean-shaven except for a two- or three-day growth of whiskers. "He could be any farmer you'd meet travelin' down the road."

Mrs. Archer said, "He was overcome with grief and remorse. Like a father who has just lost his son."

Andy said, "You know, don't you, that he has a price on his head?"

"So we heard, but he did not strike us as the badman the sheriff described him to be. You should have seen how gentle he was with that boy. Had I not known otherwise, I could more easily have taken him for a preacher than an outlaw." Mrs. Archer looked to her husband for confirmation, and he nodded in solemn agreement.

Archer said, "He swore to us that he never killed anybody. He acted like a man who truly wants to change his ways. We know you consider it your duty to capture him, but couldn't you somehow just lose his trail and let him get out of the country? He wouldn't be the first outlaw who ever got away."

Mrs. Archer said, "We have heard that under extreme circumstances the Rangers have been known to act as judge and jury. Couldn't you be a judge in this case? A lenient one?"

The suggestion left Andy off-balance. "That would be against the oath I took as a Ranger. Anyway, somebody killed one of the best friends I ever had. Maybe it was Cordell, and maybe it wasn't. Either way, I've got to find out for myself. That means stayin' on his trail."

Archer said, "Then I'm afraid we can't wish you luck."

Mrs. Archer added, "If you do find him, please try to take him without bloodshed. I believe he's a better man than you give him credit for. Perhaps better even than he knows."

The couple walked away arm in arm, leaving Andy shaking his head. How could a man with a record like Cordell's so easily turn strangers into friends?

9

The horse was wearying. Even at a walk, it labored to keep moving. Cordell had put many miles behind him in the days since Buster had died. They had been melancholy miles, for his burden of guilt had lost little of its weight. Again and again, memory punished him by bringing him the face of the dying kid.

Cordell was aware that carrying Buster to a doctor had exposed his whereabouts, giving the law a fresh start in its search for him. He had traveled hard to put several county lines between him and that town, pushing his mount to the edge of its endurance. Now he had to find a place to lay up, or he had to make a trade. Under the circumstances he disliked having to steal a fresh horse. It was not that he had moral objections, but he knew it would put the locals on his trail as well as possibly alerting the Rangers. Not even bank robbery stirred people's dander as violently as horse theft.

He had carefully avoided towns, so he did not know exactly where he was. He knew only that he had reached the central part of Texas. The landscape of chalky hills suggested that he was probably somewhere north of Austin. A cousin named Jedediah Fergus lived near Lampasas. Jedediah had his faults, but surely he would be willing to hide his kin a week or two while Cordell and his mount rested.

Lampasas had a rough reputation. The Rangers had been called in more than once to put down a savage feud between families and to break up gangs that made life precarious for people caught in the middle. It had been Cordell's kind of place. A man who knew his way around could profit from that sort of situation without actually being drawn up in the funnel of the cyclone. During the feud, he and Jedediah had sold horses to one side, then taken them back under cover of darkness and resold them to the other. The cousin had then branched out on his own, succumbing to an ambition that outmatched his abilities. Caught, he had served a couple of years of involuntary employment with the state down at Huntsville.

Cordell, on the other hand, had sensed that the risk had begun to outweigh the potential profit and had sought his fortune elsewhere. Though willing to take a gamble, he always made it a point to hold back some chips.

Jedediah had married a farm, the only way he would ever have acquired one. He had survived an attempted assassination only because his father-in-law was a poor shot. He had the good fortune to see the enraged old man die of a massive heart seizure immediately afterward. Sometimes, Cordell thought, it was more profitable to be lucky than to be smart.

Following a deeply rutted wagon trail, he came to a fork and was stymied. He did not know which direction to take. A farmhouse stood on a hill a quarter mile away, but he was wary about going up and asking directions. Some people in this part of the country surely remembered him and possibly knew the law was looking for him. He was about to make an arbitrary decision and hope for the best. Then he saw a young black man approaching, riding a mule. He was probably too young to remember Cordell's horse-swapping days here. Because of his color he would be out of the mainstream of local society and likely knew nothing about the current manhunt.

Cordell greeted him with a nod. "Boy, does one of these roads go to Lampasas?"

"Why, yes, sir, they both does. One sashays a little to the north and the other sashays a little to the south. But they both gets to the same place."

"Which one is the shortest?"

"I reckon they're pretty much the same."

"Which one is the best?"

The young man pondered a moment. "Neither one. Whichever you take, you'll wish you'd taken the other."

Cordell flipped the youngster a fifty-cent piece. "You've been a lot of help."

The youngster smiled as broadly as if it had been ten dollars.

Cordell remembered that his cousin's farm lay among hills more or less north of Lampasas, so he took the right-hand fork. As he had done for days, he pulled off the trail and sought cover when he saw someone coming. In due time he spotted the town ahead, on low ground along Sulphur Creek. It appeared to have grown some since he had been here last. He quit the trail and cut across country, for now he recognized landmarks. He counted more houses than he had seen before, and new fields in places where the land was flat enough to plow. Cattle grazed on the hills. Rain had brought up more grass than he remembered, but that was likely to be temporary. From here west, dry spells outnumbered the wet ones. Prosperity was elusive.

He hoped it had touched his cousin, for Jedediah was prone to hard luck and bad times, mostly self-imposed through lack of good judgment and avoidance of sweat. He was one of those people who seemed addicted to wrong choices. One of his few good choices had been when he managed to marry a plain-looking woman whose father owned property, and whose sudden death left it in her possession.

Cordell's impression was that Irmadell never let Jedediah forget it. Whatever material benefit the marriage had brought him, he had earned it by having to live with that barren, demanding shrew.

Smoke rising from a metal chimney told him she was in the kitchen and reminded him how long it had been since he had eaten anything substantial. The thought of food tempted him to rush, but better judgment prevailed. Caution made him approach slowly from the farm's back side, keeping the large red barn between himself and the modest frame house.

He heard cursing and stepped quickly down from the horse, his hand on his pistol. He held still, listening, until he was confident the cursing was not aimed at him. The voice was Jedediah's. The comments were directed toward a brindle cow he was milking beneath a low shed. "Hold still, you damned old slut! I'll take a whip to you."

Cordell said, "Do, and you'll get clabbered milk."

Jedediah jerked around in surprise, tipping the bucket and spilling milk on one leg of his overalls. A little brown tobacco juice trickled down his long, bewhiskered jaw. "Luther! What the hell you doin' here?"

"Just come to visit my kin."

Jedediah was large, like Cordell, except that he ran more to fat than to muscle. It took him a bit to steady down. He seemed to have lost his breath. At last he said, "Good thing you didn't come yesterday. We had John Laws goin' over this place like a swarm of bees, lookin' for you."

Cordell felt a letdown. He had hoped he was far enough

west to put the excitement behind him. "Then the news has gotten here."

"And gone a lot further, I'd wager. They're sayin' you murdered a sheriff."

"They're mistaken. It wasn't me that done it."

"They say it was, and that's what counts. They got a reward out for you. Three thousand dollars, dead or alive."

"Three thousand." Cordell was surprised. "That's more than I've ever been worth." Before the bank robbery in Galveston, at least.

Jedediah went back to his milking. "There was somebody else here lookin' for you. Said you and him was partners."

"Did he give you a name?"

"Milt. I don't remember the last name."

"Hayward. Milt Hayward." Cordell cursed under his breath. He knew he should not be surprised. "We done a couple of jobs together, but he wasn't no partner of mine."

"He said you mentioned me one time as bein' kin. Seemed anxious to find you, more anxious even than the law."

Cordell didn't need this when he already had more than enough to worry about. Milt would be looking for his share of the Galveston money. He would probably be happy to take it all if he could. Even by Cordell's liberal standards, he was a scoundrel, a criminal of the lowest degree.

Jedediah stopped milking and turned the cow's calf in with her to finish what was left in her udder. He said, "There's folks around here who don't remember you too kindly. They'd jump like a bullfrog at a chance to collect. If I was you, I'd keep ridin'." Jedediah looked hopeful.

"Been ridin' too long already. My horse is about wore

out, and I ain't far behind him. I need a place where we can rest for a few days."

Jedediah declared with alarm, "Not here."

"We're kin. I figure you owe me. You made good money when we worked together."

"But then you rode off and left, and pretty soon the laws had me by the short hair. When I got out of the pen, Irmadell like to've not let me come home. She was mad at me, but she was a hell of a lot madder at you."

"Do you always let that little bitty woman tell you what to do?"

"I have to. Everything around here has got her name on it."

Jedediah never did have the backbone of a lizard, Cordell thought. He had been handy in their business transactions because he was a natural follower. He did what Cordell told him to. When he tried to do something on his own, it usually collapsed in a puff of dust.

Cordell said, "Since the law has already given this farm a goin' over, maybe they won't be back."

"Irmadell still don't like you, Luther."

"Maybe the sight of a little money would make her like me better."

Jedediah's interest perked up. "You still got what you raised in that bank robbery?"

"Ain't had a chance to spend much of it."

Jedediah began looking hungry. "I'll bet you got it right there in them saddlebags."

Cordell frowned in suspicion. They were cousins, but only by an accident of birth, not by choice. When money was involved, blood ties could easily develop a slipknot. "Never you mind where I've got it. Just tell Irmadell I'll make it worth you-all's while to put me up."

Jedediah became as friendly as a pot-licking dog. "You

got me all wrong, Luther. I was just thinkin' of the danger to you. Of course we'll take you in. What're kinfolks for, anyway? The thought of you givin' us money never entered my mind."

"Of course not." Cordell led his horse into a corral next to the barn and unsaddled him. He carried the saddle into the barn and dropped it on the floor. He detached the saddlebags and hung them over his left arm. Finding a barrel of oats, he scooped up a good serving in a bucket and dumped it into a trough. Cordell listened to the horse's teeth eagerly grinding the grain and thought again of his own stomach.

"How long till Irmadell serves supper?"

Worry returned to Jedediah's face. "Maybe you better let me go in the house and talk to her first. She'll need a little softenin' up."

"Tell her about the money. That ought to smooth out her ruffles."

As Cordell remembered, Irmadell had always expressed moral opposition to his and her husband's horse dealings, though she had never shown any reservations about the money they brought in. She had grabbed Jedediah's share and held it like a miser. He would not have had whiskey money if he had not held out some.

Cordell waited outside the door, listening. He heard Irmadell's strident voice raised in indignation. He could not hear what Jedediah was saying, but Irmadell slowly calmed down. Cordell assumed the talk about money was what did it. He entered the kitchen and said, "Howdy, Irmadell. You look like you've lost some weight."

Women had usually responded with a smile when he made a comment like that, but Irmadell had no excess weight to lose. In contrast to her husband, she was short and scrawny. Dynamite sticks were small too, yet they could yield fire and brimstone. Her mouth tried to smile while her eyes stayed cold. "No more than this old place produces with Jedediah farmin' it, a body is bound to lose weight. But you can share what little we got."

He sensed that she was already counting the money.

She said, "If you was to see fit to share a few dollars, I could go fetch some extra groceries from town."

Cordell did not have to study long on that proposal. If Irmadell showed up in town with money, the law would immediately be on the alert. It would not take much persuasion to wring the truth out of her. "We'll get by on what's here," he said. "I'll pay you for it when I leave." Maybe anticipation would keep her pacified, even if a long way short of happy.

She made a poor effort to keep her resentment from showing. "Then it'll be beans and corn bread, and little else."

"That's more than I been gettin'."

She walked to the door and looked out. "I reckon Jedediah told you, the law's been out nosin' around. They could go hard on us if they catch you here."

"They ain't goin' to catch me. And if they was to, I'd tell them I forced you to take me in."

"Then you can sleep in the barn, and burrow under the hay if they come lookin' again."

Jedediah offered, "We can hide them saddlebags under the house." He looked too eager for Cordell's taste.

Cordell said, "I'm much obliged, but I sleep better when I use them for a pillow."

ANDY WAS STUMPED. He wished he still had Len at his side, not that it would make much difference in picking up Cordell's trail. It had gone as cold as January.

Andy could not be sure whether the fugitive had gone north, south, east, or west. He could have gone straight up for all the trace he had left. But because his direction from the first had generally been westward, Andy took that as the highest probability. He would go that way, checking with the sheriff in each county seat he came to. Since most such towns had finally been connected by telegraph wire, perhaps some word would turn up.

Anyway, Austin would want him to keep moving. The state office did not cheerfully pay a Ranger's expenses while he sat around waiting for something to happen. He feared his superiors might decide to pull him in and let Cordell go, leaving Tom's death unpunished. They probably would anyway were they not under pressure from the Galveston bank to get its money back.

He had already sent one wire notifying Austin about David Jackson's death and asking if there might be some record of him or his family. Maybe his relatives could shed light on Cordell's possible whereabouts.

The answer had been no help. It simply said, "Too many Jacksons, need more particulars."

Now he sent another wire saying that he had accompanied sheriffs' posses while they searched the county. Writing was labor for Andy. His schooling had come in fits and spurts, usually undertaken with reluctance. "No sine of fugitive," he wrote, struggling over the words. The telegrapher corrected his spelling and sent the message.

The sheriff was apologetic. He swiveled around in his big wooden chair and stretched out a bad leg in an effort to find some comfort. "We done our best, but Cordell is too slippery a fish."

Andy said, "We'll land him yet. He's got a lot to answer for."

"We'd've gotten him if Doc and the Archers hadn't waited till way up in the mornin' to tell us about him. But they're good people. I guess they had their reasons."

"Too bad they never knew Tom Blessing. They'd've felt different."

"They all took a likin' to Cordell. They were impressed with how concerned he was about that boy." The sheriff handed Andy a letter. "Stage driver brought me a message while ago. Sheriff over in San Saba County says he's got a prisoner you might want to talk to."

Andy's spine tingled. "Cordell's partner, maybe?"

"Feller claims he's ridden with Cordell in the past. Knows his habits. He may just be tryin' to buy a softer punishment, or he might be of real help to you."

Andy's spirits picked up. This might be the third man in the jailbreak. "I'm leavin' right now. If Austin sends an answer to my wire, can you forward it to me?"

"Sure. I like to play with that new telegraph." The lawman got up and reached for his cane. "Anytime you get tired of takin' orders from them state-office clerks, I could use a good deputy. I've got the goods on the county commissioners, so the pay ain't bad."

Andy had seen over the years that many Rangers grew weary of the travel and hardships and took a less demanding job in local law enforcement. It would be something for him to think about when that time came. It might ease his saddle sores, though at this point he had rather put up with saddle sores than try to convince Bethel. He feared she was still too deeply rooted to that farm.

But sooner or later she would have to leave it or else shoot her brother Farley in exasperation. Unless somebody else did it first. Andy had rather be tied to two wild horses running in opposite directions than to try to live again with Farley, especially as his brother-in-law.

The trip carried him into the second day. The clock in the courthouse cupola struck ten times as he rode up and tied his horse to a rail in the town square. He saw what passed for a restaurant and was tempted to stop there first. He decided to postpone eating until he finished what he came for. He walked up the steps to the limestone courthouse and stopped inside to look for the sheriff's office.

The lawman recognized him as a Ranger right away. Andy wondered how some people did that. Something in the way Rangers carried themselves, he supposed. The sheriff was tall and lanky, a generation older than Andy. He said, "Old man Ames wired me that you were on your way. You want to see the prisoner now?"

Andy said, "Sure enough. I've lost a lot of time already, tryin' to follow a cold trail."

"I can't promise this'll heat it up much, but you might want to see what he can tell you about the man you're lookin' for."

The sheriff led him outside to the jail, built of the same stone as the courthouse but without the style. It was square and plain, as befitted a prison. The cells were shut off from the front office by a heavy, barred door that the sheriff unlocked with a large key. He motioned toward a cell holding a balding, forlorn-looking man well into middle age. "This here is him, Maxwell Hawkins, alias John Smith, John Jones, and other such names. He got caught breakin' into a store the other night and gatherin' up a sackful of grub. He's got a record that'd reach from here to the San Saba River, but he doesn't look very ferocious now."

The man had the subdued look of a whipped dog. Andy had to strain to hear, for the prisoner spoke barely above a whisper. "I was hungry. I've come on hard times."

Andy flipped through the pages of the Ranger fugitive

book Len had left with him. "Sure enough, he's in here. Served time once for attempted bank robbery. Another time for attempted horse theft. Looks like he's good at attemptin'."

"Hard luck has followed me all of my life," the prisoner said almost apologetically.

Andy asked, "When was the last time you saw Luther Cordell?"

The prisoner considered. "Been a year, maybe a little more. I rode with him off and on till he took up with Milt Hayward. Coldest man I ever saw, Milt was. Didn't have a speck of moral character."

Milt! Tom's young deputy had said he heard a word that sounded to him like *milk*. Andy felt a stirring of excitement. He asked, "Do you have any idea where this Hayward might have gone to?"

"No notion at all. He never was one to talk much. I don't know where he come from. He might've crawled out of a rattlesnake den."

"What about Cordell?"

"He was raised in Louisiana or Mississippi or one of them other Confederate states. I got the idea some bad things had happened to him. They made him what he is now."

"A sheriff killer?"

"I never knowed of him killin' anybody. Not while I was with him, for sure. That was more Milt's style. When Luther hooked up with him, I decided to leave. Sooner or later Milt was bound to do somethin' awful and get us all caught. He's got a criminal mind."

Andy said, "We believe he was part of the jailbreak and split off from Cordell when the posse got too close. Do you know anything about the kid who was with Cordell at the time?"

"You mean Buster?"

"His real name was David Jackson."

The prisoner shook his head. "I didn't know that. Buster was all I ever heard. He showed up in camp one day, beggin' for somethin' to eat. Talked like he got tired of the farm and ran off from home. I never heard him say exactly where he came from. I did hear him say somethin' once about the Clear Fork."

Andy recounted the circumstances of the boy's wounding, and his death. Morosely the prisoner said, "That could've been me if I'd stayed with Luther. I'm sorry about the kid, but I'm glad it wasn't me."

"Too bad Cordell didn't give him a meal and send him on his way."

"You know how it is. Feed a hungry pup, and you can't get rid of him. Luther always had a weak spot for folks down on their luck. He had been there himself a lot of his life."

Andy mused, "He doesn't sound like most outlaws I ever knew. There ain't one in ten ever cares about anybody except themselves."

"Luther did. That's why I can't believe he shot that sheriff. My guess is that Milt done it. He wasn't goin' to get his share of the bank money if he didn't bust Cordell out of jail. He wasn't goin' to let no small-town law stand in his way."

Outside, the sheriff said, "Maybe you've been chasin' the wrong man. You might ought to be lookin' for Hayward."

"I don't know what he looks like, and I've got no idea where he went to. But it appears he ran off without his share of the bank loot. If I can find where Cordell is, maybe Hayward will show up. Then I can get them both."

The sheriff said, "You'd better find Cordell before

Hayward does. For ten thousand dollars, I suspect Hayward would shoot him without blinkin' an eye."

The lawman accompanied Andy to the restaurant and watched him put away a hearty meal of beef stew, beans, and biscuits. The sheriff said, "The boy spoke about the Clear Fork country. You reckon Cordell might be headed that way?"

Andy said, "It's hard to guess what he might do."

"I followed a trail herd through that country once. I hear it's settled up a right smart since."

Andy had known the area a few years ago. The Clear Fork was a tributary of the Brazos River, originating in rough breaks that marked the eastern edge of the staked plains. East of the escarpment and the breaks lay a rolling country that had once teemed with buffalo and now furnished grazing for thousands of cattle. In flatter areas its deep soil offered an opportunity for farming, though it was often beset by extended periods of too little rain.

Andy said, "I'll ease up that way and take a look. I'll have to be careful not to flush the quail too quick, though. If he hears that a Ranger is askin' questions, he'll take to the tules."

"Don't tell anybody you're a Ranger. Just act like an ignorant cowboy lookin' for a job. You can look ignorant, can't you?"

"I often do. Right now, for instance."

10

Cordell had never considered Irmadell much of a cook, but he was so hungry that raw prairie dog would have tasted like beefsteak. He attacked a plate of red beans, shoveling them onto his spoon with a large piece of corn bread. Jedediah and Irmadell picked at their supper and watched him with poorly concealed resentment.

"This is mighty good fixin's," he said. "A man in my business has to put up with a lot of lean days."

Irmadell said, "It's the Lord's punishment for bein' in that kind of business. You'd be way ahead today if you'd got yourself married and took up real work instead of robbin' honest people of the fruits of their labor."

"I ain't never robbed honest people, just banks and such."

"What about the horse stealin' you lured Jedediah into? It got him sent away for a couple of years."

"Them wasn't honest people. They was tryin' to kill one another. Anyway, I did get married once." He stopped there, for he didn't want to talk about it.

"I've heard. You picked the wrong woman, is all." Irmadell went silent, staring darkly at her plate.

Jedediah thought he heard something and jumped up, striding anxiously to the window. He slumped in relief.

"Wasn't nothin' but that fool tomcat. He knocked the milk bucket off of the rack."

Cordell said, "Sit down, Jedediah. You're too nervous."

"And I'll stay nervous as long as you're here. I'm sure you've got better places to go."

"I'll leave when I feel like my horse has rested enough. I don't guess you've got one you could trade me? I'd be on my way a lot sooner."

"Ain't got but one, and he's a plow horse. You'd just as well walk."

Cordell felt Irmadell's narrowed eyes burning him. She said, "Looks like your cup's empty. Want some more coffee?"

"I'd be much obliged."

She got up from the table and fetched the coffeepot from the top of the cast-iron stove. She brought it around behind him and poured coffee into his cup, then splashed it on his arm. It was scalding hot. In reflex he rose halfway to his feet, shouting in surprise and gripping the burned arm. She took advantage of the distraction and yanked his pistol from its holster. He whirled around, but not in time to catch her. She stepped back, the pistol in both hands and aimed at his nose. She had dropped the pot. Its remaining coffee spread dark across the floor.

She declared, "Now, by God, you'll raise your hands. Jedediah, come around here and take this gun."

Jedediah seemed as shocked as Cordell. He was slow in rising from the table. She spoke more sharply, "I said get yourself up here, damn you, and act like a man for a change."

Relieved of the pistol, she stood with her hands on her narrow hips, her eyes crackling. "So you thought you'd just waltz in here and take over, did you? My old daddy didn't put up with that kind of treatment, and neither does his daughter. Put your hands flat on the table and keep them there. Else I'll tell Jedediah to shoot you. That reward is paid dead or alive."

Cordell was too taken aback to answer. He saw two possibilities. They could turn him in for the three thousand dollars, or they could kill him and bury him in secret, hoping to keep the nearly ten thousand he carried from that Galveston transaction.

Irmadell had already made her choice. "You keep him sittin' there, Jedediah. I'll saddle a horse and ride for the sheriff. That three thousand would really fix up this old place."

Jedediah said, "They claim he took ten thousand from that bank. If we was to kill him, we could keep all of it."

She shook her head. "The law would come down on us as soon as we started to spend it. This way we get it legal. Three thousand in the hand is better than ten thousand that we can't use."

Jedediah said, "Have it your way. Take our horse. Luther's is wore out."

She hurried through the door. Shortly Cordell heard the plodding hooves of a plow horse, galloping away in the direction of Lampasas.

Cordell felt like a fool, letting that witch of a woman get the better of him. He rubbed his burned arm and studied his cousin, looking for weakness. He said, "That woman of yours could make Jesus Christ use God's name in vain."

"But as long as she's got property, I've got property."

"You pay a hell of a price for it. You ought not to let a scrawny little woman like that run over you the way she does. I'll bet she don't weigh a hundred pounds."

"But it's a hundred pounds of pure hell."

Cordell looked his cousin squarely in the eyes. "She'll get you killed someday."

"Not me. I figure on outlivin' her. Then everything'll be mine."

"By that time, you'll be trippin' over a long gray beard."

"No, I won't. When she's gone, I'll sell this damned old farm and go to San Antone or someplace. Maybe even Chicago. I'll live high, wide, and handsome."

"High and wide, maybe, but you'll never be handsome." Cordell coughed. "My throat's dry, and my coffee's gettin' cold."

"Let it. Keep your hands on the table, like she said."

Cordell frowned. "She's gone now. Without her bein' here to tell you to, I don't believe you'd really shoot me."

"For three thousand dollars, I'd shoot Irmadell."

"More than likely, she'd shoot you first. Money or not, she ought to anyway, just on general principles. You ain't worth a bucket of cold spit."

"But I'll soon be worth three thousand more than I am, and you'll be sittin' behind bars. I never did like you, Luther. You always acted like you was better than the rest of us."

"Hell, I *was* better than the rest of you."

Cordell struck the coffee cup and sent it flying across the table. Instinctively Jedediah ducked. Cordell wrested the pistol from his hands before his cousin could regain his wits. He said, "Jedediah, you're too easy. A man can't take any pride in outsmartin' you." He pointed the pistol in his cousin's face.

Jedediah pushed trembling hands forward in supplication, eyes brimming with tears. "For God's sake, don't shoot me."

"I ought to, but it'd be too big a favor to Irmadell.

I want her to be stuck with you till you're both shriveled and old." Cordell motioned for Jedediah to stand, then motioned again toward the door. "We're goin' out to the barn together. You got any more guns in the house?"

Jedediah stammered. "Just that shotgun over the fireplace."

Cordell retrieved it. "I wouldn't want you to shoot me as I ride off." He dropped a little money on the table. "This is for the groceries you're fixin' to sack up for me. Some coffee, some beans, all of that corn bread."

"Anything you want. Just don't keep pointin' that six-shooter at me."

Jedediah gathered up most of the food that was in the kitchen. Then Cordell marched his cousin outside. "Too bad you ain't got a decent horse. Saddle mine for me."

Jedediah complied, still trembling. Cordell checked to be certain the girth was tight enough. It would be like Jedediah to leave it loose, hoping for the saddle to slip. Mounting, Cordell said, "I'll take the shotgun with me. Tell the sheriff I'm sorry not to make his acquaintance. And if Milt Hayward comes back, tell him he ought to've gone to Mexico and stayed there. It's on account of him that they got a murder charge out on me."

Jedediah stood with shoulders drooped, his mouth sagging open. Cordell took pleasure in picturing the blistering he would get from Irmadell when she returned and found herself three thousand dollars short of expectations.

Cordell said, "I can't hardly believe we had the same granddaddy. Maybe old Granny wasn't quite the lady she made out to be."

Riding away, he was aware that the horse was still tired. "Sorry, old friend," he said. "Them people didn't give me any choice. Be glad *you've* got no relations."

Without wanting to, he began to dwell on what Irmadell had said about his not being married. The memories always brought him pain. He had married a neighbor girl named Martha back in Louisiana just prior to the war of Northern aggression. She had given him a son before he marched away with a local company of Confederate volunteers. He had never lost the memory of the boy's face, the eyes blue, sparkling with laughter.

Wounded in the last year of the conflict, he had been left behind by his retreating brothers-in-arms. He suffered through the rest of the war in a miserable prisoner of war camp, staying alive only by the force of his will. He had finally limped home, only to find he no longer had a home. Yankee troops had burned the house, and carpetbaggers had confiscated the land. His wife's family had been nervously evasive about her whereabouts. A sympathetic neighbor broke the news as gently as he could. Martha had taken up with another man. They had left with the intention of going to California, far from the war. Naturally, she had taken their son.

Cordell had followed in the vain hope of finding them, but California was far larger than he had realized. He never found any sign. For all he knew, they might not have made it that far. They might have changed their plans, or Indians might have gotten them somewhere along the way. They came close once to getting Cordell.

He had drifted back as far as Texas, bitter and disillusioned, looking for a new life. Times were hard after the war, and an honest man had a tough time making a living. So he had given up being an honest man. There was money to be made for those who were bold, and Cordell had thought he had nothing to lose.

Now he was in his fifties, weary, hungry, hounded by the law. He had close to ten thousand dollars in his saddlebags, but at this point he would trade it all for a safe place to stay.

Irmadell had been right about the wasting of his life. He *had* had something to lose, and he had lost it.

Perhaps when the heat died down, he could take a new name and start a fresh life somewhere far away, like California, where nobody knew of him. In San Francisco he had seen ships in port. He might even book passage on one and sail to the west. He had heard talk about an island named Hawaii, where a man could lie around all day on a warm and sandy beach, just waiting for coconuts to fall from a tree.

That sounded like his kind of life. It wouldn't matter whether they had banks there or not.

But first he owed Buster's family the boy's share of the ten thousand. As to telling them about Buster's death, he had plenty of time to build up a plausible story. Many miles of travel lay ahead of him before he reached the Clear Fork.

Darkness came as a friend. He let the horse slow its pace to a walk. Even at that rate, he could make a lot of miles before daylight gave the law a chance to pick up his trail.

THE LAMPASAS SHERIFF had predisposed Andy to dislike Jedediah and Irmadell Fergus on sight, and they met his expectations. Having no family himself, he put great stock in blood kinship and could not fathom how a man could betray one of his own and live with his conscience.

Stopping to consult local law enforcement officers in each county through which he rode, he had learned of Cordell's visit to the Fergus farm. The sheriff guided

Andy there, giving him a lengthy and uncomplimentary history of the pair.

He said, "You remember what the Bible said about a tongue that biteth like an adder? That's Irmadell. And if ever anybody deserved her, Jedediah is that man."

Irmadell dominated the conversation. Though she weighed hardly a hundred pounds, it was easy to see that her two-hundred-pound husband was cowed by her. He stood half a pace behind her and a little to the side. If he had been a dog, he would have had his tail between his legs. Across his cheekbone he bore a severe bruise of recent origin. His eye was swollen. Andy first thought Cordell was responsible, though he soon became convinced that Irmadell was the culprit. The longer he listened to her tirade against her husband's cousin, the more she seemed capable of inflicting injuries far out of proportion to her diminutive size.

She said, "We didn't invite Luther to come here. He took advantage of our hospitality, then rode off without a word of thanks. Didn't leave us nothin' for what we was out on groceries."

Jedediah looked at the floor as if he had something to hide.

She declared, "Not a widow's mite did he leave us. On top of everything, he carried off our only shotgun. Now we've got no way to guard our chickens against the varmints. I lost two hens last night."

Andy tried to look sympathetic, but it was not in him. He said, "The way I heard it, you were on your way to town to fetch the sheriff."

"Yes, I was. Luther's got a lot to answer for when he stands at them pearly gates. The sooner he gets there, the better it'll suit me."

The Lampasas sheriff had said Jedediah's past did not stand close scrutiny either.

Andy asked, "Did he give you any idea where he was goin' from here?"

She turned to her husband. Her eyes had the sting of a wasp. "Jedediah was the last one to talk to him. He played the fool and let Luther get away."

Jedediah did not look Andy in the eyes. "I was scared he was fixin' to shoot me, so I didn't ask him no foolish questions. He just cussed me out and rode off west." He pointed in that general direction.

Irmadell said, "I had him captured dead to rights, right here in my kitchen. And it was me that put the sheriff on his trail. Looks like when you catch him, I ought to be due part of the reward."

Andy figured she didn't stand a snowball's chance in hell. "You'll have to argue with the law about that."

"You bet I'll argue with them. It ain't my fault this fool sheriff couldn't follow the trail past the top of the hill." She shifted her accusing gaze to the local lawman. His face reddened, but he did not waste breath trying to argue with her.

Andy had already learned that Cordell and Jedediah had spent time together as boys and had reconnected some years after the war. Irmadell assured him that they had nothing in common except blood kinship. "And that ain't no way our fault," she said. "A man can't choose his relations."

If they could, Andy thought, Cordell and Jedediah might both have chosen different limbs on the family tree.

Leaving the house, the sheriff said, "I'm afraid you didn't gain much by comin' out here. If they knew anything, they didn't spill it."

Andy shook his head. "Cordell would've been too shrewd to tell them what he figured to do. He had to know they'd go runnin' to you for the reward."

"At least you've got a fresh start. You know he was right here a day or so ago."

Andy had been even closer when Buster died, but he saw no reason to dwell on the negative. "He left on a tired horse, so he can't push too hard. Thanks to you and that stableman in town, I've got a fresh horse. And grub aplenty on my mule."

"Nothin's too good for the Rangers. I wish I could go with you, but there's enough wild men around here to keep me busy. Have you got any notion as to where he might be goin'?"

"It's a thin one, but it's all I've got." Andy explained about the kid who had ridden with Cordell, and the possibility that the outlaw might be headed toward the Clear Fork in search of the kid's family.

Even if Andy had been an expert tracker, he would have had difficulty in following Cordell's trail. The sheriff's posse had ridden all over the place, trying to pick it up. They had ruined whatever sign Cordell might have left.

"Sorry about that," the sheriff said, "but I had to deputize anybody I could find that had a horse."

"I'm not much of a tracker anyway."

"The Clear Fork country is big, especially if you don't know just where to look."

Andy said, "I only know that the family's name is Jackson."

"The world is full of Jacksons. Even if you find the family, you can't be sure Cordell is headed that way. If I was him and had all that money, I'd light out for parts unknown."

"Cordell's a robber and a thief, but accordin' to an old partner named Hawkins, he's got his own notions about honor."

"Yeah, he probably says 'Pardon me' before he steals your money. But he takes it just the same."

The sheriff rode with him a couple of miles until they cut into a well-worn wagon road that led northwestward. He said, "You'd best watch yourself. You're in the land of the forty thieves. There's boys around here can steal your socks without takin' your boots off."

Andy nodded. "I've met some of those boys. I've still got my socks."

He suspected that Cordell might have taken the same road. He had observed that the outlaw liked to follow well-traveled roads from time to time, which allowed his tracks to be lost among the many others. Yet nobody ever seemed to see him. He evidently saw them first.

Andy had become used to riding long distances alone, but nevertheless he wished for Len Tanner's company. Len could make a man's ears ring with all his talking. Still, his stories were entertaining if sometimes suspect. His long experience as a Ranger made him a good man to have along. He knew how to cover a partner's back.

Another reason for liking him was that Farley Brackett didn't.

The sheriff was about to ride back toward town but stopped abruptly. "Looks like somebody's comin'. I'll wait and find out if he's seen anything."

Approaching from the west, the rider proved to be an agitated man of considerable bulk. His ruddy face was flushed with stress and indignation. "Sheriff," he shouted before he was within good talking distance, "I was on my way to town to fetch you. Somebody's stole that good black stud of mine."

Andy immediately thought of Cordell. "Did you get a look at the thief?"

The rider gave Andy a suspicious frown, as if he thought he might be the sheriff's prisoner. "No, he made a swap out in my pasture. Left a horse that looked like he'd been ridden to a fare-thee-well."

"When did this happen?"

"Could've been anytime in the last day or two. I had the stud turned out with some mares." The man squinted, giving Andy a close scrutiny. "Who are you to be askin' me questions? My business is with the sheriff."

Andy was put off by the man's belligerent attitude. The sheriff answered for him. "Andy Pickard is a Ranger. He's been trailin' a fugitive who might be your horse thief."

The red-faced man said accusingly, "The trouble with you people that work for the government is, you're always a day late. Damned pity you didn't catch your man before he stole my horse."

The sheriff said, "Just be glad you didn't run into the thief yourself, Thaddeus Hunnicutt. He's accused of killin' a sheriff."

"I wish I *had* run into him. I'd've shot him so full of holes that he couldn't hold his water."

Andy took that for idle bluster. Hunnicutt struck him as a man who talked a good game but folded quickly.

Hunnicutt declared, "I paid five hundred dollars for that stud. Best I ever owned. You'd better get him back, Sheriff, if you expect any financial support from me at the next election."

The sheriff looked as if Hunnicutt had stepped on his sore toe. "I didn't have any financial support from you in the last one. But I'll do what I can. Me and the Ranger." He looked at Andy. "Are you with me?"

Andy nodded and gave his attention to Hunnicutt. "Show us where the stud was stolen from."

Hunnicutt reined around and started back west. He grumbled, "A man pays his taxes and expects the law to protect him, but he's got to do most of it for himself." He rode on ahead, leaving Andy and the sheriff behind.

Andy said, "Except for you, everybody I've met around here so far has been about as agreeable as a badger with its foot caught. Is there somethin' wrong with the water?"

"This county has got the best folks you could ever hope to meet. It's also some that ought to've been drowned at birth like a sackful of kittens. It takes a few of those to make you appreciate the rest."

Except for the possibility that Cordell was the thief, Andy would be content to let Hunnicutt hunt his horse by himself.

They traveled several miles before coming to a barbed-wire fence that ran parallel to the wagon road. Such fences were going up in a lot of places, enclosing private property. Sometimes they illegally enclosed state land as well, leading to all manner of disputes and problems for local law enforcement. Andy saw the practical side of the fences, though he would be better suited had the wire never been invented. They went against all the free-roaming instincts fostered by his youthful years with the Comanches.

Hunnicutt said, "I spent a wagonload of money buildin' this fence so I could keep my breedin' program clean. I don't want no wild studs gettin' in amongst those good mares of mine."

Andy doubted that even barbed wire would stop a determined stallion if it saw mares on the other side.

They came to a barbed-wire gate. Hunnicutt waited as if he expected Andy or the sheriff to dismount and open it. Neither offered, so he got down and did it himself, mumbling under his breath. His temper was not improved by his having to strain to get the tight gate open, then closed again after the horses passed through. He said, "Soon as I saw a strange horse in this pasture, I had a hunch that somebody had made a trade. I wish he'd taken a mare. None of them cost me more than fifty dollars."

Andy could see horse tracks everywhere. It would be futile to try to pick out one set and follow them, even if he knew which belonged to the missing stud. "The thief wouldn't have stayed in this pasture long. Do you know where he went out?"

"He broke my fence about a mile up the way. Didn't have a proper cutter, so he twisted the wires till they busted in two. Some of my mares got out, is how I come to see I'd been robbed."

The three riders followed the fence line until they reached the place where the wires were broken. They had been patched in haste. Hunnicutt said, "If he'd only known it, there's another gate about a mile farther on. He didn't have to leave my fence in this shape."

Andy could see by the tracks that several horses had strayed out through the opening. He told the sheriff, "I hope you're a better tracker than I am."

"I couldn't track a freight wagon through a mudhole."

Hunnicutt's frustration reached a new level, his face redder than before. "You mean you're both drawin' wages from the taxpayers, and you can't do the job you're hired for?"

The sheriff said, "I know somebody who's a tracker, and he's already on your payroll. Choctaw John."

"That damned half-breed? He ain't on my payroll. I fired his insolent ass."

"Looks like you'd better hire him back if you want us to find that stud."

"I'd rather take a whippin' with a wet rope." Hunnicutt mulled the proposition awhile. "All right, but I ain't payin' that Indian more than a dollar a day. And if he gives me any of his sass, I'll fire him again."

The sheriff said, perhaps a bit too hopefully, "You won't need to go with us. Just John and me and the Ranger."

"It's my stud horse we're talkin' about. Damned right I'm goin' with you. I hope I can shoot whoever's got him."

The sheriff took his disappointment in stride. "Then you'd better plug your ears and bite your tongue where John is concerned. Lose him and you've like as not lost your horse."

Hunnicutt grumbled, "The indignities a man has to put up with just to get back what belongs to him . . ." He pointed southwestward. "He's livin' in that miserable shack he built over on the creek."

The sheriff said, "Lead off. We'll follow you."

Trailing behind the rancher, Andy asked the sheriff, "Is this John really an Indian?"

"Half of one. His old daddy was a Scotchman. He brought a Choctaw wife down from the Territory. Pleasant woman, she was, and plumb white in her ways, but folks around here didn't cotton to her much. They remembered the Comanches and couldn't see the difference. John had to whip most of the boys his age before they quit aggravatin' him about his Indian blood."

Andy could relate to that. Though he was not Indian by blood, he had lived with them as a boy captive and picked up many of their ways. As a youth returned to the white man's road, he had bruised his fists many times in defending his right to walk with shoulders straight as anyone else's.

From Hunnicutt's description, Andy had expected Choctaw John's cabin to be as dilapidated as Fowler Gaskin's. It was small, but it was sturdily built of sawmill lumber and bore a coat of white paint, a luxury many houses lacked in rural Texas. It had been set in the midst of several live-oak trees, which would help shelter it from the worst of sun and wind. Andy thought he would not mind having a house like that for himself, though Bethel would probably want its size doubled or tripled. Several varmint hides were stretched and hanging along the outside walls.

Hunnicutt said, "He was always off runnin' traplines and such when I needed him. Claimed he made more money from them than he made workin' for me. Looks to me like the man payin' the wages ought to be the one who says how much he'll give, and the workin' class ought to be grateful to get it."

Two hounds came running out from under the house to announce the visitors. A man appeared in the open door, gave them a moment's study, then stepped out onto a narrow front porch. His arms were folded, and a deep frown creased his face.

"Thaddeus Hunnicutt," he said in a deep, booming voice, "I run you off of my place ten days ago. You sure don't learn very good."

Hunnicutt sputtered something unintelligible.

The sheriff said, "Howdy, John. We need your help."

"Poor way to ask for it, the kind of company you're keepin'." John shifted his attention to Andy, his black eyes questioning.

The sheriff made the introductions. "This here is Andy

Pickard. He's a Ranger. We need your help to trail a horse thief."

"One of Thaddeus's horses? That sorry black stud of his, I hope."

Hunnicutt glowered, seeming to puff up like a prairie chicken on its stomping ground. "It wouldn't surprise me if we was to find that stud right here on this place."

John said, "Now, what use would I have for a stallion, even if it was a good one? I don't own no mares, and if I did, I'd think more of them than to turn that stumble-footed black in with them." He paused, staring hard at the rancher. "What's the pay?"

Hunnicutt said, "I'll give you seventy-five cents a day."

The sheriff put in, "You said a dollar."

Hunnicutt turned on him angrily but seemed to have second thoughts about antagonizing the lawman more than he already had. "All right, a dollar, but he furnishes his own horse."

John took his time before agreeing. "Mind you, I'm just trackin'. I ain't doin' no camp cookin'. And the first time Thaddeus raises his voice at me, my price goes to a dollar and a half."

The sheriff told Hunnicutt, "Maybe you'd better go home and leave it to us, or this trip is liable to cost you more than you'll want to pay."

Sullenly Hunnicutt said, "I'm goin' with you, but I'll try to keep my mouth shut."

The sheriff gave Andy a look that said he did not believe in miracles.

11

Cordell considered himself a good judge of horses, but he had been dealt a joker on this black stallion. He had spotted it in a fenced pasture with several mares and had thought it one of the best-looking animals he had seen in a long time. He knew the risk he took in making an involuntary trade, but that was outweighed by the fact that the horse he had ridden so long was nearing the limits of its endurance. He did not want the poor animal to die beneath him.

He had had the devil's own time catching and saddling the stallion, and now he was having the devil's own time riding it. The animal had an iron jaw, an unbending neck, and a will that matched Cordell's own. It seemed well aware that it outweighed him five or six times over.

"You're a damned hoodoo," he declared. "I'd sooner ride a burro."

The black shook its head violently, as if it understood. It had stumbled more than once. It responded to the tickle of Cordell's spurs by trying to pitch him off. He had no credentials as a bronc rider, but he knew what would result if he let the animal get away from him. Afoot, he would be easy pickings for whatever lawmen were surely following him, and the money in his saddlebags would go where the stallion went. His big right hand took a death grip on the saddle horn.

I ought to've known better than to pick a stud, he thought. *They've just got their mind on one thing.*

He knew he had to make another horse trade whatever the risk. This stallion was going to get him caught.

They've probably already got a noose sized for my neck. They can't hang me any higher for stealing another horse than for stealing this one.

He and the stud feuded until they came after a time to a creek lined sporadically with pecan trees. He saw a horse standing in the shade. At the distance, he could tell little about age or conformation, but so long as it had four legs and none of them were lame, it had to be an improvement over the stallion. Riding closer, he saw that the animal was a bay, tethered on a long rope to allow it to graze. An old buggy stood idle not far away, its wheels sprung a little out of line.

He brought his hand down to his pistol, for someone was camped on the creek. The stallion began acting up, curious about the tied horse. Cordell hoped it was not another stud, for he might be caught in the middle of a vigorous horse fight. He felt some relief when he saw that the other animal was a mare. Even so, he could have trouble on his hands if she happened to be in heat.

She wasn't, for the black's interest waned. Cordell tied him some distance from the mare and moved cautiously along the creek bank. Halfway down, he saw a small canvas tent. At the water's edge, a man sat with a pole in his hand, intently studying the point where his fishing line met the river. It began bobbing up and down. He gave the pole a yank to set the hook, then swung it around, dropping a large catfish on the ground nearby. It flopped about, struggling for life.

Not until then did the fisherman notice Cordell. His eyes widened in surprise, but he offered no threat. If he had any kind of firearm, it must be in the tent or the buggy, for Cordell saw none.

He opened the conversation. "Looks like you've got the makin's of a good supper."

The fisherman looked to be seventy or more, with friendly eyes and a smiling countenance. He said, "It's big enough for both of us if you're of a mind to stay. I'd admire some company for a change."

Cordell could not remember the last time he had enjoyed a good bait of catfish. Back in Louisiana it had frequently graced the family table. And he, too, would admire some company. "Wish I could, but I've got places to go."

The fisherman shoved his hand forward. "Dobson's my name. *Son,* better known. They hung that nickname on me when I was a kid so they could tell me from my old daddy."

That must have been a long time ago, Cordell thought. He shook hands but did not offer his name. Gray whiskers and bent shoulders told him the fisherman was past being able to do heavy work. He suspected the old fellow was whiling away the twilight of his life, sustaining himself and getting by the best he could.

The old-timer said, "I had to wait a spell before he finally took the bait, but hours don't matter much to an old, wore-out farmer. It's the days that I've got to count. Sure you won't stay for supper? I'll have this fish cut up and fried in about two shakes of a lamb's tail."

Though he felt the pressure of pursuit, Cordell also felt the pressure of hunger. "I reckon I could stay for just a little while."

He dragged in some dead tree limbs to stoke up the

fire while the old man gutted the fish. Soon it was sizzling in a cast-iron frying pan well greased with bacon
drippings.

Cordell asked, "Doesn't it worry you, campin' out here
by yourself? No tellin' who might come by."

"Nobody would want to hurt me. I'm an old man, just
about useless to anybody but myself. I've got nothin'
worth stealin'. Got nothin' but time."

"But what if your heart was to give out with nobody
around?"

"I don't know a better way to go, or a better place to
go from. I like it out here all by myself. Don't get me
wrong, I love my grandkids, but damned if they can't
make enough noise sometimes to wake up everybody in
the cemetery. You ever have any kids?"

The question brought a stab of pain. "Just one. Lost
him." Cordell saw no point in further explanation.

"Sorry. I had four kids. One boy died. Two daughters
got married and went wanderin' off with their husbands,
one to Arizona, one to California. Ain't seen them in years.
My oldest son runs the farm now. Does a better job of it
than I ever did. I ain't of much use to him anymore, so I
do a lot of fishin' when the weather is favorable."

"Sounds like a good way to spend your declinin'
years." Cordell had given little thought to his own declin-
ing years. In his occupation, he had doubted he would
have any.

Dobson said, "The fish is about done. I've got some
cold biscuits I made in the skillet this mornin'. Help yourself to the coffee."

"Much obliged." Cordell could not remember when
anything had tasted better, certainly nothing at Irmadell's
table. He could have eaten the whole fish, but he did not
want to deprive Dobson. It was his camp, and his catfish.

He found himself envying the farmer. He wished he could relax here on the creek bank, watching a line in the water instead of watching his back trail for evidence of pursuit. Such a worry-free life would fit him like a well-worn pair of boots, he thought. He knew he could not rob a harmless old man like this, one willing to share his supper with a stranger and wanting nothing in return but a little company. He said, "I was wonderin' what you might ask for that buggy mare. I'm pretty near afoot."

The fisherman had seen the black, tied up on top of the creek bank. "That's a right smart lookin' stud. You're a long ways from bein' afoot."

"He's got some habits that I can't abide."

"I'd swap my mare for him, but I wouldn't want to beat you. She's past her prime."

"I'd need to pay you cash. That stud ain't mine to swap. There's some question about his ownership."

The old farmer seemed to catch on. His pale eyes twinkled, "Got him kind of cheap, did you?"

"You could look at it that way. Would a hundred dollars be enough for your mare?"

"I'd be cheatin' you. I could buy me two good horses for that."

"It's worth it. I've already got enough people mad at me without you bein' another one." Cordell frowned. "There's liable to be somebody behind me, kind of anxious about that stud. If they was to ask you, you could tell them you've got no idea how he come to be here."

The farmer smiled. "I've never seen you in my life." His smile spread even wider when Cordell paid him.

Cordell said, "I hate to leave you afoot. That stud is too much horse for you to try to ride, and he'd probably tear up your buggy."

"I wasn't goin' nowhere. My son'll come to see about

me when I don't show up in two or three days." The farmer watched Cordell put his saddle on the mare. "You don't look like the type to've killed somebody. Have you?"

"They claim I did, but they're wrong. I've made myself unpopular with a few moneylenders, but I ain't killed nobody."

"I've seen some outlaws in my time. Most of them didn't look any worse than the sheriffs that trailed after them. They just crossed the line somewhere."

"It's a thin line. Easy to cross over and hard to cross back."

Cordell rode the mare in a circle to be sure she was not lame.

The old man said, "She's seen better days, but ain't we all? She's still got lots of heart."

"Much obliged for the supper." Waving his hand, Cordell crossed the creek and headed westward. The stallion followed him and the mare for a hundred yards or so, then lost interest, lowered his head, and began to graze.

Cordell liked the mare from the first. She had a smoother trot than the stallion, setting a steady pace that could cover ground without pounding his rump raw. She had been worth the price, especially considering that he bought her with someone else's money. He halfway wished he had paid the old man more.

THADDEUS HUNNICUTT HAD promised not to abuse Choctaw John, but that promise soon evaporated. John was slow and careful in picking the stallion's tracks from those of the mares that had followed him out through the opening the fugitive had left in the fence. And he lost the tracks a couple of times where the stallion had been ridden over rocky ground.

Hunnicutt said, "If you cause me to lose that black stud, I'll whip you all the way back up to Indian Territory where you belong."

John responded, "You'd better be ready to eat that whip, handle and all. Sheriff, I wish you'd send Thaddeus home before the Indian side of me decides to scalp what little hair he's still got under that hat."

Hunnicutt said, "You can't send me home. It's a free country, and I got a right to look for my horse."

The sheriff's voice was clipped. "You'll be lookin' for him all by yourself if you don't tighten the rein on that mouth of yours."

Andy had been listening without comment. His interest was not in the stallion but in the man who might be riding him. Local quarrels were none of his business. Hunnicutt and the sheriff dropped back twenty or thirty yards, giving John plenty of room. Andy was curious about the tracker and remained beside him, trying to study his method. John had picked up the tracks again.

"They're pretty old," he said. "I figure a couple of days. There ain't much left of them." He looked back at Hunnicutt. "I don't care if the old dickens never finds his stud horse, long as he pays me. And the longer we keep trackin', the longer he's got to pay me."

Now and again the tracks were plain enough that Andy could have followed them himself. Other times he wondered at John's ability to see that which was not there. For a while he suspected that John was stringing Hunnicutt along for the money. Then the tracks would show up again.

John's face showed little that seemed distinctly Indian beyond being a shade darker than average.

Andy said, "You don't look like most Indians I've known."

"I'm just half, from my mama."

"That's what I heard. Some people say I'm half-Indian, too. When I was a boy, the Comanches captured me. I lived with them for several years."

John was not impressed. "They're wild men. We ain't nothin' like them."

"You don't talk like an Indian either."

"Us Choctaws've been civilized since my great-granddaddy's time." He frowned. "I've heard Comanches talk. They're savages. I never could make any sense of what they was sayin'."

"I used to speak Comanche. I'm afraid I've forgotten some of it."

"Just as well. They ain't likely to rise again."

Andy was momentarily miffed at John's prejudice against those Andy considered his adopted people. On reflection he remembered that the Comanches regarded all others as inferior to themselves. He remembered hearing Comanche warriors boast about killing Choctaws. They regarded them as being almost white. Prejudice was not the sole property of one race.

He said, "I take it you've worked for Hunnicutt before."

"Several times. We get mad at one another, and he fires me or I quit. Then he needs me again."

"And you keep goin' back to him?"

"Money ain't overly plentiful around here."

"He's not payin' you much."

"But when I'm at his place I carry enough home out of his kitchen to make up the difference. I can still eat durin' the times I ain't got a job."

Andy considered. "If I had to be around him much, I'd sooner or later want to kill him."

"I get even in my own way, like sometimes I pee in his coffeepot. The old hayshaker never knows."

"Where's the revenge in it if he doesn't know?"

"The point is, *I* know."

Andy wished Len were here. He would appreciate John's off-center logic. Andy liked it himself.

They camped at an abandoned homesite where a dug well provided passable water. John gathered wood for a fire but did not offer to contribute to the cooking. Neither did Hunnicutt, so Andy and the sheriff took care of supper. The lawman opened a couple of airtights of tomatoes. Andy managed to burn Hunnicutt's bacon, frying it down to a shrunken and blackened sliver. He boiled a pot of coffee and kept an eye on John in case he might seek a little revenge on his employer.

The next morning John said the trail was becoming fresher. Andy had to take his word for it. John pointed to a small area where the ground was disturbed. "Looks to me like that black stud tried to pitch him off."

Hunnicutt took heart. "Maybe he got away."

John shook his head. "No, the rider managed to stay on him. Probably knew he'd be in bad trouble if he lost him. The tracks straighten out afterwards and head west like before, and a little to the north."

They came in the afternoon to a tree-lined creek, where an old buggy stood on the bank. John said, "I smell woodsmoke. Somebody's camped down yonder." He swore in surprise. "Well, I'll be damned. Yonder's that sorry black of yours." He pointed toward the stallion, which raised its head from the shin-high grass and nickered at the oncoming horses. "I guess you just owe me for two days, Thaddeus."

Hunnicutt demanded, "How do you figure two days? It's no more than a day and a half."

Andy drew his rifle. "It don't seem likely that Cordell would be layin' around in camp, but we'd better go slow. We don't know who's down there."

He remained in the saddle, keeping a tight grip on the weapon. A fishing pole was wedged between two stones. He saw someone lying on the creek bank, evidently napping. Andy rode within touching distance before he spoke. "Raise up easy. Don't make a move toward a gun."

An elderly man blinked the sleep from his eyes and stared up at Andy, or more precisely at his rifle. He said in a shaky voice, "Ain't no use pointin' that thing at me. I ain't got a gun. And there ain't much here that's worth stealin'."

The sheriff's tension eased. He said, "Don't worry, Andy. This is old man Dobson. I've known him forever."

The fisherman managed a weak smile but did not look away from Andy's rifle. "Son, better known. Howdy, Sheriff."

Hunnicutt swung his bulk down from the saddle and approached Dobson with red-faced belligerence. "What the hell are you doin' with my stallion?"

Dobson got to his feet. The move appeared to stir up arthritis, for he winced in pain. "I ain't doin' nothin' with him. He just showed up here. I wish you'd take him home. Every time he goes down to the creek for a drink, he paws the water and scares away the fish."

Hunnicutt shook his finger in Dobson's face. "If you was thinkin' about breedin' him to one of your mares . . ."

"I don't own but two mares, and I doubt they'd associate with that stud horse of yours. They're too prideful for that."

Andy pushed in front of Hunnicutt, stopping his attempt at argument. "What're you doin' out here all by yourself, Mr. Dobson? I see a buggy, but I don't see a buggy horse."

"Since my wife passed on to a better life, I like to get away from my son's family once in a while and camp here on the creek, where it's quiet. Sometimes a man is his own best company. My son'll fetch me a buggy horse when I get ready to go home."

Andy thought the story plausible, as far as it went, but he suspected there was more to it. "That stud didn't just stray in here, it was ridden. We've been followin' its tracks."

John put in, "Not *we*, *me*. You'd just as well tell him, Son. This young man is a Ranger."

Andy could see that his three companions knew Dobson. Two had respect for him. Hunnicutt did not, but that was a point in Dobson's favor. "Tell us about the man who rode in here on the stud."

Dobson rubbed his gray-whiskered chin and looked from one visitor to the other. Reluctantly he said, "I don't want to get anybody in trouble."

Andy said, "He's already in trouble."

"Seemed like a nice feller. An outlaw, I suppose, but he was square with me. Bought my buggy mare and paid me double what she was worth."

If the fugitive was indeed Cordell, that payment was made with stolen money. Andy knew that he should by law confiscate it, but he had no intention of taking it away from this old man who did not appear to be overly endowed with the world's goods. He asked, "What did this man look like?"

"He was a big one. Not fat, mind you, just had shoulders on him like that black studhorse. Hands that looked like they could choke a mule. Black eyes, but friendly, the kind you feel like trustin'. I'd've been willin' to lend him that mare if he hadn't offered to buy her from me."

Hunnicutt said, "You'd've never got her back."

"I've lost things a lot more valuable than the mare. Anyway, *you* got your stud back."

John looked straight at Hunnicutt. "Thanks to me. You owe me for two days."

Hunnicutt shrugged. "All right, two days. But that's where it stops."

Dobson looked on quizzically, not understanding the exchange.

The sheriff said, "Here's where I have to leave you, Andy. The county line is just ahead, and my authority stops there. I'll help Thaddeus take his horse home."

Andy hated to bid the lawman good-bye. He said, "Maybe I'll see you again, next time some lawbreaker passes through your county."

"You're welcome to all you can catch. We've already got enough that we don't need any more."

Andy said to Dobson, "I don't suppose you'd want to tell us which way he went from here."

Dobson glanced at Choctaw John. "I gave him a half-way promise. Anyway, with John to do the trackin', you don't need me to tell you. He can follow a crow's shadow for ten miles."

John said modestly, "Maybe five."

Hunnicutt looked suddenly alarmed. "I ain't payin' that Indian past today. If he goes with you, it's up to the state or the county to foot the bill." He reconsidered. "Not the county either. Your fugitive did his dirty work some-place else. I don't see why us Lampasas County taxpayers ought to ante up for it."

Andy turned to John. "How about it? Are you goin' on with me?"

"Trappin' season is over, so I got nothin' better to do. The state's money is as good as his." He nodded at Hunnicutt. "Better, because I won't have to listen to the state bellyachin' all the time."

Dobson seemed downcast. He said, "If you catch up to him, I hope you don't shoot him. I feel like he ain't a bad man at heart."

Andy said, "We don't shoot people for the fun of it. Only if they force it on us." It continued to puzzle him that almost everyone whose trail Cordell crossed bore kindly feelings toward him. Damn it all, the man was a bank robber. And even if he might not actually have fired the shot that killed Tom Blessing, he was partially responsible. It happened while he was being broken out of jail. And there was that kid, Buster. Cordell was at fault in his death as well. He had given Andy a double load of guilt: part for being late in coming to Tom's aid, and part for knowing that it was his bullet that ultimately killed the youngster.

He said, "Let's go, John. We've got an outlaw to catch."

12

Cordell was pleased with the bay mare. True, she was long past being a colt, but she still had enough *go* about her to carry him miles into the night without acting up as the stud had done. He made a dry and fireless camp. He would have liked some coffee, but that could wait. He would stop somewhere after daylight and boil a pot without much risk that his campfire would attract attention. He had no specific reason to believe anyone was actually on his trail, but he trusted his hunches. They told him it was likely that someone was. They just didn't tell him how far behind the pursuit might be. He had no intention of making it easy for them.

The stallion had been so feisty that it had been a constant fight to make it go where Cordell wanted it to. The mare was more pliable. He guided her onto hard, rocky ground where the terrain offered any. Unlike the stallion, she never stumbled. His snaky trail would be difficult for even an expert tracker and impossible for anyone less apt.

He had begun to notice a considerable scattering of buffalo bones bleaching on the prairie. He realized that this was all that remained of the vast shaggy herds that had once roamed the country. No one could have believed beforehand how quickly they would be decimated once a market developed for the hides.

"All wiped out," he told the mare. "Their time has come and gone."

He tried not to dwell on it, but he could not help thinking that his own time would probably soon be gone, too. With John Laws of all kinds covering Texas like horseflies, little room was left for free spirits like himself. Before long, bankers would be able to rob the public without having to worry about somebody robbing *them*. He would have no choice but to change his occupation. Maybe he could make a living gathering up buffalo bones.

In a couple of days he came to the crumbled ruins of what he took to be a frontier military fort. Partial stone walls gave him some idea of the post's original configuration. He recognized one small structure as having been a powder magazine, constructed at a distance from the other buildings as a precaution in event of an accidental explosion. Remnants of charred wood told him the fort had been burned in the distant past.

From stories he had heard, he realized this was probably what remained of Fort Phantom Hill, built as an outpost against Comanche and Kiowa, then abandoned. It would have been logical to assume that Indians had burned it, but Cordell had been told that departing soldiers hated the place so much that they had set it on fire to make certain they never had to return.

He had seen maps of this area. He tried to visualize them from memory and determine where he was in relation to the farm from which Buster had come. Unfortunately, he was stumped.

The sun was going down, and he was hungry, so he decided to camp here. He could build a small campfire within one of the ruined buildings. The partially crumbled walls should protect the modest flames from view. He loosed an unwieldy bundle from behind the cantle, along with his rolled blanket. In the bundle were coffee beans from Irmadell's kitchen and part of a ham from Jedediah's smokehouse. He was glad he had had the foresight to take them. All that Galveston money in his saddlebags would do him no good if he starved.

He had found a stream below the hill and assumed it to be the Clear Fork of the Brazos. He could follow it and find Fort Griffin, but it was as crooked as a snake's track. It stood to reason that he had bypassed Griffin and now was to the west or southwest of it. After the mare had drunk her fill, he staked her where he found the grass tall and moderately green for this part of the country. Here rainfall was chancy, and grass had to be hardy to survive long periods of drought. But the struggle seemed to give the vegetation more strength than was common farther east. Animals thrived on it.

The ham, though good, was getting to be monotonous. Sitting beside the tiny campfire, he sipped from what was left of his coffee. He reflected darkly that he seemed to have spent most of his adult life like this, alone, hungry, sleeping with a single blanket on the hard ground. Usually, like tonight, he had wondered who might be coming behind him and how close they might be to catching up.

He thought about Son Dobson and how much he would give to trade places with the old farmer-fisherman, worried about nothing more than his noisy grandchildren. If they were Cordell's, they could make all the noise they wanted. That would be far preferable to the eerie silence of this old fort, where stone chimneys stood like tombstones over broken-down walls. The place was about as welcoming as a cemetery.

He dozed off, only to be awakened suddenly by the sound of horses moving through the grass. His heart hammered as he drew his pistol and sprinted out through an opening. He flattened himself against the highest part of the wall opposite the source of the sound.

Someone shouted, "Hello, the camp!"

Cordell remained silent. He heard a young voice say, "Told you I smelled smoke. There's a campfire in that old buildin'. What's left of one, anyway."

"Maybe they got some coffee," another replied.

Cordell held his breath. He heard the creak of leather as the riders dismounted on the far side of the ruined structure. The first voice said, "Don't seem to be anybody here. Must've fixed supper and left."

"Naw, there's a blanket yonder, and a saddle. And I seen a horse staked outside. Somebody's still around."

Cordell stepped back through the opening, pistol in his hand. "Somethin' I can do for you fellers?"

The pistol caught their immediate attention. Both men raised their hands to shoulder height. One stammered, "You don't need to point that thing at us, mister. We don't mean you no harm."

Cordell made his voice sound severe. "Did you come lookin' for me?"

"We don't even know who you are. We was just lookin' for some coffee, and maybe somethin' to eat."

Cordell placed several small pieces of dry wood on the fire to make it flare up. In its dancing light, he saw that both men were young, probably twenty years old or less. They looked like cowboys, possibly out of a job and riding the chuck line, depending upon others' hospitality. He lowered the pistol but did not immediately return it to its holster. Young or not, they could hurt a man. "Sorry if I gave you-all a fright, but you never know who might come ridin' in out of the night. Fort Griffin and the Clear Fork country have raised some hard characters."

"We're a ways past Griffin."

That told Cordell he had indeed ridden too far. It was by no means the first wrong guess he had made. In case someone should ask these two later, he decided to throw them off the track. "I know. Already been there. I'm headin' west, out to El Paso."

"They've got hard characters there, too."

Though not convinced, Cordell decided to give the pair the benefit of the doubt. He holstered the pistol but did not let his hand drift far from it. "The pot's empty, but you're welcome to boil some fresh coffee if you're of a mind to. Got smoked ham, too. Feel free to eat it all up. I'm tired of it."

He watched as they wolfed down what was left of his ham and drank coffee steaming hot. One had soft, patchy whiskers. He looked as if his next shave would be his first. The other's whiskers were just beginning to darken. Cordell asked, "You-all work around here?"

They looked at one another before the older of the two answered. "We're drovers. Came up from south of San Antonio with a herd but got fired at Griffin. It wasn't our fault. We wasn't the ones started the fight."

"Anybody killed?"

"Not quite, but pert near. We decided not to stay around. Folks in Fort Griffin have been known to hang people."

Cordell noticed that the younger-looking one, who had spoken little, seemed to be studying Cordell's saddle with much interest. Perhaps he sensed that the bulging saddlebags held something more than grub.

"Much obliged for the supper," the older one said as he got to his feet. "If you don't mind, we'll stake our horses and camp the night here."

Reluctantly Cordell said, "It's a free country."

He watched them as they walked out to where they had tied their horses. The youngest seemed all of a sudden to be doing a lot of talking. The other nodded a couple of times and glanced back over his shoulder. Cordell wished he could hear what was being said. He had a hunch they were not discussing his health.

He knew he would not sleep tonight.

He spread his blanket outside the wall. They remained inside. While they settled in for the night, he kept watching them through an opening that had been a doorway. He waited until he heard snoring, then arose, rolled his blanket and tied it behind his saddle along with his little bit of camp equipment. So the pair would be less likely to hear, he led the mare out fifty yards or so before he saddled her. He circled back around and quietly untied the youths' horses. He led them westward about a mile before turning them loose. Not quite qualifying as horse theft, it was his favorite way of stalling pursuit.

By the time the pair found their mounts, he would be miles away.

He was still uncertain about their intentions. Odds were that they would have tried to rob him during the night. In that case he had no cause to regret setting them afoot. On the other hand there was a chance they were just what they appeared to be, a couple of luckless cowboys. If so, he had done them a wrong. But at least it was only a nuisance that would result in nothing worse than sore feet. Some people he had known, like Milt Hayward, would have shot them just to be safe.

He made little effort in the night to hide his tracks, for he could not see the terrain well enough to pick his ground. Much of it was sandy. Judging direction by the North Star, he kept riding west to confuse pursuers until he came into a dry wash with a gravel base. That ought to make him hard to track, he thought. He followed the wash in a northwesterly direction for several miles until it played out. He cut back to the northeast to compensate for the wide circle he had made.

At daylight he did not know where he was except in a general way. Far to the west stretched the rough breaks that led to the base of the high-plains escarpment. Somewhere to the east was notorious Fort Griffin, legendary first as a military post and buffalo hunters' rendezvous, then later as host to cattle drives on their way north to Kansas. He felt that its tales of violence had been exaggerated. Such stories almost always were, for most people were more interested in raw meat than in the facts. Still, there must be at least some fire to yield so much smoke. Perhaps in such an environment his past transgressions might be overlooked.

He was unaware of the half dozen riders until they topped a small rise in front of him, not fifty yards away. To run would be useless, for they had seen him. Dropping his hand to the grip of his pistol, he reined in the mare and waited. They had the grim and purposeful look of a posse. Had they come from behind him, he would not have been surprised, but their appearance head-on gave him a start. He resisted the temptation to draw the weapon. They could perforate him before he got off more than a shot or two.

The leader was a gaunt man with a severe expression and a black beard that hid his collar button, or would if he were wearing a collar. He said sternly, "I do wish you'd take your hand away from that six-shooter."

Cordell decided to try bluffing his way through. "Not till I know your intentions."

The leader beckoned to a rider whose hat was precariously perched atop a bandaged head. "Does he look like one of them, Hez?"

The little man called Hez gave Cordell only a brief inspection. "Naw, this feller is as big as the both of them put together. He don't look like no drover, and he sure as hell ain't no kid anymore."

"You're certain?"

"Damn right. They had their faces covered, but I could tell from their voices that they were a couple of young'uns. One of them no-good little bastards laid the barrel of a pistol upside my head. Like to've brained me."

The man with the beard turned apologetically to Cordell. "Sorry for the inconvenience, friend. We're lookin' for a couple of cowboys that robbed a saloon in Fort Griffin after closin' time the other night. Probably came off of a cattle drive and knew there'd be a lot of money in the saloon. Got themselves a road stake before they lit out for parts unknown."

Cordell knew whom he was talking about, but he saw no reason to say so. An honorable outlaw did not inform on others. It was a courtesy of the trade. He didn't see a badge among this bunch anyway. They looked more like a mob bent on vengeance. Citizens of Griffin had been known to mete out rough justice without waiting for the law. Waiting required patience.

He said, "I ain't seen anybody that fits your description. Fact is, I ain't seen anybody at all."

"They had a good head start. They're probably long gone." The bearded man frowned. "If you happen to run into a pair of that description, though, you'd better ride way around them. A young rattlesnake's bite is as dangerous as an old one's. Hez's partner is laid up with a cracked skull. They're liable to kill somebody the next time."

Cordell said, "It's been some years since I was in Fort Griffin. What's it like these days?"

"It's seen better times. With railroads comin' across Texas, the trail drives are slowin' down. Since the Indians were put away, things are quiet up at the army post. Worst of all, Albany's the county seat now. Griffin ain't like it used to be, and sometimes I begin to wonder if it ever was."

Cordell had no interest in the fortunes or misfortunes of Fort Griffin except as they might apply to the Jackson family. He was doubly relieved when the posse rode on. First of all, they had not recognized him. Maybe the alarm hadn't reached this far west. Second, his suspicions about his visitors last night had proven well-founded. If he had relaxed his guard, he might be lying dead amid the ruins of Phantom Hill, and they might be marveling at their great luck in becoming suddenly rich.

Inasmuch as these possemen had looked him over without realizing who he was, he felt emboldened to visit Fort Griffin and ask about the Jacksons. He would finish his mission here, then move on. Perhaps that new life he had hoped for was finally within his reach.

CHOCTAW JOHN CHEWED vigorously on a wad of tobacco as he squatted on his heels and studied the ground. "Ain't there been a storybook about a flyin' horse?"

Andy replied, "Can't say. I never read many storybooks."

"I'm afraid that's what we got here. For all the trace I can find, that horse just up and flew away."

John's tracking had led them to an abandoned military post, its walls crumbled, the brush growing up on what had been a parade ground. It was Phantom Hill, John said. Fresh ashes and charred wood showed that someone had built a campfire. Boot tracks were still visible where remnants of old walls had protected them from wind.

John said, "Looks like your man met up with two others here. Hard to figure what happened. All three horses started off together. Looks like somebody was followin' after them afoot. Damned peculiar."

A mile or so from the post, two horses had split off and headed north. The third, its tracks the same ones Andy and John had followed all along, had continued westward for a short time, then suddenly vanished. John and Andy spent several hours circling and searching but found no more sign.

Andy had heard stories among the Comanches about medicine men supposedly able to transform themselves into birds and fly to distant places. He had never believed those tales. Anyway, Cordell was no medicine man, but years of experience in escaping from the law appeared to have made him part coyote.

John said, "Maybe your Cordell is usin' an old Choctaw trick, wrappin' his horse's feet with leather so the hoofs don't cut deep."

Andy could not leave unanswered the implication that Choctaws were smarter. "Comanches did it, too."

He thought it more likely that Cordell simply had a strong instinct for finding ground where he would not leave a trail. Andy had developed a grudging respect for the fugitive's perverse ability to evade pursuit.

John said, "If you ever capture this one, they ought to promote you. He's about as slippery as I've ever seen not to have some Choctaw blood in him."

"That wouldn't surprise me. I don't know a lot about him except he's slicker than a greased pig."

John arose to a stand and leaned against his horse. "I'm afraid we've lost him for good. He'll eventually come to ground in one place or another, and some sheriff will grab him."

"I've been on his trail too long to quit. I couldn't go back and look at Tom Blessing's grave, knowin' I'd failed him. I wish you'd stay with me awhile longer."

John shrugged. "I hate to take money under false pretenses, except when it belongs to Thaddeus Hunnicutt. I get a kick out of aggravatin' that old skinflint."

"What if I offered you three dollars a day instead of two?"

John brightened. "Now, Ranger, you're speakin' the Choctaw language. But you know there ain't a Chinaman's chance I'll pick up that trail again."

"At least it's a chance, no matter how small."

"I like a man who makes up his mind to do a job and sticks with it even when it goes to hell. Must be the Comanche in you. They're the stubbornest damned people I ever knew."

"You might be right."

"As I remember it, though, every time us Choctaws had a fight with the Comanches, we won."

Andy grinned. "Like hell you did."

He knew that by tradition a Ranger was always supposed to be sure of himself, but he was undecided about what to do next. All he could think of was to keep going in a westerly direction and hope. Maybe they would get lucky and cut into Cordell's trail. Andy had a general sense of where he and John were. He had passed through this region during his time with the nomadic Comanches and later in his growing-up years. This was a transition area where the Cross Timbers yielded to the rolling plains. Somewhere back to the northeast would be Fort

Griffin. The town and the army post for which it was named lay along the south side of a Brazos River tributary known as the Clear Fork. It had been a favorite hunting ground for the Comanches before they were driven north of the Red River. Cattlemen had brought in their herds after hide hunters had killed off the buffalo. Now farmers were taking up the more arable portions, turning the native sod under. He had heard rumors of plans for a railroad.

Cordell had avoided towns for the most part, so Andy thought it unlikely he would go to Griffin and risk being recognized. More likely he would continue west, up over the caprock and out onto the open plains. On the vast Llano Estacado, Indian raiders had usually been able simply to disappear, confounding those who pursued them. Andy decided to keep moving that way and hope.

He saw half a dozen riders ahead, coming from the direction of the distant caprock. They slouched in their saddles as if they had almost reached the end of their endurance. He said, "Let's wait and see who they are. Maybe they've seen somebody."

The apparent leader was a man with a black beard not unlike the one Andy remembered seeing on Cordell, though this beard was better trimmed. The man gave Andy and John a quick but critical study, then asked, "Mind tellin' me who you-all are?"

"I'm Andy Pickard, Texas Ranger. John's my tracker."

"A Ranger?" The man looked frustrated. "We could've sure used you yesterday. I reckon now it's too late. They've given us the slip."

"They?"

"Two men, probably drovers. Robbed a saloon in Fort Griffin, pistol-whipped the owner and the bartender. Come nigh killin' them."

Andy's hopes surged. "Was one of them a big feller, forty or so?"

"No, these were young. Not much more than kids, the way the bartender told it."

Andy's hopes sagged.

The leader asked, "You're lookin' for a big man?"

"A man named Cordell. I've been on his trail all the way from southeast Texas."

The leader stroked his beard. "We may have seen him. We came upon a big feller yesterday and asked if he'd crossed trails with the two we're after. He said he hadn't."

"Was he ridin' a bay mare?"

"Sure was. What's he done?"

"It'd take an hour to tell you what all. Which way was he travelin'?"

"West." The posse leader frowned. "If you was to chance upon those two young scoundrels, we'd appreciate you puttin' them under arrest and bringin' them to Fort Griffin. We'd see that they never rob anybody again."

"I couldn't stand still for a hangin', if that's what you've got in mind."

"You ain't likely to see them anyhow. They're probably halfway across the plains by now, to Mobeetie or Tascosa."

Andy said, "I don't think so." He told how John had read the tracks. "Two riders turned north. I'll bet they're the ones you're lookin' for."

The leader looked puzzled. "We missed that. But why would they turn north after comin' so far west?"

"Maybe they figured to circle around and throw you off."

One of the possemen said worriedly, "They could be

back in Fort Griffin right now, robbin' somebody else. They had their faces covered. Nobody would know them."

The leader said, "Then we'd better use our spurs and get back. Comin' with us, Ranger?"

"No. We've got our own job to do."

Andy strongly suspected that the posse had unknowingly come upon Cordell. Living up to the outlaw fraternity's code of ethics, he had lied when he told them he had not seen the young riders.

The riders pushed their horses into a reluctant trot. Andy and John continued in their westward direction. Late in the afternoon Andy noticed that John kept looking back. Andy saw nothing behind him. Finally John said, "I thought you Comanches had a guardian spirit to tell you about things you can't see."

"It doesn't always work. Choctaws are supposed to have one, too."

"I don't need any spirit to talk to me. My eyesight's good enough. I'll bet you hadn't noticed there's somebody followin' us."

Andy's first thought was of Cordell, but that made no sense. "If there is, how do you know he's followin' us? He might have a good reason to be travelin' in the same direction that we are."

"We can find out. Let's jog to the north and see if he keeps on comin'."

John's uneasiness was contagious. Andy had still not seen anyone, but he knew John's eyesight was sharp. Perhaps he had a sixth sense as well. "We'll try it. I hope you're wrong."

They made a sharp change in direction and rode on for a mile or so. John said, "Like I figured, he's trailin' us."

Andy had hoped it would not happen. He said, "There's brush up ahead. We can pull up there and lay for him."

"What'll we do with him when we get him?"

"Unless he's Cordell, I've got no idea."

Showing caution, the rider slowed as he approached the brushy draw where Andy and John had concealed themselves. He stopped to study the way ahead. By this time Andy could see that the man was large, somewhat as he remembered Cordell. But Cordell should be somewhere ahead of them. It made no sense for him to have fallen behind.

The rider overcame his doubts and came on. Pistols drawn, Andy and John rode out to confront him. Andy said, "Keep those hands up where we can see them."

Startled, the man instinctively reached for his pistol but saw he was covered. He raised his hands to shoulder height and blurted, "What the hell?"

"That's what we want to know. How come you're trailin' us?"

The rider shook his head. "I ain't trailin' you. I don't even know who you are. If you figure to rob me, you won't get much."

"We're not robbers. I'm a Ranger. Now, who are you?"

The man looked around as if gauging his chance of breaking away. "Name's Smith. John Smith."

Andy said, "My horse could come up with a better name than that." He saw that the man had a sizable blanket roll tied behind his saddle, as if he were traveling far. He probably had camp supplies bundled in it. His saddlebags bulged. "You're pretty well fixed for travelin'."

The man's eyes had a hard and defiant look. "It's a long ways between towns."

Andy said, "I wouldn't be surprised to find you in my fugitive book. Keep him covered, John."

Andy holstered his pistol and reached into his saddle-bag, where he kept Len's list of wanted men. He cut his gaze away from the stranger for a moment. The stranger sank spurs into his horse and rammed into John, throwing him off-balance. John grabbed for the saddle horn, dropping his pistol. In an instant the rider had his own pistol out. He snapped off a shot at John and swung the muzzle around. For a couple of seconds he aimed point-blank at Andy. For some reason he did not squeeze the trigger.

Startled by the shot, Andy's horse danced in confusion. Andy drew his pistol but was unable to steady it enough for a clean shot. The shooter wheeled his horse around and quickly vanished from sight in the thick brush. Andy was about to spur after him when he saw that John was on the ground. Fearfully he swung out of the saddle and dropped to one knee. "Are you hit?"

John pressed his hand against his side, then raised it for Andy to see the blood. "Damn right I'm hit." He sucked in a sharp breath, his face twisting. "Feels like I've got a broke rib. Maybe a bunch of them."

The two horses ran off a short way, then stopped to look back. The little pack mule followed them. Andy hoped that was as far as they would go, but he could not take time to catch them now. He had to see about John. Kneeling at the tracker's side, he pulled John's shirt open. The wound was bleeding.

After a brisk examination he said, "Looks like that bullet glanced off of your ribs and went on. Probably broke one or two."

John wheezed, "Hell of a way to earn three dollars."

"Think you can ride?"

John pressed his hand against his ribs and tried, with Andy's help, to get to his feet. He groaned and settled back down to a sitting position. "I don't think so."

It occurred to Andy that if one or two ribs were broken, which appeared likely, a sharp edge could puncture John's lung. He said, "I can't just leave you out here and ride for help. No tellin' how far it'd be or how long it'd take."

"There ain't no way in hell that I can ride a horse."

Andy weighed another possibility. "Maybe I can rig a travois like the Indians used."

John considered. "Sounds like a Comanche torture trick, but I don't want to stay here."

Andy rolled John's shirt and used it to bind the ribs as best he could. John grunted when Andy drew the makeshift wrapping tight. Face pinched with pain, he asked, "Who do you reckon that was?"

"Somebody who was afraid I'd find him listed in the book, I guess. It was just chance that we ran into each other."

"But he *was* followin' us."

"That I can't explain." There was something else Andy could not explain. "He drew a perfect bead on me but didn't shoot."

"I wish he hadn't shot at me either."

"He could've killed me, but he didn't."

"Count your blessin's. Anyway, I'm afraid I've cost you any chance to catch up with Cordell."

"It appears we'd lost him anyway."

Andy slowly approached the horses, talking gently in hope they would not run away. He caught his own, then John's. It took a while to find two branches long enough and strong enough to carry John's weight. He ran them through his stirrups and tied them, then secured shorter pieces as cross braces behind the horse. He placed his and John's blankets on as padding. "It's a long ways from a feather bed," he said.

Slowly and cautiously he eased John onto this awkward conveyance. Hurting, John said, "Don't you bounce me off of this thing."

Andy tied John's horse to the pack mule, knowing the mule would follow like a dog. He asked, "Are you ready?"

"No, but let's go anyway."

Andy sensed that his horse was uneasy. Allowing it time to accept this odd attachment it was expected to drag, he started in a slow walk. The horse kept looking back at first. Andy feared it might kick at the travois. But the animal calmed, and Andy felt secure enough to pick up the pace.

It was going to be a rough ride for John. Andy could only guess how far it was to Fort Griffin.

13

Cordell was skittish about riding into Fort Griffin in broad daylight. He staked the mare to graze near the narrow river and took his ease beneath the shade of heavy trees while he waited for darkness. Three people rode by but gave him no more than a glance. He took that for a favorable sign. Maybe this town was not given to asking a lot of questions.

At dark he rode down the dirt street, looking first of all for a place to eat, one not crowded with customers. He found a small joint that seemed to have no business at all. The cook was the only person in the place, and he was skinny as a snake. That should have been a warning about the food, Cordell decided once he bit into the steak. It must have come from a tough, old bull, and the biscuits were hard enough to hurt his teeth. But it was the first time in a while that he ate his fill.

Carrying his saddlebags, he walked down a couple of doors to a saloon that suffered the same lack of customers and decided to give it a little of his business. Two men stood at the bar. More accurately, they leaned on it and gave every appearance of having been there too long. Cordell walked to a dark corner well away from the kerosene lamp that sat on the bar. He intended to have a quiet drink or two and, when nobody was close enough to hear and remember, to ask the bartender about the Jackson family.

The barkeep brought Cordell a drink. Cordell said, "Kind of quiet here tonight."

"Yeah, been a couple of days since a trail herd hit town. There's several just south of here, though. It'll get busier in a night or two."

Bits and pieces of the two drunks' conversation came to Cordell, but he could not hear enough to piece together any meaning, not that it mattered. They became louder when they argued over which had the fastest horse.

Their voices were drowned out by boisterous laughter from the street. Three young men pushed through the door, two jamming shoulders together as they tried to enter at the same time. A third trailed a couple of steps behind, dragging his feet. He looked to be the youngest, perhaps seventeen or eighteen. As the three approached the lamp and its full light shone on their faces, Cordell was startled. The two in the lead were the ones he had encountered at Phantom Hill. He remembered that their tracks had veered north a mile or so from the abandoned post. The posse had been wrong in assuming they went on west. They had circled and taken a roundabout way back to Griffin.

The third youth remained in a dim area well away from the lamplight. Cordell could not see his face clearly.

The oldest of the youths began to harass the two drunks. "How long has it been since you old farts took a bath? You stink."

The older men tried to ignore him. The one who had spoken grabbed the nearest drunk by the shoulder and turned him half around. "It'd be a service to the town if we was to drag you down to the river and throw you in. A soakin' would do you both a world of good."

The other youth shouted in gleeful agreement. The pair grabbed the two men by their arms and pulled them toward the door.

The bartender's face darkened. He slammed both hands down on the bar to get their attention. It sounded almost like a pistol shot. "Boys, I won't have you manhandlin' my customers. If you want a drink and have the money to pay for it, put it here where I can see it. Otherwise, go back outside and get you some fresh air."

The oldest of the three said, "Now, Oscar, you better be careful what you say. You just might get a bath yourself." He made a move as if to grab the bartender by the collar. Oscar stepped back out of reach, bent down, and came up with a double-barreled shotgun. His voice was angry. "Like I said, the air's fresher outside."

The challenger stared at the weapon but did not back away. Cordell had not intended to meddle, but he thought he saw serious intention in the bartender's face. If someone didn't yield, there was about to be a mess of blood on the floor and all kinds of people rushing in here to see what happened. A crowd like that was the last thing he wanted.

He said sternly, "Son, maybe you've never seen what a shotgun blast can do to a man."

The youths' attention shifted. The one who had challenged the bartender took a step toward Cordell's table. "Ain't I seen you somewhere?"

The two drunks took advantage of the distraction to stumble out through the door.

Cordell laid his pistol on the table, where it immediately gained the youths' full attention. "Not as I recall."

The second young man said, "Sully, ain't he the one that—"

"Shut up, Finn," the older one snapped.

Cordell said, "I believe it'll be better all around if you take your business down the street. The whiskey here ain't that good anyway."

The youngest of the three said, "I never did like this joint. Let's git."

Sully said grudgingly, "All right. I don't care to spend my money where it ain't appreciated." To the bartender he said, "We heard what happened to Old Shep at his bar the other night, him and Hez. You might want to be careful how you talk to people, Oscar. It could happen to you." He turned. The other two followed him out.

The bartender waited to be sure they were gone, then placed the shotgun back beneath the bar. Bringing a bottle and a glass, he sat down at the table, refilled Cordell's drink, and downed one himself. "You said my whiskey ain't very good. What's wrong with it?"

"Nothin'. I had to say somethin'. It was about to get serious."

"We got some wild kids around here."

Cordell knew better, but he said, "Maybe they were just funnin'."

"Their kind of fun ain't funny. Sooner or later it'll get somebody hurt."

"Who are they?"

"The oldest two are the Keeler brothers. Got no mother, and their old daddy is too busy stayin' drunk to pay them much mind. They're like two young studs that nobody's managed to put a saddle on."

The Keelers were the ones Cordell had left afoot. "And the other?"

"Name's Dobie Jackson. Got no daddy, just a widowed mother. She's workin' herself into the grave to keep the farm goin'. That boy needs a quirt taken to him. If he keeps runnin' with them Keeler brothers, he'll end up dead or killin' somebody."

Jackson! Cordell had found out most of what he wanted without having to ask for it. He hoped it was the right family. Trying to be casual, he said, "Ain't she got any other sons to help her?"

"She used to have. She's afraid Dobie's liable to up and leave like her other boy did. If he keeps lettin' them Keelers lead him around, he may *have* to."

"What about that other son?"

"Name's David. He hung around with the Keelers too much, too. Got in a little trouble and took to the brush. Aurelia has no idea where he's at."

Cordell felt a wrenching in his gut. Probably the whiskey, he tried to tell himself, but he knew the cause.

Oscar said, "It's a damned shame to see a boy throw his life away. Like as not, David is in jail someplace. The way he's goin', Dobie is apt to follow right after him." The bartender leaned forward, lowering his voice. "I got a strong suspicion it wasn't no drovers that robbed Old Shep's bar. Wouldn't surprise me none if it was them Keeler boys."

"They can't be very smart if they think they can pull a stunt like that in their own town and not be recognized."

"They covered their faces with sacks, but they ain't half as smart as they think they are. If they was to try that trick on me, I'd know them. They wouldn't get six feet inside the door."

Cordell swallowed another drink, emptying the bottle. He tried in vain to drive away the image of Buster lying dead in a doctor's office, taken down by a lawman's bullet.

Oscar said, "All of a sudden you don't look so good."

"Somethin' I ate."

"Must've been in that joint down the street. I ain't surprised. I wouldn't let my dog eat what comes out of that kitchen."

"I think I'd better go out and get me some air." Cordell thought of a way around having to ask the question directly. "I wouldn't want to run into those boys and have trouble with them. Whichaway will they be goin' home?"

"East, down the river. The Jackson farm is three or four miles, the Keeler place a ways further. But they won't be leavin' town till they run out of money or they're fallin'-down drunk." Oscar picked up Cordell's empty bottle from the table. "I wish we had chain gangs here like we had back home in Alabama. It'd do them boys a heap of good to work on the roads awhile. Maybe it'd sweat some of the meanness out of them. You ever see a chain gang?"

Suppressed memories and old emotions enveloped Cordell like a malevolent dark cloud. He winced. "Once."

He felt unsteady, making his way out the door. He leaned on the outside wall until he had his feet under him. He knew he had drunk too much. That was dangerous for a man on the dodge. He would be an easy catch should a lawman show up, or a thief coveting what he carried in his saddlebags. He found a wooden bench in front of a darkened store and slumped there, hoping the effects of the whiskey would soon pass. He dozed off, wakened when the saddlebags slipped from his lap, then dozed again.

His sleep was again interrupted by loud talking and a voice raised in what was meant to be a song. Down the street he saw three shadowy figures stumbling around a hitching rail. Trying to mount his horse, one let his foot slip from the stirrup. He fell on his back while the other two laughed. Though he could not see them clearly, their voices told him that they were the Keeler brothers and Dobie Jackson.

A thought penetrated the fog that had enveloped his brain. He had wanted to know where the Jackson family lived without having to ask directly. All he had to do was follow these three. He hoped they were on their way home and not simply looking for another place to carouse.

The mare snorted as he untied her. She probably did not like the awkward way he approached her, or perhaps it was the smell of the whiskey. "You're right, old girl," he muttered. "I don't like myself very much right now either." He managed to get into the saddle on the first try. He had the presence of mind to be sure he had tied the saddle-bags down securely. As the three riders pulled away from town, he put the mare into a walk. They sometimes moved out of sight despite the full moon, but he could follow the sound of their voices. They talked and laughed and sang. They occasionally stopped, passing a bottle around. As he gradually sobered, he felt some concern that they might not make it home.

Eventually he saw light ahead. A lantern was suspended from the roof of a farmhouse porch. It was a mother's way of helping her boy find his way home, he supposed. He reined up to prevent overtaking the three. They stopped and talked a few minutes before two rode on. One made his way to a barn and started to dismount, then fell like a sack of grain. He lay on the ground a minute or two before he pushed shakily to his feet and removed the saddle, blanket, and bridle. Slapping his horse on the rump, he dragged his tack into the barn. He did not come out. Cordell suspected he had collapsed on the floor. He would probably spend the night there without going to the house.

Damned fool kid, Cordell thought. He remembered what the barkeep had said. *Ought to have a quirt taken to him.*

Now he knew where the Jackson family lived. He would retreat a little way and finish the night sleeping on the ground. Ever since Buster had died, he had tried to decide how to go about what had to be done. Now that he was here, all the options he had considered seemed to have evaporated. Maybe the morning sun would clear his head. Then he could make up his mind what to do next.

He slept fitfully, his stomach not taking kindly to the abuse he had given it. *It's bad enough when some chuckle-headed kid drinks too much, but a man my age ought to know better,* he thought. After sunup he boiled coffee. It helped clear his head but did nothing for his stomach. His whiskers had been allowed to grow for several days. He feared his appearance might frighten Buster's mother, so he took time to boil river water and shave. He knew he was still a long way from handsome, but he had done the best he could.

If he betrayed his true identity immediately, he might not be allowed to enter the house. Buster's mother would have every right to blame him for losing her son, though the bartender had said the boy was already under a cloud when he left here. Cordell decided to play his cards close to the vest until the time felt right for show-ing his hand.

Riding toward the unpainted frame farmhouse, he could see that it was badly in need of work. A side win-dow was broken out, a piece of cardboard put up in its place. Some roof shingles were broken, probably by a hailstorm. Out back, at the barn, a door hung by a single hinge. These were all things her son Dobie could repair if he were more inclined toward work.

Buster's rightful share of the bank money would come to just over three thousand dollars. Cordell could see that the farm badly needed patching up, starting with the unpainted frame house. That kind of money could do this place a world of good. He wondered about Mrs. Jackson's reaction. Would she eagerly grab the cash, as Irmadell almost certainly would, or coldly reject both it and him? He halfway hoped she would turn it down. He admired honesty and courage wherever he saw them. In that case, he would hide the money so she would find it later, after he was gone. A debt of honor had to be paid whatever the cost.

A picket fence surrounded the house, though like everything else around here, it needed work. He tied his horse and walked up to the front door. It was open, but it would be rude to enter without invitation, especially with the knowledge that a woman was inside. He knocked on the doorframe. He could hear the wooden floor creak as someone walked across it. A woman appeared at the door, wiping her hands on an apron. She said, "Yes?"

Taking off his hat, he had to look at her a moment before he could say anything. She was in her forties but by his estimation was still a handsome woman despite worry tracks around her tired eyes and gray beginning to streak the hair tied in a bun at the back of her head. "Ma'am," he said, "my name is . . . Walter Goodson. I'm lookin' for work, and I see your place could stand some fixin' up."

She gave him as intense a looking-over as he had given her. "That it does, but I can't afford to hire anybody."

He said, "That don't need to stand in the way. I've been hungry awhile. I'd work for meals and a place to sleep out of the rain."

He could see her struggling over the proposition. She said, "I wouldn't want to take advantage of you, asking you to work for nothing."

"It wouldn't be for nothin', ma'am. I'm takin' it on faith that you're a good cook."

"Fair to middling, but you won't see any fat people around here."

"I'd regard it as a real favor if you'd let me stay at least a little while. I promise you I'd earn my keep."

She was weakening. "I never like to turn anybody away from the door hungry, and it's a fact that we could use some help." She smiled. It was just a half smile, but it was a pleasant one. "All right, for a little while. And if there's any way I can do it, I'll pay you. I warn you, it may not be much."

"I don't need for much."

"You'll find hay in the shed for your mare. You can turn her loose in the corral. And there's an old cot in the barn where you can lay out your bedding. It'll still be a while before dinner."

"I'll find somethin' useful to do till then." He put his hat back on. "I thank you, ma'am."

"By the way, my name is Aurelia Jackson."

"Mighty pleased to know you, ma'am." He took the hat off again.

He noticed a large woodpile in back of the house, but only a small stack had been chopped into the right length for a cookstove. He turned the bay mare into the corral and put out some hay for her. He found a folding steel cot and dropped his blanket roll on it. He hid his saddlebags beneath the pile of hay, then returned to the woodpile and began swinging the ax. His hands were tender, not used to hard manual labor. They soon became sore. He could feel a blister rising, but he was determined to get himself into the widow's good graces. Then, at the proper time, he would tell her why he was here.

He became so absorbed in the work that he did not hear someone walk up behind him until he saw a shadow. He whirled, dropping his hand to his hip.

Dobie Jackson stood there, looking considerably less cheerful than in the saloon last night. His eyes were bloodshot. He sweated profusely though the day had not turned more than moderately warm. He demanded, "Who the hell are you, and what're you doin' here?"

"My name's Walter Goodson, and I've hired on to work." Though he knew, he asked, "And who are you?"

"I'm Dobie." The youth frowned darkly, squinting one eye. "Ain't I seen you someplace?"

"Maybe. I've been lots of places."

"You wasn't in Oscar's place last night, was you?"

"I believe I was. And I believe I saw you there, too."

Dobie's voice carried a bit of resentment. "You busted up a little innocent fun. Me and the Keeler boys wasn't really goin' to throw anybody in the river. We were just hoorawin' a couple of drunks."

"It looked to me like you were a little drunk yourself."

Concern crept into Dobie's eyes. "You won't tell Maw about that, will you?"

"I won't tell her about you if you won't tell her about me."

"Fair deal." Dobie started toward the house, then turned back. "What did you say you're doin' here?"

"Just hired on to do some fixin' up. The place needs it." Accusation slipped into his voice. "Been needin' it for some time, looks like."

"Yeah. I been meanin' to get around to it."

Cordell leaned on the ax. "Who are those Keeler boys?"

"They're neighbors." Dobie jerked his thumb toward the east. "We used to go to school together till we all decided to quit. Got tired of teachers tryin' to tell us what to do."

"Do those Keelers tell *you* what to do?"

"Nobody tells me what to do. I do my own thinkin'."

And a damned poor job of it, Cordell thought. *Well, you're none of my worry. But I feel sorry for your mother.*

He chopped what he thought would be enough wood for at least four or five days, then drove the blade of the ax into a log he had used for a chopping block. He picked up an armload and carried it into the kitchen to replenish the woodbox beside the hot cast-iron range. He could smell bread baking in the oven.

Aurelia Jackson poked a couple of sticks of wood into the stove and said, "You'd just as well quit and wash up. Dinner'll be ready pretty soon. I expect you're hungry."

He breathed a bit heavily from the exertion. "Yes, ma'am, I sure am."

"I wish you'd call my son. He's workin' at the barn, I think."

Cordell saw no reason to tell her that Dobie was slumped on a bench in the shade at the side of the house. "I'll fetch him."

He told Dobie what she had said. He did not look up but said, "I don't know as I can eat anything. My stomach is all tore up."

"Whiskey'll do that to you every time. What you need is good hard work to sweat it out of your blood. I saw a stack of shingles out yonder. After dinner we'll climb up and patch your mother's roof."

"It don't rain here all that much."

"We'll fix it just the same." Cordell's own hangover

made him short of patience. "Get off your butt and wash for dinner."

"Who do you think you are, orderin' me around?"

"I'm a man who can kick you from here to Fort Griffin. Now go wash up for dinner."

Resentfully Dobie left the bench and walked to a small back porch where a bucket of water and a basin sat on a waist-high shelf. He glared at Cordell as he washed his hands, then splashed his face with water.

Cordell said, "Wouldn't hurt none if you combed your hair. You look like a woolly booger."

"You ain't no rose yourself."

Cordell washed up and went into the kitchen. He was greeted by the smell of fresh bread and roast pork. He had already noted a pen of hogs out back of the barn.

Mrs. Jackson said, "It's a rare thing when we have beef around here, but hog meat is plentiful enough."

Cordell had eaten his fill of ham out of the Fergus smokehouse. Roast, however, was a different matter. "It looks mighty good," he said.

He was pleased to see Dobie walk into the kitchen with his hair combed. The youth flashed him a quick frown, then glanced away. Cordell said, "Me and your son are goin' to work on your roof after dinner. Looks like it might have a few leaks in it."

"That it does," she agreed. "I'd be much obliged if you'd show Dobie how it's done. Since his daddy died, there hasn't been anybody here to teach him things like that."

"We'll get along just fine, him and me." He gave Dobie a hard glance that told him there would be no argument.

He started to reach for the biscuits but saw Mrs. Jackson bow her head and begin giving thanks. That caught him off guard. It had been a long time since he had given the blessing or even heard someone else do it. Flustered, he looked down at the table and followed her "Amen" with a barely audible one of his own.

She said, "Dobie doesn't know how fortunate he is to have someone show him how to do things. I wish there had been somebody here for David."

Cordell felt a jolt but tried not to show it. "David?"

"My older son. He went kind of wild after he lost his father. Then one day he just up and rode away. We had a couple of short letters from him, but that was all. I wish I knew where he is."

Cordell could not look at her.

She said, "I keep hopin' he'll come ridin' in here someday, all grown-up, ready to settle down and start a family. That dream is about all that keeps me goin'."

Cordell lost his taste for biscuits and roast pork.

14

Andy wondered how Choctaw John kept from crying out as the crude travois bumped along the broken ground. He tried to avoid the rougher places, but the uneven terrain was a constant challenge. He stopped from time to time, dismounted, and went back to make sure John was still breathing. A punctured lung, should that come to pass, might well kill him.

He said, "Maybe we'd better stop awhile and let you rest."

John's face had paled. His eyes were pinched in pain, or perhaps from the burning of sweat that ran down his forehead. "The sooner we get to where we're goin', the sooner I can get off of this devilish drag."

Andy could only guess the distance to Fort Griffin. At this slow rate, it was a cinch they would not reach there before sometime tomorrow, if then.

John asked, "Are you sure they got a doctor in that town?"

"I'm not sure of anything except that it's a long way."

"They've probably got an undertaker. That may be what I need by the time we get there."

"Don't talk about dyin'. You haven't earned your money yet."

"I've got no interest in dyin'. I wouldn't give Thaddeus that satisfaction."

At least John had not lost his sardonic sense of humor. Andy took comfort in that.

Toward sundown he decided John had had about all he should have to stand for one day. They had enough canteen water that they could camp without traveling farther to find a creek.

John protested, "The day ain't finished yet."

"No, but you are, just about." Andy helped him off the travois and spread his blanket in the shade of a tree. "I'll try to whip up a little supper."

"I doubt I can eat much. Lord, but these ribs do hurt." John stretched himself slowly and carefully on the doubled blanket. He let out a long breath as if he had been holding it all day. He closed his eyes and said, "I almost wish that jaybird was a better shot. I wouldn't be feelin' anything now."

"Think about the money," Andy suggested. "Three dollars a day."

"Money's good for nothin' except gettin' you things you want, and I don't want much. I'd give up the wages just to get my ribs fixed back the way they was. Hell, I'd even kiss Thaddeus Hunnicutt."

"I'd give ten dollars to see that. He'd fall down in a dead faint."

"If I didn't beat him to it." John squinted one eye. "Who's goin' to foot my doctor bill?"

Andy said, "Me, like as not. You know how the state hates to pay up. The politicians get their hands into the pot first, and they don't leave much."

"I wish it was them ridin' on that drag instead of me."

Pain kept John awake most of the night, so Andy did not sleep much either. At sunup he boiled coffee and fried bacon. He could persuade John to eat only a little. John said, "It tastes better when a woman fixes it."

"You've got no woman."

"Now and again I do. They stay till we can't stand one another. That don't generally take long."

Andy caught up the horses, packed the mule, and helped John settle onto the travois. The second-day hurting was more severe than the first. His face contorted, John said, "Next time I get shot, I'll try to be closer to town."

Andy felt like groaning with John as the travois dragged across rough ground. About midmorning he saw a wagon moving eastward on a path parallel to his own. Its hoops were partially covered by canvas. A milk cow plodded along behind at the end of a short rope.

He said, "Hold on tight, John. We may get you a better ride."

The people with the wagon gave no sign that they had seen this makeshift procession. Andy realized they were going to outdistance him. He drew his pistol and fired a couple of shots into the air. The wagon stopped. People who had walked alongside quickly disappeared behind it.

John muttered, "They may think we're Indians."

Andy said, "We are, aren't we? You anyway."

"Just half. We better move up slow, or they're liable to shoot us both. I don't need any more of that."

Andy tied a handkerchief to his rifle barrel and waved it over his head. He heard a faint shout from the wagon but could not decipher the words. He assumed they meant for him to come on in but do nothing sudden. Moving closer, he saw a man half hidden behind the rear of the wagon, his rifle aimed and ready. The voice was clearer now. "That's close enough. State your business."

"I'm a Ranger," Andy shouted back. "Got a wounded man here. He needs help."

The man beckoned him to move closer, but he held the rifle steady. "You got anything to show that you're a Ranger?"

"Just my word."

The man stepped hesitantly into plain view. He appeared to be in early middle age, wearing an untrimmed salt-and-pepper beard, a plain cotton shirt without a collar, and faded bib overalls. He lowered the rifle. "I'm takin' you at your word. Just be careful that whatever you're draggin' don't booger my team. Got my wife and youngest baby in the wagon."

"Would you be headin' for Fort Griffin?"

"I'm sorry to say that we are. We'd prefer to go around that Sodom and Gomorrah, but we've got to pick up a few provisions to carry us back to East Texas."

Andy thought the description of the town was exaggerated, but this was not the time to argue the point. "Have you got room to carry this man? The travois is about to kill him."

The farmer frowned. "Is he a prisoner?"

"No, he's been helpin' me. Got shot in the line of duty."

Easing, the farmer said, "I reckon we could shuffle things around and make room."

Three pairs of young eyes peered with great curiosity from beneath the wagon bed. A boy of about twelve stepped out and asked, "Are you really and truly a Ranger? We never seen a Ranger before."

"Yes, and there's no need for you to be scared. Me and John don't have any horns."

The farmer said, "I'm Henry Orville. My wife Hannalee is in the wagon." A bonneted woman looked out from beneath the canvas cover. Orville climbed into the wagon. Andy could hear the pair moving things around. The farmer finished tying the cover down over the hoops so the entire wagon was covered. He said, "We've got a bed of sorts fixed for your deputy."

He helped Andy lift John up over the end gate. John winced but did not cry out. Andy could hear Mrs. Orville beneath the canvas, telling him to lie down gently. "Poor man," she said. "Seems like there's no end of misfortune in this godforsaken part of the world."

It was obvious the family was moving. Belongings of various kinds were tied to the sides of the wagon and even beneath its bed, including two crude coops containing several chickens. Andy said, "Most people these days are movin' west. How come you're goin' east?"

"We already been west," Orville said, frowning as if he had bitten into something sour. "Out on them plains yonder, up over the caprock. A new land, they said. A new start. A barren desert, I call it. Fit only for Indians, and I doubt even they would want it back."

Andy could argue about that, but he had more important things on his mind.

Orville said, "We had us a few cattle. What the four-legged wolves didn't kill, the two-legged ones stole. We tried to farm, but the wheat was so short I'd've had to lather it before I could cut it. We had to dig for our water. And trees? There wasn't none, just wide-open plains for miles in every direction. Made a man feel buck naked in front of the world."

"Henry," his wife admonished. "The children . . ."

"I'm just tellin' it the way it is. We're goin' back to where it knows how to rain once in a while, where a man can raise a garden and rest in the shade of a tree when he's tired from his labor."

Andy had strong memories of the plains from his years with the Comanches. They differed from this disheartened farmer's description. There had been water if one knew where to look for it. Game had been plentiful most of the time, so meat had seldom been short. Bushes and shrubs in the canyons and draws offered wild berries and nuts of many varieties. The strong grass supported not only the buffalo but vast numbers of horses, both wild and tame. These people who came from a much different environment did not recognize the bounty nature placed there for the taking. The Indian had known, and it had served him well. Andy feared white men had already begun to spoil it, trying to turn it into the image of what they had left behind.

The two oldest children stared at him openly and without reserve. A little girl of four or five years stayed hidden behind a wheel, peeking out with one eye.

Andy beckoned the oldest boy. "Would you like to ride my deputy's horse so I don't have to lead him?"

The boy agreed with a broad grin. He quickly climbed into the saddle as if he feared Andy might change his mind. Orville returned to the wagon seat. "You young'uns stay clear of the wagon now. Everybody set? Here we go." The first forward movement caught the milk cow unprepared and almost jerked her off her feet. The two younger children walked alongside the wagon. The pack mule followed.

Orville's wife sat beside him on the wagon seat, the baby in her lap. Andy pulled his horse up beside them. He asked, "Where did you-all live before you came out here?"

Orville said, "The piney woods, over by Nacogdoches. I reckon that's why we couldn't find comfort out on that open prairie. You could see for ten miles in any direction, only there wasn't nothin' to look at. Had to hunt high and low for firewood. And lonesome? Now and then some cowboy came by, was all. Hannalee went for four months once without seein' another woman."

She nodded grimly.

Orville continued, "Folks weren't meant to live like that, white folks anyway. Hannalee was always afraid the Indians might show up, and I wasn't none too sure myself."

"They've been on the reservation for years now."

"They might decide to come back, though for the life of me I can't see why." Orville glanced at the sleeping baby in its mother's lap. "We decided to go home to East Texas and raise our young'uns in a civilized country." He rode in silence awhile, then asked, "How did your helper come to get hisself shot?"

Andy explained the circumstances without going into detail.

Orville said, "You never saw the shooter before?"

"Not that I know of. Odd thing, though, he seemed to be followin' us."

"He probably thought you were lookin' for *him,* and he decided to get you first."

"After he shot John, he was all set to shoot me between the eyes, but he didn't do it. I've got no idea why."

"There's no way of knowin' what goes on in the minds of men like that. They ain't normal."

Andy had searched the fugitive book, but the physical descriptions in it were sometimes vague. Besides, he had seen the outlaw close up for only a few wild and confused moments. The man could have been any one of fifty on the list.

Orville said, "That's another good reason for us to leave. Too many wild and lawless heathens out this way."

"There's good people here, too."

"Maybe so, but they're scattered too thin for my taste."

Andy was disappointed that Fort Griffin was still not in sight at dusk. The Orvilles made camp. Andy spread blankets on the ground for John and helped him down from the wagon. He had seen at noon that the family did not carry much food with them, certainly none to waste. He said, "Maybe the deer will come out in the cool of the evenin'. I'll see if I can get us some fresh meat."

He had not ridden far before he spotted three does easing warily into the open. They reached down to graze a patch of weeds, then jerked their heads up, chewing while they watched for danger. Andy knelt with his rifle, steadying one elbow on his knee. He aimed at the fattest of the three and fired. All the does jumped, but one fell kicking while the other two sprinted back into the brush. Andy gutted her on the ground, then tried to lift her up in front of his saddle. The horse shied away, spooking at the smell of fresh blood. Andy kept trying until he managed to get her into place and swing into the saddle. He feared for a while that the horse would pitch, throwing both him and the doe. Holding a tight rein, he reached camp just before dark.

The family welcomed the venison as a change from their meager fare on the trail. John had recovered his appetite, asking for a second helping. Andy took that for a good sign. John walked around a little, easing the stiffness in his legs, though he kept one hand pressed against his ribs. He coughed a few times. Andy hoped the cough was just caused by dust.

He asked, "How's the wagon ride?"

John considered his answer. "Better than that damned travois, but it's still hard on the constitution. How much further do you suppose we have to go?"

"We ought to be in Griffin tomorrow."

"It's damned sure time."

The next morning they moved along the upwind side of a trail herd, keeping away from dust stirred by the cattle. The trail boss was a young man of barely more than twenty, but he had already made two trips up the trail. He told Andy the wagon should reach Griffin by afternoon.

He turned out to be right. Reaching town, Andy inquired about a doctor and was pointed toward an upstairs office. Orville pulled the wagon as close as he could. Andy helped John up the steps, taking them one at a time. The doctor was an all-business little man wearing an old gray vest with tiny holes burned in front, indicating carelessness with his smoking. He gave John a thorough feeling-over without regard to the pain he caused.

His voice sounded critical. "Who wrapped you up so tight?"

Andy dreaded the lecture he was sure was coming, but he said, "I did."

"It's a good thing. He's just got one broken rib," the doctor declared, "but it's enough." He said to John, "If the Ranger hadn't taken good care of you, you could be hammering on the pearly gates by now because of a punctured lung. Or you could be dead of blood poisoning from the wound. Either way, you'd be trying to look up through six feet of dirt."

Andy asked, "What should I do with him now?"

"There's a hotel down the street. It's not the Brown Palace, but it's got no bedbugs as far as I know. Put him there where I can keep looking in on him for a few days."

"A few days?" Andy had not counted on such a delay.

"A broken rib is not like a broken spoke in a wheel. It can't be fixed in an hour."

Andy knew the state office would complain about paying for the doctor, much less the hotel, especially inasmuch as John was not a state employee. If it came to that, Andy would pay the bills out of his own pocket. He owed John that much for getting him into this fix. To make things worse, he had lost all track of Luther Cordell.

The family wasted no time in buying the supplies they needed and preparing to get under way. Orville said, "I'd like to put this town several miles behind us before we stop for the night. I want none of its corruption rubbin' off on the children."

Andy had seen no corruption yet, but he supposed if he were a family man, his viewpoint might be more critical. He felt that the Orvilles had given up their farm too soon, but perhaps it was for the best. Some people would never adapt to the dry and open plains. He bade the family good-bye and good luck, then watched their wagon pull out toward the east. The milk cow struggled against the rope that forced her to follow.

The hotel manager moved a cot into John's room for Andy. "Nothing is too good for the Rangers," he said. "It will be good, having you here in case some of the drovers stay too long in the barroom. We had a bad robbery in one of the saloons a few nights ago."

Andy said, "I heard about that. Folks seem to think a couple of drovers did it."

"Maybe yes, maybe no. There are some suspicions about that. Cowboys are free spenders. That money is a temptation to vultures who hover about, looking to reap where they have not sown."

"It takes a low class of criminal to hold up a saloon."

"The petty criminal will settle for less if he can get it with little risk. You say you have been hunting for a man who robbed a bank?"

Andy nodded. "I guess you could consider him a higher class of criminal. Not only was it a bank, but it was in one of the biggest towns in Texas."

"A man of high ambition."

"It's my ambition to catch him."

Andy was hard put to decide what to do. Loyalty to Choctaw John would require him to remain here at least until he knew John was going to recover without complications. Loyalty to the Rangers, on the other hand, would require him to go back where they had lost Cordell's trail and try again to discover some trace.

John had found that Cordell turned northward a while after leaving the ruins of Phantom Hill. It might have been only a temporary change of direction in an effort to throw off pursuit, or it could mean Cordell had not meant to travel farther west in the first place. It could mean he had circled back around, that he could even be here in Fort Griffin. It was a long shot, about as likely as Andy's getting an apology from Farley Brackett. Still, it was an intriguing possibility, enough to argue for his staying around at least a few days should the state office question his decision. He might see or hear something.

His first order of business, after seeing to John's needs, was to visit the local law. He found that the sheriff's office was in Albany, but a deputy was assigned to Fort Griffin. He introduced himself and told about his search.

The deputy gave him scant comfort. He said, "Sure, I could've seen your man. In the last couple of weeks, with the cattle herds comin' through, I've probably seen twenty that would match your description. Been a lot of strangers passed this way. As long as they haven't caused a row, I haven't paid much attention. Except for a pair that robbed Old Shep's saloon the other night, there hasn't been much excitement. In spite of the stories people tell about us, we're pretty good folks here in Griffin Town."

Andy told about meeting an impromptu posse on the trail of the two. The deputy grunted. "They were a hangin' party. They didn't have any authority from me or the sheriff. It's probably a good thing they didn't find those men. Somebody would've gotten killed, and it wouldn't have been just the robbers."

Andy agreed. A group of gun-toting citizens on the hunt could be more danger to themselves than to their quarry. "I'll probably hang around a few days," he said. "If you see or hear anything suspicious, I hope you'll let me know."

"Sure 'nuff. And if you spot your man and need help, all you've got to do is holler."

15

Cordell felt satisfaction in a job well done as he looked at the repaired corral fence. Only the blind would call it pretty, but it was strong, and it would hold just about any animal bigger than a house cat.

Dobie Jackson leaned on a shovel, sleeves rolled up and shirt stained with sweat. His voice was antagonistic. "I hope you're satisfied now. I don't see why we had to build the whole thing over. A little patchin' would've done it."

Cordell said, "A job worth doin' at all is worth doin' right. It's too bad we had to use old lumber, but at least you won't have to be ashamed of it now."

"I wasn't ashamed of it in the first place."

"It ought to give you a warm feelin', knowin' you've finished a good piece of work."

"All I feel is tired."

Cordell's good mood began to sour. He didn't know what it would take to straighten this boy out. Maybe a roof needed to fall in on him, or something. *His paw ought to've taken a razor strap to him a long time ago,* he thought. But he remembered that Dobie's father had been dead for some years. *He's too big for his maw to whip him, and it's not my place to do it, bad as I'd like to.* It bothered him that Dobie looked a little like his brother, and he was showing signs of following in Buster's wayward footsteps.

Cordell had not found a way to tell Aurelia Jackson that her oldest son was dead. He had meant every day to do it, but every day he had put it off, dreading the pain it would cause her. He had immersed himself in work, repairing much around here that had long needed fixing. He had bullied Dobie into helping him, hoping some healthy sweat would bring the youngster around to a greater appreciation for the home he had. Dobie had been a competent worker, though not an eager one. He took no initiative. He had to be told what to do, and sometimes how to do it.

Cordell liked this farm. It stirred up half-forgotten memories of one long ago in Louisiana. What he would give, he thought, if he could turn back the years and start over. Seeing Mrs. Jackson every day made him think of the wife he had lost by going off to war, and the empty years he had spent alone. He barely remembered anymore what she had looked like. It had been a long time since he had been able to conjure up a clear vision of her as she had been the last time they were together. But he remembered well the long and futile search he had made for her and their son.

If he still lived, that boy would be fully grown now, older than Dobie. Cordell had often tried to imagine what he would look like, what kind of man he would be. A better man, surely, than his father. It was just as well that the boy never got to know him, or to know what his father had become. Even if he chanced to hear the name Cordell, he would not recognize it, for that was not the name he had been born with.

So far he had not felt comfortable enough to use Aurelia's given name, though she had indicated that he need not continue being formal. He was hesitant to call her anything except Mrs. Jackson. Buster still haunted him, especially here where the boy had once been at home. He was sure that when he finally told Aurelia what had happened, she would hate him.

He said, "We'd just as well go to the house. I expect supper will be ready before long."

"No readier than I am," Dobie replied.

"Nothin' like hard work to give you an appetite."

"Or blisters." Dobie looked at his hands and frowned. "Before the war, did you have any slaves?"

"I never had money enough."

"Too bad. You'd've been a good slave driver."

Cordell pretended to take that for a joke, though he knew it was not meant to be. He had suffered about as much of Dobie's attitude as his patience would endure. He felt a strong urge to tell Mrs. Jackson about Buster, then ride on. Any day now, a Ranger or other lawman might show up at the door. Though he had seen no sign of pursuit, he had a nagging feeling that it was there, somewhere. It was time he headed west again, or he might become so attached to this place that he would stay and let himself be captured.

Halfway to the house, he heard a holler. Two horsemen approached from the east. He recognized them as the Keeler brothers. One shouted, "Hey, Dobie, wait up."

Dobie grinned and turned to face the pair. Cordell felt his stomach draw into a knot. He had seen the brothers twice before, and they had given him indigestion both times.

Keeler said, "Come and go with us to town. We'll have us a time."

Cordell did not give Dobie a chance to accept. He said, "Dobie ain't had his supper."

Keeler gave Cordell a hard look. "He can eat supper in town."

"Costs too much. He'll stay here."

Dobie turned hostile eyes on him. "Who are you to tell me what I can't do? You're not my daddy."

Keeler asked Dobie, "Is this old man kin to you?"

"Not kin to me or to anybody else I know of. He just came here to bum a meal and decided to stay."

Keeler demanded of Cordell, "Who the hell are you, anyway?"

Cordell clenched his big fists and rested them on his hips. "It don't matter who I am. Just know that I'm a man who can whip the both of you." He glanced at Dobie. "Three of you, if it comes to that."

The three young men tried to stare him down, but they could not hold their gaze long. They all cut their eyes away.

Keeler said, "We're goin' on, Dobie, with or without you."

Cordell said, "It'll be without him."

As the brothers rode away, Cordell said, "You ought to steer clear of people like that. They'll do nothin' but get you in trouble."

"Who I choose for friends is none of your business. I'm a grown man."

"Lackin' a few years."

"We wouldn't do anything but have a little fun. Ain't been much fun around here lately with all the work you've found to do."

"There's nothin' wrong with a little fun as long as it's the right kind. But people like those Keelers, they've got peculiar ideas about what that is." He was convinced the two brothers had held up and pistol-whipped the saloon-keeper in town. "Let yourself step onto the outlaw trail, and pretty soon you find you can't get off of it. You're trapped there, like . . ." Catching himself, he broke off. He had been about to blurt *like your brother.*

For a moment he hoped he was beginning to get through to Dobie, but the young man asked, "How much longer do you figure to stay here?"

"I haven't decided."

Eyes narrowed, Dobie said, "Maybe you figure to stay from now on. Maybe you think you'll smooth-talk my mother till she decides to marry you, and you'll have this farm real cheap."

Heat rose in Cordell's face. "I've got no such notion. You have a dirty mind, boy. And a dirty mouth."

Dobie's eyes blazed with defiance. "You goin' to try to wash it out with soap?"

"Not even lye soap would be strong enough. Your mother is wavin' us in for supper. Get yourself into the house."

They ate supper in strained silence. Aurelia looked from her son to Cordell and back again. It was clear that she felt the tension between them. Dobie left some of the food on his plate and strode out onto the front porch to flop in an old wooden chair and sulk.

Worriedly Aurelia said, "I saw the Keeler boys ride up to talk to Dobie. What did they want?"

"Wanted him to go to town with them."

"I have a feeling he would have gone had it not been for you. What did you say to him?"

Cordell felt as if he were trapped in a narrow chute. "Just told him it wouldn't be a good idea. Those boys are no-account."

"I know. I've tried to talk to Dobie, but he's drawn to them somehow. He doesn't want to listen to what I say.

I'm glad you're here, Mr. Goodson. You can talk to him better than I can."

"It's not because he likes what I tell him, but because he's half-afraid of me."

"He's still more a boy than a man. He'll come around when he gets a little older and has more experience."

He may not last that long, Cordell thought. *Buster didn't.*

Aurelia sipped a little coffee and put down the cup. "Cold," she said, her face twisting a little.

She probably meant the coffee, but she could have meant her son, Cordell thought.

She said, "I'm glad you're here to keep him away from trouble."

"There's reasons why I'll have to be movin' on pretty soon. I may have stayed too long already."

He had noticed her dark brown eyes the first time he saw her. Now they looked even darker, and much troubled. She said, "Whatever your reasons, can't they wait? I need you here. Dobie needs you."

He felt himself melting under her steady gaze. He knew he should end it right here. He should saddle up and leave without spending another night in the barn. He knew also that he would not.

He said, "I believe I'll have another cup of coffee. Can I bring you one?"

A few nights later he sat on the edge of his cot in the barn, yawning as he mended harness by lantern light. He heard horses approaching the corral, and the low murmur of voices. He put out the light and stepped through the open barn door into the darkness. He recognized Dobie by the way he moved, catching and saddling his horse. Two other men on horseback waited outside the corral. He could not see their features, but he sensed that they were the Keeler brothers. Unable to make out what they were saying, he moved closer, careful that his footsteps not be heard.

Dobie was saying, "Good thing Maw went to bed early. Otherwise I couldn't have slipped out of the house. She'll raise hell when I come home."

One of the Keelers said, "You'll be back before daylight. It's time you cut loose from the apron strings anyway. You're a man, ain't you?"

The other said, "You'll come back with your pockets full. We figure there's a lot of drover money piled up in old Oscar Counts's saloon. He was pretty snotty to us the last time we was in his joint. We'll pay him a visit as he closes up."

"You meanin' to rob him?"

"Let's don't say *rob*. Let's just say we don't like to see an old man havin' to tote all that extra weight around. We'll lighten his load."

Dobie argued, "People in town know us too well. They'll be comin' to get us."

"Not if we cover our faces, like before." One of the Keelers pulled a small cloth sack from his pocket. It had slits cut for the eyes. "Oscar'll think we're some of them drovers, takin' their money back."

The second Keeler said, "You like money, don't you?"

"Sure, I do. But . . ."

"But nothin'. All you'll have to do is stay outside and hold the horses for us. Now git in the saddle and let's be movin'."

Dobie took the reins and started to mount. Cordell saw that he had made up his mind. He shouted, "Dobie, you get down from there. You're not goin' anyplace." He ran to stop the boy.

One of the Keelers jumped his horse out in front of him. "Where did he come from?" he demanded. Cordell's first reflex was to dodge the horse. Before he could do anything else, Keeler swung a pistol barrel and struck a glancing blow to the side of his head. Cordell staggered and went down.

He heard Dobie say anxiously, "You didn't kill him, did you?"

Keeler replied, "His head is too hard. I just dizzied him a little. Let's go."

Cordell pushed to his knees, choking on the dust the horses raised as they loped away. He saw Aurelia step out onto the porch in her nightgown. She looked in the direction the three young men had gone. Then she saw Cordell, bracing himself against the fence. She ran toward him. "Mr. Goodson! What happened?"

Cordell rubbed his pounding head. He felt a small tickle of sticky blood where the pistol had struck. "Those Keelers." His voice sounded raspy.

"Dobie went with them, didn't he?" she demanded.

Reluctantly he said, "I'm afraid he did."

"They'll be the death of him one of these days."

And this could be that day, he thought. "I'll saddle my horse and go fetch him back." He stepped away from the fence and almost fell. She grabbed his arm and steadied him. "I don't think you're in any condition to ride. I'll hitch up the wagon and go myself."

He helped her with the team, then went into the barn. He had not worn his pistol since he had come here, but he buckled his gun belt around his waist and climbed up into the wagon. "We'll both go," he said. He let her take the reins. He held on to the seat the first mile or so until he felt steady enough not to fall.

She said, "You find him for me. I'll take him by the

ear and drag him out. Maybe that'll shame him enough
to bring him to his senses."

"Or make him run away for good," he cautioned her.

"What else can we do?"

"I don't know. I'll figure it out when the time comes."

Approaching town, they circled around a trail herd
bedded down for the night. Cordell saw what appeared
to be the chuck wagon, a lighted lantern atop the box, like
a beacon to guide the cowboys to camp. They passed a
festive group of riders who had evidently finished their
evening in town and were returning to the herd.

"Cowboys," she said. "Most of them aren't much older
than Dobie. They're David's age, a lot of them." She became pensive. "I wish I could hear from David. You don't
know how hard it is, not knowing where your son has
gone."

Cordell knew. He had done a lot of thinking about his
own lost son, especially since Buster's death. He felt that
it would ease his pain a little if he could talk to her about
it, but he did not want to burden this good woman with
his problem. She had too many of her own.

Most of the town was dark. The streets were almost
deserted. A few horses were still tied in front of the saloons, but Cordell figured most of the visiting drovers had
quit for the night and returned to their herds. The last
stragglers would soon give up and allow the saloons to
close. That, he knew, was when the Keelers would strike.

"Pull in at the wagon yard," he said, "but leave the
team hitched. We may want to leave town kind of quick."

She did as he directed. "What do we do now?" she
asked.

"I'll see if I can find Dobie. You wait right here. It may
take a while."

"He won't want to come with you."

"I know. But he'll come." He climbed down from the wagon and tested his balance. His head still hurt a little, but his legs were steady.

He thought it unlikely that the Keelers would enter Oscar's place until they were ready to rob him, for he would remember them by the way they were dressed, even if they covered their faces. If they were smart, they would not be drinking at all tonight. Whiskey was dangerous when a man set out to do a job that was risky even for somebody cold sober. Whiskey had allowed Sheriff Tom Blessing to capture Cordell after that Galveston bank job.

No, if the boys had the judgment God gave a jackrabbit, they would be lurking in the dark, waiting for Oscar to close up. Still, Cordell had not figured them for high intelligence. Most criminals he had known were longer on nerve than on brains. He stopped in front of the first saloon he came to and peered through the door. He counted two customers he surmised were drovers. The bartender was watching them impatiently, evidently hoping they were about ready to call it a night. A small white bandage on the side of his head told Cordell he was the one the Keelers had robbed sometime back. When he stepped out from behind the bar, Cordell saw that he had a pistol belt strapped around his waist. He was not going to accept a second robbery without a fight.

Cordell remembered that Oscar kept a shotgun within easy reach behind his bar. The Keelers might not find him to be easy pickings.

He walked past several darkened buildings until he reached Oscar's place. A lighted lantern hung beneath the porch roof. As before, a lamp stood on the bar. It furnished the only light inside the saloon. Cordell eased up to the window and looked through. He did not expect to see the Keelers and Dobie there, but he had to be sure. He saw only two customers, sitting at a table halfway toward the back door. Cordell gave them a cursory glance, then felt a sudden alarm and looked again. One face was vaguely familiar. Cordell searched his memory. He had seen it somewhere weeks ago. But where?

Realization struck him like the kick of a mule. This man had visited Tom Blessing in the jail just before Blessing was killed. Cordell was not certain, but this could have been one of those shooting at him during the jail-break. He could even be the one whose bullet struck Buster. He must be a lawman of some kind, perhaps a Ranger.

Cordell's first instinct was to grab a horse and run. He went so far as to survey the few horses that remained tied on the street, wondering which he should take. But he hesitated, his mind going back to that woman waiting at the wagon yard. She depended on him to save her son from himself. He could not leave until he fulfilled his obligation to her. He retreated to a dark space between two buildings and waited, his stomach in turmoil as he re-thought his options: to run or to stay.

The two customers left the saloon. Oscar came onto the narrow porch and blew out the lantern. The lamp on the bar still burned. Cordell heard horses and saw three riders coming down the dark street in a walk. Two, wearing sacks for masks, dismounted in front of the saloon and handed their reins to the third. Cordell knew that would be Dobie.

He waited until the two Keelers entered the saloon, then stepped out into the street. He swung up onto one of the Keelers' horses while Dobie froze in astonishment. He said, "Come on, boy, we're gettin' away from here."

Dobie started to protest. Cordell swung his fist with

all the strength he could muster and connected with Dobie's chin. He held Dobie to prevent him from falling, though the boy lost his hat and the mask. Cordell grabbed Dobie's reins and moved into a run back up the street. Behind him, he heard a shotgun blast and a scream. Pistol shots quickly followed.

By the time he reached the wagon yard, people were spilling out onto the street. He led Dobie's horse up against the wagon and gave the stunned boy a shove that tumbled him out of the saddle and into the wagon bed. He swung to the ground and gave the Keeler horse a slap on the rump. It trotted down the street. He tied Dobie's to the tailgate and climbed up beside Aurelia.

Wide-eyed, she said, "I heard shooting. Is he . . . ?"

"He's not shot. I hit him with my fist because he was fixin' to get himself into bad trouble, and I didn't have time for argument."

"It sounded like *somebody* got shot."

Grimly he said, "Them Keeler boys, I expect. But as far as anybody needs to know, Dobie never came to town. Us neither."

"Thank God." She laid her head against his arm. "And thank you too, Mr. Goodson. I'll always owe you for this."

"You don't owe me nothin'." He flipped the reins to put the team into a trot. "I had a boy once, but I lost him. You lost a boy, too. I didn't want to see you lose another."

The wagon bumped along the road. As they neared the house, she broke a long silence. "You don't have a home, do you, Mr. Goodson?"

"I used to have, a long time ago."

"Since you've been here, a lot of things have changed for the better. I do wish you'd stay."

He felt his throat tighten. Regret weighed on him like

a stone. "Aurelia, there's no place I'd rather be than right here. It's like I've found what I've been lookin' for the last twenty-thirty years. There's reasons I can't stay, but this isn't the time to talk about them. Right now let's get Dobie home. If somebody comes askin' after him, we can say he's been there all night."

16

Andy was itching to leave town. Choctaw John said he was not sure he was healed enough to ride, though Andy suspected he simply liked the wages. He was walking around on his own and had discovered Oscar Counts's saloon without help from Andy. He claimed whiskey eased the pain.

Andy said, "I thought it was against the law to sell liquor to Indians."

"I ain't but half of one. It's the other half that drinks."

With aid of the deputy sheriff, Andy had contacted other lawmen in the region, alerting them to be on the lookout for Cordell. He decided Griffin was as good a place as any to await developments. He passed the time by visiting drovers who came by with northbound herds, learning about the areas from which they had started, the chances of going into ranching for himself. Perhaps if he found the right place, he could wean Bethel away from the family farm and shed himself of Farley Brackett for once and for all.

Oscar was a flowing fountain of information, though little of it was of help to Andy. He had been in Fort Griffin since buffalo-hunting days. He told Andy and John, "You ain't smelled smells till you've smelled a big stack of buffalo hides from the downwind side. They'd blister your nose. And flies? They'd swarm to where you couldn't see the sun, hardly. There wasn't but one savin' grace to the buffalo trade. That was the money. We had flush times here while they lasted."

Andy observed, "Looks like you've been doin' pretty good with the trail herds comin' by."

"Durin' spring and part of the summer. It shuts off then because they want to get to Kansas before the snow flies. Them South Texas cattle don't take kindly to a blizzard, and neither do South Texas cowboys. So I've got to make hay while the sun shines." He frowned. "I'm afraid it ain't goin' to shine much longer here. The railroads are soon goin' to finish the trail drives."

"We've heard about the robbery that took place some nights ago. Have you taken precautions?"

Oscar stepped behind the bar and brought up a double-barreled shotgun. "I've got old Chickamauga here. Kicks like a mule, but it blows a hole big enough to drive a wagon through."

"If they give you a chance to use it."

"I never get far from it when there's suspicious-lookin' characters in here."

Andy described Cordell as best he could. "Been anybody in here who looked like that?"

Oscar shrugged. "There's half a dozen of them any night. Hell, you've come close to describin' me, except I'm too old to fit." He considered for a moment. "Come to think of it, I remember one man in particular. He was sittin' back yonder mindin' his own business when them Keeler boys come in one night and started hoorawin' a couple of my customers. Me and him, we set them straight. He looked like he could chew them up and spit them out. I think he put the Indian sign on them, because they ain't been back."

Andy sat up straight. "What did he look like?"

"About the way you described, only he didn't have no beard. Just a few days' whiskers, was all. He put away enough whiskey to bring a mule to its knees, but it didn't faze him none that I could see."

"Do you know where he came from, or where he went?"

"Never seen him before or since. I judged that he might be bossin' a trail herd. He looked like one of them tough cowmen from down in the brush country. If so, he's close to the Red River by now, or across it."

Andy eased. It seemed unlikely that Cordell would be with a trail drive. Cattle herds traveled no more than about ten miles a day, and that only on the good days. Cordell would want to move faster.

Oscar brought Andy a beer and filled John's whiskey glass. "You fellers are welcome to sit here as long as you like. It's on the house. If they hear there's a Ranger and his helper around, them robbers are apt to steer clear of Griffin."

Andy said, "I can't stay in town much longer. I've got to get out and look for Cordell."

"You don't have any idea where he's at, do you?"

"No."

"So any direction you go, you're apt to be movin' farther away from him instead of closer. Ain't that right?"

"That's a way of lookin' at it."

"So, if I was you, I'd stay right here till I heard somethin'. That makes sense, don't it?"

Andy knew it made sense to Oscar, but he had a vested interest in keeping a Ranger here. The state office might not feel the same way. "Well, maybe just a little bit longer."

Andy had about made up his mind to leave town. He had received a wire from Austin telling him to continue the search for Cordell at his own discretion, though the state office offered no new leads to help him. He had satisfied himself that Cordell was not in Fort Griffin. He was undecided where to go from here. He told John, "I'll write a voucher for what the state owes you. You can submit it from back home."

John took the news in good nature. "I guess my vacation is over, and so is Thaddeus's. I've missed bein' able to wart that old skinflint. How about we go down to Oscar's place and have a last drink together? Or maybe two."

By the time Andy had finished one beer and John had downed three whiskeys, the evening's cowboy crowd was gone. A local citizen came in and visited with Oscar a couple of minutes, his expression grim. He spoke in a voice so low that Andy could not make out what he was saying. Oscar came to Andy, his face troubled. "I hope you-all ain't in a hurry to go to bed."

Andy asked, "What's the trouble?"

"None yet, but a friend of mine just told me he saw them Keeler boys down by the river."

Andy remembered Oscar talking about the Keelers before. "You think they may be up to no good?"

"I never seen them when they wasn't. And I hear there's another one with them. Probably that Jackson kid."

Jackson. Andy wondered why that name sounded familiar. He tried to remember where he had heard it.

Oscar said, "I've suspicioned all along that it wasn't no drovers that pistol-whipped and robbed Old Shep. I believe it was them Keelers. I suspect they've held a grudge agin me since the night me and that stranger ran them out of here."

"Have you got your money in a safe place?"

"I keep enough behind the bar to make change. The rest is in a steel box under a trapdoor back here. Ain't but three or four people besides me know that."

Andy considered. "If they're plannin' to rob you, they probably figure to do it as you close up, when you're by yourself. So me and John will let them see us leave, but we won't go far."

Oscar checked the shotgun. "This town has put up with their shenanigans long enough. If they come here on mischief, they've got a surprise waitin', and it ain't a birthday present."

Andy said, "Just be sure you don't shoot me or John." He moved to the door. He told John quietly, "You cut around and cover the back door in case they try to go in that way. I'll watch the front."

John said, "This sounds a little dangerous. Reckon you can get me extra pay for it?"

"Just remember how many free drinks Oscar has given you."

They turned into the darkness at the side of Oscar's saloon. John walked down to the far end, near the back door. Andy saw Oscar blow out the lantern that hung on the front porch. That threw the area outside the saloon into near darkness, compromised only by a pale light from the lamp on the bar.

Andy found himself sweating. He usually did when he faced the probability of a fight. It was something he had never talked to other Rangers about. He feared they would take it as a sign of weakness and have less confidence in him. He rubbed a clammy hand on a trouser leg and concentrated on the street.

He did not wait long. He saw three horsemen moving in the darkness. In front of the saloon, two with faces covered dismounted and handed their bridle reins to the third rider. His face was masked, but his wiry form indicated he was young. The two stepped up onto Oscar's porch, paused a moment as if summoning their nerve, and walked through the door.

Seemingly from nowhere, a large man appeared on foot, grabbed the reins to one of the horses and swung quickly into the saddle. He said something sharp, then drove a hard fist against the rider's jaw. He grabbed the young man to keep him from falling, then set both horses into a run back up the street.

Andy froze. He could almost swear he had seen Cordell. It was like reliving the jailbreak.

Oscar's shotgun blast reverberated like a cannon inside the saloon. An agonized scream followed the shot. One of the robbers rushed out the door and turned to fire his pistol back into the saloon.

Andy shouted, "Halt! Drop the gun!"

Instead, the man whirled and triggered a quick shot in Andy's direction. Andy fired. The man doubled over, staggered, then sprawled on the porch.

Oscar yelled from inside, "Everything all right out there?"

His body shaking, Andy answered, "It's over with." John came running around the corner, pistol in his hand. He stopped when he saw the would-be robber lying on his stomach. The man groaned. Andy turned him over and pulled off the sack that had hidden his face. The robber was young, his eyes full of terror. Spitting blood, he spoke in a raspy voice Andy could barely hear. "It wasn't supposed . . . to happen like this." He cried in desperation, "Somebody help me!" He reached out a hand, then let it drop. He trembled and went still.

Andy shuddered. Rusty Shannon had told him he should never become so hardened that it did not disturb him to kill someone, even in self-defense. He doubted that he ever would. He *hoped* he never would.

Oscar came onto the porch, holding the bar lamp. Shaken, he said, "It was the Keelers, all right. But where's Dobie Jackson? I figured he was with them."

Andy considered telling what he had seen, but instinct told him to wait. The name Jackson nagged at him until he remembered where he had heard it. That was the name of the young outlaw he had shot when Cordell was being broken out of jail. Andy had helped bury him. The pieces began coming together.

He said, "Looks like you might've figured wrong."

Oscar replied, "I suppose I did. These two were all that I saw. But it wouldn't hurt to talk to Dobie. He might know somethin' about this."

"I'll talk to him. Where does he live?"

Oscar said Jackson and his mother lived east of town, on the river. "A widow. Nice woman, but she raised two wild sons. The older one ran away from home. I been expecting the younger one to do the same thing."

"The older one . . . what was his name?"

"David. Seemed like a decent kid till he took to the wild bunch. Why, do you know somethin' about him?"

"Just curious."

By this time an excited crowd had gathered, including the grim-faced deputy. Oscar explained to him what had happened. The lawman said, "Too bad, but those boys've been tryin' to get through the penitentiary gates for a long time. Or the gates of hell. There wasn't anybody with them?"

"I just saw these two," Oscar said. "Soon as they came

in with their faces covered, I knew what they was fixin'
to do. I let go with old Chickamauga. Cut the first one in
two. The other one turned and ran, but he taken a shot
at the Ranger. Worst mistake he ever made."

The deputy turned to Andy. "Lucky thing you were
close by."

Andy looked down at the body on the porch. "Not for
this boy." He shuddered again. He felt as if he might throw
up, and he fought to bring the nausea under control.

The deputy shook his head. "I dread ridin' out to tell
old man Keeler. He'll just sink deeper into the bottle
after this."

Oscar said with some bitterness, "That boy died callin'
for help. He needed it a long time ago, him and his
brother both. Damned little they got from the old man."

Andy beckoned to John. "We've got to take us a ride."

"Right now?"

"We won't sleep tonight anyway, not after this. Let's
go saddle up."

LAMPLIGHT SHONE THROUGH the farmhouse window.
Approaching it, Andy said, "No respectable farmer is
awake this long after midnight unless somebody's sick."

John remained skeptical. "Maybe you've been huntin'
Cordell so long that everybody has started to look like
him."

"Maybe. We're fixin' to find out." Andy moved up to
a window propped open with a stick. In the dull light of
a lamp he saw a woman sitting with a young man at a
kitchen table. He assumed from what Oscar had told him
that they were Mrs. Jackson and her son Dobie. A large
man stood nearby, turned away so that Andy could not
see his face.

The young man was complaining, "But they'll think I went coward and ran out on them."

The woman said, "Son, those Keelers are of bad blood. It makes no difference what they think. The main thing is that Mr. Goodson probably saved you from going to the penitentiary. Or to your grave."

Dobie cried, "Who is he to be runnin' my life? He ain't my paw, and he ain't your husband. He ain't nobody."

The man said gravely, "Boy, you were fixin' to set foot on the road to perdition."

Dobie shouted, "What would you know about it? Are you a preacher or somethin'?"

"I'm a long ways from bein' a preacher, but I know that road. I've been on it. I'm still on it. It's hard to get off of." He placed a hand on Dobie's shoulder. Dobie twisted away from him.

Mrs. Jackson told her son, "It was my doing as much as his. I asked Mr. Goodson to stop you."

Dobie lashed out at her, "Why don't you mind your own business? You're naggin' me like you nagged David. It was you that made him run away from home."

She said, "I was trying to keep him from making a bad mistake. The same kind you were about to make tonight."

"So he got a bellyful of it and left. Now you have no idea where he's at."

"I wish to God I did."

"I've had it in mind to go and find him. That's why I went with the Keelers, to get me some travelin' money."

Mrs. Jackson began to weep. The man stepped up closer and moved a hand as if to touch her, then changed his mind and drew it away. "Aurelia, there's somethin' I've got to tell you. I've been meanin' to from the first, but I couldn't bring myself to do it." He paused as if gathering courage. "Dobie, there's no use in you lookin' for David. He's dead."

Mrs. Jackson gasped. Dobie froze.

The man said, "David made the mistake of throwin' in with a bad man. That mistake got him killed."

Mrs. Jackson seemed too stunned to speak. Dobie demanded, "What bad man?"

"Me."

Andy had heard enough. Though he had not seen the face, he knew this was Cordell. Drawing his pistol, he motioned for John to follow him through the kitchen door. He declared, "Luther Cordell, I'm a Ranger, and you're under arrest."

Cordell turned slowly, raising his hands. Andy had not seen him without the dark beard he had worn in jail. Nothing in his face showed him to be the same man except perhaps the piercing dark eyes. Cordell appeared more resigned than surprised. He said, "You're that friend of Sheriff Blessing's."

"That's right. I am."

"You've been followin' me all along, ain't you?"

"I have." Andy wondered at Cordell's unflinching acceptance of his capture.

"I didn't know who it was, but I felt in my bones that somebody was doggin' me. I stayed on the move till I got to this place. I kept meanin' to go on, but I couldn't." Cordell looked regretfully at Mrs. Jackson. "The longer I stayed, the harder it was to do what I came for."

Her eyes were sad. "And what did you come for?"

"To tell you about your boy David. I owed it to you to tell you where he's buried. And I was goin' to give you the money that rightfully belonged to him."

Andy said, "If it's the Galveston money, it's not yours

to give." He reached out and lifted Cordell's pistol from its holster.

Cordell said, "Don't worry. I won't try to get away. I won't bring trouble to this good lady's house. She's already had enough." He lowered his hands and sat down at the table. "Aurelia, I'm a wanted man. Been one for a long time. But I didn't lie to you about my name. It's really Walter Goodson. I borrowed the name Cordell from a man I knew that got killed in the war. I didn't figure it could hurt him none."

"What about David?" she asked anxiously.

"I called him Buster. Didn't even know his rightful name for a long time. He was pitiful as a lost pup, broke and hungry, lookin' for somebody to join up with. I fed him and tried to run him off, but he kept followin' me. I got to where I liked havin' him around. I've wished a thousand times that I'd turned him away. It would've been a kindness." Cordell looked at Dobie. "That's why I stopped you tonight. I didn't want you to end up like your brother."

Andy said, "I saw what you did in town. It was the right thing. The Keeler brothers are dead."

Dobie's jaw dropped. "Dead? Sully and Finn both?"

"Both of them."

Dobie seemed to wilt.

Cordell said, "You don't have to arrest Dobie, do you, Ranger? He never set foot in that saloon, and he was gone before the shootin' took place."

Andy saw grief and fear in Mrs. Jackson's eyes. His voice was severe as he spoke to Dobie. "Boy, you came within an inch of bein' killed. If it wasn't for Cordell, you'd likely be laid out at the undertaker's right now, alongside the Keelers."

Dobie was still stunned. In a breaking voice, he asked Cordell, "Do you know for sure that my brother is dead?"

Cordell said with regret, "I was with him when he died."

Andy said, "And I was there at his buryin'."

Dobie broke down and cried. His mother put her arms around his shoulders and cried with him.

Cordell's question was still unanswered. He said, "If you'll let the boy go, I promise I won't try to get away from you. Not now, and not later."

Andy said, "I don't see the harm. Maybe he's learned somethin', and I wouldn't want to see the lady lose another son."

Cordell attempted a smile, but it did not quite come off. "I'm much obliged. What do we do now?"

Andy snapped the cuffs over Cordell's wrists. "We get that Galveston money, and then we head east."

John asked, "What about me? Don't you think I ought to go along to help you guard him?"

Andy knew John was mainly interested in getting paid a while longer. "You heard him promise he won't try to get away."

"Ain't you ever had an outlaw lie to you?"

"All right, you're still on the payroll, even if it comes out of my pocket."

"Just till we get to my place. If you need help after that, you'll have to hire somebody else. I've got things of my own to do."

Mrs. Jackson took control of her emotions and set about making breakfast. "It'll be daylight pretty soon," she said. "You-all shouldn't start a long trip on an empty stomach." The way she looked at Cordell told Andy she wished he would never go.

Andy wondered again what it was about the man that

drew so many people to him. He *was* an outlaw, after all, yet people instinctively liked him. Andy said, "Cordell, I can't figure you out. At the start, I took it for granted that you shot Tom Blessing. Now, the way folks keep takin' up for you, I wonder."

"Milt Hayward done it. I didn't intend for him and the boy to bust me loose. I've never seen a jail I couldn't get out of by myself. But Milt was anxious for his share of the Galveston take, and he never was one for waitin'. I cussed him good for shootin' the sheriff. There wasn't no need in it."

"Where do you suppose he is now?"

"With Milt, there's no tellin'. He could be anyplace."

"If I could catch him and make him talk, the law might go easier on you. As it is, all I've got is your word that you didn't shoot Tom."

"And I don't reckon my word is worth a plugged nickel."

Andy pondered, then admitted, "It is to me, but it might not be enough for a court."

"Looks like my goose is cooked."

Mrs. Jackson poured coffee and brought scrambled eggs and bacon to the table. She looked in the oven. "Biscuits are almost ready."

Andy noticed that her eyes were on Cordell except when she had to tend to her cooking. He saw there a look that he had sometimes seen in Bethel's.

He said to Cordell, "You look like a man who could do anything he wanted to. How did you come to get started on the wrong side of the law?"

"It was after the war. I'd lost everything that meant anything to me. Didn't have coin enough in my pocket to buy coffee. I came onto this little old country bank just sittin' there doin' nothin'. I thought about all the money in it just sittin' there doin' nothin', and I decided to put it to work. I'd've been happy to quit after that, but the law wouldn't let me stop anywhere long enough to hold an honest job. Pretty soon I was broke and hungry again, and I found me another bank. It's been like that ever since."

"Think you could ever have got yourself straight?"

"I've wanted to. I'd do it in a minute if the law wasn't crowdin' me. If I could start over fresh, I'd be the happiest dirt farmer you ever saw." He turned to Dobie. "I've been tryin' to tell you about the road to perdition. I've been on it a long time and tryin' hard to get off."

Mrs. Jackson pleaded, "He means it, Ranger, can't you see that?"

Andy felt himself caught in a bind. "I'm sorry, but I'm honorbound to bring in Luther Cordell."

He and John had tied their horses thirty yards from the house. John went out to fetch them while Andy and Cordell walked to the barn. The sun was just coming up, hitting Andy in the eyes. Cordell said, "That's my mare in the pen. She won't leave the barn at night. The feed has got her spoiled." He opened the gate. "Don't worry, I didn't steal her. I bought her fair and square."

With stolen money, Andy thought. "I met the old man you bought her from. He stood up for you, said you're on the square."

"I've always tried to be, after my fashion. I never robbed anybody that didn't have too much money for his own good."

Andy had holstered his pistol, but he kept his hand on the butt of it. Though Cordell had promised not to try to get away, Andy had observed that even the most honest of men would lie now and again if the stakes were high enough. "Get her saddled, then tell me where you hid the money."

Cordell said, "In the barn. I found a loose board under the saddle rack. Lift it up and there'll be my saddlebags." John had arrived, leading his and Andy's horses. Andy motioned to him, and John entered the barn. In a minute he was back with the saddlebags. He opened one and whistled in surprise. "I never saw so much money in all my life."

Cordell said, "It should be somethin' over nine thousand dollars. I've had to spend a little along the way. It costs a right smart to live nowadays. Have you seen the price of flour and coffee?"

John said, "Do we really have to turn it in? We could split it and say he spent it all. I'd be almost as rich as old Thaddeus."

Andy was not sure John was joking until he saw a boyish grin spread across the man's face. "Don't even talk about it unless you want to find out if a Comanche can whip a Choctaw."

Mrs. Jackson and Dobie came up together from the house. She had her hands clasped in front of her, and her eyes glistened. "Mr. Goodson, when you get free, you'll always be welcome here."

Cordell's expression was downcast. "Ranger, I owe her a decent good-bye."

Andy nodded. "Go ahead."

The outlaw walked to her, leading the mare. Despite the cuffs around his wrists, he took her hands in a tight grip. "Aurelia, I'd give anything . . ."

Her eyes filled with tears. She grasped his shoulders and kissed him. "I know."

Dobie watched with amazement. Cordell turned to him and said, "Remember what I told you about the road to perdition. And take good care of your mother. She needs you real bad."

Dobie looked dazed. He said nothing.

Cordell told Mrs. Jackson, "He's learned a lot today. Once he's sorted it all out, I believe he'll be all right."

A bewhiskered horseman rode out from behind the barn, taking Andy by surprise. Brandishing a pistol, he ordered, "Everybody raise your hands to where I can see them." He poked the muzzle in Andy's and John's direction. "You two, drop them guns on the ground. Do it with your left hands."

He was almost as large as Cordell. Andy recognized him.

John muttered, "That's the jaybird that busted my ribs."

The man said, "I'll do worse if anybody messes with me." He turned his attention to Cordell. "Howdy, Luther. I've wore out three horses tryin' to find you."

Cordell said sullenly, "Thought you ran off to Mexico, Milt."

Milt Hayward replied, "Started to, but I kept thinkin' about the money you was supposed to hold for me. You still got it in them saddlebags?" He motioned toward the pouches Andy had just tied to his saddle.

Cordell said, "Except for what little I spent. How did you manage to trail me so far?"

"I couldn't. You were too slippery. But I figured the Ranger was trailin' you, so I followed *him*. I hoped he'd catch up to you sooner or later."

Andy realized why Hayward had avoided shooting him when he wounded John. He had needed Andy to lead him to Cordell.

Cordell said, "You left before we could make the split. I always intended to give you your share."

Hayward made a crooked smile. "I'll bet you did. Luther, I like the way them handcuffs fit you. As long as the law has got you, I don't have to worry about you comin' after me. And I don't have to settle for part of that money. I can take all of it."

Cordell's jaw tightened with anger.

Hayward said, "That woman'll be good insurance for me. I'm takin' her along. If anybody crowds me, she's dead."

Dobie shouted, "No." He moved protectively in front of his mother. "Take me if you need somebody, but leave her alone."

Hayward said, "You're a fool, kid. Move aside, or I'll have to shoot you."

Mrs. Jackson gently pushed her son away. "Do what he says."

Andy declared, "You're the man that shot Tom Blessing."

"You mean that clodhopper sheriff? Damn fool got in my way."

Andy trembled with anger. "You'd better ride far and fast, because I'll be comin' after you."

Hayward's eyes had a poisonous look. "There's one way to take care of that." He pointed the pistol into Andy's face.

Cordell took a quick step forward, placing himself between Andy and Hayward. "Killin' a Ranger will bring all the law in Texas down on us. Leave him to me. Let me pick up one of the guns, and I'll see that he gives you a long head start."

Hayward shook his head. "Or maybe you'd shoot me and him both and keep the money yourself. I ain't no tenderfoot. Step out of the way."

Cordell did not move. Hayward began to look flustered. He said, "All right, Luther, I won't shoot the Ranger.

You can bring them saddlebags to me yourself. And woman, get on that mare."

Dobie again stepped in front of his mother. Cordell told him, "He means what he says. For your mother's sake, you'd better do it." Cordell's voice crackled with hatred as he warned Hayward, "Don't you hurt this woman, or I'll follow you to hell's far side."

Hayward grumbled, "Fetch me that money, or I *will* shoot somebody."

Hampered by the cuffs, Cordell fumbled in detaching the bags from Andy's saddle. He moved toward Hayward. "Here they are, and be damned."

As the outlaw reached for them, Cordell flung them at the horse. The startled animal jumped, slinging its head and squealing. Almost unseated, Hayward cursed and grabbed at the saddle horn.

Cordell shouted, "Let's get him, Ranger!" He grabbed up the pistol John had dropped, but Hayward fired first. Cordell grunted at the impact.

Hayward's frightened horse kicked up clods of earth as it pitched out from under him. The outlaw fell heavily but kept his grip on the pistol. In the moment of confusion Andy retrieved his own weapon and fired. Hayward jerked as the bullet drove into his chest, but he did not drop the pistol. Andy fired again. Hayward pitched forward beside the saddlebags. Struggling for breath, he murmured, "Burn in hell, all of you." He reached for the bags, but his clawing fingers could not find them. A long sigh escaped from deep in his chest. He did not breathe again.

Andy felt no nausea this time. Instead, he felt satisfaction and a sense of closure. Now maybe Tom Blessing could rest easy.

He said, "Thanks, Cordell. You made a good try."

Aurelia Jackson grabbed her son and gave him a sweeping glance up and down. "Did he hit you, Son?"

Dobie's voice trembled. "No, but I think he got Mr. Goodson."

Andy had been too busy to see Cordell fall. He took two long strides, dropped to one knee, and turned Cordell over onto his back. Blood pumped from a wound in his shoulder. Andy said, "At least he missed the heart. John, you'd better hitch up the wagon. We have to get him to town pretty quick, or we'll lose him." He tried to stanch the blood with a handkerchief, but it was not enough.

Aurelia was on her knees, her arm around Cordell. Tears in her eyes, she said, "That might be better than spending the rest of his life in the penitentiary." Then she cried, "I didn't mean it. Hold on, Mr. Goodson. Please hold on."

Andy drew back, addled by the way a situation that seemed so simple and straightforward had taken such an unexpected turn.

Dobie hurried to the house and brought back a couple of towels. Andy tore Cordell's shirt open and pressed one against the wound. He told Mrs. Jackson, "Hold it tight so he won't bleed to death."

John brought up the wagon. He said, "Andy, if you know any Comanche medicine songs, this might be a good time to sing them."

"I don't remember one. You know any?"

"Us Choctaws don't believe in that foolishness."

Andy and John lifted Cordell into the bed of the wagon. The strain of the man's weight caused John to clutch at the side where his rib was still bandaged. Andy said, "Mrs. Jackson, you and Dobie get started. Me and

John will be right behind you." He turned his attention to Hayward's still form. "We've got to take Cordell's body in to show the deputy."

John blinked. "What do you mean, Cordell's body? Cordell is in the wagon."

"No, that's Mr. Goodson." Andy pointed with his chin toward the man on the ground. "This is Cordell."

It took John a moment to absorb what Andy was saying. "You went to a lot of trouble to find him. Now you're lettin' him go?"

"I was after the man who killed Tom Blessing. I got him. That's as much as anybody needs to know."

"You're takin' a hell of a chance. If Cordell ever goes outlaw again, they won't only be lookin' for him, they'll be lookin' for you."

Andy watched the wagon move away, Dobie driving the team. Aurelia Jackson sat in the wagon bed. The man she knew as Goodson lay with his head in her lap. Andy said, "The dead don't come back to life. Luther Cordell is dead, and we'll give him a tombstone to prove it."

JUDGE TOMPKINS STOOD up from his paper-strewn desk and took a half-smoked cigar from his mouth as Andy walked into his office. "The prodigal has returned," he said, beaming. "Ranger headquarters sent us a wire saying you got your man."

Andy said, "Dead and buried. Anything new around here?"

The judge said, "A little. You been out to the Brackett farm yet?"

Andy shook his head. "No, I've been sort of dreadin' it."

"I suspect that little girl will be glad to see you."

"But her brother won't. I had one fistfight with him. I

left to keep from havin' another. I doubt his temperament has changed much."

"He's got more things to worry about than a little argument with you. We've set the date for a special election to fill Tom Blessing's job as sheriff. Farley Brackett was the first to file."

Andy grunted in resignation. "I figured as much."

"But he's got opposition. A group of us convinced Rusty Shannon that the county needs a better sheriff than Farley. From what I can tell, most people around here agree with us. On election day, Farley is going to feel like a cyclone hit him. I think he already senses it."

Andy took pleasure in the thought that Rusty would be the next sheriff. But defeat would probably make Farley even more antagonistic than he already was.

The judge fingered through several papers on his desk. "I've got a wire here from the state Ranger office. It's for you." He found it and handed it over. "They're pleased with what you've done. They're offering you a new station."

Andy read the wire. It should have been good news, but it left him feeling cold. "Kerrville's a long way from here. A long way from Bethel."

"And from Farley," the judge pointed out.

"That part I like."

"There's something else. Being gone, you couldn't have heard. Old Mrs. Brackett died a couple of days after you left. Bethel's feeling pretty low. She's lost her mother, and she figures she's lost you." He paused. "Has she?"

"Not if I can help it."

A dog met Andy a hundred yards from the Brackett farmhouse and escorted him in, barking an announcement all the way. Farley walked out onto the front porch and waited for him. Glum-faced, he grunted, "Back, are you?"

Andy tensed, half expecting Farley to order him off the place. "For just a little while."

Farley frowned. "I expect you came to see Bethel. She's inside."

Andy stepped down and tied his horse to a post.

Farley said, "I suppose you heard that your friend Rusty Shannon is runnin' against me."

"So I've been told."

"From everything I hear, I'd just as well withdraw. I can't understand what people around here have got against me." Farley stepped down from the porch and started toward the barn. He stopped and turned half around. "This county has got more sunshine, more sunflowers, and more sons of bitches than any place I've ever been." He stalked away, his shoulders hunched.

Bethel met Andy at the door. He thought he had remembered how beautiful she was, but she looked even better as she moved eagerly into his arms. He said, "I just now heard about your mother. I'm sorry."

A tear moved down Bethel's cheek. "It was her time. She was ready to go. Now it's just Farley and Teresa and me. And you."

He lifted the message from his shirt pocket and unfolded it. "I won't be here for long." He handed her the paper. "They're sendin' me way off to West Texas, to Kerrville."

"I've heard you talk a lot about the hill country. You loved it when you were stationed there."

"I always figured to have a place of my own someday. Maybe I'll find it out in the hills."

She read the wire and looked up at him. "When are we leaving?"

"We?"

"Farley can run the farm to suit himself. With Mother gone, there's nothing to keep me here."

"But what would people say, us goin' off together and not even married?"

She clasped her hands behind his neck, pulled him down, and kissed him. "That should be easy to fix."